SENATOR

ALSO BY RICHARD BOWKER

Summit

Dover Beach

Marlborough Street

Replica

Forbidden Sanctuary

Senator

A NOVEL

Richard Bowker

William Morrow and Company, Inc.
New York

It is the policy of William Morrow and Company, Inc., and its imprints and affiliates, recognizing the importance of preserving what has been written, to print the books we publish on acid-free paper, and we exert our best efforts to that end.

Library of Congress Cataloging-in-Publication Data

Bowker, Richard.
    Senator : a novel / Richard Bowker.
        p.   cm.
    ISBN 0-688-12454-2
    1. Senators—United States—Fiction.   I. Title.
PS3552.08739S46   1994
813'.54—dc20   93-32521
                                                                                 CIP

Printed in the United States of America

First Edition

1 2 3 4 5 6 7 8 9 10

BOOK DESIGN BY SRS DESIGN

For James Robert Bowker

SENATOR

CHAPTER I

I am a politician.

I stare at the blank screen, and that is the first thing I can think of to write.

It's astonishing, really. I have never thought of myself as a politician. I certainly didn't plan to become one. Even as I campaigned, as I shook hands and kissed babies, gave canned speeches and attended endless fund raisers, it didn't occur to me that these activities were defining me; I always thought of them as simply a means to an end. Until now. Now, when it has all changed forever.

I'm a politician, and I have just finished the toughest campaign of my life. But it isn't just the campaign I want to write about in this unfamiliar room, on this intimidating machine. Because I want to be something more than a politician, and that will require an understanding of far more than the mechanics of running for public office. It won't be easy to find that understanding.

But this is where I have to start.

The battle had been shaping up ever since Bobby Finn announced in late spring that he was going to run against me, but the public didn't pay attention until after the primary. Couldn't blame them; we were both lying low—raising funds, doing research, plotting strategy. Neither of us had opposition in the pri-

9

mary, so we spent our time stockpiling ammunition; better to do that than to use it up early and risk having nothing left for the final struggle.

But even when we started in earnest, people were slow to react to the legendary confrontation. The pros blamed it on the weather. It was a soggy September. Flights were delayed, parades canceled; people at factory entrances and subway stops rushed past us to get out of the perpetual rain. Even indoors the crowds were small and inattentive, worried more about whether their basements were flooding than about who would get their vote for senator. Maybe after the baseball season, the pros thought. Eventually they would have to take an interest.

Eventually they did, but Lord, it wasn't the way I wanted.

I may as well start with the Friday evening it all began. Just another speech—this one to the Newton Republican Women's Club. Not an especially important event; I was preaching to the converted, and there were only a couple of local reporters there to take my message to the masses. My mind was far away, but still, it went well; the fine ladies laughed at the jokes and applauded at the proper places and were generally thrilled to be in my presence. A politician is an actor whose performance never ends.

Kevin Feeney was with me. It was his job to grab me away from the fine ladies as soon as possible after my speech. Let them blame him, not me, for not staying longer. *Sorry, ladies. I'm a slave to my schedule, and Kevin is its keeper.*

He did his job—he always does—and together we headed out into the fog and drizzle. He held an umbrella over the two of us as we stood in the parking lot. "Let me drive you home, Senator," he said.

"Don't be silly. What'll we do with the extra car? Take the night off. Relax."

"You should have let me drive you here."

By using my own car, I had provided the evening with a logistical complication that Kevin found unnerving. He was supposed to take care of me, and I wasn't cooperating. "I managed to get here by myself, Kevin," I said. "I'm sure I can make it back. Go home. Introduce yourself to Barbara and the kids. I'll see you in the morning."

Kevin still didn't look happy. His wife and children came in a distant second in his loyalties. But I wasn't going to argue with him; I had more important things to do. I got into my Buick and opened the window. "Go home, Kevin," I repeated. And then I left him standing forlornly in the parking lot.

I didn't feel sorry for him; in fact, I didn't give him another thought. Kevin would always be there. I drove along Commonwealth Avenue, an oldies station on low, the windshield wipers keeping time with Neil Sedaka. Generally I like driving alone— offstage, if only for a while. But tonight the pleasure was soured. I had a problem, and I had to solve it by myself.

At a stoplight I picked up the car phone and dialed a number. After the fourth ring the answering machine clicked on: "Hi, this is Amanda Taylor. I can't come to the phone right now, but—" The light turned green, and I slammed the receiver down.

Maybe she's there, I thought. Maybe she just isn't answering.

But maybe it would be better if she weren't there. I had a key.

Newton turned into Brighton, and the big old Victorian houses gave way to dorms and apartment buildings, Laundromats and convenience stores and bars. I come from Brighton, but not this part; this was academic territory. First Boston College and then Boston University, the campus sprawling in urban disarray on both sides of the road for a mile or two before petering out in the dance clubs and record stores and pizza joints of Kenmore Square. To the right, the light towers above Fenway Park blazed in the darkness; the Red Sox were trying to get the game in despite the fog. Big advance sale, probably. I cursed silently: ten thousand extra cars in the neighborhood.

I made my way through the chaos of Kenmore Square traffic and into the Back Bay, where Commonwealth Avenue became elegant once again. I didn't pay attention to the stately elms and old brick town houses, though; like everyone else in the Back Bay, I was looking for a place to park.

The best I could find was a "residents only" space on Gloucester Street. I decided that I didn't have a choice, so I pulled into it. I got out of the car and opened my umbrella. At least the fog would make it less likely that I'd be recognized; I didn't need a conversation about abortion or someone's Social Security benefits just now. I started walking.

If she was there, what would I say? It was important not to lose my temper. I didn't need an argument. Above all, I didn't need her angry at me. And I did need to know what was going on.

If she wasn't there, I would have to wait for her. This couldn't be put off.

The building was on Commonwealth, between Gloucester and Fairfield. Out front a low hedge surrounded a magnolia tree, glistening in the light from an old-fashioned streetlamp. Black wrought-iron bars enclosed the windows in the basement and first floor. In the basement I could see the flicker of a black-and-white TV through the bars. A woman approached, walking a Doberman. The Doberman paused at the streetlamp; the woman stared at me. Where had she seen that face before? I hurried up the front steps and inside.

I closed the umbrella and glanced around. A row of mailboxes to the right. On the wall next to them, a handwritten notice about a lost cat. On the floor beneath, a few faded sheets advertising a Scientology lecture. The ever-present smell of disinfectant. I had caught a whiff of the same disinfectant once in a bathroom at a fund raiser and found myself becoming aroused. I expect that will happen to me again someday. I rang her bell; no answer. I didn't want to hang around the lobby. As usual someone had left the inner door unlocked. I opened it and hurried up the stairs.

I never took the elevator. You can avoid being seen if you pass someone on the stairs; it's impossible in an elevator. I took out my keys and started looking for the one I wanted. By the time I reached the third floor, I had found it. The door was there in front of me. My heart was pounding—from racing up the stairs; from the tension of the coming confrontation. I put the key into the lock, and that's when I knew that something was wrong.

The wood around the lock had been splintered and gouged, as if someone had attacked it with a hammer. I tried the knob; the door was locked. I turned the key, and the door swung open.

"Amanda?" I called out, closing the door behind me.

No answer. I moved into the living room. My heart sank. The place had been ransacked: books and tapes and compact disks pulled off shelves, papers scattered on the rug, the glass coffee table upended. A spider plant lay on its side, its pot cracked, dirt trailing from it like blood from a wound. "Amanda?" I whispered, a prayer now: She wasn't here; she was at a friend's place; she was at the police station. "Amanda?"

On the floor next to the bookshelves I saw several large shards of glass. It took me a moment to recognize them; they were the remains of her crystal ball. "I wish I knew where all this was going to end up," she had said to me once, smiling wistfully. "I wish I had a crystal ball I could look into and see the future." So I had bought one for her. A joke. It was the only present I had ever given her. It had never done her much good, and now, shattered into a dozen pieces, it looked more useless than ever.

I wanted to run away. I wanted to rewind the tape and start over again. This wasn't it. The scene was suppposed to be entirely different. She should be standing here, beautiful, frightened, apologetic. She had made a mistake. She could explain everything. Nothing for me to worry about.

But my will wasn't strong enough to change reality, and I knew that running away would only make things worse. So I forced myself to move through the apartment, pleading with God to make it empty.

Her bedroom seemed untouched. So was the bathroom. The little second bedroom she used for an office was a mess; the desk drawers were all open, and her floppy disks were scattered on the floor like shingles ripped from a roof by a hurricane. But her computer was on, humming softly in the silence. On the screen, white words against a black background. I stepped into the room and read the words:

> she had to die she had to die she had to die she had to
> die she had to die she had to die she had to die she had
> to die she had to die she had to die she had to die she . . .

They swam in my vision; they merged and twisted as I stared at them and tried to change their meaning. They are only words, I thought. Words can lie. Or they can just be words, sound without content, a speech to nice Republican ladies.

One last room.

I walked past the words and into the kitchen, and that's where I found her.

She was sprawled on the black tile floor. Her white shirt was torn and bloody; her eyes were open, and they stared unblinking at the ceiling. They seemed amazed that this was the last thing they would see. I reached down and touched her wrist; she was cold.

I looked around wildly. Was her murderer lying in wait for me as well? But I had searched already; I was alone. I closed her eyes, and then I closed my own, slumping down beside her on the floor. The apartment, the city were silent; the only sounds were the hum of the computer in the next room and the thumping of my heart. She was cold. She was dead.

Amanda.

At that moment I would have given back everything I had accomplished, everything I had achieved, for Amanda to be alive again.

But it wasn't going to happen. My life ticked inexorably onward, and gradually my grief yielded to the pressures of the moment. After a while I forced myself to open my eyes. I haven't been to a great many crime scenes in my life, but I'm not unfamiliar with murder. I tried to look at Amanda clinically. No rigor mortis, so she'd been dead less than eight hours. On the floor, the bottom of her arm was purplish from the blood settling there, so lividity had started. That meant she'd been dead at least a couple of hours.

Someone had murdered Amanda in the late afternoon.

And I thought: Exact time of death is going to be important.

Her clothes were intact, except for where she had been stabbed. At least she hadn't been raped, thank God. There was a bruise on her right forearm—where her attacker had held her? There were cuts on her hands and arms—where she had tried to defend herself?

On the floor near the sink I saw a kitchen knife, its blade dark with dried blood. I recalled using that knife to chop celery one evening.

Oh, Lord, I thought: fingerprints. And then the pressures started to overwhelm me. I had to do something. I was in terrible trouble.

I crawled over to the knife. I took out my handkerchief and wiped the handle—

—and immediately felt stupid and evil. It had been months since I had used the knife. My fingerprints couldn't possibly have been on it. What mattered more: saving my career or finding out who had murdered Amanda?

But then I realized that finding out who had murdered Amanda was just as likely to end my career as having my fingerprints on the knife. This murder couldn't be a coincidence.

So what should I do? Run away? Go outside and howl in the fog? I couldn't think of anything that would help. I don't deserve any credit for it, but finally I decided to do what civilization had taught me to do. I went into the bedroom and called the police.

I gave the dispatcher the address and told her there had been a murder. She asked for my name, and I gave that to her as well. She didn't seem surprised. There are plenty of James O'Connors in Boston.

Then, continuing to be responsible, I called Harold White. No answer. I tried Roger Simmons next. He was home. "Hi, Roger. Jim."

"Jim, how are you? What can I—"

"I'm at a murder scene, Roger. I discovered the body. I just called the police. They haven't arrived yet."

"Jesus Christ," he whispered.

"I need you," I said. I gave him the address.

"Jim," he said, "I'm not sure I'm the person you want. You know I haven't done criminal in—"

"That's okay. Between the two of us it'll all come back. And get hold of Harold if you can. He isn't answering."

"All right, but—"

I hung up. I didn't feel like chatting with Roger.

I sat on the edge of the bed and looked around. Lights were on, I noticed: in the living room, here in the bedroom. Did that mean she had been alive into the evening? *The time of death matters.*

But it had been foggy all day, and the apartment was dark anyway, so—

So what? Amanda was dead.

I looked down at the black comforter on the bed. Black comforter, black rugs, white walls. "Why is everything black and white?" I asked her the first time I saw her apartment. I was nervous; I needed to talk.

"I have no style," she said. "Decorating's easier if you stick to black and white."

I didn't believe her. She oozed style. "I think it's because you're a journalist," I said. "Journalists like extremes. Good guys and bad guys. Saints and sinners."

"All right," she said. "Have it your way."

"So am I a good guy or a bad guy?" I persisted.

And then she smiled at me. That sensuous, knowing smile, the smile of a prom queen watching the gawky boy try to ask her for a dance. "I don't know," she said. "But I intend to find out."

The words were filled with menace in the remembering. I thought of her white shirt, now stained red. I thought of her white skin turning purple against the black floor. I heard sirens.

I thought of what I had come here to find out. Too late for that now. If it was here, hidden somewhere in the computer or the pile of floppy disks, I was ruined. But I thought: At least I can't let them find out we were lovers.

We had been careful, I knew. No presents, no mementos. No risks. Was there anything—

Yes. A Polaroid snapshot we had taken with a timer one night after a bottle of wine: the two of us kissing openmouthed on the edge of the bed. Where I was sitting now. We didn't stop kissing when the flash went off and the camera spat out the photo. Afterward I suggested that we burn it, but she refused. "I need something to remind me of you when you're not here," she insisted. Were those words another lie? I hadn't thought so at the time. She kissed me again, and I didn't object when she kept the photo.

She had put it in the drawer of her night table, beneath her birth control pills. Could it still be there? Perhaps she had thrown it away in anger or despair; more likely she was saving it for evidence. I opened the drawer. The pills were where I remembered them; I picked them up, and there was the photograph. I stuck it in my pocket without looking at it. And then I held my head in my hands and started to cry for the first time since I was twelve years old.

CHAPTER 2

There was a knock on the door. I went and let the police in.

Two cops: one young and black, the other middle-aged and white. They recognized me, and they couldn't disguise their surprise—or their anxiety. Oh, shit, I could feel them thinking, this is gonna be a messy one. And suddenly I was performing. It was as if the politician in me had simply been waiting for an audience to arrive for him to take over once again. He couldn't be denied; he was a force of nature. Here was the audience, and now every gesture, every word counted.

I took charge. "The victim is in the kitchen, Officers. Her name is Amanda Taylor. She's a reporter for *Hub* magazine. I came here a few minutes ago to be interviewed. I found the place like this." I waved at the chaos in the living room.

They looked at the chaos, then at each other. The older officer motioned to the younger one, who headed for the kitchen. Then the older one took out a notebook and started jotting things down. He had black, oily hair with graying sideburns, unstylishly long. He was left-handed. His stomach bulged out over his belt. "Did you touch anything, sir?" he asked.

"No—well, yes. I closed her eyes . . . and felt for a pulse. And I kind of searched through the apartment—in case, you know, the murderer was still here. And of course, I used the phone to call nine-one-one."

The lies had begun. They felt easy, effortless. Politicians get so used to lying sometimes that they start mistaking it for the truth.

The cop nodded and wrote some more. He didn't know how to act. He was just waiting for the homicide people to show up and let him off the hook. The young black policeman returned from the kitchen. "She's dead," he said. "Look like she was stabbed. A few hours ago maybe."

This obviously made the older cop feel better. Here I was being cooperative. I was still wearing a wet raincoat; my wet umbrella was lying beside the door. At least he didn't have to worry about arresting me. The black officer glanced at me. I'm not a big favorite with blacks. Was he disappointed that I didn't appear to be a suspect? Impossible to tell.

We heard the elevator stop, then footsteps along the corridor and a knock on the door. "Mackey," a voice said.

The cops relaxed. It was Mackey's problem now. I knew Mackey; I didn't know if that was good or bad. The older cop opened the door.

Mackey entered and saw me. "Hi, Jim," he said, as if we were passing on the street.

"Hi, Mack."

He glanced quickly around. "So, uh, what the fuck is going on?" he asked of no one in particular.

So the law enforcement machinery rumbled into motion. People showed up: EMTs, in case Amanda was alive; a medical examiner, to determine how and when she died; assorted technicians, to record everything and sift for evidence; and an assistant DA, to make sure the investigation went by the book. The two cops went down to handle the crowd gathering outside. Mackey started taking his own notes. Amanda became a case; her death became a job.

I find this comforting in the abstract. The quest for justice shouldn't be the stuff of newspaper crusades and popular uprisings. It should be institutionalized; it should belong to bureaucrats. Justice should happen because that's the way things work, like sending out tax bills or holding elections. Someone's paycheck should depend on it. That, really, is what civilization is all about.

Well.

Mackey is a thin Irishman with a pointed nose and a pointed chin and a few strands of hair that stick like thin, limp spaghetti to an ever-growing bald spot. He was wearing a rumpled green raincoat, an old brown suit, and rubbers over his wing tips. If he was surprised to see me at the scene of a homicide, he didn't show it. Of course, he wouldn't have shown any surprise if he had come across his mother naked in a schoolyard with an assault rifle.

When things were under control, he turned his notebook to me. "Wanna start from the beginning, Jim?" he said.

"She was writing a book about me, Mack," I responded. Too quickly? "I've come here a few times to be interviewed. Tonight I gave a speech in Newton and then drove over. I found the body and called the police. And that's it."

Mackey wrote everything down. "Good-lookin' woman, Jim," he said.

I nodded my agreement. "Exactly what my wife said when she introduced us."

Mackey smiled. "How is Liz?"

"Couldn't be better. She went back to school, you know. Getting her doctorate."

"I read about that. The brains in the family."

"Our kid's the one with brains, Mack. We're just trying to keep pace."

Mackey smiled again. He liked kids. He had about a dozen of them.

Roger showed up at that point, wet and breathless; he had put on a lot of weight in the couple of years since his wife died. He was wearing one of those floppy canvas rain hats that can make even a legal scholar look like a dim-witted country club drunk. I hoped he hadn't been drinking. He looked nervous. "Ball game traffic," he explained. "They lost. Hi, Mack."

Mackey nodded to Roger. "Lemme get Mr. Tobin," he said, "and we can take care of the formalities." The way he said "Mr. Tobin" told us exactly what he thought of the assistant DA. He went into the next room.

Roger looked at me. "Harold's on his way," he said.

"Great."

"Are there going to be any problems here, Jim?"

I thought about it. "Not right now," I said truthfully.

Roger nodded. It was obvious that this was going to be bad

for us, even under the most innocent of interpretations. I wasn't going to tell him that those innocent interpretations would be far from the truth. That made me a typical client, of course—lying from the moment he starts talking to his lawyer. "We'll handle it, Jim," he said. But he still looked nervous.

Mackey came back with the assistant DA. "Jerry Tobin, meet Jim O'Connor and Roger Simmons."

Tobin shook our hands firmly. "Shall we get started, gentlemen?" he said. It didn't come out sounding quite as matter-of-fact and in control as he undoubtedly hoped it would. He looked about eighteen years old, even with the pin-striped suit and horn-rimmed glasses that were supposed to make him appear mature and distinguished. I knew the type. Not quite as smart as good old Dad, who had probably pushed him through BC and Suffolk Law through sheer force of will. Good old Dad probably knew Francis Cavanaugh from the Knights of Columbus or Kiwanis, probably contributed to his campaigns every four years (even though Francis never had any opponents). And when little Jerry needed a job after eking out his J.D., Dad knew whom to call. And poor Jerry just had the bad luck to be on duty for this.

Not that Jerry was a loser. No matter how much we dislike each other, I have to admit that Cavanaugh isn't stupid, and he knows better than to hire losers. Lots of these green Suffolk Law grads become wily, tenacious prosecutors. But clearly young Tobin was in over his head when it came to dealing with this particular situation. So why was he going to handle this crucial first interview with me? Why not keep me on ice until the boss could show up?

I figured I knew. Surely Tobin was bright enough to call Cavanaugh as soon as he took one look at me. And the Monsignor (as everyone refers to him behind his back) would understand how delicate the situation was. This was the opportunity of a lifetime, but he couldn't afford to overplay it. I was in enough trouble. No sense in giving me the sympathy vote by having it look as if his office were out to get me. So let Jerry handle things for now, but keep him on a short leash. And I imagined I could hear the sound of phones ringing all over the state as the Monsignor spread the news, as the people who live and breathe politics suddenly found new meaning in their existence.

The four of us found some privacy in the dim stairwell. Mackey stationed a cop at the door to keep people from barging in. Roger sat on the stairs heading up to the next floor; the rest of us remained standing. I went over my story once again.

"But why would you come to her apartment to be interviewed?" Mackey asked, reasonably enough, when I had finished. "Why wouldn't she go to your house or your office or campaign headquarters—someplace more convenient for *you?*"

"Well, as I said, I happened to be in the neighborhood tonight, so this *was* convenient for me."

"But in general, Jim. You said you've been here a few times."

"I didn't say I came here exclusively, Mack. Sometimes it made sense for me to come here, so I did."

"Why is this an issue?" Roger interrupted.

"Well, we're gonna have to piece together this woman's life, aren't we? And Jim happens to be standing here, so I figure, let's start with him."

"But why do you have to piece together her life?" Roger persisted. "Her apartment's a mess. It looks to me like someone broke into the place and robbed her."

Mackey shrugged. "Maybe. Her wallet's empty. But the ME gives me a time of death of four-thirty, five o'clock. You generally don't have break-ins in the late afternoon. Too many people around."

Four-thirty, five. No, that was not a good time of death. Oh, Lord.

"And then there's the stuff on the computer," Mackey added.

"What stuff?" Roger asked.

Mackey told him.

"That's weird," Roger said. "But why doesn't it also suggest a robbery? Some crazy breaks in, kills her, sees the computer on, and decides to leave a message."

"Maybe," Mackey said again. "But your average crazy doesn't stick around to leave messages."

"Well, there's the door, Mack," I said. "It looked to me like someone attacked the lock."

"Looked to me like someone did a bad job of making it appear that the lock had been forced. Whacked at it with a hammer or something—didn't do any real damage. Probably got scared by the noise. Was the door locked when you got here, Jim?"

I could have lied, but I didn't have time to think through the consequences. Under the circumstances I figured it was better to tell as much of the truth as I could. "Yes," I said.

"How'd you get in?"

"I have a key."

I thought I noticed Tobin twitch. The assistant DA knew what would make his boss happy. My opinion of him went up. "How come you have a key?" he demanded.

Mackey sighed.

"Because I asked for it," I said. "Once she got delayed coming to the interview, so there was nothing for me to do but leave. Waste of my time. I got pretty angry about that. I said, 'If we're going to meet here, at least give me a key, let me go in and get some work done if you're late.' So she did."

Not bad, I thought, for spur of the moment. But the key was obviously a problem; just one of many. "Didn't you think it might look bad," Tobin persisted, "meeting a single woman alone in her apartment?"

"Oh, come on," Roger said. I glared self-righteously at Tobin. Mackey laid a hand on my arm. Tobin looked away.

"Anyone see you coming in?" Mackey asked.

"No. I mean, out on Comm. Ave., maybe. There was a woman walking her dog. But not in the building, not that I know of."

"Any reason not to believe him, Mack?" Roger asked.

"Heck, I've got a hundred witnesses who saw me in Newton half an hour before I got here," I pointed out. "Of course, they're all Republicans."

Everyone laughed except Tobin.

"Do you know if this woman had any enemies?" Mackey asked. "*Hub* magazine—they can get pretty nasty."

"True, but she wasn't one of the nasty ones. We wouldn't have agreed to the biography if we thought she was out to savage me. She did mainly human-interest–type stuff—you know, quadriplegic with AIDS volunteering at a homeless shelter, that sort of thing."

"So you don't think she had enemies."

I shrugged. "Look, Mack, anyone in the public eye can have enemies. You know that. She writes something unflattering about the quadriplegic's dog, and he rams her with his wheelchair. But no one told me about any enemies."

"Were you two close, Jim?"

Jerry Tobin perked up.

"Not especially," I said. "I mean, we were friendly—once again, I wouldn't have gone ahead with this if I didn't feel there was some rapport. But that was it. I don't need that kind of trouble, Mack."

I stared at Mackey. He stared back. Two old pros. He scribbled some notes. "Anything else you can think of might help us, Jim?"

Plenty. But nothing I was going to share with Mackey or Tobin. Or Roger. "Sorry, Mack. I really don't know anything."

Roger stood up. "Okay, gentlemen?"

Mackey shrugged. "Sure."

"We may, of course, need to question you further at a later time," Jerry Tobin said.

"Oh, I'm confident there'll be scenes on the news of me heading into the Monsignor's office to be grilled by his crack staff," I said. "These things have a way of happening."

Tobin's face turned crimson, but he didn't respond.

"So long, Mack," I said. "Give my love to Tricia." If I had been a better politician, I would have remembered the names of his kids, too.

"See you, Jim. Same to Liz."

Mackey and the assistant DA went back to Amanda's apartment. Roger and I headed downstairs. "You want to face 'em," he asked, "or should I handle it?"

"No, I'll have to do it. This looks bad enough without me hiding behind a lawyer." I glanced at my watch, "Perfect for the eleven o'clock news. You think any TV stations'll be out there?"

Roger laughed. "Nah, this sort of thing wouldn't interest them. They're all at Logan Airport, probably, doing live reports about the fog. I bet Harold'll be out there somewhere, though."

Harold. I didn't feel like dealing with Harold now. "Won't that be a thrill," I muttered.

Roger looked at me. "Are you okay, Jim?"

"I'm okay," I said. "Considering."

"It must've been quite a shock."

We reached the lobby. Roger was out of breath; he couldn't even walk *downstairs*? The smell of disinfectant hit me once again. White shirt, black floor. Eyes staring at the ceiling. Quite a shock. "Roger, would you do me a favor?" I said.

"Sure thing, Jim. What?"

"Take your hat off."

Roger took his hat off. We walked through the lobby, past the cop at the door, and outside.

It wasn't raining anymore. The TV lights made everything

as bright as morning in the tropics. The yellow police lines out on the sidewalk gave us a little breathing room, but eventually we had to cross them and enter the jungle beyond. And when we did, the microphones jabbed at us, the cameras tracked us, the questions roared in our ears. I stopped and waited in the middle of the frenzy. I felt calm; I could handle this sort of thing. Eventually the roar subsided. "I'd like to make a statement," I said.

Silence, except for the clicking and whirring of cameras, the jockeying for position. "This evening I went to the apartment of Ms. Amanda Taylor," I said. "Ms. Taylor was a highly regarded reporter for *Hub* magazine. She was conducting a series of interviews with me for a book she was writing. When I arrived, I discovered her body. She had been murdered, and her apartment had been ransacked. Of course, I called the police immediately, and I have just finished talking with them. This is a terrible tragedy. Ms. Taylor was a fine writer and a good human being, and my heart goes out to her family and friends. I intend to assist the police in any way I can to bring the perpetrator of this brutal, senseless crime to justice."

The questions exploded at me as soon as I finished. I picked out one that asked how Amanda had died. "I know you'll understand that it's inappropriate for me to speculate about this crime," I responded, "or to reveal any details that might jeopardize the police's investigation. I'm sure the police and the district attorney's office will provide you with all the appropriate information."

"Could you tell us more about your relationship with the victim?" someone shouted.

Might as well get it over with, I figured. "Well, my staff has received several requests over the past year or so from people who wanted our cooperation in writing books about me. My wife recommended Ms. Taylor. As you may know, Liz is a graduate student at Cabot College, and she became acquainted with Ms. Taylor while she was writing an article about the college for *Hub*. We were all impressed by Ms. Taylor's enthusiasm and objectivity, so we gave her the go-ahead. I guess you could say the result was to have been a semiauthorized biography. She had conducted several interviews with me as part of her research, and I was supposed to talk with her again tonight."

More questions. I could make out one of Mackey's among them: Why were the interviews conducted in her apartment? I didn't want to handle that one now; I was running out of steam, and I was afraid I would make a mistake. I raised a hand. "As you can well imagine, this had been a deeply distressing experience for me. I'll be happy to answer more questions at a later date, but that's all for now."

The questions didn't stop, but I started walking with Roger at my side, and the seas parted for us, more or less. And there was Harold, at the edge of the crowd, motioning to us. I headed for him. As usual, he was wearing a tweed jacket, a starched white shirt, and a bow tie. He was carrying an expensive umbrella that looked like a walking stick. A dandy out for an evening stroll. "I'm double-parked down the block," he said.

"Great," I replied. "Just drive me to my car."

"All right. We're meeting at my place if you can make it, Roger."

Roger nodded. "Nice work back there, Jim."

I shrugged and followed Harold. Roger put his hat back on and went off to his own car. A meeting was the last thing I wanted, but there was no way to avoid it. We had to figure out what to do.

Harold was silent as we got into his Porsche. He was angry at me, I knew; he had every right to be, from his point of view. I loosened my tie and closed my eyes. "I'm parked on Gloucester," I said. "Near Marlborough."

Harold started the car. After a few turns on the one-way streets we pulled up next to my Buick. "Thanks," I said, opening my eyes.

Harold was staring at me—the stare that had reduced many a campaign worker to jelly. "Did you kill her?" he demanded.

I stared back. "No," I said. "Did you?" I didn't bother waiting for an answer. I got out of the car and slammed the door shut. Harold paused for a moment and then drove slowly away.

I unlocked my car and got in. It was only then that I noticed the parking ticket stuck beneath the driver-side windshield wiper. I opened my window, grabbed it, and flung it onto the seat next to me. Staring at it, I felt a twinge of guilt for breaking the law.

What a joke.

I started the car and headed off to Harold's place.

CHAPTER 3

My campaign manager lives in a waterfront condo that perversely faces the city instead of the ocean. There is much about Harold White himself that could be considered perverse. Why does he own a sports car if he never drives over fifty miles an hour? Why does he think tax rates are too high if he won't deduct his charitable contributions on Schedule A? Why does he constantly rail against me, my political acumen, and my general fitness as a human being if he won't consider working for anyone else?

I sit here and look out the window at the bare trees, their branches swaying in the wind, and I try to understand Harold, along with everyone and everything else. Occasionally I think it's all clear, but then the understanding seems to slip away, like a dream dissolving with the dawn. Harold enjoys being perverse, obviously. But he really is different from the rest of us, and the way he lives is far less an act than the way I live. I have heard staff members joke about getting him drunk so they could see the real Harold at last. Would he run naked through Downtown Crossing? Proposition a state trooper? Write out a check to the ACLU? But I suspect that none of those things would happen; he would still be Harold, and the mystery would remain.

One thing is clear to me about Harold. It is said of some liberals that they love The People; it's people they can't stand.

Well, Harold is a conservative embodiment of that contradiction. He believes that government should get off the backs of the working stiff and the small businessman and the entrepreneur, he is passionate in his support for the victims of crime, but he hasn't the slightest interest in the poor souls he is trying to help. I don't think he wants to come much closer to them than the view from his tenth-story window. And that's why he enjoys being a political operative. I'm the one who has to deal with the sweating, belching, dull-eyed masses, with their fears and prejudices and mindless yearnings. Harold has to deal only with me.

And the brain trust.

I was the last one to arrive. Everyone else was in the living room, watching me on the news. Harold has three television sets, for just such occasions as this. It's important to compare coverage during a crisis: The raising of one anchorman's eyebrow might be an isolated reaction; the raising of three eyebrows could portend disaster. I went into the kitchen and got a beer. I didn't need to study the eyebrows; the people in the living room would do that for me. And I didn't want to see shots of the body sliding into the ambulance, the interview with the grief-stricken parents, the pontifications of the political commentators.

Harold doesn't drink, but he always keeps some Coors around on general principle. I opened a bottle and waited for someone to come and get me.

Kevin—who else?—was the one they designated. He was wearing the mournful expression of the typical fatalistic Irishman. *Sure, there'll be pestilence and destruction a-comin' now.* Kevin often reminds me of my father. "Senator," he whispered. "They're wondering if—"

"Of course." I stood up. Did he feel betrayed, with me heading to this woman's apartment instead of going home? Did he wonder what other lies I had been telling? No, not Kevin. Kevin was trying to figure out some way in which this was his fault. After all, it couldn't be mine. I patted him on the shoulder and went into the living room.

The TVs were still on, but the sound was muted. Roger sat by the windows, sipping what looked like whiskey; he must have brought it with him. Poor Roger, I thought. He had the beginnings of a problem. Harold was talking on the phone in the corner.

Marge Terry was sitting on the couch opposite the TVs. She was wearing jeans, a Cornell sweatshirt, and no makeup—not the standard uniform for a media coordinator. There were circles under her eyes. Harold had probably rousted her out of bed. A lot of people would be losing sleep tonight. She didn't meet my gaze as I came into the room. I hadn't thought about her reaction. Would she be as bad as Harold?

Yes, I realized, she would.

Standing next to the TVs was Sam Fisher, our media consultant. I don't think I've ever seen him sitting down. He is as expansive as Harold is buttoned down. His frizzy hair seems to explode from his head in a kind of Jewish Afro; Marge claims she saw birds nesting in it once. I could smell his cologne from across the room.

"Nice job back there, Jim," Sam said. "I particularly liked the way you said 'we,' 'the campaign,' so on. Keep it all objective, impersonal. You're distressed, of course, anyone would be, but this really has nothing to do with you."

If a politician ever has the audacity to think he's real, talking to someone like Sam will put him in his place. Sam sees only the image, cares only about the image. He does like to start out by buttering you up, though, in case there are real feelings lurking inside; this is especially true when he has bad news. I was too tired and worried to play games, however. "But?" I said, knowing full well what the "but" was.

"But it's a disaster," he said, spreading his arms, as if trying to encompass the magnitude of the debacle. "An absolute fucking disaster. You've put yourself in the hands of your worst enemies. Bobby Finn is probably doing backflips through the streets of Belmont even as we speak."

"If they try and pull anything, it'll backfire on them," Kevin said. "No one'll believe the senator's a murderer."

Good old Kevin. Like a mother shielding her young. "Doesn't matter, Kevin," Marge explained. "He was alone in the apartment of an attractive single woman who happened to get herself murdered. That's sordid on the face of it. The *Herald*'s on our side, but even they'll have to put this on the front page for a week. Cavanaugh doesn't have to arrest Jim. He just has to string things out so he gets maximum publicity."

"What is the essence of Jim's appeal?" Sam asked, pacing back and forth as he started his lecture. More of the obvious, I was sure. "How can a Republican like him be elected to the Senate from such a heavily Democratic state? First and foremost, it's his integrity. People trust him. Trust his commitment to family values, honesty in government, so on. They're voting the man, not the party. But if people sense there's something wrong with the man, then there's no reason left to vote for him."

"But someone like Ted Kennedy—" Kevin protested.

"Different story. People don't mind if a politician isn't a saint so long as he doesn't pretend he's one. But they don't like being taken in. They'll vote for scoundrels, but not for hypocrites."

"Well, I think it's clear what the problem is," Roger said. "Why don't we start trying to figure out a solution?"

"There's just one thing I want to get clear," Sam replied. "How come I didn't know about this book deal? No offense, but books are media, and that's what you're paying me for. How come no one asked *me* what I thought about Jim showing up alone at the apartment of an attractive young reporter?"

Silence.

"There was no book deal," Harold said finally. He was off the phone now but still standing in the corner of the room.

"Oh," Sam said. He stroked his bushy mustache, for once at a loss for words.

The phone rang. Harold answered it. It wouldn't stop ringing for a long time. The people who had my home number would be calling it, too, but I doubted that Liz was answering. She liked to unplug the bedroom phone and go to sleep early. So she probably didn't know yet. Poor Liz. It was time to start thinking about her.

I sat down in a cushy wing chair next to the sofa and took a swig of my Coors. "Harold and Marge here didn't like Amanda's proposal," I said.

"If there had to be a book, we preferred a ghostwritten autobiography," Marge said. "We didn't know what this woman's agenda was, and she wouldn't give us approval over her manuscript. So we thought it was a bad idea. The discussion never reached the point where we had to bring it up with you, Sam."

"I went ahead with it on my own," I said.

"Oh." Sam was tugging at his mustache now. "Of course, no one in the campaign is going to say that this was all Jim's—"

Marge waved the idea away. "Of course not. We were behind this project a hundred percent. Best thing that ever happened to the campaign. Hell, we practically had to bludgeon Jim into going along with it." She fumbled in her Coach bag for her cigarettes, then stopped and tossed the bag aside in disgust. This was probably one of the weeks when she had quit.

I noticed an ugly bruise on her forearm. She noticed me notice and quickly pushed the sleeve of her sweatshirt down. Had that bruise been there at the meeting this afternoon?

"And is it true what you said on TV," Sam asked, "that Liz introduced—"

"That's true," I said. This was painful, but there was worse to come. *Liz, wake up, we've got to talk.*

The phone rang again. Harold ignored it this time. Sam moved over next to Roger and leaned against the windowsill. Sweat stains had appeared under the arms of his shirt. On TV, Jay Leno and Ted Koppel and David Letterman were all talking soundlessly at me. "Jim," Sam said, "maybe you don't want to answer this, but believe me, complete honesty is the only way we're going to figure out the best thing to do here. Were you and this woman having an affair?"

Complete honesty. I considered it for a microsecond and then rejected it. I wasn't just dealing with a campaign strategy here; I was also dealing with a murder investigation. What if I told these people the truth and Cavanaugh subpoenaed them? How many of them would commit perjury for me? Harold and Marge, at least, knew some of the truth without my telling them. If they knew the rest, would they turn me in, even without a subpoena? I couldn't afford to find out. "Sam," I said, "she was writing a book about me. Maybe I got carried away and disagreed with my staff because she was young and good-looking. And I'll grant you that going to her apartment by myself was stupid. But the police aren't going to uncover any evidence of some torrid love affair between us."

"Did she have a contract for this book?"

I shrugged. "I don't think so. She told me she wanted to finish it before trying to sell it. Thought she'd get a better deal that way."

"How far along was she in the manuscript?"

"I don't know."

Sam tried not to look suspicious. "Will the police find a manuscript, Jim?"

"I don't know. She might not have started it yet."

"Well, did she tape the interviews, take notes, what?"

"What's going on here?" Kevin interrupted. "This isn't a trial. We should be helping the senator, not cross-examining him."

"You think we're in hot water now," Roger said to Kevin, "but it'll really start to boil if Cavanaugh claims Jim is lying about this book." He took out a flask and poured more whiskey into his glass.

The phone rang. Why didn't Harold unplug it if he wasn't going to answer it? Probably just trying to annoy me. I couldn't stand talking about the book anymore. "All I'm saying is that I didn't pay attention to her writing methods," I said. "She didn't take notes during the interviews. She didn't say anything about taping. Maybe she did it secretly. Maybe she took notes afterward. Some reporters do that to make it seem more like a conversation, so you let your guard down. I'm sure this won't be a problem, Sam."

"If you say so, Jim." He didn't sound convinced. I wasn't convinced myself. "Jim, I think you know as well as I do who holds the key to our survival right now."

I nodded. Not District Attorney Cavanaugh, not Detective Mackey, not Governor Finn. Not even Senator James O'Connor; it was out of my hands, too. "Liz," I said. I finished the beer and set it down next to the chair.

"Can I get you another?" Kevin asked immediately.

"I guess not, Kevin," I replied. Marge was looking at me. She has big, easy-to-trust green eyes that she uses to good effect when she's trying to put one over on a reporter. Now they were boring into me, blazing messages that were not difficult to interpret. "What do we want Liz to do for us?" I asked softly.

"You should hold a press conference tomorrow," Sam said, his hands framing the scene. "On the lawn outside your home. Liz by your side. Kathleen's bicycle parked in camera range. Liz talks about how she introduced this reporter to you. Make it sound as if she was Liz's friend, not yours—or at least a friend of the family. Liz, of course, is as distraught as you are by this tragedy, so on. If some insensitive boor asks her if she was jealous of the victim, she reaches for your hand—you know, surreptitiously, but so the cameras can pick up the gesture—squeezes it, says, 'Jim and I have been married for fifteen years, twenty years, whatever, and we know each other too well to be jealous. We have a good marriage, and I believe this tragedy will only strengthen the bond between us.' See what I mean?"

We were silent for a moment, indulging in the fantasy that

we could actually get Liz to say something like that. "What if we just draft a statement for her?" Roger asked, trying to be practical.

Sam shook his head. "Not good enough. We need the visuals. We need the loyal wife by the candidate's side. It's not what she says but how she says it."

The phone rang. This time Harold picked up the receiver and immediately put it back down again. "She should go to the funeral, too," he said.

I closed my eyes. That was really asking too much; Harold was trying to rub it in. "It might seem inappropriate for either of us to go to the funeral," I suggested. "You know, concern for the victim's family. We don't want to turn it into a media circus after all."

"You think it won't be a media circus anyway?" Sam asked.

He had a point.

"The family doesn't have anything against you, do they?" Marge asked.

"I don't see why they should."

"Then you have to go," she said. "It'll look bad if you don't. And if you go, Liz should go. Think you can get her to do it, Jim?"

"I don't know," I replied. In fact, I doubted it very much.

Sam held his hands up over his head, like a referee signaling a touchdown. "Tell her this is it," he said. "This is the ball game, right here. That's the truth, and we all know it. The election's neck and neck now. You're popular, but so is Finn. If this gives Finn some momentum, we may never catch up to him."

Sam was right, but the important question was: Did Liz care? Would she care even less after I got home and had my talk with her? "We should do some polling," I noted, changing the subject.

"I've already talked to Steadman," Harold said. "We'll have numbers tomorrow night."

"I suppose you've talked to Washington, too," I said, not doubting it.

Harold nodded. "I told Art to refer all inquiries to the campaign. He knows how to handle this sort of thing."

"Fine." On TV a comedian was laughing at his own joke. A bearded guy in a tweed jacket gestured at a map of eastern Europe. A baby squeezed a roll of toilet paper. "I'll talk to Liz," I said. "I can't promise anything."

"Good," Sam said. "Now, I think we should cancel your schedule for tomorrow. Focus everything on the one event. Hold the press conference at, say, two. I can come over ahead of time and talk to Liz, give her some pointers."

"Fine," I said. "Call me first thing in the morning. Now if there's nothing else—"

Kevin spoke up. "Aren't we leaving out the most important topic?"

People looked at him in surprise. Kevin is not the kind to add his own items to the agenda. "What's that, Kevin?" I asked.

"Well, I think we should talk about who murdered Amanda Taylor."

Blank looks all around—except, perhaps, on Harold's face. But he was still in shadows in the corner, and I couldn't make out his expression. "Okay, Kevin," Sam said. "But I don't see what there is to talk about. On TV they thought maybe robbery—"

"Mackey doesn't think it's robbery," Roger said.

"What then?" Sam asked.

"Jim has a lot of enemies," Kevin said. "Isn't it possible one of them is behind her murder?"

"But why?" Roger asked. "Why kill this woman to get at Jim?"

"To put him in precisely this situation," Kevin said. "They found out he was going to her apartment alone, and they decided to take advantage of it. Maybe they didn't mean to kill her. Say they broke in looking for compromising photographs or something, and she surprised them." His eyes glistened with righteous indignation. I thought about the Polaroid in my raincoat.

"I'm the first one to believe the Democrats are evil," Sam remarked, "but I don't think they're *that* evil."

"Not necessarily Finn's people," Kevin said. "But someone with a grudge. Donato must be out, right? If it weren't for Jim sending him to prison back when he was attorney general, Donato might be governor now; he might be running for senator instead of Finn."

I hadn't thought of Donato in years. It was true, he'd be out now. I wondered what kind of grudge he carried.

"Jim does have his enemies," Roger admitted.

"But let's be realistic," Sam said. "What do we do with this, even if we have our suspicions? We can't exactly make an accusation at the press conference. I suppose we could float a rumor, have a friendly columnist do some speculating. But that doesn't get us very far."

"I think we should look into this murder ourselves," Kevin said. "Cavanaugh is going to try and pin this on the senator, right? He's not going to care about who the real murderer is. So why not do our own investigating?" Clearly Kevin was enamored of the idea: the good guys fighting back against the bad guys. More satisfying, at any rate, than contemplating random urban violence that just happened to put our whole future in jeopardy.

"Cavanaugh's bound to find out," Roger said, "and that will make things messy. He'd probably accuse us of trying to obstruct justice. I think we should lay off. We can always take some potshots at him later if we think he's playing politics with the investigation."

Good old Roger, the voice of prudence. People looked at me. In a way I wanted to side with Kevin. I wanted to know who killed Amanda. But the thought of my campaign investigating Amanda's death wasn't much more palatable than the thought of Cavanaugh investigating it. I nodded at Roger. "I think you're right," I said. "Let's see how things go. Mackey won't be anyone's puppet. He'd arrest the police commissioner if he had the evidence. And anyway, we probably won't get very far solving the murder on our own. More likely we'll just remind people like Donato how much they hate me."

Kevin looked glum, but he didn't argue; his god had spoken. I stood up. "Look, I'm exhausted," I said. "If anyone has any more angles on this, let's talk about them in the morning."

"Would you like someone to drive you home?" Harold asked from the corner of the room. I had a feeling there was more sarcasm than solicitousness in the question, but at this point I didn't really care.

"I can make it," I said. "Thanks for your concern, though. Good night, all."

I was almost out the door when I realized that I had left my raincoat in the kitchen. I retrieved it and felt in the pocket; the photograph was still there. As I left, the phone started ringing.

By the time I reached my car, I wasn't at all sure that I could make it home. Amanda was dead, and my emotions were still lying in wait for me, assassins seeking the right moment to strike. What better moment than this—the only time I'd be alone for God knows how long?

I felt unclean as well as exhausted. Amanda was dead, but I had spent most of the time since I had discovered her corpse worrying about the effect her death would have on me. It was inevitable, but it wasn't right.

I drove slowly out of the garage and onto the streets of the city. At a stoplight I took out the photograph and stared at it, at us. We made quite a couple.

There was me, of course, with my curly black hair and pale Irish complexion—the gray haze of my late-night beard just visible in the flash of the camera. I have seen so many photographs and editorial cartoons of this face of mine over the years that it scarcely registers on my consciousness anymore. But I never saw it like this—eyes closed, mouth passionately pressed against the mouth of a beautiful woman, a hint of bare shoulder in the corner of the photo—and the sight still made my heart skip a beat. This will not do, the politician inside me said. This will get me into trouble.

But my face was not worth studying. It was still there; the eyes still stared back at me from the rearview mirror. But, oh, Amanda . . .

She was blond, and her hair was straight; she kept it cut to just beneath her chin, in an angular style that complemented her fine, high cheekbones. Her eyes were closed in the photo and slightly slanted in a vaguely Oriental way. When they were open, they could seem cold and appraising—her whole face had the icy, haughty beauty of a *Vogue* model—but when she was happy, when her wide mouth stretched into an impossibly brilliant smile, then the eyes would sparkle with a joy that could leave you breathless.

And her hands, one of which caressed the line of my jaw: the long, ringless fingers, the perfect tapering nails—

A horn blared behind me. I put the photograph down and accelerated away from the light. Probably a good thing I didn't have a chance to think about the rest of her body, naked next to mine on the bed, about to open like a flower for me after the camera had done its job. . . .

The body that now lay in a bag in a locker in the Southern Mortuary, that would soon be cut up by the medical examiner as he dispassionately recited what he found into a tape recorder. How little the tape recorder would know. How much the camera had seen.

Somehow I made my way onto the Southeast Expressway. The rain had started again, and I was having difficulty seeing the road. A car wreck would be a fitting end to the day.

Kevin's theory was not absurd. I was sure that it was because of me that Amanda had died.

I didn't know what had happened. It had all turned bad, and I wanted to blame her, had every reason to blame her, but I couldn't. The punishment was far worse than the crime. And I remembered the beginning, before the lies and the betrayal and the blood on the kitchen floor.

"Do you know what you're getting yourself in for?" I asked her before we made love for the first time, as we stood by her bed and I struggled to unbutton her blouse, my hands trembling with excitement, my eyes blurring with desire. A Brandenburg Concerto played in the background; our brandies sat undrunk on the glass coffee table in the living room.

Her dark eyes stared at me, judged me. "But the risk is all yours, isn't it?" she said. She unhooked her skirt, and it fell to the floor with a ripple of silk.

"I've made my choice to live in front of the public. You haven't."

She shrugged out of her blouse and unhooked her bra, which joined the pile of clothing on the floor. "I think I'm making my choice right now," she murmured, and she moved into my embrace. White breasts, black panties. Eyes that had judged me and found me worthy. Giving herself to me.

Oh God, life is cruel.

I was south of the city now, heading home. *Liz, you have every right to be angry at me, but my future—our future—is at stake here.* No, not so pompous. *We've got a problem, Liz, a big problem. I'm begging you to help me solve it.*

And Kathleen. I hadn't even thought about her yet. *There'll be stuff in the papers, on the news, Kathleen. I'm sorry if any of this will hurt you.* No, she didn't like apologies. Just give her the facts and let her make up her mind. Would she understand? Could she forgive?

I'd have to find out. Fighting sleep, I got off the highway and onto the long dark road that led into Hingham. My nice, affluent suburb. Went for me three to one in the last election. Amanda was dead. How many points would that lose me in Hingham? Would my wife help me? Would my daughter hate me? Steadman would have numbers tomorrow night. Amanda was dead. My wife and daughter were safely asleep in our cozy home, and Amanda lay in a bag in a locker. Harold apparently thought I had killed her, Marge probably did, too, and the Democrats were overjoyed. Amanda was dead, and I didn't want to do anything but think about that, think about her, but I couldn't, because the campaign never stopped, and my problems were only beginning.

I turned up the long drive that led through the mist and the pines to my house. I stopped in front of the garage and looked at the place, in darkness except for the light on over the side door leading to the kitchen. I was too tired to move, but I had to go in there, had to face Liz.

I looked down at the photo on the seat next to me. On top of the parking ticket. I sighed. We were such a beautiful couple. I pushed in the cigarette lighter. When it clicked, I pulled it out and laid a corner of the photo on it. The corner glowed for a while, and then the photo flamed up in the darkness as the fire consumed us, and I dropped it into the ashtray. The flame died away quickly, leaving behind only brittle black paper that crumbled to dust beneath my touch.

Then I got out of the car and went inside to talk to my wife.

CHAPTER 4

I stood in the middle of my safe, homey kitchen. I gazed at the refrigerator door covered with school notices and postcards and comic strips torn out of the newspaper; the ragged cookbooks on the shelf above the counter; the peeling paint in one corner of the ceiling, where water had leaked in past a rotting gutter during a summer storm; Kathleen's denim jacket slung over the back of a chair. No murders here.

I decided that I was hungry. I tried to remember when I'd eaten last. I should have grabbed something at Harold's, but food had seemed irrelevant until now, in my own kitchen, as I looked for ways to delay facing Liz.

I opened the refrigerator, and the sight of the familiar shelves of food seemed to add an extra layer to my sorrow and confusion. Amanda was dead. I would eat leftover tuna for the thousandth time, only it wouldn't matter, it was just the need to survive, to keep going, like lying to the press, like hiding my secrets from my campaign staff, like begging Liz for a favor she had no reason to grant. I added some mayonnaise—Liz never puts in enough mayonnaise—and ate the tuna right out of the plastic bowl. "Oh, Daddy, yuech," Kathleen would say. Well, she'd never know. When the tuna was gone, I rinsed out the bowl and left it in the dish drainer by the sink. Then I went upstairs.

I felt like an intruder, a criminal sneaking from one misdeed to the next. That hadn't been my tuna—Kathleen had probably been counting on it for her lunch—and this scarcely seemed to be my house anymore, no matter how much time I spent in it. And the sleeping woman I was about to disturb—well, things were better once, Liz, weren't they?

I turned the bathroom light on so that I could see my way along the hall to our bedroom. The door was closed. I opened it and stood just inside the room for a moment, staring in at Liz as she slept. In the dim light she looked scarcely different from when I first met her, the same short blond hair framing the same thin, pretty face. The hair was frosted now, and the skin on her pretty face was not as smooth as it had once been. But I couldn't claim in my defense that she had let herself go. The beginnings of middle age had affected her no more than they had affected me.

What, then? What did I claim? *My wife doesn't understand me.* Hardly. After all this time she probably understood me better than anyone in the world. And perhaps that was it, although it wasn't an argument I'd like to make to a jury. *My wife understands me too well.* In her eyes I wasn't the glamorous young senator, one of the most powerful men in America, his name already bandied about for the presidential race two years down the road. No, I was Jimmy O'Connor, the mick lawyer from the seedy side of Brighton, begging her to marry him, making a fool of himself trying to talk about no-load mutual funds with her father, throwing up from nervousness the night before a big trial, always trying to be a little tougher and smoother than he really was. I was the guy who couldn't change a flat, who forgot birthdays and anniversaries, who put too much mayonnaise in his tuna. I was the guy who turned his back on a six-figure income and dragged her to candidates' nights in drab school auditoriums and parades in decaying industrial cities, who forced her to be the frozen-smiled hostess at countless fund raisers, who demanded that she do all sorts of things she hated doing with every fiber of her being—all in order to satisfy some silly ambition that had more to do with hormones than a desire to fix what was wrong with the world.

Ladies and gentlemen of the jury, can you see why I tried to escape from that kind of understanding?

Can you see why she did her own escaping when she got the chance—with me in Washington most of the time and Kathleen in school? Going back to school herself, to study . . . whatever it was that Cabot College was teaching her—humanistic studies or something. As far as I could tell, her program consisted of reading pop psychology books and dabbling in the occult. Coping Strategies 101. Practicum in Astral Projection. "I'm inner-directed and you're outer-directed," she explained once, with the condescension of a grad student who has recently learned the mysteries of the universe. "This can be a source of conflict between us, but it can also be the source of great strength."

I had told her the same thing (only without the jargon) when I was trying to convince her to marry me. So why hadn't we found the strength?

My fault, of course. No sense in even bringing up the question. She was willing to work on our relationship. Perhaps, it occurs to me now, going back to school was her way of working on it. If she could learn enough about the human heart, she could fix what was wrong between us. But I had to go to a committee meeting, to a caucus, to a roll call; I had to talk to constituents, to my staff, to the President; I had to do my homework on air pollution, on national health insurance, on mandatory sentencing. Above all, I had to campaign, always campaign. So what was I supposed to do?

Well, I wasn't supposed to have an affair; I was inner-directed enough to understand that much. *Liz, I guess you know that things haven't been right between us for—*

I walked over to my side of the bed and turned the light on. The phone next to the light was unplugged, as I had suspected. So she didn't know. "Liz," I said. My voice quavered; I'm not the sort whose voice quavers. She didn't stir. "Liz," I said. "Wake up." I sat on the bed and put a hand on her arm.

Liz opened an eye and shut it again. "Time is it?" she mumbled.

I shook her arm. "It's after one. Liz, I've got to talk to you."

Both eyes opened and blinked against the light. She pulled herself up to a sitting position and stared at me. She was wearing panties and one of my pajama tops. I mentioned once that I thought this was a sexy outfit to wear to bed, and she rarely wears anything else now—at least when I'm around. "What's going on?" she asked.

"Amanda Taylor," I said. All my mental rehearsals, and those were the only words that would come out.

Liz stared at me. If there was a reaction to the name, I couldn't detect it. "What about her?"

"She's dead. She was murdered. I discovered the body tonight."

Liz brushed a strand of hair out of her face. How many times had I seen her do that? This time was it a reaction? *Oh, my God. Poor Amanda. It must've been awful for you.* Nothing. Just her eyes, studying me. "Dead," she repeated finally, as if she were learning a word in a foreign language. And then: "Why did you discover the body?"

The time had come. I stood up. Lies wouldn't help, and delaying would only make it worse. "Amanda and I had an affair," I said. "It was over between us—I swear it was—but I heard that she might be going to write something about me. So I went to see her after the speech tonight, to try and talk her out of it, and that's when I found her. I'm sorry, Liz. You know how things have been between us. I never wanted to hurt you, but . . . I'm sorry."

Couldn't I have done better? The speech sounded hollow— lines from old movies. Liz looked away, as if embarrassed at my performance. She pulled up her knees and pressed her hands together in front of her face. *How could you? What have I ever done to deserve this? I hate you.* No. Not from Liz. "Am I the last person to find out?" she asked.

"About the affair? I don't know," I said. "You're the first person I've told anyway. I guess Harold and some of the others suspected, but they didn't say anything to me. At least not directly."

She shook her head. That wasn't it. "I mean, was it on the news? Do our neighbors know? Does my hairdresser know? Do Kathleen's teachers know?"

"The murder was on the news. I was on the news. I don't think they'll find any conclusive evidence about the affair. But there'll be suspicions, of course. There'll be rumors. You know how it is." Yes, she knew how it was. I realized that I had moved to the foot of the bed, to try to get her to look at me again. It was so difficult talking to her nowadays, even on topics much less dangerous than this. I sometimes thought a Ouija board would have been more effective.

And I thought: If only the affair was all I had to worry about.

She gazed at me over her knees for a moment, then lowered her eyes. "Is Amanda the only one?" she asked.

"Yes, Liz. I swear it. I won't deny that I've had opportunities, down in Washington all by myself. But there haven't been any others."

She looked at me again, and I could see that she didn't believe me, and then her disbelief turned into misery. More than misery: terror. I got a dizzying glimpse of what must have been going on inside her before she lowered her eyes once more. She had been hurt, and now she would have to live in fear that she would be hurt again. You can't be married as long as we have without developing the capacity to inflict enormous pain on each other, I realized. Without being hurt by the pain that you yourself inflict.

"So this means trouble," she whispered to her lap.

Trouble for us or trouble for me? I decided she meant the latter. "Liz, something like this can destroy a campaign, even when there isn't any impropriety. Particularly when you're a candidate like me. You know what I'm talking about. I won't be able to bring up the issues or talk about my record. All people will be thinking about is the murder, the scandal."

"I'm sorry to hear that," Liz said.

Was she being sarcastic? Probably, but maybe not. I just couldn't tell anymore. I had to press forward. I went over and sat next to her on her side of the bed. I put a hand on her knee, half expecting her to brush it away. She didn't move. "You probably hate me right now," I said. "But I'm going to ask you to do something for me, and I want you to think about it very carefully before you answer." She crossed her arms, protecting herself. She met my gaze. "I want you to stand by me for the next couple of days," I said. "Answer questions at a press conference with me tomorrow. Go to Amanda's funeral. Show the world that you believe in your husband. I know this sort of thing is hard for you in the best of times, but see, you just aren't going to be able to escape it now. If you don't go to the press conference, they'll just track you down at school or wherever and make your life hell until you tell them what they want to know. The only chance you have to get things back the way they were is to say that everything is fine, as forcefully and as publicly and as soon as you can."

The argument had come to me only as I started speaking. Appeal to her self-interest. Not the self-interest that her husband would be disgraced and out of a job if she didn't cooperate, but that cooperating was the only way to get the world to leave her alone. It was a risky approach, but my lawyer's instincts felt good about it.

"Why should I bother?" she said. "I could kick you out of the house and demand a divorce. Once you've lost the election, no one will care about me anymore."

I nodded. "I know that would give you some satisfaction," I said, "and I'm not saying I don't deserve that sort of treatment. But think about Kathleen."

Didn't want to make too big a point about Kathleen. That would just give Liz an opening to accuse me of using our daughter as a weapon. "Did you think about Kathleen while you were screwing Amanda Taylor?" she asked.

I spread my hands in a peacemaking gesture. "I can't offer you a defense for what I did, Liz. I can only ask your forgiveness."

"You don't want my forgiveness," she said. "You want my help."

"I'd like both. But if I can't have your forgiveness, yes, your help is still important to me. Please, Liz."

Her face took on that exasperated, put-upon look I had seen so often over the years. *How did I let this guy into my life?* it seemed to say. The expression had been there even the first time I asked her to marry me, as we danced at my brother's wedding reception.

Marry you, Jim? Don't ruin everything. I'd just be asking for trouble.

Nonsense. You'd be asking for glory. Riches beyond the dreams of avarice. Great sex. And of course, my scintillating personality and Irish wit, twenty-four hours a day.

Trouble, James O'Connor. Nothing but trouble.

The band played "Sunrise, Sunset"; the rotating globe on the ceiling threw splashes of gold on the dancers; Liz was warm and luscious in my arms. In the middle of the floor my brother Danny nuzzled his bride as he balanced a glass of champagne behind her back. My father looked on from the head table, nodding benignly in time to the music. The world was filled with promise. Liz's reluctance only increased my resolve. I would conquer her; I would conquer the world.

She said yes then . . . finally; she said yes now. "I suppose so," actually. Sighing, slumping down in bed, closing her eyes to block out the sight of me.

"It's only for a couple of days," I said. "Till the initial excitement dies down. It'll die down a lot faster with you by my side."

"Of course," she said to the pillow. "Just a couple of days."

"Thank you, Liz. You've saved my life."

"Turn out the light," she said.

I got up from the bed and did as I was told. "Maybe I should sleep in the —"

"Sleep wherever you like," she said. "You've been doing that all along. No reason to stop now."

"Right." I went into the bathroom, sat on the toilet, and held my head in my hands. I was trembling. I felt as if I'd been beaten up. And yet she hadn't raised her voice to me, hadn't even seemed especially angry or surprised. We could've been discussing what to have for breakfast tomorrow morning. It was my own sense of guilt, I supposed. I was beating myself up. But still—

I couldn't think about it. I had to get some sleep. Today had been bad, but tomorrow could only be worse. After a while I got up and brushed my teeth, then returned to the bedroom and changed into my pajamas in the darkness. Liz lay motionless in bed. I couldn't tell if she was asleep or just faking, unwilling to deal with me anymore.

Finally I padded silently into Kathleen's room down the hall. She was lost under the covers somewhere, one arm thrust out into the night, as if reaching for help. Her cat, Angelica, was a dark blob at the foot of the bed. I went over, found the top of my daughter's head, and kissed it. She stirred and turned away from me, drawing back her arm. *Don't need any help. I can do it myself.* I smiled. Angelica sleepily changed positions to accommodate herself to the new state of affairs. I hesitated by the bed for a moment, wondering if I should get it over with now, then decided not to. I had used up all my courage for the night. I didn't even bother rehearsing what I would say; it would come out differently anyway. I considered going to the guest room or the couch downstairs in the living room, then walked back to my bedroom and lay down next to Liz. Was it penance, or did I really want to try to get things back to normal between us? I don't know; I was too tired to think straight.

As soon as I closed my eyes, Amanda's corpse appeared, on the floor in her kitchen, staring past me at the ceiling. I have to sleep, I told myself, but I knew that even asleep I wasn't likely to forget that sight.

And then I realized what had been odd about my conversation with Liz. She hadn't seemed interested at all in the topic of Amanda's death. Why hadn't she asked me, like Harold, if I had killed Amanda? Because she couldn't believe such a thing about me? Because my adultery was enough pain for her to deal with? Because my adultery had more to do with *her*? Or—

I turned my head and stared at the back of the person who had slept beside me for so many years. What's going on in that inner-directed mind of yours? I wondered. But if she understood me too well, I was no longer sure I understood her at all.

I did know this, though, from the hunch of the shoulders, or the tilt of the head, or some mysterious rearrangement of the molecules in the air around her: She was still awake, eyes staring into the darkness as she fumed or coped or plotted or despaired. In the old days I would have snuggled up close, rubbed her behind, nuzzled her neck. I would have murmured random reassurances in the hope that one would hit the mark. I wouldn't have left her alone until I had made things better.

But now I could do none of that, and I was too tired even to try. Liz would have to fight her own battles in the darkness. My eyes closed once again, and the nightmares came, and they didn't leave until morning.

CHAPTER 5

I got up before Liz, but after Kathleen. The *Globe* was on the kitchen table, along with a carton of orange juice; Kathleen wasn't good about putting things away. I poured myself some juice, put the carton away, and sat down to study the coverage; it was reasonably fair, considering that the *Globe* hated me. Finally I went back upstairs to find Kathleen.

She was in her room, her back to me, sitting in front of her computer. It was Saturday, no school, yet here she was, at seven-thirty in the morning, already at work. Just the way I had been. And yet nothing like the way I had been. "Good morning, angel princess," I said.

"Good morning, snookie-wookums," she replied without turning to look at me. She had grown out of pet names a long time ago, so she had decided to give as well as she got.

"Can I come in?" I asked.

"Sure."

I entered her room. It was a mess. Einstein looked down at me from above Kathleen's bed; next to him was some dreamy-eyed pop star whose name I could never seem to remember. There were several red-white-and-blue "Senator O'Connor" bumper stickers plastered on the walls and the furniture, and more clothes than I could imagine one person ever wearing piled on the floor

46

and spilling out of the closet. From all that, she had chosen to wear a Harvard sweatshirt and faded jeans with the knees worn away. I kissed the top of her head and looked over her shoulder at the computer screen. On it an abstract gray sea-horse tail spiraled inward while layers of brown and black waves swirled around it. "That's gorgeous," I said. "Did you draw that?"

"It's a Mandelbrot set," she said, as if that made everything clear.

"Oh," I said. I sat on the edge of her bed. Angelica was still curled up at the foot of the bed; Angelica was getting old. *Kathleen, we've got to talk.* No. I couldn't do it. "So, um, what's a Mandelbrot set?"

Kathleen swiveled in her chair and looked at me. She was always very patient with my ignorance. "It's a collection of complex numbers. They form all sorts of spectacular patterns. I've got a program that generates them. It's got to do with fractals."

"Oh," I said. She was wearing her hair in a ponytail. She had her mother's blond hair and good looks, except for my strong chin, which seemed to make her face a little too broad. She was starting to worry about how pretty she was; I wanted to tell her that she needn't bother, that the boys were undoubtedly lusting after her already, but why should she believe her father?

The silence became uncomfortable. "Do you know about fractals?" Kathleen asked finally.

I shook my head.

"Do you want to learn?"

"Sure." Better than talking about adultery and murder. Probably she was thinking the same thing. She kept things in, like her mother—like me, in a way. I could hear the phone start ringing in my office downstairs. I ignored it.

"Um, think of the coastline of Massachusetts," she said. "From outer space it looks pretty much like the maps—you know, just a few wiggles. Well, the closer in you get, the more detail you see, right? Someone walking along Cape Cod will notice little, I don't know, inlets and stuff that the mapmakers ignore. And an ant crawling along the beach will pick up even more detail. So the ant's estimate of how long the coastline is will be a lot larger than that of someone looking at it from outer space, right?"

"Right." Her eyes sparkled when she talked about stuff like this.

"So it's basically meaningless to talk about how long the Massachusetts coastline is, right?"

"Well, I guess. So what's a fractal?"

"A fractal is a measure of how irregular something is. How complex it is. How rough around the edges. And the Mandelbrot set shows what happens when you focus in on the irregularity. No matter how close you look at things, there's always more complexity. This could be, like, an ant's-eye view of things," she said, gesturing at the computer screen. "We could step back and get a person's-eye view, or we could zoom in and get, you know, a molecule's-eye view. If molecules had eyes." She started to giggle, suddenly self-conscious.

"And it would always be different," I said.

"Uh-huh. Except it's always there. You just can't see it if you're back too far."

I shook my head in wonder. "How come I don't know any of this stuff?"

"They hadn't thought it up when you were in school," she pointed out.

"Back in the Dark Ages."

"The sixties," she whispered, making the decade sound distant and mysterious.

I laughed. And my heart ached, thinking about what I had missed of my daughter's life while I fought my battles down in Washington. We fell silent again, and I knew it was time. "You read the newspaper this morning," I said.

She nodded. The sparkle went out of her eyes.

"I have to talk to you about what happened. It'll be in the news a lot, and people will be saying things, and—"

"I know that, Daddy," she said. "It's okay." She was blushing.

"Well, I want you to understand that I won't hide anything from you. I know this affects you, and your feelings are important to me."

"It's okay," she repeated. Her hands clasped and unclasped in her lap. She didn't want to talk about it, but if she didn't, she'd brood about it and gnaw at it, and eventually it would become worse than it really was—if that were possible.

"Do you want to ask me anything? I know this is awkward for both of us, but it's important."

She shook her head. "It's—" she started to say, then stopped. She knew that it wasn't okay. She turned and looked at the sea horse tail on her screen. "You were having an affair with her, right?"

I took a breath. "Yes," I said.

"Did you use a condom?"

That hadn't come up in my mental rehearsals. "Huh?"

"They hadn't thought up AIDS in the sixties either," she said.

"Right," I whispered. And my heart ached once again. The world was a terrifying place, and my daughter was just starting to venture out into it. Crime and pestilence threatened on all sides. Toxic waste lay buried beneath us; acid rain fell on top of us. Boys were beginning to compete with computers in her thoughts, but boys were hairy and wild and dangerous, and maybe it would be safer just to stare at the pretty patterns on her screen. I wanted to embrace her, to tell her I would protect her from everything, but how could I? I was part of the danger. "I didn't use a condom," I said. "I'm sorry."

"Don't apologize," she responded reflexively. She hated it when I apologized.

"I'm sure there isn't a problem" I said.

"Why?"

"Because—because I knew her."

"How do you know you knew her?"

I spread my hands helplessly. It was an excellent question. One I had asked myself. "She was a good person, Kathleen. I wouldn't have gotten involved with someone who wasn't a good person."

"It's okay," she said, retreating.

"Your mother and I—"

"Don't worry about that. I understand about that."

Did she? Then she understood more than I did—which was not impossible. Certainly she wanted Liz and me to work out our problems. The three of us had posed for a family photograph in the summer—Harold thought it would be good to use in some direct-mail pieces—and afterward Kathleen was full of sly comments: "Boy, I sure enjoyed being together with *both* of you." "Isn't it great that we *look* like a family?" But she never confronted us directly about how it was all affecting her. And clearly she didn't want to talk about it now.

"I love you, Kathleen," I said. "I know this must hurt you, but I don't want to hurt you anymore. Please let me know if I do. Okay?"

"Sure, Daddy."

I got up and kissed her. "There'll be a press conference here later on," I said. "I hope that won't—"

"No problem"

"Thanks, dumpling."

She smiled. "You're welcome, pudding."

I was on my way out of the room when she called after me. "Daddy?"

"Yes?"

"I'm sorry she died, Daddy."

And then she turned back to her computer.

I went downstairs once again. I made myself a cup of instant coffee, grabbed a couple of semistale doughnuts out of the bread box, then went into my office and shut the door. It was time to go to work.

I was glad I didn't have to campaign; it would have been hell out there. But the alternative wasn't likely to be much better. Nothing to be done about it, though. The damage had to be contained.

But there was something I had to do even before that. I drank some of the coffee and called my brother.

His wife, Melissa, answered. "Hi, Lissa," I said. "It's Jim."

"Oh. Jim. Hi. Um—"

"I'm sorry to bother you so early, but I've got to talk to Danny."

"Danny? Well, he's asleep, Jim. He's been really sick lately, he hasn't been out of bed in two three days, and I don't want to bother him if I don't have to. It's the flu, you know. He keeps picking it up from the kids. He doesn't take good care of himself, and he comes down with something, and then he's like blaming the world. It seems like he's out of work half the time lately, and I don't know—"

"Okay, Lissa. I understand." She sounded half hysterical; living with Danny would do that to a person. "Tell him when he wakes up that he's got to call me. It's very important. All right?"

"All right, Jim, but—"

"You have the number of my car phone, right?"

"Um, sure, yes, we've got it. Jim?"

"Yes?"

"I'm so sorry about what happened yesterday."

"Thanks, Lissa."

"Is everything going to be all right, do you think? You know, with the election and—and everything."

"Oh, sure, I can take care of that," I said lightly. "But have Danny call me as soon as possible."

Danny, I thought after I hung up. What have you done to me now?

And then I turned my attention back to politics.

A raft of messages had come in on my private line. I played them back, meanwhile making a list of the people to be called. It was important to get to them before they had a chance to panic—before the rumors could start, before momentum could shift. "Everything is under control," the senator's call would tell them. This is just a minor pothole on the highway to victory. The confident sound of my voice would counteract the raising of the anchorman's eyebrow, the gloating of the Democrats, the mention of the word "Chappaquiddick" in the *Globe*'s op-ed columns, and everything would be back on track once again.

And so I made the calls, and I picked up the lying where I had left off the night before. My strategy was simple and intuitive; I scarcely had to think it through. Admit the stupidity. Gloss over the possibility of an affair; certainly gloss over the murder. Emphasize Liz. "I could kick myself," I told them, one after another. "I've been around long enough to know that the appearance of impropriety matters as much as impropriety itself. But it honestly never occurred to me. I mean, I know she was good-looking, but she was a reporter, for God's sake. I was stupid to go to her apartment, but I'm not stupid enough to have an affair with a reporter. Incidentally, Liz is behind me a hundred percent on this. After all, having Amanda Taylor write the book was Liz's idea in the first place."

It worked, as lying often does. People were pleased and relieved to hear from me, and their dismay and anger and fear couldn't withstand my blarney for long. Lying is necessary for politicians, and finally it becomes easy.

And here is the central question: Does the politician come to believe his lies? Or—worse, perhaps—does he lose all sense of what is true and what is false? Are the categories simply irrelevant to the words he utters?

I am trying to tell the truth here. If I don't tell it here, where will I tell it?

Kevin was the first of my staff to arrive at the house. He looked even more lugubrious than usual. He showed up early for a reason, it turned out. "Senator," he said, "I feel terrible about yesterday."

"That makes two of us, at least, Kevin."

"The thing is," he went on, "about the time of death. It was in the paper, you know."

The time of death. Yes, I knew about the time of death. "What about it, Kevin?"

"Well, I was thinking . . . Cavanaugh's gonna make a big deal about this unless you've got a good alibi. So I was thinking I could vouch for you if you wanted. Say I drove you from the meeting yesterday afternoon. You know, if you thought it would help."

He wouldn't meet my eyes. I expected him to starting pulling at his collar and scuffing his shoes on the floor. Did he, too, think I was guilty? Obviously I had misled him last night, making him think I was going home when, in fact, I was heading off to this blond woman's apartment. How deeply was his faith in me shaken? Not enough to make him turn his back on me at any rate. Would any of the rest of them do what Kevin was offering to do?

I patted him on the shoulder. "Thanks, Kevin. It's all right, though. We'll get through this."

"It's just that the Democrats are jumping all over you," he said "They make it sound—"

"Don't worry about the Democrats. We're still gonna whip 'em."

Kevin grinned. "I know we are, Senator. I know we are."

The rest of them arrived one by one after Kevin, and it began to feel like business as usual. If Harold still thought I had murdered Amanda, if Marge was still planning to murder *me,* you couldn't detect it from the brisk professionalism with which they did their jobs.

Roger showed up around noontime. He was wearing white shoes, plaid pants, and a jersey that stretched over his bulging middle. "I got a call from Tobin," he informed me. "They want to see you again."

"Why am I not surprised? They have anything new?"

"Not that Tobin said. Of course, why would he confide in me? Jim, I really think you'd be better off if you got someone—"

"Forget it, Roger. I want you. Set something up for later on."

"But not for immediately after the press conference," Sam

Fisher said. "We don't want the media to get shots of Jim jumping in a car to go be questioned by the police."

"Okay," Roger said. "I'll do my best."

"If the DA's got anything," Harold pointed out, "he'll probably leak it to a friendly reporter, see if he can nail you in front of everyone."

"They won't have anything," I said, not at all sure I was telling the truth.

For lunch I had a sandwich in the kitchen. Out front the media people started setting up on my lawn. It wasn't much of a lawn, but this wasn't going to do it any good. Sam Fisher was prepping Liz, who looked as if she were having bamboo shoots stuck under her fingernails. Sam had already picked out my clothes: chinos, casual shirt, sweater. The family man at home on a typical Saturday in the fall. Angelica wandered through, looking disgusted with all the activity. I glanced over the talking points Marge had written up for my opening statement. This would be okay—if Liz cooperated, if the police hadn't come up with anything. I just had to assume that's the way it would be.

Danny didn't return my call. I suppressed the urge to call him again; it would just make Melissa unhappier.

"I don't think I can go through with it," Liz said as the moment approached.

Sam looked at me. He was gnawing a knuckle. Harold gazed at the kitchen ceiling. Marge was out with the media people; she and Liz didn't get along.

"You don't have to do it if you don't want to," I said carefully. "You understand that. But we would all be grateful if you did."

"I don't know," she whispered. She was wearing a wool skirt, a white blouse, and a powder blue sweater. She looked as if she had stepped out of a Talbot's catalog. Her forehead had creases in it that appeared only when she was at her most tense. Her arms were folded tight across her chest. I thought she might be about to throw up.

"Oh, for God's sake, Liz," Roger said from the kitchen table. "Just stand there and look beautiful and say you love your husband. That's all you have to do. You'll be great. Trust me."

She looked at Roger. I expected her to bolt from the room— to lock herself in the bathroom, maybe, and leave me to deal by

myself with the unwashed hordes waiting outside. But she didn't.
"Okay," she whispered.

Sam clapped his hands together. "That's the spirit," he said.
"Whenever you two are ready, then . . ."

I went over to her. "Thanks, Liz," I said. She didn't reply.
"Shall we do it?"

She didn't move. "Do it," Roger said. I held out my hand.
She hesitated a moment longer, then took it. I led her through
the hallway and out the front door. Her hand was moist. The sun
was trying to break through the clouds. The cameras clicked and
whirred. We stepped up to the microphones.

"Let me just make a brief statement before taking your questions," I began. "As I said to you last night, this has been a terrible,
senseless tragedy, and Liz and I want to help in any way we can
to bring Amanda Taylor's murderer to justice. I also understand
the public's curiosity about my role in the tragedy, and so I've
called this press conference to try to clarify it. It really wasn't
much of a role, I'm afraid, and people looking for scandals and
sizzling headlines are going to be disappointed. But it's important
to get the truth out, and that's what I want to do today."

I stopped, and the questions assaulted us. I pointed at a
friendly reporter from the Quincy *Patriot Ledger;* I knew she'd
give us an easy one. "Senator, have you been in touch with the
victim's family?"

"No, I didn't want to intrude on their grief at this time. They
do have my deepest sympathy, of course, and if they want to speak
with me—in person or by phone—I would be happy to share with
them what I know. Liz and I are also planning to attend the
funeral, which I understand is scheduled for Monday morning."

A slick young reporter from Channel 4 was next. "Are you
afraid the district attorney will use the investigation of this murder
to embarrass you politically?"

I shook my head. "I've known Francis Cavanaugh for a long
time. We've had our battles, but I respect him, and I'm sure he
knows that the public would not stand for any attempt to politicize
a murder investigation. We want this campaign to be about the
issues, and I hope the Democrats want the same thing."

See, Liz? Nothing to it. The next one was for her. "Mrs.
O'Connor, your husband said last night that it was on your rec-
ommendation that he agreed to let Amanda Taylor write a book
about him. Is that true, and if so, could you tell us why?"

"Well, of course it's true," Liz said with just the right touch of asperity at the question. Good girl! "Ms. Taylor interviewed me as part of a story she was doing about Cabot College. During the interview she expressed her admiration for my husband and mentioned that she had considered writing a book about him. She asked me if I wouldn't mind finding out from Jim what the chances were of getting his cooperation. I was happy to oblige. I thought she did a good job on her article about Cabot, so why not?"

"What was your reaction when you found out that your husband had discovered Amanda Taylor's body?" another reporter called out.

"What do you think it was?" she shot back. And then she paused—too long. I glanced at her. *You can do it, Liz. Please.* "I suppose you want me to say I was jealous or something," she said. "That's the sort of thing that sells newspapers, right? Well, I'm sorry to disappoint you. I love my husband, and I stand by him. He is a good senator and a good man. You should believe what he says."

There it was then. Not what Sam Fisher had fantasized, but as good as we were going to get. She had told the reporters to believe me, but she hadn't quite said she believed me herself. I had the feeling that her statement had been scrupulously truthful, and that was tough to pull off under the circumstances. So what would happen if someone else noticed what I had noticed? What if she was asked what *she* believed about me and Amanda Taylor, not what she thought everyone else should believe? Would she feel obliged to go on being truthful?

I waited for the follow-up to come. I did a mediocre job of handling a couple of questions directed at me: Why were the interviews conducted in her apartment? Did I have a theory about who murdered her? And then I began to relax. No one was going to follow up on Liz's response. It would sound too obnoxious, perhaps, although that usually didn't stop reporters. Perhaps there were just too many interesting aspects to the scandal to concentrate on one of them. I wasn't going to worry about the explanation, though. They had let it pass, and so would I.

Meanwhile, the questions kept coming. Had I seen Amanda Taylor socially? *No.* Didn't I think it was a bad idea to be alone with her in her apartment? *In hindsight, it apparently was.* How did I think her murder would affect the election? *I have every confidence in the voters, blah blah blah...*

And more for Liz: How friendly had she been with Amanda Taylor? *I didn't really know her at all, except for that interview.* Did she resent my relationship with the victim? *Absolutely not.*

It became clear that we had won the battle. No one had a smoking gun to show the world. Liz was holding up well enough. The worst thing the media could pin on me—today, at least—was an error in judgment in going alone to a single woman's apartment. What the voters would think, of course, was still open to question.

Finally Sam Fisher signaled, and I called a halt to things. We had given them enough. Liz and I retreated to the house as the print reporters headed off to file and the TV reporters hung around to do their wrap-ups.

Kathleen was the first to congratulate us. "You guys were great," she said, hugging us each in turn.

"Thanks, kitten," I said. Liz looked embarrassed.

"How come you don't campaign more, Mom?"

"Your father does just fine without me," Liz replied, and she went upstairs.

Kathleen shook her head. "Mom really was good, you know," she said.

"She saved my life," I said.

"Are you campaigning tomorrow?"

"Looks like it."

"Can I come?"

"You know your mother doesn't want you to."

"Maybe if you insisted—"

I rolled my eyes. "I'm in no position to insist on anything right now."

Kathleen shrugged. "And then you go back to Washington?"

"Monday. After the funeral. I'm sor— I mean, that's the way it is. I'm a busy guy."

"I know," she said. She looked as if she wanted to say something more, but then she thought better of it and followed her mother upstairs. She was probably hoping that this murder would make things better between her mother and me: the family pulling together in the face of adversity. It didn't seem likely.

I went into the kitchen, where my staff was busy dissecting the performance. The consensus was favorable. We hadn't been overwhelming, but we had done the job. After half an hour of rehashing I went upstairs and found Liz in our bedroom, reading a book about reincarnation. "I just wanted to thank you," I said. "You were great out there. Everyone says so."

She looked up from the book. "I go to the funeral," she said, "and that's it."

"Okay," I said. "The funeral is all we need. So, um, I have to see the DA now."

Good luck, dear. Liz stared at me. "Will you be back tonight?"

"Yes. I'll be back."

She nodded and returned to her book.

I stayed standing in the doorway for a moment, and then I went back downstairs.

It was time to find out just how much trouble I was in.

CHAPTER 6

$\mathcal{T}$he press was waiting when Roger and I arrived at the Suffolk County Courthouse. Cavanaugh had made sure my triumph earlier in the afternoon wouldn't go unchallenged; the late news would show me as a potential murder suspect as well as a suburban family man. I no-commented my way through the reporters and met Tobin and Mackey in a dreary conference room; I had undoubtedly been in it a lifetime ago for some plea-bargaining session with one of Tobin's innumerable predecessors.

Mackey looked uncomfortable; Tobin looked wired. This could be the big case that would make his career, he was probably thinking. You need only one after all; he didn't have to look further than my own career for evidence of that.

For Mackey, on the other hand, I was sure that this case was nothing but a pain. He didn't need headlines; he didn't need a career. Above all, he didn't need everyone in the state looking over his shoulder. And he liked me, I was sure; most cops did. I was on their side after all. I wanted to put the scum in prison, where they belonged. Mackey didn't want to think of me as being part of the scum.

"Thank you for coming in to see us this afternoon, Senator," Tobin said when we were all seated.

58

"My pleasure, Jerry."

"There are just a few things we'd like to go over with you, if you don't mind."

"I'd like to get it established at the outset whether or not my client is a suspect," Roger said.

"It's much too early for us to have any suspects," Tobin replied. "We're still just trying to get the facts straight here."

"Fine," Roger said. We could tell the press that the DA's office had stated unequivocally that I wasn't a suspect.

"There are a couple of points we wanted to clear up," Tobin said. "First, we haven't found any tapes of these interviews the victim was supposed to be carrying out with you."

I had known that one was coming. "Well, I'm not aware that she was necessarily taping those interviews," I said. "Maybe she just took notes afterward or something."

"We haven't found much in the way of notes either," Mackey pointed out. "How long has she been at this?"

"We had our first discussions around the beginning of this year," I responded. "But you say there are notes," I added quickly.

"Some," Mackey admitted.

"And were there tapes of other interviews?"

"There appear to be," he said.

My heart sank. I thought of the tapes scattered on the floor of her office. Were those the ones? In any case their existence meant I would win this battle and probably lose the war. Damn you, Amanda, I thought. You didn't deserve to die, but I didn't exactly deserve what you did—or are going to do—to me.

"So we've established that there are notes and tapes," Roger said. "Is there a problem?"

"Just trying to clear up a point," Tobin replied, smiling. "And there's this one other point has us puzzled. We've been looking through Amanda Taylor's articles for *Hub*. Frankly, they don't seem to be written from, let's say, the conservative point of view. Lots of, you know, look at the poor oppressed people whose needs are being ignored. Just wondering why you'd pick that kind of person to write your biography."

That was another obvious one. They weren't having much difficulty building their case, and it was only going to get easier. "Sympathy for the poor and the oppressed is not incompatible with conservatism," I responded pompously. "It was precisely Ms.

Taylor's sympathetic response to other people that attracted us to her. We didn't want a doctrinaire right-wing tract. We wanted a portrait of me as a human being."

"Isn't it possible you got more than you bargained for?"

"This is absurd," I said. "Do you think I killed Amanda Taylor to steal these supposed tapes, then came back a few hours later to discover the body and call the whole world's attention to her death?"

"We haven't reached the point of having any theories," Tobin responded. "But I suppose it's possible to imagine a cool, calculating killer who might do something like that just to throw suspicion off himself."

"Oh, for God's sake," Roger said. "We don't have to put up with this nonsense."

He got up as if to go. Mackey was staring out the window, tapping his pencil against his knuckles. I gestured for Roger to sit back down. "Well, I can see that this campaign is going to get very interesting," I said. "So what else have we got to talk about?"

Tobin reddened but didn't respond.

"Jim, we need to find out where you were late yesterday afternoon," Mackey said.

And there was my main problem. "We have a staff meeting at campaign headquarters on Friday afternoons," I said. "I think the one yesterday got out, oh, fourish." It had ended at precisely four o'clock, I knew. Harold told us he had another meeting to get to—in the Back Bay, I realized with a shudder.

"We're interested in your whereabouts specifically at four forty-five yesterday afternoon," Tobin said.

"Your ME must be pretty good if he can pinpoint the time of death that accurately," I said—as if I could avoid answering the question by criticizing the investigation.

"We've got a witness," Mackey said. "A lady on the fourth floor. Said she saw a well-dressed white man, wearing a hat and carrying a black umbrella, enter the building at quarter to five."

"How could she tell he was a white man," Roger asked, "if he was wearing a hat and she's way up on the fourth floor?"

Good old Roger might not have wanted this case, but he hadn't lost his savvy. "She saw his hand when he opened the door," Tobin said.

"Do you know this man was involved in the murder? Did your

witness hears sounds of a struggle? Did she see the guy leave?"

Tobin should have told Roger to go to hell. At this point it was none of our business what they'd gotten out of their witness. But he let himself get drawn into it. "She didn't have to hear anything for this to be significant," he said. "She sees someone enter the building at around the time when the ME says the victim died, and no one else who lived there claimed to have had a visitor at the time. I think that's worth pinning down."

"Could've been an insurance salesman," Roger said. "Or the person who put up that sign I saw about a lost cat."

"Rest assured we'll look into those possibilities," Tobin replied. "In the meantime, I'd appreciate an answer from your client."

All eyes turned to me. If I had an alibi, we could end this torture right now. "Let's see," I said. "I'd say that at quarter to five I was sitting in my car at Wollaston Beach, looking out at the ocean."

The room was silent. I think Tobin was too stunned to gloat. Only a confession would have been better for him. "Do you have any witnesses who saw you there?" he asked after a few moments.

I shook my head. "Oh, somebody may have noticed me, but no one that I'm aware of. I didn't have anything on my schedule from the time the meeting ended till the speech in Newton, so I was driving home. But the traffic was brutal, what with Friday rush hour and the bad weather and all, so I decided to get off the expressway at Neponset and just work on my speech somewhere for a while. Otherwise, as soon as I got home, I'd just have had to turn around and leave."

"And no one saw you until you showed up in Newton?"

"That's right."

"And your campaign headquarters are in the city somewhere."

I nodded. "We've got office space over at International Place."

Tobin appeared to think it over, but how much thinking was required? I could easily have gotten from the meeting to Amanda's place in time to be the mysterious stranger with the umbrella and the hat. In time to murder her. Tobin had even seen the umbrella.

So no alibi; not even close. A United States senator, someone whose every waking minute was managed by a zealous staff—in the middle of a brutal reelection campaign—had a three-hour hole in his life during which a beautiful woman he had known under suspicious circumstances had been murdered. Tobin didn't have to be Hercule Poirot to figure out that this was pretty damaging.

"Jim, what was your speech about?" Mackey asked. He was still playing with his pencil, not looking at me.

"Oh, values, issues, the future—that sort of thing."

"Pretty standard stuff?"

I saw where he was heading. I shrugged. "I suppose so."

"I mean," Mackey went on, "don't candidates work up a kind of all-occasions speech to give during a campaign? Why was this speech so different you had to work on it for a couple of hours?"

"Well, I suppose it wasn't, Mack. But I didn't feel like driving all the way home. I was at loose ends."

Mackey nodded gloomily; Tobin twitched. He had undoubtedly found out that my wife and I weren't getting along especially well. Did that help his search for a motive? It probably did, I realized. "So you weren't telling the truth when you said you were working on your speech?" Tobin demanded.

"Oh, now, Jerry," I responded. "I sat in my car and stared out at the ocean and worked on my Democrat jokes. Want to hear some?"

"I'd like to go into more detail about your relationship with the victim," he said.

And so it went. Tobin and Mackey probed, and I gave them what I had to. The lack of an alibi was the only real damage, but it was serious enough. Tobin excused himself at one point, and I figured he went to tell Cavanaugh the good news. Whether or not they could pin the murder on me, they could certainly justify making me a suspect. And that would make Cavanaugh's life worth living once again.

"I think that will be all for now," Tobin said finally.

I stood up immediately. "I enjoyed it, Jerry," I said. "Keep in touch."

"Don't worry, Senator. I will."

I nodded to Mackey, who didn't look happy. "Mack."

"Jim."

Roger and I left the room. "How long till they leak it?" I asked him as we walked along the musty corridor.

"Wouldn't surprise me if they already did," Roger replied. "Tobin wasn't going to the bathroom when he left the room that time."

"As I live and breathe, if it isn't Jim O'Connor," we heard a cheery baritone voice say. We looked up to see Francis X. Cavanaugh grinning at us from a doorway.

Even on a Saturday afternoon the district attorney was wearing his usual three-piece suit and starched white shirt. He always looked as if he were on his way to a wedding. And he always looked as if he were just back from Florida; his tan verged on the miraculous. It has never been entirely clear to me why everyone refers to him as the Monsignor. It isn't that he is especially holy, although he spends virtually every Sunday morning of his life speaking at a communion breakfast somewhere in the county. Possibly it's because, with his tan and his head of curly white hair, he looks like the pastor of some affluent suburban parish, the kind of priest who spends his days working on his backswing rather than saving souls. He is in his early sixties now, but he looks almost exactly the same as he did almost twenty years ago, when I came to him and asked for a job.

I didn't get it, and that was only the start of the problems between the Monsignor and me. I'll have to bring up the rest of them before very long.

"Here on a Saturday afternoon, Francis?" I said. "I'm impressed. You just don't slow down."

"The criminals don't slow down," he said, "so how can I?"

"You should leave more of the work to your trusted assistants. I was just talking to one of them—Jerry Tobin? Nice kid."

"He speaks very highly of you as well."

"He does? Well, that makes my day. Be seeing you, Francis."

"Jim?" The Monsignor smiled. "I just wanted to assure you that we are going to be scrupulously fair in this investigation. Politics and personal history will have no place in it."

I smiled back. "Francis, that's good to hear. And I appreciate your taking the time to tell me."

"I thought you'd want to know."

Cavanaugh retreated into his office with a friendly wave. Roger and I continued down the corridor. "The bastard smells blood," I murmured.

"Maybe you should tell the press about this alibi business," Roger suggested. "Launch a preemptive strike."

"I suppose I should."

"How come you didn't mention it in the meeting last night? Harold will be—"

"Yeah, yeah. How was I supposed to know the exact time of death? How was I supposed to know what kind of witness they'd come up with? This is just bad luck."

"Okay, Jim," Roger said. "Take it easy."

Bad luck. I have never believed in luck.

I faced the reporters yet again and gave them my version of what had just taken place. It was tricky this time: I had to plant the first hints that the DA's office was politicizing the murder case, but I couldn't sound as if I were whining. The public still probably perceived Cavanaugh as only doing his job. However, I wanted to help the moment along when the public's perception would change.

The questions weren't hard. There was nothing much to ask me once I'd explained about my hours at the beach. All in all I figured the day would turn out to be a draw.

Afterward Roger and I drove over to campaign headquarters. A lot of people were there, and I gave them a pep talk. "Get the word out," I said. "We're going to work harder than ever. We're not going to let the Democrats steal this election with innuendos and false accusations. We're going to fight back, we're going to get our message across, and we're going to win." They loved it.

Then another meeting of the brain trust. Art Chandler had flown in from Washington. He is the head of my Senate staff down there; gaunt and brilliant, he isn't much on campaigning, but he's a whiz on the intricacies of the Senate. And Ronald Steadman was there, bringing with him the results of his polling.

Steadman wears thick glasses, and his face always has a slightly puzzled look on it, as if he can't quite remember why he is talking to you. Today he was wearing hiking boots, a plaid shirt, and a black leather tie about a millimeter wide. He looks like the kind of guy who never leaves his computer, but his appearance is at least partially deceiving; you can't do what Steadman does without understanding people as well as you understand numbers.

Someone had ordered in a bunch of hamburgers and Cokes. We passed out the food, and I started the meeting off on a depressing note by summarizing what had gone on with Tobin and Mackey, in case anyone hadn't already heard. Then Harold turned to Steadman. "What have you got for us, Ron?"

Steadman passed around copies of a few pages of printouts. "First, I should point out that the nightly tracking polls weren't scheduled to start for a couple of weeks," he began, "so we had to put this together on the fly."

"We should start tracking immediately," Harold said.

"If you've got the money, I certainly recommend it. This looks like it's going to be a very volatile situation."

We would have the money, unless things got really bad; Republicans can almost always outspend Democrats. They generally have to, actually, because Democrats tend to attract more volunteers. Anyway, tracking polls were going to be crucial in a close race like this. Every day you find out: Is your message getting across? Is your opponent making inroads? What groups do you have to concentrate on? Crucial and expensive.

"Let's do it," I said. I glanced at the results. "What's significant here?"

"Well, looking at the big picture, we can see that there's not much movement from the last poll," Steadman replied. "A couple percent more undecided, but that's well within the margin of error. You still hold a ten-point lead, your favorables are still quite high across the spectrum, but so are Governor Finn's. So there hasn't been a catastrophic shift, at least not yet. But remember what I told you before, that a senator's favorability rating is likely to drop more than a governor's in the course of a campaign. Everyone knows their governor, and they've pretty much made up their minds what they think of him before the race. But they have no idea what their senator is up to down in Washington. Finn starts publicizing some of your votes, and suddenly people realize they don't agree with you about a lot of things. So your numbers start to erode."

I nodded. You could hide for six years, but eventually you had to come out into the light of day.

"Women," Harold said, staring at the numbers.

Steadman looked at him with the respect of one professional for another. "Women," he agreed, sipping his Coke. "They're the potential problem, Senator. When we asked if last night's incident would have an effect on their vote, eighteen percent of women said yes or maybe, compared with only four percent for men. Of course, most people say they're just going to wait and see, but the numbers are interesting anyway. Women like you, Senator. You're young, good-looking, dynamic—but also maybe a little dangerous. And they like Finn, too. He's not that much older than you, but he's got more of a fatherly feel to him. They think they understand him; they think they can trust him. So now they begin to have their doubts about you. Maybe you're not so nice after all. Maybe you're a bit too dangerous. And if Finn begins pounding away at your votes on abortion, family leave, day care, that sort of issue, you have a problem."

I bit into a hamburger. It was cold. Yes, I had a problem. "I think we've gotten everything from Liz we're going to get," I said, "except the funeral."

"Well, that could be enough," Steadman said. "We did the phoning this morning, so the effect won't show up until tomorrow. Of course, you also have this alibi thing to contend with now."

"And meanwhile, we're losing the whole focus of our campaign," Sam Fisher complained. He got up and began pacing. "We've got an event set up tomorrow at the Hampden County Jail. We bring the TV crews in, show how overcrowded it is, make a pitch for Jim's plan to offer federal aid for prison construction. So do we go through with it or not? We show Jim inside a prison, maybe people get a totally different message from the one we want to send them."

"Art, what's the prognosis for the bill?" Marge Terry asked.

Art shrugged. "Tough to call at this point. We want to offer it as an amendment to the omnibus crime bill, but it's not even clear the crime bill will come to a vote before the end of the session. We're getting squeezed from the left and the right, and of course, the President is opposed. I'm not wildly optimistic."

"Maybe we shouldn't make such a big deal about it then. If we lose, it makes us look incompetent, even if people agree with us."

"Crime is our key issue, though," Sam pointed out. "Voters blame Finn for the rising crime rate. Your car gets stolen, it's gotta be someone's fault, right? Jim's the guy who puts criminals in prison. Problem is, it's tough to put anyone in prison when you're a senator."

"We've done our best," Art said.

People laughed.

I looked over at Harold, who was doodling on Steadman's printout: a series of vertical lines. Then he connected them with two horizontal lines. Prison bars.

"So what do we do?" Kevin asked.

"We go on the offensive," Harold replied, not looking up.

"Make Amanda Taylor's murder a symbol of our campaign, not theirs. Dare them to solve it. Voice the outrage of the people when they fail. Ignore Jim's involvement. That's just accidental, and anyone who says different is heartlessly using this tragedy for political gain. 'Look,' we say, 'nice young white girls are getting murdered in their apartments in broad daylight. The state's going to hell. And who's been in charge? Bobby Finn. And now he wants to be your senator. Well, Bobby Finn doesn't deserve a promotion. He deserves retirement.' "

Everyone was silent for a moment, pondering that strategy. It was tempting. We had to counterattack. If your opponent can keep you on the defensive, you lose. On the other hand . . . "What if they do solve the murder?" I asked Harold finally.

"Then you're in the clear," he replied, still not looking up from his doodle, "and we don't have a problem. Right?"

"You're so clever, Harold," I said. I reached for another hamburger, and the debate began.

CHAPTER 7

"*P*resident Kenton says he's against crime, but he's consistently opposed my bill to provide federal aid for construction of new prisons. Governor Finn says he's against crime, but what has he done to solve the crime problem in Massachusetts? Where are the bold new ideas he promised us once upon a time? It's easy to say you're against crime. It's a lot tougher to do something about it.

"As you know, violent crime has touched my life quite recently, as it has touched almost everyone's life in this state. We all want to get the criminals off the streets, but we can't do that if there's nowhere to put them. That's why it's so important to pass this bill. That's why it's so frustrating to have President Kenton and Governor Finn oppose it. And that's why I'm so pleased to have Sheriff Amado's endorsement. He shares my frustration with the Democrats' inaction at the state and national level, and he shares my resolve to do something about crime once and for all. Thank you very much."

I shook hands with the sheriff in front of the cameras. Reporters shouted questions about Amanda Taylor at me, but I ignored them. I had said what I had to say about the murder; now it was time to move on.

*   *   *

We had bought into Harold's idea. There wasn't much choice, we decided. We had to define what the race was about. It had to be about the condition of the state, about my defense of traditional values. We couldn't let it be about my voting record in the Senate or my possible involvement in a sensational murder.

I didn't want to bring Amanda into the campaign, even though I believed what I said about violent crime. Usually when I bring up the issue, I talk about how my grandmother was mugged more than thirty years ago on her way to Good Friday services. But I have told that story so many times that I can scarcely summon up the real memories of those events anymore; all that comes are the words I use to recount them. Would Amanda's murder follow suit? Probably. If lies can seem like the truth when you're a politician, the truth can come to seem like a lie. I had protected Amanda—and us—while she was alive, but now that she was dead it was no longer possible.

The Sunday coverage of the murder was more or less what we had expected. Our press conference and the revelation about my lack of an alibi got equal play. The *Globe* interviewed Amanda's father, who said that she spoke highly of me. Friends and co-workers remembered her as bright, popular, and ambitious. No one could think of a reason why she would be murdered. She hadn't talked about the book very much, but she had talked about it. No one mentioned anything about a boyfriend. "She always seemed to be too busy to date," one of her fellow reporters remarked. " 'There'll be time for that later,' she used to say." No one said anything about her politics.

The *Herald* found out about the strange message the murderer had left on Amanda's computer and shrieked it to the world: "SHE HAD TO DIE," MURDERER SAYS! If my involvement hadn't been enough to keep the case alive in the papers, that message would have done the trick by itself.

I called Danny from the car phone on the way back from the media event at the prison. "Oh, Jim, he's out," Melissa said. "I told him to call you, but—"

I pounded the dashboard in frustration. Startled, Kevin looked over at me. "Damn it," I said, "this is important, Lissa."

Melissa started to cry. "I'm sorry, Jim," she sobbed. "I tried to—I said—but you know how he gets."

"Okay, Lissa. Okay. I know you tried. I'm sorry. I'll call again later."

I hung up and stared out the window, trying to control my temper. Only Danny could make me this angry.

After the campaigning was over for the day, I dropped Kevin off and took the car. There was no problem this time; he knew where I went on Sunday evenings.

My father lives in a pleasant garden apartment in the pleasant Boston neighborhood of West Roxbury. The apartment complex is not exactly elderly housing, but it has more than its share of old people. "Full of old divils like me," as my father puts it. "But at least there's a few normal people here, too." My father is opposed to housing for the elderly. Actually he's opposed to the elderly as well. Campaign consultants always recommend getting him out on the road talking to senior citizens' groups about what a swell guy I am and how the Republicans aren't really going to steal their Social Security checks. But he's as bad as Liz about campaigning for me. In the first place, he's not at all sure that the Republicans won't steal people's Social Security checks. In the second place, he hates senior citizens' groups. "Bunch of boring people sitting around complaining about their kids and their arthritis," he explained to Harold once. "Or they play stupid games and go on stupid outings like they're in kindergarten. All they're doing is taking up space until they die."

Harold decided that my father would not be an asset to the campaign.

My father is in reasonably good health, considering that he hates doctors and goes to them only under duress. Nevertheless, he has convinced himself that he is not long for this world. "I'm rereading Dickens, Jimmy," he told me. "When I'm through with Dickens, I have this feeling I'll be through with everything."

When I showed up on Sunday night, he was in the middle of *Bleak House*. "Lawyers, Jimmy. Dickens had them pegged."

"Scum of the earth," I agreed. I got out the bottle of bourbon and poured us each a drink. "Only thing worse is politicians. Cheers."

"Cheers." He sipped the bourbon. In my middle age I have taken to wondering what I'll look like when I grow old. My father gives me a foreshadowing: black hair gone gray and thin, ears sticking out more, a road map of broken blood vessels visible beneath the skin. He looks more Irish than he has ever looked, as if his heritage is finally asserting itself as he heads toward the grave. He will probably end up a shriveled leprechaun of a man, hunched over in his favorite chair and bewailing the sorry state of the world.

And beneath all the complaints he will probably be content.

"Tough couple of days, sounds like," he said.

Which was his way of saying that he had followed everything that had happened over the weekend, and his heart went out to me, and if there was anything he could do, I had only to ask. Except that, as a card-carrying Irishman, he would never dream of saying any of that.

"I've had better," I agreed. I'm a card-carrying Irishman, too.

"How's Kathleen?" *Is my granddaughter taking this all right? You can't ignore your family, Jimmy. Your family is more important than anything.*

"Kathleen is doing okay. She was explaining to me about fractals yesterday. A fractal is a measure of something's complexity. I thought you'd want to know. She showed me some wild patterns you can create on a computer with them. I don't know how she does it." *I'm paying attention to her, Dad. You don't have to worry about that.*

"Fractals, huh? I had enough trouble with fractions. And those word problems. Someone's filling the pool while someone else is emptying it. Could never figure that stuff out."

"She's way beyond both of us, I think." I had set his mind at ease. I had survived; Kathleen had survived; the world would go on.

He took another sip of his drink. "I never met a person who got murdered before," he said. "At least not that I know of."

"You met her?"

"Sure. She came out here to interview me—two, three weeks ago." I tried not to look as if this news surprised me, but my father could tell. "I would've cleared it with you," he hastened to add, "but you know I don't like bothering you. You haven't minded before when I give interviews. And then it just slipped my mind."

"Oh, no, it's okay, it's just that . . . maybe you'll have to talk to the police now. I hate to get you involved in all this."

"Don't worry about it. It's too bad, though, about her. She seemed very nice."

"Did you tell her good things about me?"

"Oh, I said you were all right for a Republican. She thought that was very funny."

"Swell."

We sat in near darkness and continued our visit, although I found it hard to concentrate. *Amanda had been here, had probably sat in this chair.* What was she looking for? What did she think she could get from my father?

I asked about his health; he complained. He asked about the campaign; I told funny stories. We talked about Dickens, whom I hadn't glanced at since college. I offered to do any chores that needed doing; he couldn't think of any. These Sunday evening visits had been going on for so long that they were now like a ritual. They were probably the most important thing in my father's life, although he wouldn't dream of telling me that, any more than I would tell him the truth about Amanda.

He went to the bathroom, and I looked around the apartment. His world was so small now: a few rooms filled with faded furniture from our old house in Brighton; a few old friends—every year fewer. And memories, although it was impossible to tell if he spent his days drifting through the past. Where was the evidence? There was only one photograph of me in the place: of the two of us, actually, on the Capitol steps after my swearing in. And one of Danny, scoring the winning touchdown against South Boston High.

And none of my mother.

But what did that prove? Gramma told me once that he never got over my mother's death. Of course, she was as sentimental as my father is gruff. But I think she was probably right. What do you need photographs for if your past is so much more powerful than the present that it is what seems real, while the present is just a vague succession of TV shows and novels and nagging ailments?

"Another?" my father asked as he emerged from the bathroom.

I shook my head, as I almost always did when he made the ritual offer. "I'm driving."

"Well, I'm not going anywhere," he said, and he poured himself some more bourbon.

"You should take a trip," I said. "Go on a cruise maybe."

"I've been everywhere I want to go."

"You've never been anywhere."

"Well, that sums me up in a nutshell, wouldn't you say?"

"You could come with Liz and Kathleen and me. We'll go to Bermuda after the election."

"Liz would just love that, wouldn't she? No, I'll just stay here and tackle *Little Dorrit.*"

"Bring *Little Dorrit* with you."

My father just laughed. "Imagine my bony knees in those shorts." He laughed some more. "Imagine *your* bony knees."

"My knees are exquisite," I said. "Some magazine named me one of the ten sexiest politicians in Washington."

"Don't believe everything you read, Jimmy. You'll never get anywhere in life if you do."

"I'll try to remember that."

There was a loud knocking on the door. My father and I exchanged a glance. "I wonder who that could be," he murmured.

"I'll put the bottle away," I replied. We knew who it was. Danny was aware of our Sunday evening ritual and had been known to butt in, especially when he'd been drinking. I was relieved that I would finally get a chance to talk to him, but I was also frightened of what he might have to tell me.

I shoved the bourbon into the kitchen cabinet next to the refrigerator while my father answered the door. "Why, Daniel, what a pleasant surprise," I heard him say.

I came out of the kitchen and saw my brother grinning his world-class grin at my father. "Dad," he said. "And Jim," he added when he saw me. "Our little family, together again."

"Hi, Danny," I said.

He was wearing a raincoat that looked vaguely familiar. I could smell the liquor on his breath from across the room. He walked past my father and ensconced himself in my father's favorite armchair. Under the raincoat he was wearing a white dress shirt, open at the collar, and faded jeans. "Any more of that?" he asked, pointing to my father's glass of bourbon.

"Fresh out," I said.

Danny looked as if he were deciding whether to be an obnoxious drunk or an obliging one. He pulled at his ear and sneezed and chose to be obliging. He waved a hand as if to say that it was okay, he'd forgive us this once. "Doesn't matter, long as I'm in the bosom of my family," he said. He blew his nose, then folded his hands on his stomach and smiled beatifically.

When I look at my father, I see myself grown old; when I look at Danny, I see myself gone bad. Well, not bad, exactly: tired; defeated; helpless.

He was born less than a year before me; we were "Irish twins," as they used to refer to such siblings. And our appearance has always been as close as our age: the same black, curly hair and pale skin, the same dark eyes. He had the readier smile, although I had proved that I could smile with the best of them, too. But now there were slight differences between us, perhaps only noticeable to a twin: the sprinkle of gray in his sideburns, the bulge of his belly over his pants. The deadness in his eyes, even when smiling. The slight tremor in his hand when he reached for his glass. The difference between success and failure, between someone who is trying to keep winning and someone who is trying desperately to stop losing.

"A little glitch in the campaign, eh, Jimmy?" he said.

"Nothing we can't handle."

"Wouldn't be so sure," he said. "Voters can turn on a guy real fast nowadays." Danny liked to pretend that he knew something about politics. What he said was right, of course, but that didn't mean anything. It's easy to pontificate. "You were looking for me, Jim?" he asked innocently.

"We need to talk," I said.

"What about?"

I gave him a stare that would have reduced most of my staff to tears. Danny was oblivious.

"Can I get you some coffee, Danny?" my father broke in. He looked nervous. This obscure conflict between his children was more than he could handle.

"Coffee. Great," Danny said.

Relieved, my father headed off to the kitchen.

Danny got up and gazed at the two photographs: me on the steps of the Capitol, him on the football field, long ago. What must he have felt when he looked at them, side by side? "She was a stunner, wasn't she?" he said, his back to me. "Amanda Taylor. Name reeks of money. Where'd the paper say she was from? Wayland? Weston? Probably rode horses, you think? Lunch at the country club, put it on Daddy's bill. Want a little condo in the Back Bay? Sure, princess. Whatever makes you happy."

"You talked to her, didn't you?" I said.

He turned and looked at me. "You didn't tell me not to, did you?"

"You bastard," I whispered.

"Milk and sugar, right?" my father asked, returning to the room.

"Great," Danny replied. He blew his nose again. He really did look sick.

"How about those Patriots, huh?" my father said. "Gonna stink it up again this year?"

Danny didn't respond. I could feel both of them looking at me. My father counted on me to take care of things. Why wasn't I doing that now?

"How's business, Danny?" my father tried. "Picking up now that summer's over?"

"Business sucks," Danny said.

I stood up. "I'm driving Danny home," I said.

"But what'll he do about—"

"He can come back and get his car when he's sober. He's got no business driving in this condition anyway. Right, Danny?"

Once again he faced a choice, and miraculously he chose not to be obnoxious. "Whatever you say, Jim. Wouldn't look good to have your brother picked up for drunk driving, right?"

"I have a funeral to attend tomorrow," I said. "I don't want to go to one the day after, too."

A cloud seemed to pass over his face, but then he shrugged and got to his feet.

"I could drive Danny's car," my father said, "but my eyes . . . after dark—"

"Don't worry about it," I said. "It's his problem. I'll see you next Sunday. Let me know how *Bleak House* turns out."

"Oh, the lawyers'll win," he replied. "The lawyers always win."

"Will *our* lawyer win?" Danny asked, gesturing at me. "Things don't look so great for him all of a sudden."

"Don't worry about Jim," my father said. "You just take care of yourself."

"But I'm my brother's keeper, am I not? My brother's keeper."

"You've got it backwards, I think," I said, as I hustled him out the door, with my father gazing anxiously after us. As he closed the door behind us, I realized where I had seen Danny's raincoat before. It used to be mine. Liz must've given it to Melissa at some point when things were especially bad. Did Danny realize that? He couldn't have known, or he would never have worn it.

We walked out of the courtyard and into the parking lot. "Good old Buick," Danny said when he saw my car. "Wouldn't do for a senator to be driving around in some foreign car, would it?"

Right again. He could be right forever, though, and it wouldn't make a bit of difference, because I was the senator. We got in the car and headed off to Brighton, and finally I had the chance to find out just what my brother had done to me.

"Why the hell did you tell her about Jackie Scanlon?" I demanded.

"What makes you think I did that?" Danny said.

"Because Scanlon told me Amanda knew about the *Sea-Star,* and she was interviewing people and trying to get a confirmation about me and him. He's telling me this in Southie at the same time she's being murdered in the Back Bay. So what am I supposed to tell the police? Oh, I've got an alibi, all right. I was in a meeting with the second biggest mobster in New England, trying to figure out how to keep the murder victim from writing a story that would destroy my career. The Democrats would love to know that."

That shut Danny up for a moment. "I guess I should have told you," he muttered finally.

"But why the hell did you say anything to her in the first place? How could you be that stupid? It's your ass, too."

"She knew already," Danny replied, on the defensive now. "She said: 'Your brother and Scanlon had a deal, right? He kept Scanlon out of prison while he was attorney general, right?' So what was I supposed to do? I had to give our side. Your side. I was just protecting you."

"What do you mean, she knew already? How could she have found out? I didn't tell her, and Scanlon certainly had no reason to tell her."

"I don't know how she knew. Maybe it was one of Scanlon's buddies; those guys are always knifing each other in the back."

"Scanlon swears it wasn't his people. None of them know. It was too important to tell any of them. He figured it had to be you. Did you ask her how she knew?"

"Of course I did. She was real cagey. Protecting her sources, she said."

"Sources? Plural? More than one?"

"Source, sources, I don't know. Jesus, don't play your lawyer games with me."

"This isn't a game, Danny. I need to know everything. Did she say what she was going to do with the information?"

"No. I assumed it was for this book she was writing."

And then I asked the most important questions of all. "Did she tape the interview, Danny? Did she takes notes?"

He didn't respond. I looked over at him. He was chewing on a knuckle. "I don't know," he said. "Maybe. I don't remember."

"That's great. Try re-creating the scene in your mind. Where was it?"

"Her apartment," he replied grudgingly.

"Okay. You're sitting in her living room. White walls, book-shelves, glass coffee table. She puts a little black machine on the table between you and her, says you shouldn't let it intimidate you—"

"I don't fucking remember, all right?"

"Were you drinking before the interview?"

"Jesus Christ, I don't know. Nothing out of the usual."

"So you'd been drinking."

"Drinking, drinking. I'm always drinking. What else is there to do?"

"I don't know. Ask Melissa. Ask your children."

If there was a tape, if there were notes, why hadn't Mackey and Tobin arrested me by now? All they had to do was listen to the tape and they had their motive. Were they taking their time, digging deeper?

I wanted to cross-examine my brother some more. I wanted to bludgeon him into submission, into telling the truth. But it suddenly seemed like a waste of time. "What exactly did you say, Danny?" I asked, as calmly as I could. "What exactly did she say? I've got to know. I've got to know what might be on the tape."

"I said enough," he replied. "She said enough. I mean . . . it's there. Okay?"

What else was there to say? "Okay."

We were silent for a moment. "You're going to lose the election, aren't you?" Danny said finally.

"If they find out about Scanlon and me, of course I am."

"Maybe we'll both be out of work before long."

I shook my head. "That's the least of our worries at this point, Danny."

We headed into Brighton, a working-class neighborhood in the northwest corner of Boston. Irish Catholic in our day, now increasingly occupied by Cambodians and Vietnamese. My father and I had gotten out long ago; Danny had been left behind. Or, rather, he had chosen to stay behind. He could complain all he wanted about fate and bad luck, but all his life he had made choices that had brought him to where he was today.

"Look," Danny said. "They've put in a video store where Callahan's pharmacy used to be. Remember those Coke floats we used to get there for a nickel?"

I didn't respond. Danny was always filled with memories, especially when the present was painful—as it usually was for him. I gazed at the convenience stores and the ATMs and the shabby condos as we headed toward Danny's home; I saw the signs printed in Vietnamese; I saw black kids with strange patterns cut in their hair hanging on the corner and staring back at us. Brighton had been a different place back then—and yet not so different. It was still a dreary urban neighborhood that people got out of when they had the chance.

Returning to Brighton always made me uneasy, as if the choices I had made were not irreversible, and I could end up back here with my Irish twin, Hingham and the Senate and everything else just a memory or a fantasy.

It was utterly improbable in the first place. Danny was the one who should have made it big; Danny was the one who should have been in politics. After all, he was named after Daniel O'Connell, the Irish statesman. After all, he was the one who had girls adoring him and guys admiring him from as early as I can remember. I was the shy one, resigned to living in his shadow. All I wanted to do was to get good grades, to be well behaved, to please Gramma and my father. I had so much to make up for.

It was all my fault, you see. I don't know when or how I figured this out. I certainly can't believe that my family would have consciously instilled this belief in me—although perhaps Danny, in a bullying mood . . . At any rate, I believed it. Believed it was my fault that my mother died. In the deepest recesses of my soul I still believe it today.

And it's true in a sense. She died from giving birth to me. Puerperal fever. It sounds so Victorian; in fact, it was on its way out back in my mother's day, with the discovery of antibiotics. I never learned the details; my father was not the kind to volunteer them, and I was afraid to ask. All I knew was that after she had me, she got sick, and then she died of that disease with the awful name. For years I thought it was called "purple" fever, and I imagined my mother turning a deep bloody color in the course of dying, as if she had held her breath for far too long. I would stand in front of a mirror and hold my own breath, imagining that I, too, could come down with puerperal fever if I had the courage to keep from exhaling for long enough.

Danny had no such morbid thoughts, I believe. If anything, he figured that the world owed him, having taken away his mother at such an early age. He did whatever came easily to him, whatever had the surest reward. In school that was athletics. So he became a football star.

And oh, the glory! What can compare with those adolescent triumphs? When you're an adult, you know too much, your triumphs are always tinged with sadness, tempered by wisdom. This, too, will pass. They love me in November; they'll forget my name by January. But when you're in high school, you don't think like that; certainly Danny didn't. He was great then, and he assumed that he would always be great.

He was mistaken.

The high point came when he got a football scholarship to Notre Dame. Notre Dame! My father didn't have much use for Catholic education, but he couldn't very well object to Notre Dame or to a scholarship; a postal worker's salary wasn't going to put the two of us through college.

But the leap from Brighton High to the real world, to the big leagues, proved to be too much for Danny; he didn't make it through his freshman year at South Bend. He complained about the coaches; he complained about the hicks out in Indiana; he complained about the boring courses and the boring professors. He was homesick, obviously. His attachment to his home was far stronger than mine, even though I went to college just across the river in Cambridge.

But if that was his only problem, why didn't he transfer to a school nearer home and try again—at Boston College up the street, for example, or Holy Cross a few miles away in Worcester? The problem was clear enough, at least to me: In college he would have to work to succeed, and he was unwilling to do that.

Instead he enlisted in the Navy. What was left of his good luck kept him away from Vietnam, but other than that the service didn't do him much good. He certainly didn't come back with a maturer perspective on life. He didn't come back ready to leave Brighton behind and make his way in the real world. He came back wanting to own a bar.

Nothing wrong with that. Except that Danny's idea of owning a bar was to sit around all night swapping stories about the glory days with his buddies, then empty the cash register into his pockets at closing time. No work, no worries. An easy life. Danny Boy's, he called the place he bought in Brighton Center. I never found out if my father helped him with the down payment. If he did, it was not the best investment he made in his life.

Danny Boy's. The name was apt. If I was old before my time, Danny was young long after his—or at least he tried to be, he longed to be. Even when he first bought the place, when I was still just a law student and it was too soon to tell if he or the bar would be successful, I felt vaguely embarrassed whenever I went in there and saw the framed photographs of his triumphs on the walls. A man in his mid-twenties, with his best days already behind him.

He would have proved me wrong if Danny Boy's had become popular, but it never did. He could never choose between the working-class crowd and the college crowd; he wanted both, and most of the time he ended up with neither. He tried live entertainment; he tried big-screen TVs; he tried wet T-shirt nights. Nothing worked for long.

And that's when the resentment began: resentment of the world; resentment, especially, of me, as my career progressed and his floundered. He resented me, I think, not simply because I was successful, but because I represented something about the world that he didn't want to believe: that it does sometimes reward hard work and perseverance.

He resented me even as he started to flaunt his relationship to me. My photos joined his behind the bar. My infrequent appearances there were cause for a round on the house.

And that's when the drinking began, too. He had always been drinking, actually, but when he was an indestructible youth, it hadn't mattered. Now it did. "Two sons," my father mourned, "one a lush, the other a Republican. Where did I go wrong?" Except that he really did worry about Danny, his firstborn, his pride and joy; me, he only felt obliged to cut down to size, in case my success made me forget my beginnings. What could he do to help Danny?

Nothing, really. I was the one in a position to help. And that was why I now faced defeat, disgrace, and prison. The tragedy of Danny's life had overtaken my own; perhaps I had been foolish to think that I could escape it, just as I had been foolish to think I could leave Brighton behind.

Danny lived just a couple of blocks from where we had grown up. Every tree, every curbstone, every telephone pole seemed familiar to me, even though all the faces were new. A Cambodian family rented the upstairs from Danny, and he never said anything good about them; I think he was afraid they would end up more successful than he was, and that would just give him something more to resent.

I pulled up in front of his house.

"So what do we do?" Danny said.

"I don't know. I was hoping you'd explain it all away somehow. Give me a reason not to worry."

Danny blew his nose. "Maybe there isn't a tape," he said.

"Maybe."

"It's too bad about the alibi."

I sighed.

"Maybe Scanlon had her murdered to shut her up," Danny suggested.

"Gangland murderers don't leave strange messages on their victims' computers," I said. "Anyway, if Scanlon was behind it, that doesn't help me very much."

"True." He looked out the window. "I'm sorry, Jim," he said. "But she knew already. Honest she did."

I tried to get past my anger and frustration and think rationally. "This is important, Danny. You didn't tell her you had any specific knowledge of a relationship between me and Scanlon, right?"

He looked puzzled. "Well, I mean, it's obvious, isn't it?"

"It may be obvious to you, but I've never told you anything, right? And you've never personally observed anything, right? You just have this supposition. It may be right, it may be wrong."

Danny caught on. "Sure, I guess so. Only, talking to her, I sort of assumed—"

"Okay, but she didn't present you with any facts, did she?

Beyond, you know, the *Sea-Star* and that business. And if she did, you couldn't confirm or deny them—at least as far as my relationship with Scanlon is concerned."

"I guess she didn't have that much in the way of facts," he admitted.

"All right. Look. The police will probably want to talk to you. Just tell them the truth. Don't try to hide anything; don't try to justify anything; don't try to protect me. It won't help. The only thing will help is that you don't know anything." I took out a notepad and scribbled down the names of a few lawyers. "The police'll try to scare you into thinking you're in trouble, but they don't have a case. It was a long time ago, and it's all pretty stale by now." I ripped off the page and handed it to him. "Talk to one of these guys if they start reading you your rights or if you feel you're getting in over your head. Understand?"

Danny stared at the list. The reality of it seemed to befuddle him. "Okay, Jimmy," he said finally. "Okay." He shoved the list into his shirt pocket.

"All right, Danny. Let's go inside."

He got out of the car and walked up the front steps. I followed, almost tripping over an upended tricycle on the porch. Melissa opened the door before Danny had a chance to find his key. She must have been watching as we pulled up—worried, as usual, about what her husband was up to. She didn't look happy to see either of us; my presence was a sure sign that Danny had been misbehaving. I thought about turning on the charm and smoothing things over, but I didn't feel like it. This was Danny's problem.

"You could've called," she said to him.

He pushed past her without replying. Melissa looked at me for a moment, as if trying to decide if decorum would win out over her anger; decorum lost. She left the door open for me and followed her husband into the kitchen. I went into the living room and listened without much interest to their argument. Melissa was angry at him for getting out of his sickbed and going off drinking without so much as a word. Well, what was he supposed to do, Danny wanted to know, hang around here with a bunch of screaming kids? Why didn't she just leave him alone? Why didn't everyone just leave him alone?

I sat on the sofa in the tired living room amid the scattered toys, and I wondered if the kids were awake, listening. I looked at their photographs on the mantel of the walled-over fireplace.

They weren't bad kids. But what was a life like this going to do to them?

What had it done to Melissa? Their wedding picture was on the mantel as well: the dashing groom, the happy bride. She wasn't happy anymore; she was filled with a rage that I found frightening whenever I caught a glimpse of it. Life had been full of promise back then. She had a good job; she had a small inheritance; she had a gorgeous guy. But her inheritance disappeared without a trace into the bar, and she gave up her job when Daniel junior came along and life married to the gorgeous guy turned out to be a lot less fun than life dating him. And now she was trapped.

Having a famous brother-in-law gave her some solace. Certainly she couldn't understand Liz's problems with me. What did Liz have to complain about? I was inclined to agree with Melissa about that, naturally. But we all find our own way to suffer.

Doors slammed finally, and Melissa appeared in the living room. She had lost her figure having the children, and the cheap sweat suit she was wearing didn't flatter her. There were perpetual creases in her forehead from frowning. She was probably not happy that I was seeing her like this, without makeup, wearing unattractive clothes, in a messy house. She nervously scooped a magazine off a chair. "I'm sorry, Jim," she said. "Was he very bad?"

"Not really. But we thought it'd be a good idea if he didn't drive. His car's over at Dad's."

She nodded. "We'll get it back. Can I, uh, get you a cup of tea or something?"

"That's okay, Lissa. I've got to be going."

"You have that funeral in the morning," she said.

"That's right."

She sat down on the chair. She was still clutching the magazine. "Is everything going to be all right with you?"

Not likely, I thought. "You never can tell," I said.

"It sounded on the news like the district attorney might be out to get you."

"Cavanaugh's been out to get me for as long as I can remember, and he hasn't succeeded yet. I wouldn't worry about it, Lissa."

She rolled the magazine into a tight cylinder and squeezed it. "I worry about everything," she said. "Dan won't see a doctor. I wish he'd see a doctor."

"Just like his old man," I said. Had Danny told Melissa about Amanda—or about Jackie Scanlon? *That* would give her something to worry about. No, it wasn't any of her business, Danny would insist.

"I think he might get fired," Melissa was saying. "He's used up all his sick days. And I don't think he does a very good job when he does show up. It would serve him right."

"Now, Lissa. It wouldn't serve you and the kids right. And if he's been sick—"

"He's sick because he doesn't take care of himself. And maybe having him lose his job is what I need to—to do something. I wouldn't have any choice then."

Her voice had risen; the magazine was crumpled in her hands. I couldn't recall seeing her this bad. Her anger at Danny was warping her thinking. She could divorce him anytime. And if she didn't divorce him, did she think life would be better with her out working at some awful minimum-wage job while he sat at home, drunk and sullen? "It's always better to have a choice," I said. "Look, if you need advice, if you need help, be sure to let me know, okay? I can't straighten out Danny, but maybe I can do something for you."

Melissa started to cry. She dropped the magazine and turned her head away, embarrasssed. I was embarrassed, too. It was my brother who was causing her this pain. "You shouldn't have to worry about us," she sobbed. "You've got enough to worry about."

That was certainly true. "Well, you're worrying about me," I pointed out lightly. "We're all worrying about each other. That's life, right?"

"Danny's a shit," she replied.

No, he wasn't. But he was a problem neither of us could solve. I went over and kissed my sister-in-law on the top of the head. "I'm sorry, Lissa," I said. "I'll talk to you soon."

Sniffling, she looked up at me. "I'm sorry, too, Jim," she whispered.

I let myself out. The ride back to Hingham was long and unpleasant. For once I would have preferred some company to being alone with my thoughts. *Danny. Amanda. Jackie Scanlon.*

Why hadn't Danny told me Amanda was questioning him about Jackie Scanlon? Did he really think he had been protecting me? It wasn't impossible. He turns on the Irish charm, and Amanda pretends to succumb; she was very good at pretending. He thinks he's talked her out of writing the story when, in fact, he has just given her the confirmation she needs to make the story real.

But how—and how much—did she know in the first place?

Unless Danny was lying to me—also not impossible. She calls him up for an interview, expecting nothing unusual, and instead he gives her the scoop of a lifetime. Why? Well, why would Melissa want him to lose his job? The desire to hurt can be stronger than the instinct for self-preservation. He had seemed drunkenly pleased with himself at my father's until he found out that I could be charged with murder as a result of all this. Besides, how much harm would Amanda's story have done him? He had a crime to conceal, but it was nothing compared with what I had on my conscience: a U.S. senator who was once in the back pocket of a mobster. Just how much resentment did he have festering inside him?

I tired eventually of trying to understand Danny; that was a lifetime project. What mattered now was the tape of his interview—if it existed—or any other evidence that Amanda knew my guilty secret. If Cavanaugh had the evidence, I was done for. Danny's ignorance might be helpful, but I doubted it would stop Cavanaugh for long.

Liz and Kathleen were asleep when I got home, and I soon joined them. I dreamed I was listening to a tape, and all that was on the tape was the endless scream of a woman, dying. In the morning I woke up expecting to be arrested.

CHAPTER 8

The police weren't waiting on my doorstep. The papers said that attention was being focused on the victim's acquaintances. The stories all mentioned the weird message on the computer and the mysterious stranger with the hat and the black umbrella. No mention of any suspects.

What was Cavanaugh up to? I began to feel a little better. Surely by now Mackey had listened to Amanda's tapes and read her notes. If the police had evidence that Amanda knew about Scanlon and me, why not haul me in?

Well, maybe Amanda hadn't been able to come up with the whole story. Danny had part of it. But who had the rest—except for Scanlon and me? And Scanlon swore he hadn't talked. Without the whole story my motive might not be entirely clear. So maybe the police had to do a little more digging.

In any event I had to proceed on the assumption that I was in the clear, that I was dealing with a political problem, not a criminal one. The only way you can get anything accomplished, I have found, is by assuming that it can be done. So I put on a somber suit, and my wife and I went off in the rain to my lover's funeral.

I was happy to have Kevin drive us in a campaign car—someone to talk to besides Liz, who looked and acted as if she'd rather have been going to *my* funeral. We sat on opposite sides of the back seat and stared out at the traffic as Kevin tried to make conversation.

The brain trust had decided that I should go to the funeral home first to offer my condolences to the family. We didn't want Mr. and Mrs. Taylor to give a sobbing interview to some newspaper and say I never once told them I was sorry their daughter died. Every nuance counted.

Our arrival caused a predictable stir. Heads turned; conversations stopped. The sickly sweet smell of flower arrangements in the crowded room made me want to gag, but instead I forged ahead to the closed casket. I can't remember if I felt anything as I looked at it; I was too nervous. It wasn't Amanda anyway; Amanda was in my memories, not in the casket.

Liz and I knelt and pretended to say a prayer, then blessed ourselves and stood up. Amanda's parents and younger sister were standing a couple of feet away, greeting the mourners. The people they were talking to seemed to melt away, and the family was facing us. Mr. Taylor was tall, graying, and handsome—an investment banker to the marrow of his well-bred bones. He stood stiffly next to his wife, as if someone were grading his posture. Mrs. Taylor— blond, tanned, smooth-skinned—was the image of her daughter grown older, although the slightly dazed look in her eyes suggested that she lacked Amanda's brains. She was a volunteer, a tennis player, a gardener, according to Amanda. She looked a trifle too serene under the circumstances; probably an extra Valium was helping her make it through the day. And finally there was Lauren—was I supposed to know her name?—who had missed out on the family's good looks and compensated for it by being an intellectual; she was a grad student at Chicago or Northwestern or someplace. I wondered what she would have given for Amanda's cheekbones. She eyed me suspiciously through thick glasses; she and Amanda had not been close.

"Jim O'Connor," I said to Mr. Taylor, meeting his gaze, "and this is my wife, Liz. I just wanted to tell you how deeply sorry we are about your daughter. This must be a terribly trying time for all of you, and I want you to know, if there's anything we can do, please just tell us." I gazed at Mrs. Taylor; she smiled a little woozily.

"Thank you for coming, Senator," Mr. Taylor said. "I've always been an admirer of yours." Amanda had told me of his admiration, said he was pleased Massachusetts had finally come to its senses and elected a good conservative Republican to the Senate. He took my hand in a bone-crushing grip and shook it, then passed me on to his wife while Liz murmured something to him.

Mrs. Taylor had a limp, ladylike half grip that surprised me in a tennis player. "Oh, Senator," she crooned, "how awful for you to discover . . . you know—"

I put my left hand lightly on her arm. "Mrs. Taylor, what I went through was nothing compared to what you've had to endure. I lost a friend; you've lost a daughter. I don't know how you're managing so well."

Her face lit up at the compliment. "Oh, well, you know, one must—you know. It's important that you—you know, don't you think?"

"Exactly. And this must be Amanda's sister."

"That's right," Mrs. Taylor said, still smiling. "Senator O'Connor, this is my daughter Lauren."

The suspicion in Lauren's eyes had deepened into obvious distaste. She didn't offer her hand. Did she know something? Amanda couldn't have confided in her—or could she? "I just want to tell you, Senator," she said, "that I think your reactionary views on crime are despicable."

"De'-spic-able"—accent on the first syllable, like a true intellectual. Was that all that was bothering her? "I'm sorry you feel that way, Ms. Taylor," I replied. "I'd be happy to discuss my views with you at a more appropriate time."

"Why isn't this an appropriate time?" she persisted. "Poor people and people of color are suffering at this very instant because of policies you support."

I sent out telepathic signals for someone to rescue me. "Senator, could I speak to you for a moment?" It was Kevin, matchless Kevin, at my elbow, leading me away from danger.

"Excuse me, won't you?" I said to Amanda's sister. "I really do hope we have a chance to talk sometime."

She turned away from me in disgust and shook Liz's hand perfunctorily.

"Thanks, Kevin," I murmured as we moved away. Could have been worse. Lauren hated me, but not because she thought I had something to do with Amanda's death. People like her can crop up anywhere; they're an occupational hazard for politicians. Liz joined us. "The sister didn't nail you?" I asked her.

"She said she pities me," Liz replied.

I rolled my eyes.

There were a few minutes to kill, so I shook some hands on the periphery of the funeral parlor. Didn't want to look as if I were campaigning, but I didn't want to appear unsociable either. No one had anything nasty to say to me. I noticed a young man with greased-back hair and rimless glasses angling for me, and finally there was no avoiding him. "Brad Williams, Senator," he said, shaking my hand. His palm was moist; his smile was phony. "I'm another Adams House alum—a few years after you, of course."

I cringed. I don't like it when people claim kinship with me because we're fellow Harvard grads; what do I care if they went to the same school or shared the same undergraduate house? "Great to meet you, Brad," I said, and tried to move on.

He wouldn't let go. "I was a colleague of Amanda's at *Hub*," he continued. "Such a tragic loss."

Oh, *that* Brad Williams. Why wasn't I better with names? Amanda had mentioned him to me. The former *Crimson* editor, now doing dreary articles about Boston's hottest singles bars and the fifty most eligible bachelors in the city. What a comedown. For some people the real world is never as exciting as Cambridge. He had lusted after Amanda. She had dated him a couple of times, she told me, and decided he was a pig. "Yes, indeed," I said, trying to extricate my hand. "Such a tragedy."

"Did she ever mention me, Senator?"

"Mention you? Why, no, I don't believe so." You self-important loser.

"Just wondering. And this is your wife?"

He was pushing it. Why? Was he just a jerk? Was he going to ask for an interview? Did he expect to get the real inside scoop on the murder from his fellow Harvard grad? "That's right," I said. I didn't offer to introduce Liz.

"Great job at the press conference Saturday, Mrs. O'Connor," he said to her. "Wish I could've been there, but *Hub* has someone else covering the campaign."

"My loss, I'm sure," Liz said. She turned away.

Williams turned back to me, grinning with too many teeth. "Well, good luck in the campaign, Senator."

Go crawl back under your rock. I gave a slight nod and looked for Kevin. It was time to get out of here.

We retired to the car, and in a few minutes the procession to the church started. I stared out at the grayness, thinking about Amanda, the police, the campaign.

"Do you believe in life after death?" Liz asked me suddenly, breaking a long silence.

Kevin's head turned slightly, but then he went back to watching the road. "Sure," I said. I wasn't going to get into anything with her.

"You didn't use to."

"I'm getting older. I've decided life after death is a good idea after all."

"I think the spirits of the dead are always with us," Liz said. "There's so much they could tell us if only we could open ourselves to them." I looked across the back seat at her. Her eyes were glowing. And I thought, hardly for the first time: Does she really believe this stuff?

When Kathleen was settled in school, I more or less expected Liz to go back to teaching. She was always so obsessed with money, well, here was her chance to earn some once again. But instead she put it off and put it off: There was the election campaign for the Senate, after all, and then the abortive attempt at living in Washington with me. But then, when nothing was standing in her way, she finally announced she was going to start the program at Cabot.

Why? Perhaps she didn't think that a senator's wife should be a mere grammar school teacher. Perhaps she was doing it to get back at me in some obscure way. *See, I can screw up our finances, too.* Perhaps it was to work on our relationship, as I suggested earlier, or to escape from the burden of it. I just couldn't figure it out, so my response to Liz's course of study has been an edgy defensiveness, tinged with a sarcasm that infuriates her.

It was no different this morning. "The police would certainly like it if Amanda would tell them some things," I said.

Liz shook her head. I didn't get it; I had never gotten it. "Why should the dead care about the same things the living care about? That's why we have such difficulty communicating with them. We're too bound up in our everyday concerns. We don't have the right perspective."

"Mom, there's no scientific basis for any of this stuff. How can you possibly believe it?" Kathleen had even less patience with her mother than I did. Liz would just smile an infuriatingly knowing smile at her and say, "There are some things your scientists will never understand, dear." And that would just drive Kathleen up the wall.

"How do we find out what the right perspective is, Liz?" I asked.

"That's what life is all about," Liz said. "Finding that perspective."

We had reached the old stone church, I noticed gratefully, and the procession came to a stop. Kevin stayed behind in the car, and Liz and I walked quickly inside under the eyes of the waiting cameras. Good. We would be seen on the news tonight going to the funeral together. Liz had done her job.

We slid into a pew, and in a few moments the mass began.

The police would have their questions for Amanda, and I would have some, too, I thought. I looked at the burnished wood of the casket as it sat at the foot of the altar, facing the church filled with the grieving and the dutiful and the merely curious. Here lies Amanda Taylor: loving daughter, hardworking reporter, loyal friend. *Here lies.* The priest in his white vestments would repeat all the clichés, and maybe there would be a tear-choked graveside eulogy that would repeat them yet again. So what was the truth, Amanda? Not about the clichés, but about what mattered to me? Lover or liar? Which was the charade: the interviews with friends and relatives or the long romantic dinners, the dreamy conversations, the passionate sex?

Or was it all true? And was I just too stupid to understand?

I remembered the first time we met: fifteen minutes in my Senate office. As often happens, the meeting was delayed while I rushed off to vote in the Senate chamber and got caught up in procedural issues that wasted an hour or two. I wouldn't keep the networks waiting, but a magazine reporter wanting to write a book about me? Not important. After all, I was seeing her in the first place only as a favor to Liz.

I finally got back to my office, and Mrs. Sullivan showed her in, after first informing me that her thirty minutes had to be chopped in half if I wanted to make it to the lunch with the delegation from the South Shore Chamber of Commerce.

So Amanda Taylor came into my life: expensive black suit, white silk blouse, gold necklace, gold watch. Money, I thought when I saw her. Money, and youth, and beauty—and the self-confidence that those three things provide. Her grip was firm and her hand was cool when I shook it. "It's such a pleasure to finally meet you, Senator," she said.

I smiled. "What's your position on splitting infinitives, Ms. Taylor?"

Her slightly slanted eyes looked puzzled for a moment, and then she laughed a brilliant laugh that displayed her impossibly white teeth. "I keep a little silver hatchet in my handbag," she replied, "just in case I come across an infinitive that needs to be split."

I nodded. "It's good to be prepared. Have a seat." I motioned to a comfortable upholstered chair in one corner of my office. She sat and crossed her legs, showing enough thigh to convince me that she was aware of the power of her beauty and willing to use it. I sat opposite her. I didn't like sitting behind my desk for this sort of thing: too formal, too intimidating—although sometimes intimidation is useful. "So, why should I cooperate with you on this book project, Ms. Taylor?"

"Please, call me Amanda." Another smile. "You should cooperate with me, Senator, because I think you want to run for President, and a book like this will help establish your reputation nationally. It will make you look like a serious contender to the people whose opinions count."

"A book like what?"

"A book that examines your philosophy and, more importantly, the man behind the philosophy. Why do you believe the things you do? Why have you been so successful? What makes Jim O'Connor tick?"

I considered. "Shouldn't that be 'more important,' not 'more importantly'?" I asked. Amanda reddened; she didn't know. I felt pleased with myself, but I let the victory pass. "Why should *you* write the book, Ms.—Amanda? Why don't I write it myself or have it ghostwritten? Are you interested in ghostwriting?"

She shook her head. "No, it would be my book. But that would be to your advantage, Senator. No one pays any attention to candidates' autobiographies; they're so obviously tendentious. But a book written by an objective outsider would be taken seriously."

Tendentious. No one uses "tendentious" in conversation. She was trying to make up for "more importantly." All right, that told me something. "Don't I run the risk that you'll be *too* objective, Amanda? Or perhaps you have your own agenda here. I don't know anything about you. What if you decide to trash me in this book?"

"I assure you that I'm not out to trash you, Senator. But if I were, wouldn't it be better to at least let me interview you, so you can have your point of view represented?"

I shrugged. "Not necessarily—not if I have no control over how you do the representing. Besides, if I don't cooperate, you don't have a book. I assume you haven't sold your proposal yet, right?"

"No, but I have a lot of publishing contacts, and—" Amanda stopped short, as if she realized that she simply didn't have the arguments to convince me. She uncrossed her legs and leaned forward. "Think of it as a challenge," she said. "To win me over. To make me believe in you. I've read a lot about you: working your way through Harvard, the spectacular legal career, then giving it up to run for office. . . . You've been taking on challenges all your life. This is just one more."

Her expensive perfume wafted over me, and I almost laughed, the appeal was so blatant. But of all the important things I could be doing with my time, why should I want to spend it trying to win over Amanda Taylor? Why this challenge and not another?

I didn't bother asking. Instead I stood up. "Let me think about it," I said. "I'll get back to you."

Amanda's smile disappeared. "I take that as a polite rejection."

"Then you take it wrong. Politicians aren't allowed to make decisions like this on their own. They're required by law to consult their advisers and get twenty-six different opinions about it before they make up their minds. I'll be in touch."

Amanda stood up. "Then I'll keep hoping," she said. She held out her hand. "Thanks for 'more important,' " she said.

I took her hand and held it a fraction of a second longer than I meant to. "My pleasure," I said.

And then it was time for lunch with the Chamber of Commerce.

We both were acting at that point, I assume, although Amanda later swore otherwise. For my part I was impressed by her, but I didn't feel especially tempted. Beauty, intelligence, and good breeding might be worth flirting over, but they were hardly worth risking my career over. Amanda's charm did get her something out of the meeting, though: I relayed her request to Harold and Marge instead of rejecting it outright, as I had assumed I would before meeting her. They were as dubious as I had been—Marge, especially—but they agreed to check her out.

What they came up with wasn't encouraging.

"She comes from good Republican stock," Harold reported. "Her father's a banker, and there's family money besides; she's got a trust fund she's using to underwrite her little venture into the work world. But there's no evidence that she's ideologically compatible with us. She's a reporter."

From Harold that was not a compliment. "But she's got brains, right?" I asked.

He shrugged. "She graduated from Smith magna cum laude in government, then got a fellowship to Oxford for a year. She's no dope."

"What about her work at *Hub*?"

Marge answered that. "She's been there for three years. She's done all right, I guess. She did an exposé of Boston building inspectors that shook things up a bit. Mostly, though, she's written fluff. Including, of course, the immortal piece on Cabot College."

I could tell that Marge and Amanda would not be best buddies.

"So why does she want to write a book about me?"

Harold shrugged. "My guess is she's bored working at the magazine, and she's looking to move on. Three years is a long time at a place like *Hub,* and there's only so many articles you can write on local colleges. She meets Liz and figures maybe she can use the contact to get involved in something more exciting. Her entrée into the glamorous world of Washington politics. A chance to use her college major."

"But who cares, Jim?" Marge broke in. "She's a lightweight. The last thing we need is someone like her trying to make a reputation off you."

Hard to disagree. And yet . . . "Right," I said. "Well, thanks for the research, guys."

"Anytime, Senator."

The priest was giving the sermon now, saying all the right, comforting things. A woman in the pew in front of us was crying silently into her handkerchief. She looked to be about Amanda's age. A classmate? Another reporter? In the front pew Mrs. Taylor leaned her head against her husband's arm. Liz stared at her folded hands as the grief for her rival welled up around her.

Amanda? Are you there, Amanda? We did stop acting eventually—didn't we?

If Amanda Taylor was the last thing we needed, why did I call her back and set up another meeting to discuss her project?

I wasn't consciously plotting a relationship with her; my virtue still felt safe. I just wanted to see her again, to talk to her some more, perhaps to find the reality beneath the perfect exterior. As she suggested, I found her a challenge, although what sort of challenge I couldn't really have said.

We met for lunch at a Back Bay café during Christmas recess. If any proof of the purity of my intentions is needed, my agreeing to meet her in a public place in Boston should be sufficient. It was something I wouldn't have dreamed of doing a couple of months later.

Amanda was dressed more casually this time, although her suede jacket hardly looked cheap. She seemed more at ease in a restaurant than in my office; the fact that I had called her back must have helped her confidence. Her smile still dazzled. "It's so good of you to see me again, Senator," she said. "Does this mean you'll let me do some interviews for the book? I'm ready to start anytime."

"I'm not sure," I said honestly. "My advisers are against it."

"Why?"

"For one thing, you're not a Republican. They don't think you're sympathetic to my views."

"Oh, but I am sympathetic," she said, leaning forward, her eyes shining with sincerity. "I'm so impressed by the emphasis you put on personal responsibility. I mean, in a perfect world maybe a criminal would have had a good upbringing and wouldn't have broken the law, but ultimately he has to accept the blame when he commits a crime. The government should get the criminals off the streets and then get out of the way and let people live their lives."

The waiter came. He was a young gay with close-cropped blond hair and a hoop earring; he recognized me. Amanda ordered a glass of white wine. I ordered a Coke.

"So, if you can't afford health insurance and you need an operation," I said, "the government should get out of the way and let you die and let your children starve." I couldn't help it; it's the lawyer in me. Someone argues one side of the case, and I start arguing the other.

Amanda seemed taken aback for a moment, but she didn't yield. "Tragedies happen," she said. "Liberals think government can prevent them. I have a sister who thinks like that. I used to think like that in college. But hasn't the experience of the past fifty years or so proved that this just isn't true? We can't provide a world where everyone is healthy and happy and has a good job. At best we can only provide the opportunity for those things."

The waiter brought our drinks. He looked as if he wanted to join in the discussion. Amanda ordered a salad. I ordered an omelet.

"All right," I said, "so you're a born-again conservative. The last time we met you said I should go along with this project because of the challenge of winning you over. So where's the challenge?"

She laughed. "I'm sure there are issues where we disagree. Abortion, for example. The death penalty. I'm no match for you as a debater, but I'll say what I think."

Why should I care what she thought? *She's a lightweight.* Well, I did seem to care. We talked. The food came, and the waiter lingered, as if hoping to put in a good word for gay rights or federal funding for the arts; we ignored him and talked some more. Amanda tried to draw me out, but I wasn't interested in hearing what I had to say. This was still a job interview. She was the one who had to make a good impression.

Looking back on it, I can say that I wasn't fooled, at least not totally. I couldn't tell if she really was a conservative or if she was just parroting some of my positions to flatter me. At the time it didn't matter. What mattered was the energy she was investing in getting me to go along with her idea, the single-mindedness with which she strove to convince me. It was refreshing. I was so used to Washington cynicism. I was so used to Liz, who seemed bored with my positions, if not outright hostile to them.

I liked her enthusiasm, and I liked her youth. I'm not old, as politicians go, and I work as hard as anyone to meet the goals I've set for myself, but a lot of that is just the routine that comes from a lifetime of overachievement. With Amanda, I could feel once again what it had been like for me, fresh out of law school, with a world to conquer and only my wits and my personality with which to conquer it. If you lie a little, if you push a little too hard, well, how else are you going to get anywhere?

By the end of the meal I had agreed to a single interview. After that we would see. If it went well, I would cooperate. If it didn't, she could use the interview for a magazine article. Fair enough?

Amanda was delighted. And I was nervous. I didn't tell Harold or Marge what I was up to—a sure sign of a guilty conscience. After some toing-and-froing, we agreed on her apartment for the interview. So that we wouldn't be interrupted, we said. I went there on a snowy night just before the end of the Christmas recess. Amazingly I found a legal parking space—a good omen, I decided. And then for the first time I walked through that lobby and smelled the disinfectant I was to smell so often; I saw the black and white of her apartment, and we had our first half-flirtatious conversation about it. And we sat down on opposite sides of her glass coffee table and had our interview.

She didn't tape it, I'm sure. She didn't take notes.

I forget what she asked me. I forget what I answered. I remember being attracted to the simplicity of the decor, in such contrast to the complexity of my life. I remember feeling warm and safe sitting there and talking to her in the middle of the storm. I remember thinking that this was starting to feel like more than an interview, thinking that if so, it was a big mistake. I remember not wanting to think.

Nothing happened. It could have. "You could've taken me right there on the coffee table," Amanda admitted later. "Actually you probably could've taken me in your office the first time we met. Not the best start for a relationship, though."

Agreed. The interview lasted for an hour, and then I said I had to go. The snow. The trip back to Washington in the morning. My busy life. She didn't protest. "Did the interview go all right?" she asked. "Can we do another?"

"I'll call you," I said, like a guy trying to dump a blind date.

But her hand lingered in mine as we said good-bye, and there was a moment when our eyes met and I thought: Now. The moment passed, though, the door closed, and I headed home.

Liz and I walked up the center aisle to receive communion. *Hypocrite.* On the way back to the pew I noticed Brad Williams staring at me. What was his problem? Didn't I look sincere enough?

I knelt and leaned my elbows on the back of the pew in front of me, and I brought my clasped hands up to my face. I wondered when I had last prayed. Right now all I could do was think impure thoughts.

When I was back in Washington, Amanda stayed on my mind, through the hearings and the markups and the roll calls and the caucuses. Through the long nights alone in my apartment, when I should have been studying the memos from my staff, trying to master the next day's issues. Around eleven-thirty on one of those long nights, I called her.

Why? I had been faithful to my wife throughout a not-always-idyllic marriage. I had done only one other thing to threaten my career, and it, too, would come back to haunt me. But that other risk had been thrust upon me; this one I took all on my own— for a reporter I had met three times.

I don't think I was in love. Infatuated, certainly, but I could have dealt with the infatuation if I had chosen to. I have dealt with stronger emotions, as Marge is happy to remind me.

Here is one explanation: The campaign was coming up, and I knew that Finn would be my opponent, and I knew that it would be brutal. I thought I deserved a fling before the long race began. Not a fling, really; a quiet place where the pressures of my life could not reach.

And here is another: Liz, lost in her books and her courses, was oblivious to the campaign planning. I was starting to get fed up with her lack of interest in my career. Perhaps this was a way of testing the limits of just how little Liz cared.

Here is one final, simpler explanation: I had tired of all my roles and wanted to try another.

When Amanda answered, it was as if she had been waiting by the phone ever since I had left her apartment. "I'll be back in Massachusetts on Saturday," I said. "I have an event to attend in Worcester at eight. I can see you afterward."

"Oh, that's wonderful," she breathed. What was she wearing? A nightgown? Pajamas? Nothing at all? Was she alone? "Where can I meet you?"

"Your apartment would be fine," I said.

"I see."

We both saw.

On Saturday I sleepwalked through the fund raiser in Worcester, then raced along the turnpike into Boston. Amanda and I pretended to have another interview, and afterward, instead of leaving, I accepted a brandy and listened to Bach. And then we left our brandies on the coffee table, went into her bedroom, and stopped pretending.

Didn't we?

I certainly did. And oh, the glory of letting go. The choice had been made, the danger and the sin were forgotten—or at least shoved into a corner of my mind, while pleasure flooded every other particle of my being. I have lived my life like a dutiful son, atoning for a sin I did not commit. For once duty didn't matter. Nothing mattered except the feel of Amanda's naked skin, the hot pressure of her lips, the movement of her hands over my body. It was wonderful. It took all my willpower afterward to shower and dress and leave, to return to the cold, complex world I no longer wished to inhabit.

After that night everything changed for a while. No more talk about the book. We met to drink in each other's bodies and souls. We were a little reckless at first; she flew down to Washington a few days later and spent the night with me in my apartment. But it was Amanda who urged caution the next morning. "You don't want to be another Gary Hart," she warned. "There are nosy neighbors. There are reporters. You can't afford to take any chances."

No, it would not have been wise to take chances.

Kneeling in the pew, I tried to remember what secrets I had told her in our conversations. Nothing terrible. Certainly nothing about Jackie Scanlon. Little about Liz and me—that had never seemed like a good topic to bring up. I had babbled on about literature, about Yeats and Hopkins and Shakespeare. I had talked a lot about my past, about growing up a motherless bookworm in the fifties, about going to Harvard in the sixties and having my world turned upside down. And I had indulged in my dreams of how to make America a better place to live. I had revealed more than I had to anyone else in years. But there was nothing, I thought, that would look terrible on the pages of *Hub* magazine— except for the hypocrisy of the affair itself. And that would be enough.

And how much had Amanda revealed to me? A lot, I realized,

looking back on it, even though I seemed to do most of the talking. "I want so much to *prove* myself," she said to me once. "Lots of things have always come easy for me because I'm nice to look at. But then there's always a barrier because people assume that what they see is all there is. It was no problem getting my editor to hire me—I just walked into his office and batted my eyes at him—but now I can't get him to give me the really good stories because he assumes I don't have what it takes. But I've shown him. *I've shown him.*" She stopped for a moment, as if to regain her composure.

" 'Only God, my dear,' " I murmured, " 'Could love you for yourself alone / And not your yellow hair.' "

"Yeats," she said quickly. She had studied up on my passions. "Very good."

"Anyway, maybe I don't have what it takes," she admitted. "Maybe life has just been too easy for me. I'm not as aggressive as I should be. You have to be a bitch sometimes to get ahead, and I just find that so hard."

I thought of our first interview; she had probably hoped I would be as easy to convince as her editor. "Was the book about me going to be a way of proving yourself?" I asked.

Amanda smiled dreamily and kissed me. "I guess it was," she said. "But look how that turned out."

We laughed and made love. We did that a lot.

She was pensive sometimes, and she talked about her future. She should go back to school. Maybe law school—what did I think? She should quit *Hub* and go free-lance. She should find a cause and work for it. What causes did I recommend? All these discussions seemed tentative and painful, I realized, because they ignored the central question facing us both: Was I part of her future?

And I realize now that the more intense our relationship became, the less self-confidence she seemed to have, as if what was happening were as troubling to her as it was to me. Or perhaps I was just uncovering the reality beneath the pose. It was a reality I was familiar with; it's hard to succeed in this world, and if you aren't tough, at the very least you have to look tough, to make the world believe you are tough, or you'll never get anywhere.

I wonder if that was ultimately Amanda's downfall.

The good part lasted from Christmas to Easter, when we managed to spend a few days together in San Francisco, at a criminal justice conference that I spoke at and she pretended to cover. Even then I was starting to wonder where it would all lead. The affair was only adding to the pressures of my life, and in a few short months the campaign would present me with all the pressure I could handle. But I couldn't imagine not seeing her anymore; I couldn't imagine life without the pleasure she brought me.

The issue of *Hub* was waiting for me in my office when I returned from the conference. Marge was happy to confess that she had put it there. It contained a story by Amanda about people on general relief, a catchall category in the Massachusetts welfare system for those who didn't qualify for any other form of assistance. There was a move afoot to cut back on it, and Amanda's article put a human face on the effect the cuts would have.

It was straightforward, heart-on-sleeve liberal journalism. Many of the people on general relief suffered from something called situational anxiety, which (Marge joked) apparently meant that working made them tense. One woman claimed to have seasonal affective disorder, which Harold interpreted as meaning that she didn't like winter. Callous Republicans could laugh about it, but there was nothing wrong with the article—if the author hadn't gushed to me about how she agreed with my views on personal responsibility and getting government out of people's lives. "Good thing we kept this woman away from you, huh, Jim?" Marge said, giving me one of her meaningful looks. "Having her writing a book about you would sure cause a little situational anxiety in the campaign."

Harold was blunter: "I don't know what exactly you're up to, but if it's what I think it is, you'd better stop it fast. I'm not going to let you throw away your career on some blonde on the prowl for a story."

So they suspected. I had probably been a lot less circumspect than I imagined, and maybe they understood me a lot better than I thought. I couldn't argue with them; the article spoke for itself. I could, however, argue with Amanda.

I drove angrily to her apartment—as I did the night she was murdered—and confronted her, as I had intended to do that awful night.

She burst into tears when I accused her of lying to me. "It's just a story," she said, sobbing. "It's my job. I do human interest. That's what I'm good at. It's what my editor gives me. That's all the story was—human interest."

"Am I part of your job? Get some dirt on the senator? Is this the big break you've been hoping for from your editor?"

"No, Jim. You don't understand."

"But you have been lying to me about your politics, right?"

Amanda squeezed her hands together as she tried to get control of herself. I had never seen her so upset. I thought: She looks gorgeous when she's upset. But I couldn't let myself be interested in how she looked. "I guess I have sort of misled you," she said carefully. "I wanted so much for you to like me, I wanted to get to know you, and that seemed to be the only way. But see, it's not that I disagree with your politics; I really don't have any politics. I—I *sympathize*. Maybe that's why I always get assigned the human-interest stories. I try to sympathize with my subjects, with the people I interview. I don't know if you're right or wrong about crime and all that, but you're an interesting person—the most interesting person I've ever met—and I wanted to find out what you had to say, I wanted to find out why you were the way you were."

"Are you planning to write about me?"

"No, Jim, no." Her eyes hardened. "I'm not a whore."

"But you're a liar."

"All right, maybe, but no more than—"

She stopped, but it was easy enough to finish her sentence. *No more than you are.* Guilty as charged. But right now she could hurt me much more than I could hurt her. She suddenly looked frightened. "I didn't mean that," she whispered.

I shrugged. "You can understand the position this puts me in," I said. A line from a script.

"I love you," she replied.

A line from a totally different script. It was the first time those words had been spoken between us. Her eyes glistened with tears. She reached out and touched my arm. I felt myself becoming aroused. I thought: If she had wanted a scoop about the sanctimonious senator's loose morals, she had long ago collected all the necessary evidence. There was no need for her to act anymore.

"Maybe it was phony at the beginning, but it's real now," she said. "Can't you feel it, Jim? Do you want me to quit my job? Do you want me to register as a Republican? What can I do to prove that it's real?"

But I was scared now. The early stages of the campaign were getting under way, and the thought of what an article about an adulterous love affair with a glamorous blond reporter would do to the campaign was enough to put a stop to any sexual urges. "Amanda," I said, "you've got to understand. I can't afford to take any chances. You said so yourself. The campaign is starting, and everyone's going to start paying attention to me and—"

Somewhere during my speech her eyes went dead. She took her hand away from my arm. "Of course," she said. "I understand. I'm sorry, Jim. Really I am."

And so was I. I left her apartment feeling as if I had just been beaten up. Worse: as if I had just beaten someone up.

I thought I would never see her again.

"May her soul, and the souls of all the faithful departed, rest in peace," the priest intoned.

The whole church seemed to be crying—including Liz. Liz? She dabbed at the corners of her eyes with a tissue. Was it just the solemnity of the occasion? Thinking about the spirits of the dead?

She noticed me looking at her, and she turned away, still sniffling.

Oh, Liz. Will you ever believe me that the affair was over? Do I believe that myself?

I was in a funk all summer.

Even mistrusting Amanda, I couldn't seem to let the affair end right away. There were still those lonely nights in Washington when she was just a phone call away. There was still the temptation to go to her apartment when I was in town and have her wrap her lovely long legs around me.

She never refused to see me when I called, but of course, everything had changed. We both were more guarded now, afraid to do or say anything that might shatter the fragile remains of our relationship. I was surprised that she didn't try harder to win me over, but the self-confidence was entirely gone now, and she had become an almost totally passive recipient of whatever affection I chose to bestow on her. I'm not sure I liked the change. Looking back on it now, I'm sure she didn't like the change either.

When she did finally say something, it was enough.

I had gone over to her apartment for dinner. I helped prepare it, as I often did, chopping celery with the knife that later killed her. We drank wine; we chatted about the campaign. She told me she was thinking of quitting her job and going back to Europe. Maybe she could write articles for travel magazines. Or maybe she wouldn't bother. After dinner we made love, an urgent, silent coupling that left us both exhausted. Then we lay in bed together, and pretty soon we knew that it was time for me to go. And each time that happened, we—or I, at least—wondered if I would ever return.

Her back was to me. I put a hand on her shoulder, the sign that I was about to leave. "Amanda—" I began.

"I don't think you should come back," she interrupted, not looking at me.

"Why?"

"Because each time you come, I think: You're doing this to humor me, just till after the election. So I won't write anything about you. So you won't have to worry about the wrath of the scorned mistress."

"That's ridiculous."

"It's no more ridiculous than what you've thought about me."

I stroked the naked curve of her back. Her body was stiff and tense beneath my hand. She was right. And that was when I truly saw that it was hopeless. There were more lines in my script: *I'm under so much pressure right now. I just need some time to sort out my feelings.* But they wouldn't make her trust me, any more than her avowals of love could make me trust her. Better just to let it go.

And that was the last time I saw her, until the night I saw her corpse.

That final scene between us put me into an even worse funk. Not just because I was worried that she would write about me— although I'll admit that crossed my mind. It was more that it had all ended so inconclusively, so messily, leaving me feeling guilty and worried and, yes, lonely. Could it have ended any differently? Differently, yes. Better? Probably not.

I realize now that other people observed me in my funk and came to other conclusions about what was going on. And that was part of the reason why I was sitting in a church on a rainy Monday morning, watching the pallbearers approach my lover's casket.

I wondered what would have happened if she hadn't died. After the election. I felt in my pocket; her key was still on my key chain. Why, if our relationship was over, did I still have the key to her apartment, ready to use it on the night she was murdered? Too busy to think about getting rid of it? Or too uncertain of my feelings to make the final break? Too selfish, Liz would say. And she would probably be right.

Amanda? I thought as they carried the casket past me. I need help, Amanda. I'm in terrible trouble. Do you still care? Did you ever care?

And that was as close as I got to praying.

Liz and I walked out of the church and into the midmorning drizzle. We stood with everyone else on the steps while the casket was being slid into the hearse. The reporters huddled in the distance, waiting to pounce on me. Liz was still sniffling; the cameras, I was sure, would notice. Sam Fisher would be thrilled.

"A moment, Senator?"

It was Brad Williams. I shook my head.

He came a step closer. "I know you were having an affair with Amanda, Senator," he murmured in my ear. "I think I should get your side of the story before I tell the world about it."

He was wearing cologne that made me think of fern bars and men wearing gold chains. There are few people whom I can't even stand the smell of; Brad Williams had joined their ranks. I looked at him. "Adams House would be very proud," I said.

He didn't appear to be bothered. "Well?"

I shook my head again. "Go fuck your mother," I said, and I headed down the steps of the church with Liz on my arm.

We didn't go to the grave. I had to get to Washington; Liz had to get to school. We had done our duty. We no-commented the reporters and made our way back to the car, where Kevin was waiting for us. He folded up his *Globe* and started the car. "Nice mass?" he asked.

"Very moving."

"Such a shame," he said. "So young. Such a future ahead of her."

Shut up, Kevin. Liz didn't seem to mind. Kevin drove us to Cambridge. "What course are you taking?" I asked Liz. Why were you crying, Liz?

"The mystic tradition," she said. "It's not till this afternoon, actually, but I've got a lot of studying to do."

"Tough one, is it?"

She looked uncomfortable. Did she suspect sarcasm? "Yes," she replied. "Besides, Professor Zacharias is a world authority on the subject, and I'd really like to do well."

"You'll wow him," I said. "No problem."

She looked at me, then quickly looked away. What had I said now?

"How'll you get home, Liz?" Kevin asked from the front seat.

"Oh, don't worry about me, Kevin. My girl friend Sally lives in Cohasset, and she can drop me off."

We started talking about logistics then: when my flight was leaving, when I was coming back, who was picking me up. My everyday hectic life took over once again, and the memories of the funeral faded.

Maybe they'll arrest me at the airport, I thought. That would be dramatic enough to suit Cavanaugh.

Cabot College is crammed onto a small campus on the fringes of Harvard; its proximity to its better-known neighbor figures prominently in its recruiting brochures. Kevin dodged his way past the lunatic Harvard Square pedestrians and pulled up in front of the student center. Liz gathered her things and prepared to get out of the car. I put my hand on her arm. "Thank you, Liz," I said. "You were wonderful."

Her cheeks reddened. I thought about kissing her, but the moment passed, and she was gone. We watched her enter the building, and then Kevin headed for the airport.

"Do you believe the spirits of the dead are always with us?" I asked Kevin on the way.

He considered. "To an Irishman the dead are more real than the living," he replied. "You know that, Senator."

"Too true," I agreed. "Too true." The memories had faded for today, but they would return, I knew. They would return as long as I was among the living. I stared out the window at the traffic, and we were silent for the rest of the ride.

CHAPTER 9

No one arrested me at Logan; no one arrested me when I arrived in Washington. I was puzzled but grateful; the longer Cavanaugh delayed, the better things looked. One of my aides was waiting for me at the airport, and he drove me to the Capitol. It was time to do my job again.

The job. Millions of dollars and thousands of people were involved in the fight over it. I had it and wanted to keep it; Bobby Finn was trying to take it away from me.

Why?

Not for the money. Finn's wife is rich, and I could make a hell of a lot more practicing law than I could being a senator, as Liz was always willing to remind me. The salary might be tolerable, actually, if the expenses weren't so appalling. The government pays your plane fare back and forth to your home state, for example, but it doesn't do much to help you maintain two residences. When we first moved down to Washington, Liz and I crunched the numbers, and they just didn't add up; we couldn't afford to keep our house in Hingham as well as own a place in D.C. That was a big part of the reason Liz eventually decided to go back to Hingham, while I moved into the kind of dreary apartment I had thought I'd left behind after law school.

And that brings up the personal cost of being a senator. Where is the time to be a father and a husband? You have a duty to your constituents; you have a duty to the nation and to history. Your personal life can wait, or it can disappear. History won't mind. Your constituents won't mind—unless they find out you're a hypocrite.

So Kathleen grew up with a father who saw her occasionally on weekends and during Senate recesses. She refuses to let me apologize, but I know that somewhere inside her she must resent this.

Ah, but surely the power a senator possesses is worth the personal struggle. How much power do I really have, though? I work all year in committee on some bill, and it gets filibustered or amended to death by some senator who wants to look good to the folks back home. Everything is watered down in the constant pressure to compromise, to find the votes, to get something passed. In the attorney general's office I had power over human lives: my employees, the people I prosecuted, the people whose interests I protected. In the Senate I am just one voice among a hundred, shouting to make myself heard.

So why be a senator? Why spend millions of dollars of other people's money, and all my time and energy, running for an office I'm not sure I want?

Because I'm a politician.

Because Harold White forces me to run.

Because I'm trying to make things up to a mother I never knew.

Because occasionally I make a difference.

Well, I may not be sure why I want to be a senator, but one thing is clear: I'm good at it. I struggled for a while when I first went down to Washington, as my preconceptions battled with reality. But then I was lucky—and privileged—to find a mentor, someone who could show me what I had to do to make my mark.

His name is Carl Hutchins. Like me, he is basically a law-and-order Republican. But he is a generation older than I am, and he has been in the Senate long enough to become an institution. He was returned for a fourth term the year I was elected. I didn't approach him at first because, for all my ignorance, I at least knew that freshmen senators don't go to the institutions; the institutions come to them—if the institutions so choose. One day he sat next to me on a sofa in the cloakroom as we waited for the Senate leaders to extricate themselves from some procedural tangle. His suit was rumpled; the cuffs of his white shirt were frayed. "This is the damnedest place, isn't it, son?" he murmured.

"I'm beginning to find that out," I replied.

He scratched the left cheek of his long, thin face; he hadn't shaved very well, and there were white hairs peeking out from the craggy skin. "Son," he said, "the Senate is made up of three kinds of horses: the workhorse, the show horse, and the horse's ass. Nowadays it's gettin' tough to tell those last two apart. But you know, it's the first kind that really gets things done around here."

"Are the workhorses the ones who get reelected?" I asked.

He chuckled. "It's never failed for me, son. Never failed for me."

It was good advice, especially because it was advice I wanted to hear. I am by nature a workhorse, even if I've had to master some of the show horse's tricks. So I was more than willing to do the studying and the preparation. The leadership put me on the Armed Services Committee, so I valiantly attempted to master the defense budget. I got the seat I wanted on the Judiciary Committee, where I did my homework on the nominees for judgeships and became an expert on federal criminal law. I soon realized that I couldn't master everything, though, so I kept my focus narrow and didn't pretend to know what I didn't.

And my strategy worked. Before long my colleagues were paying attention to me. Fellow Republicans started following my lead on my chosen issues, realizing that I wouldn't steer them wrong. Even better in some ways, the press paid attention, also understanding that I was a reliable source of information. I got a reputation as an effective legislator. People began to talk about my heading for a still-higher office.

Meanwhile, Liz was hating every moment of it.

A year or so after I was elected, Senator Hutchins wandered into my office late one night. This was a rare occurrence, I knew. Senators are too busy to go visiting each other on the spur of the moment. His tie was loose, and his suit as usual was rumpled. He looked approvingly at the mound of paper work on my desk. "Sometimes I sleep in my office," he said. "Get more done that way. Saves the commute."

His wife had died a couple of years before, his kids were grown up, and he lived by himself. He was a busy, powerful man, but he also had to be terribly lonely. "Maybe I should do the same thing," I replied. "Shower in the gym. Save the rent. My wife is moving back to Massachusetts with our daughter."

He nodded. "It's a hell of a life," he said.

I thought about that for a moment. "Do you mean that in a positive sense or a negative sense, Senator?"

He chuckled. "Hard to say, son. Hard to say." He sat down and started to talk, and we both began to feel a little less lonely.

"Mrs. Sullivan, round everyone up for a meeting at five-thirty," I said as I strode into the office.

"Yes, sir." Everyone would be rounded up. Mrs. Sullivan is a stout dynamo who has worked on the Hill all her life. She likes it that I don't call her by her first name.

I called Art Chandler and Denny Myers into my office. Denny was another aide, a hotshot just a couple of years out of Stanford Law. They brought me up-to-date on the current state of senatorial affairs. Mondays are usually fairly slow in the Senate, while its members straggle in from the weekend visits to their states. But things tend to fly out of control toward the end of the session, as everyone rushes to get some action on bills before time runs out. Tactics change from moment to moment, and if you make the wrong decision, a pet project can be lost irretrievably.

My pet project was the prison aid amendment to the crime bill. Like many pieces of legislation, it started with a staff member's bright idea and grew. The idea was simple and not even especially "law and order":

> PROBLEM: One reason our criminal justice system is failing is that states have nowhere to put the criminals.
> RELATED ISSUE: The Defense Department is closing many of its military bases as the result of budgetary cutbacks.
> SOLUTION: Why not give these bases to the states and provide the states with some money to turn them into prisons?

The difficulties with turning such a straightforward idea into a law turned out to be enormous. The Pentagon wanted to hold on to the closed bases, in case communism should rise again. Fiscal conservatives didn't want to fund another costly program. Liberals wanted the bases earmarked for the needs of the homeless. States that didn't have the closed bases complained that they would be treated unfairly—why should they be denied the federal windfall? Towns where the bases were located complained that they didn't want prisons in their backyards.

But enough people were interested so that the plan lingered, got worked on, and developed. It moved away from dealing solely with the closed bases to a general procedure for helping states build prisons. Now it set up a complicated system by which the federal government matched state funds for prison construction, gave states priority in obtaining closed bases if they were going to turn them into prisons, provided towns with incentives to accept prisons . . . and so on. Something for almost everyone.

But the plan was still a bit too controversial, and I couldn't even get it out of committee as part of the omnibus crime bill. The chairman wanted something he was sure he could shepherd through the full Senate. There is a crime bill every election year to placate the angry voters, and no one wants to see it fail because of one dubious provision. So now I had to offer the plan as an amendment when the bill came to the floor.

In the meeting in Boston on Saturday Art Chandler hadn't been optimistic about our chances. I wanted to know if anything had changed.

Art shook his head. "It's gonna be close. You may have to lean on a few people to win this one."

"What if we cut the cost projections? Lower the federal contribution or something."

"Lower it any more, and states won't think it's worth their while getting involved," Denny Myers pointed out. "The whole rationale of the plan disappears." It had been his idea in the first place, and he wasn't used to the give-and-take of the legislative process yet. He no longer recognized his brainchild, and it made him unhappy.

"Something's better than nothing," I said. "I've got to get this thing passed, especially after the little media event we staged at that county jail yesterday."

"Then you should go to work on Carl Hutchins," Art said. "There are five, maybe six senators who'll follow his lead."

I sighed. "He's got a problem, doesn't he?"

Art nodded. "A thirty-eight-year-old two-term congressman with a pretty wife and a big smile and favorability ratings that are off the chart. The congressman's up ten points in the polls, so Hutchins can't make any mistakes."

"But surely Carl can make the case on this one. It's not like we're, I dunno, trying to repeal the Fourteenth Amendment or something."

"Agreed. But all I know is that he hasn't committed yet, so you've gotta make him commit. Call in your IOUs. Turn on the charm. Just don't let him slip away."

"All right," I said. "I'll get on it. And, Denny, you figure out how to cut the cost by, let's say, twenty percent. Now, what else have we got?"

There was plenty more. And there were bells signaling votes on the Senate floor, there were photo sessions with delegations representing this and that, there was a conference call with the campaign staff back in Boston, and another day passed.

At five-thirty I met my assembled staff in the largish open area where a few poor souls answered my mail. I like my staff, and I imagine they like me, although it's impossible to say for sure. Senators spend more time with their staffs than they do with one another, but still the gap between the boss and his workers is virtually unbridgeable. The workers don't appear on national TV; they don't get invited to the White House; their names aren't familiar to millions of people. And they certainly have no hope of someday taking over their boss's job. I try to be pleasant with my people, but the Senate is too demanding and the stakes are too high for me to be especially forgiving of incompetence. So perhaps they fear me more than they like me, but that simply can't be helped.

"And how was everyone else's weekend?" I asked for starters, and they gave me an appreciative laugh. Then I launched into a version of the talk I had given to the campaign workers Saturday night, except a little less political. It was crucial that my own people see me as confident and unafraid. Otherwise rumors were bound to leak to the media: He's running scared; morale is low; things are falling apart.

I got a round of applause when I finished. Everyone was more than willing to hear good news. Their jobs depended on my re-election after all.

And then I retreated into my office again to catch up on business. I tried calling Carl Hutchins, but he wasn't available. After a couple of hours I was starving, so I decided it was time to go home.

Home. A reporter for *Town and Country* or *House & Garden* or some such magazine once wanted to do a piece on the glamorous young senator's living quarters. Marge Terry actually brought up the request at a staff meeting, to give everyone a laugh. I live in a nondescript apartment in a racially mixed neighborhood in the District. My housekeeping does not enhance the neighborhood. Kathleen visited the apartment once, and after her first view of it she said she couldn't be blamed for her sloppiness; it was clearly inherited.

What's a guy to do? I never have the time or energy to clean. Hiring someone would be more trouble than it was worth. I could have asked Liz to decorate the place, but it was a matter of pride that if she didn't want to stay in Washington, I didn't need her help.

Besides, I basically don't care. The apartment is a place to park my body at night, nothing more. I didn't come to Washington to entertain or do little household projects; I came to be a senator.

When I finally arrived at my apartment with a briefcase full of memos and a leaking bag of Chinese food, however, I could have wished for a more welcoming sight than last week's newspapers strewn across the couch and a balled-up pile of shirts that hadn't made it to the laundry on the kitchen table. "Such glamour," I muttered. I got the last beer out of the refrigerator and sat at the table in front of my dirty shirts, where I drank the beer and ate some of the Chinese food; the rest would have to do me for the week. Then I cleared a space on the sofa, sat down, and called Danny.

He was the one to answer the phone for a change. "Danny, did the police talk to you yet?" I said, without bothering with any amenities.

"No. No one's come. That's good, isn't it?"

He sounded hopeful but nervous. I heard the TV in the background; children were shouting at one another. He wanted me to tell him the danger was past. But how could I tell him that?

"Sure it's good. But it could still happen. Did you talk to any of those lawyers?"

"Uh, I didn't get around to it."

I hadn't really expected him to. "Just don't start thinking we're out of the woods," I said. "There's no telling what the police are up to."

"I understand," he said, a trifle belligerently. He didn't like lectures. "I'll call you if anything happens."

"Please, Danny. Please do that."

I hung up and stared at the phone. He was right; it was a good sign that the police hadn't come to talk to him. Why hadn't they? Grilling him was the obvious first step. Unless the police didn't have the tape.

But they had to have the tape—unless my brother was deluded. Unless whoever had killed Amanda had stolen it.

And who had told Amanda about my relationship with Jackie Scanlon? I know I hadn't, and Danny and Jackie both denied it. Who else was there?

I gave it up for the moment. The light on the answering machine was blinking. I rewound the tape and played back the messages.

And suddenly I was listening to Amanda once again.

"Hi, uh, it's Friday morning at, let's see, nine-thirty. I guess you've already left. The thing is, Jim, I'd like to see you again. I know how busy you are but—maybe just a few minutes this weekend. I know I shouldn't be calling you like this, and I promise not to be a pest but—please, Jim. It's important. Just come over anytime."

Silence and then a beep, and that was all.

It gave me an eerie feeling, to listen to her voice in my empty apartment. A message from the dead. If she had called a few minutes earlier, she would have got hold of me. Would that have changed anything? Would that have somehow kept her alive?

I played the message again and again, searching for clues. She didn't sound like a reporter on the trail of a scoop. She had the uncertain, tentative attitude I had become so familiar with, as if she weren't quite sure what to say to me, how to act. But was she in fact acting? She had her chance to break through the barriers now. *You want human interest; I'll give you human interest. And maybe get a Pulitzer for my trouble.* So why not pretend just a little and get me over to her apartment for one final, devastating interview?

It just didn't sound right.

Perhaps, I though, she was so desperate to get me back that she was going to blackmail me into continuing our relationship. But that didn't sound right either.

Finally I erased the tape. I didn't need it as evidence any more than I needed the photograph of us kissing. And I sat back and tried to figure things out.

I couldn't make sense of it. I remembered the Paul Everson case, the one that made my reputation as a defense lawyer; I remembered how I had gone over the evidence in my mind as I drove to work, as I brushed my teeth, as I lay in bed at night. How did Everson's wife die? Who had killed her? How did each piece of evidence fit into the puzzle? But it was easier as a defense lawyer; your job isn't to solve the murder, just to poke holes in the government's solution. So what if she was planning to divorce him? He could afford the alimony, and he wanted the divorce as much as she did. Of course, his fingerprints were on the knife. It was his kitchen after all. And if he was really that clever a murderer, wouldn't he have wiped the fingerprints off the knife? Poke enough holes, and you're a winner. You become famous; you become attorney general; you become a senator.

The trouble was, I could poke holes in any solution I could come up with for Amanda's murder. And so I was left with nothing except the fear that whatever the real solution was, it was bound to destroy me.

I decided to phone Detective Mackey. He liked me; maybe he would tell me something, off the record.

A couple of calls to mutual acquaintances produced his phone number. The line was busy for a while, and then a woman answered. I groped for her name. "Hi, is this Tricia?" I asked.

"Yes?" she said, with the dubious inflection of someone expecting a pitch for vinyl siding.

"Tricia, this is Jim O'Connor."

"Senator?" Still the dubious inflection. I often find it difficult to convince people that it's really me when I get them on the phone. Presumably people think I have servants taking care of all my personal business.

"Sure, Tricia. How are you doing?"

"Just fine, Senator. Um, I guess you want to talk to Bill."

Bill? It took me a second to recognize Mackey's first name. "Well, yeah, but it's sure nice to hear your voice again. Been a long time."

"I'm really sorry about this murder business, Senator," she said in a rush, as if worried she'd be overheard. "I've always admired you."

"I'm grateful for your support, Tricia. Is Bill there, by any chance?"

"Sure. Let me just go find him."

"I'd appreciate it, Tricia."

I heard the sound of the receiver clattering onto a table and a distant shout. I had to come up with something for Mackey, I realized. I couldn't just ask for information from him without easing into it. I heard footsteps, then the sound of the receiver being picked up. "Senator," Mackey said.

"Mack," I said. "Sorry to bother you at home."

"No bother, Jim. What can I do for you?"

"Well, you remember you asked me before if I had any theories about this murder."

"Sure."

"Okay, well, I don't put much stock in this, but enough people have mentioned it to me that I figured I should share it with you. Of course, you guys have probably thought about this on your own."

"What's that, Jim?"

"It's the idea—the possibility—that whoever killed Amanda Taylor did it to get me into trouble. Like someone I put away when I was AG. Is Donato out of prison, for example?"

"Oh, sure. Last I heard he was living in, uh, Lynn, I think. But jeez, Donato—"

"I'm not specifically accusing Donato, that isn't it at all. Just an example of someone who might have a grudge against me. Here's a guy, you know, might be in the Senate himself, wasn't for me."

"I don't get it, Jim. If they have a grudge, why not just kill *you* or something? What's this reporter got to do with it?"

"Precisely the way I felt when it was brought up. But say people knew she was writing this book, say someone breaks into her apartment looking for dirt about me. She surprises him, they struggle, and he kills her."

I could feel Mackey losing interest. I didn't blame him; he expected better from me. "Seems pretty farfetched, Jim. But thanks anyway."

"You're welcome. As I said, I thought I should just pass it along."

"I appreciate it."

"How are things going up there, Mack? Young Mr. Tobin still sticking his nose into everything?"

Mackey chuckled. "We're cooperating closely on the investigation. That's what I tell all the reporters anyway."

I figured that was a hint: He wasn't going to tell me anything he didn't tell reporters. Still, I had to plunge ahead. "Interesting thing about those tapes you guys found, Mack. Remember how I said she didn't appear to record our conversations?"

"Sure."

"Well, I was talking to my brother yesterday—you know my brother, Danny?"

"I've had a draft or two at Danny Boy's in my time, Jim."

"Great. Too bad he had to give the place up, huh? Well, apparently she interviewed him for the book, too, and he couldn't remember being taped either. So if you've got a tape of my brother, that suggests maybe she wasn't telling some of the people she interviewed that she was recording them. So maybe there were tapes of my interviews that someone stole."

"That's an interesting theory."

"Well, it's only interesting if you've got a tape of my brother's interview. Have you listened to all the interviews yet, Mack?"

"We're leaving no stone unturned in this investigation, Jim. That's what I tell those damn reporters."

I got the message. "Well, I'm just trying to pass along anything I think might help."

"I understand." Mack seemed to hesitate a fraction of a second. "This is a tough case, Jim," he said. "The Monsignor is very interested in this case."

"I understand, too," I murmured. "Good night, Mack. Tell Tricia it was nice talking to her again."

"She's on cloud nine, Jim. Not every day a senator calls. I think I'm on cloud nine myself. See you."

I hung up. Had it been worth it? Now Mackey undoubtedly suspected that something was amiss with Danny. What if he hadn't been going to talk to him and now decided he'd better? It wouldn't take Hercule Poirot to figure out that Danny was hiding something.

Still. If Mackey had listened to the tape, would he have been so friendly with me? Maybe this suggested that he didn't have the tape and everything was fine.

But policemen can act, too. Not as well as politicians, but well enough. Mackey wouldn't reveal anything he didn't want to reveal.

I recalled his last comment—about Cavanaugh. And I wondered: Was that a warning?

I stared at the ceiling, and I thought: Cavanaugh hates me.

He's hated me since before he had a reason to hate me. And I suddenly realized: He's going to arrest me, tape or no tape.

But Mackey's a good cop, I reasoned. Mackey won't let him. And even ignoring Mackey, Cavanaugh can't just march in and handcuff me. He's got his own career to consider.

Maybe, I thought. Maybe not.

I had to stop thinking about it. There was nothing I could do now. I tried reading the stuff I had brought home with me, but I couldn't concentrate. Get some sleep, I thought. I got up and went into the bedroom. The spread and blanket were heaped at the foot of the cheap pine bed. I could have sworn I had made the bed; could have sworn I'd brought the shirts to the laundry, for that matter. And then I remembered: the call from Scanlon last Friday. The sudden fear. Was everything about to unravel? I had every reason to be frightened, it turned out.

I thought of the phone ringing in the empty apartment, minutes after I had left that Friday. Amanda almost never called me. Too late, I thought. Too late.

And that made me feel very tired. I took my clothes off and found some clean pajamas to put on. I brushed my teeth in the bathroom, and the single toothbrush in the holder made me feel lonely as well as tired. I went back into the bedroom and lay on the filthy sheets and felt sorry for myself, and then I picked up the bedside phone and called home.

It was past Liz's bedtime, I knew, so Kathleen would answer. "Hi, princess," I said.

"Hi, duke."

"I've been thinking about fractals," I said.

"I bet," she said.

"Honest. They've been preying on my mind. What was that term you used about my apartment when you visited me?"

Kathleen thought for a moment. "Entropy?"

"Yeah, that's it. Even I know about entropy. Things falling apart. So I was wondering: Is entropy related to fractals?"

"Well, they're both *science*," she said doubtfully.

"I mean, is it like, as things get more complicated, they're more likely to fall apart?"

She considered. "It's kind of hard to follow," she said finally, in a tone that suggested *she* understood but that she despaired of making me understand. "Complex systems are really more robust than simple linear systems. I mean, the least complex state for a human being is when he's dead, right?"

"I hadn't thought of that," I admitted.

"Fractals are beautiful," she said. "Entropy is just . . . nothing. Total disorder."

"I guess I should clean up my apartment."

Kathleen giggled. "It's impossible to reverse entropy. Ultimately, I mean. We all die, for example."

"That I knew."

"Oh, Daddy, I'm sorry," she said, apparently realizing that I might not appreciate all this talk about death.

"Don't apologize," I replied. "Never apologize."

She was properly chastened. "Right," she said.

"How's your mother?"

"Fine," Kathleen said. And then: "I don't think she's very happy, actually."

I wasn't surprised. "Be nice to her," I said. "This hasn't been an easy few days for her."

"Okay." *So why aren't* you *nicer to her, Daddy?*

"Listen, I've got to go to sleep. Kiss yourself good-night for me."

She made a smacking noise into the receiver. "Good night, Daddy."

"Good night, Kathleen."

I hung up and turned out the light, feeling a little better.

And as I fell asleep in the total disorder of my apartment, I thought of something I could do.

I would get in touch with Paul Everson. He would be able to help me if anyone could.

CHAPTER 10

*E*nough for the moment. I will let myself sleep.

It is snowing, a light, delicate snow that melts as soon as it hits the windowpanes. A trial run for winter, perhaps. I watch the rivulets of moisture slide and merge across the glass; I listen to the wind blowing the snow out of the gray sky. I should go for a walk, tramp through the woods for an hour or two, feel the cold wind and snow on my face, and try to clear my brain.

But what if the snow is not a trial run? What if I become trapped in a blizzard in these strange woods? I'm a city boy. I read about stuff like that; I feel no need to experience it.

It could be a blizzard for all I know. I haven't listened to any weather reports while I've been here; I haven't had any news whatsoever of the outside world. There's no TV here, no radio; just me and the computer screen, me and a brain that won't shut itself off.

Instead of venturing outside, I have just gone into the kitchen and brewed another pot of coffee. The kitchen has marble counters, a Jenn-Air grill, a massive skylight. I'm not exactly roughing it here. If I'm cold, I turn up the thermostat. If I need food, I have a phone and a number to call. But still, I'm hidden from the world, and that was my goal. I don't need to suffer; I only need to understand. And that requires solitude.

I stood in the middle of the kitchen waiting for the coffee, and I longed to grab a newspaper, to glance through a memo, to dictate one myself. But I've made that impossible for myself because I know that this is the only way to make it work. And now I sit with the coffee mug in my hand. The snow is still falling. The cursor is still blinking. The screen waits to be filled.

It is time to think about Paul Everson.

Paul Everson and James O'Connor, Act One

It was 1969, and the world was exploding.

Not that it mattered a great deal to me. I had my student deferment to keep me out of trouble and no political beliefs to speak of. I figured I would go on to graduate school and get a Ph.D. in English. I had been successful so far reading books; why change? The job market was horrendous for English professors, but what else was I good for? I would get something. I worked hard; I would be all right.

Paul Everson was my roommate, and a radical. He had long blond hair and a scrawny beard that at least made his acne less noticeable. He wore combat boots and a black beret. He truly believed that the Revolution was about to start and that it would start here, at Harvard. Where better? He wanted to be part of it. So instead of going to classes, he passed out flyers, he marched, he protested, he attended interminable meetings to argue ever-finer points of revolutionary doctrine and fashion ever-longer lists of demands. A huge poster of a smiling Mao dominated our living room at Adams House. Copies of the *Old Mole* and the *Daily Worker* were our bathroom reading.

Despite our differences, we got along all right—mostly by ignoring each other. Everson made occasional attempts to make me see the error of my ways, but my utter lack of interest kept the conversations short.

And then one fine spring afternoon the radicals took over a building.

It was University Hall, a small administrative building in Harvard Yard. They threw the deans out and hung a sign from the windows proclaiming it Che Guevara Hall. The campus was in an uproar. Everyone had an opinion about the takeover, the demands, the administration's probable response.

Everyone except me. I wanted to stay out of it.

But my roommate was inside the building. And somehow that changed things.

Everson's parents called after dinner; the takeover had made the national news. His mother started to cry when I told them he was involved. "Please," she said, "if there's anything you can do . . ."

I couldn't think of anything, but I promised to help.

My father called next; just checking. "It's hormones, is all," he informed me. "Spring comes, and you gotta do something. If those guys had girl friends, none of this stuff would happen."

"They're totally sincere, Dad," I responded, feeling oddly defensive.

"Sincerity doesn't make up for stupidity, Jimmy. Keep your nose clean."

But that didn't seem so terribly important all of a sudden.

The Revolution required a response. That was one point Everson kept making in our infrequent political debates, and it was a point I was now beginning to accept. Neutrality, ignorance, and ironic detachment all were unacceptable. If you're not part of the solution, you're part of the problem. I couldn't wish away the horrors I saw on the nightly news. I realized that I had to make a choice.

The hours passed. Mao stared down at me from the living-room wall. There were meetings everywhere to discuss the situation, but I didn't feel like attending. If you weren't in University Hall, you might as well be alone in your room. I tried to go to sleep, but sleeping didn't seem like an acceptable choice. Finally I got dressed and went outside.

The confrontation was coming; you could smell it in the air, like an approaching thunderstorm. I walked over to the Yard. The gates had been locked that afternoon, but they weren't guarded; the police evidently had something better to do. It was easy enough to climb a wall and enter the forbidden zone.

There were plenty of other people who had done the same thing. A lot of freshmen, who lived in the Yard, were also up and about. We hung around in front of the occupied building, trading rumors and speculations, until I was tired of talking. Then I just stood there, gazing into the windows at the protesters, who looked exhausted and worried. I stood there for a long time, cold and confused. And then I no longer felt like standing still, and I walked inside.

The first-floor hallway was littered with empty Coke bottles and potato chip bags and crumpled flyers. The place smelled of unwashed adolescent. Someone had scrawled the phone number of Legal Aid on a wall. A *Crimson* reporter was interviewing a gaunt, bearded fellow on the stairway. A girl lay sleeping or passed out on the polished wooden floor.

I looked inside an office. The file cabinets were all open, and manila folders were strewn everywhere. On the windowsill was a photograph of a woman with two young children; the glass in its frame was cracked. A few hoarse-voiced students were arguing about the appropriate course of action when the pigs arrived. Should they fight? Go limp? Chain themselves to the desks? Had anyone remembered to bring chains? "Seen Paul Everson?" I asked the room.

"Upstairs, maybe," someone replied.

"We've already won this battle," the interviewee was explaining to the reporter as I passed them on the stairs. "The question is: Where do we go from here?"

Upstairs there were more bodies and more debates; the stench was even worse. I wandered around for a while and finally found my roommate sitting on the floor by himself in a corner of the ornate Faculty Room, under the grim portrait of some ancient Harvard president. Everson was smoking a cigarette; his eyes were bloodshot. I sat next to him. "Welcome to the Revolution," he said, not looking at me.

"Your mother asked me to get you out of here," I said.

"She worries too much," he replied. "Nothing's gonna happen. They'll negotiate." He said that last word with a sneer.

I shook my head. "They're gonna take the place back. Soon."

"Well, I don't give a shit. I'll survive."

We were silent for a while. Someone started playing the guitar, badly. Everson looked at me. "You didn't come here because my mother told you to," he said.

"I got bored," I replied. "This was something to do."

He nodded. "Just taking a stroll through the Yard at four in the morning and thought you'd drop in." He stubbed out his cigarette on the parquet floor and lit another one. "You don't know which fuckin' end is up, do you, O'Connor?"

"I'm trying to educate myself, Everson. That's what Harvard is all about."

"Well, this certainly has been an education. Don't know if we should let you drop in just as we're about to graduate, but what the hell. That's what anarchy is all about." He smiled, and then he started to nod off; the hand holding the cigarette dropped onto his leg and he jerked awake as the tip scorched his jeans.

"You look like shit," I remarked.

"Good of you to notice."

We fell silent again; the guitar, too, fell silent. We were waiting, I realized. Waiting for graduation. A girl started to cry and said she was going home. No one stopped her. The darkness started to lighten.

I thought of my own mother. She'd be upset, too, if she were alive. "Where did I go wrong?" she would moan, just like Mrs. Everson. But this was part of growing up. This was why you went to college. I had been a good boy all my life, I had kept my nose clean, and Danny had gotten all the girls, and the world was going to hell. Something wasn't right. Maybe we needed a revolution to fix it.

Everson had nodded off again. This time the cigarette missed his leg. I took it from his hand and stubbed it out.

"They're coming!" someone shouted.

I stood up. Everson roused himself and got to his feet, too. Everyone was at the rear of the building, looking out at the quad with Widener on the right and Memorial Church on the left. There was nothing to see. "Busloads of 'em on Quincy Street," a blond-haired kid reported. Fire alarms started going off in the dorms around the Yard. I looked up. People were gathering on the roof of Weld Hall next door. "The whole world is watching," Everson murmured.

The gaunt, bearded guy started rattling off instructions, but I didn't listen. I was too scared. I folded my arms across my chest, hoping to look determined but really trying to keep from trembling. This was what it was like every day in Vietnam, I figured. The wait continued, and I began to wonder and then to hope: false alarm. Everyone go back to sleep. Battles start at a decent hour in Cambridge.

And then, just before five, we saw them. Several cars, followed by a half dozen buses, appeared from behind Memorial Church.

We looked down into the windows of the buses; the police inside stared back at us.

The caravan came to a stop. An official-looking man got out of one of the cars and seemed to be making an announcement. We couldn't hear it. We were too busy staring at the police marching out of the buses in their boots and jodhpurs and riot helmets.

"Oh, shit," someone said. "State troopers."

There were Cambridge police, too, and Harvard police—an army, getting ready for the battle. I saw them take out their nightsticks, and I tried to imagine the pain of being hit with one of them, just as I had tried to imagine having puerperal fever. Couldn't do it. That's why I was here, right? For the experience, right?

Right?

Students in the quad were giving the Nazi salute. The police started to move.

Someone was pulling on my arm. I forced myself to look away from the advancing army. It was Everson. "Don't be a complete idiot," he said. "Let's get out of here."

I couldn't quite process this. Paul Everson? Fleeing the Revolution? He pulled me away from the window. I let myself be pulled.

We stumbled past people. Someone swore at us. We made our way downstairs and raced along the short hallway to the front door, away from where the troops were massed. Everson opened it. There was a crowd of students on the steps. A blue line of Cambridge police was heading toward us, nightsticks raised. Kids started leaping over the railing and onto the grass as the police approached. We hesitated for a second and then followed them as the police pushed their way up the steps.

So we joined the gawkers. The cowards. The steps were cleared quickly, and the police headed inside. We could hear the thunder of feet on the stairs, screams of rage and pain. I looked at Everson. He was breathing heavily. His face was expressionless.

And then people started pouring out of the building, with the police in pursuit. The blond kid who had told us about the buses on Quincy Street rushed out, his forehead dripping blood. A kid in a wheelchair shouted, "*Sieg Heil!*" and a cop overturned the wheelchair and started beating him on the ground. And I thought: Hey, this isn't right! We got out! You won! This is Harvard Yard, not Birmingham, not Chicago. A cop came straight at us and I started to run, but then I noticed that Everson wasn't with me. I turned and saw him standing his ground and shouting at the cop: *"Pig! Pig! Pig!"* The cop punched him in the face and he went down. Then the cop raised his nightstick and I rushed back, desperate to defend my roommate.

"Hey!" I shouted.

The cop looked at me. "Jimmy?" he said.

It was Bill Doherty. He lived a couple of houses up the street from us in Brighton. He had played football with Danny in high school. I used to help him write book reports for English class.

We stood on either side of my crumpled roommate. "What the fuck are you doin' here, Jimmy?" Billy asked me.

"I belong here," I said.

"Is this maggot your friend?"

I nodded.

"Well, get him the fuck out of here before he gets himself killed."

"Okay, Billy. Okay."

Billy shook his head as he looked at me. "Jesus, Jimmy. What would your father say?"

And then he rushed off to beat up someone else. I got Everson to his feet and dragged him inside the nearest dorm, while the battle continued to rage around us.

That was the Harvard Bust. It's been over twenty years now, and no one talks about it much anymore, except in the occasional retrospective article about the turbulent sixties. Are there middle-aged radicals who still remember the protesters' demands, who still seethe at the injustices that motivated the takeover? I'm sure there are, but they have long ago shuffled off the stage of history. There are new injustices now, and new demands—or perhaps they are the same ones, only in different costumes.

And yet if you were there . . . I can still close my eyes and I am standing outside University Hall in the cold predawn, trying to figure out what to do, dimly realizing that this was the biggest decision of my young life. I can still see the police getting off those buses—coming to get *me:* the lawbreaker; the enemy of society. I can still feel myself rushing toward the cop as he got ready to bludgeon my friend—and the shock of recognition when I saw that the cop, too, was my friend.

If you were there, you were changed, and the change lasts a lifetime.

Afterward the campus was shut down for a week or so, as people demonstrated and debated and held mass meetings. Things muddled along then until the school year mercifully ended.

History has shown that there were no winners out of the Bust. The Revolution didn't begin, so the protesters couldn't claim that they lost the battle but won the war. But Harvard couldn't claim victory either. It had beaten up a few of its students, and that in turn had radicalized many more. The trust and mutual respect on which the institution was based had been destroyed. It had recovered its building but lost its soul.

And what of James O'Connor and Paul Everson?

My roommate went to business school and then entered the world of high finance. Do I detect the sound of relaxed laughter from my conservative friends? Ah, yes. The young radical realizes that revolution isn't quite so glamorous after he's been socked by a cop. Making money becomes a lot more interesting than crusading for socialism. How typical.

Perhaps. But Everson was more complicated than that. He gave up on revolution, but he didn't give up his hatred for the establishment, for the smug American ruling class wallowing in its own self-interest. He decided to fight it by himself, for himself.

He became one of the earliest of the corporate raiders. He would see a company grown complacent making shoddy products for undiscerning consumers, and he would buy up its stock and take it over, usually after management had fought him till its dying breath. He would then shake the company up, turn it around, and sell it off.

I don't think he did this just to make money, although he made tons of it. He really disliked those corporate executives, safe in their boardrooms, screwing workers and consumers alike and thinking nothing could touch them, mouthing pieties about free enterprise but using every trick in the book to protect themselves from the dangers of the marketplace. Everson became the avenging demon of capitalism.

He didn't always operate entirely within the law, I'm sure. But a lot of his demonic reputation came from the hypocritical pleadings of the executives he cast aside. They became concerned about the fate of their workers and the effect on the community only when their own jobs were on the line; otherwise it was layoffs as usual. Everson didn't mind his reputation; he enjoyed it, in fact. Billy Doherty could hurt him, but these guys couldn't—not as long as he was smarter and meaner and richer than any of them.

And James O'Connor? How did he manage to avoid being radicalized?

I wasn't radicalized, I admit, but I certainly was politicized. My most immediate response to the Bust was to lose all interest in becoming an English professor. The world was too important to spend my time reading what other people thought about it— or, worse, teaching what other people thought about it. I decided to go to law school instead.

In the process I decided that, if forced to choose between the Harvard administration and the students I saw that morning in University Hall as the people I wanted to run society, I would have chosen the former, despite what they did during the Bust. What matters in the long run is the form of government, not its policies or actions at any given moment. You're always going to have cops like Billy Doherty socking punks who call them pigs. If the government is set up correctly, however, its policies can be changed, in accordance with the will of the governed. And what matters in the short run for most people, including myself, is not an abstract question about the form of government, but more prosaic concerns, like being able to go outside your home at night without fear of being assaulted. And for those concerns as well, I'd rather have Billy Doherty on my side than any of the University Hall protesters.

Billy, I'll see you later on. You've had a greater impact on my life than you'll ever know.

Anyway, I went to Harvard Law. My father was dubious about lawyers, but he liked the prestige. My chosen career was less acceptable than being an English professor, perhaps, but better than owning a bar.

And after graduation, filled with crusading spirit, I offered my services to Francis X. Cavanaugh, newly elected district attorney for Suffolk County.

Cavanaugh wasn't much older then than I am now. He had been an assistant DA for a long time, the last few years of which he basically ran the place as his boss descended into senility. When the old man decided to try for yet another term, Cavanaugh decided that he couldn't wait around for four more years and ran against him. The disloyalty didn't really shock anyone; politics is a tough business. It was clear the old man had hung on too long, and the Monsignor had earned his shot. Cavanaugh leaked some damaging stories about his boss's behavior, the old man's contributions dried up, and Cavanaugh won the Democratic primary easily. In Suffolk County in those days, that was all you needed to win.

I followed the campaign in the newspapers, and I thought: Cavanaugh's office is the place for me. Cavanaugh had a good reputation. He talked a lot during the campaign about professionalizing the DA's operations. He would surely want to recruit all the talent he could find. He would surely be overjoyed to find a local kid fresh out of Harvard Law who preferred the long hours and low pay of an assistant DA to becoming an associate in some high-powered corporate firm.

We met in his office. He was cordial. He was impressed by my credentials. He took me around to meet some of the people in his operation. We discussed what my duties might be if I came on board. I expressed my interest. He smiled encouragingly and said he would get back to me.

He never did.

After all these years that still irks me. At the time, being full of myself, with my two Harvard degrees and all, I was infuriated. Where did Cavanaugh get off, turning me down for a job? I tried to find out what the problem was, and the word came back that the Monsignor felt the chemistry was wrong. Chemistry!

My anger fueled my decision to do the opposite of what I was going to do in the DA's office. I signed on as a public defender. I would show Cavanaugh just what kind of lawyer he had turned down.

The PD's office, unfortunately, was not the place to show off one's lawyering skills. It was all I could do to keep my sanity as I dealt with the endless procession of pathetic, vicious, and crazy souls who had stumbled into the clutches of the system. They all were guilty, unless like a good liberal you believe that society itself was to blame for their misdeeds. And the most I could do for them was to bargain a little time off their sentences, or occasionally set them free on a technicality. Once in a while I felt as if I were helping society, but mostly I just felt numb.

One good thing came out of my experience in the PD's office:

I met Roger Simmons there. Roger was thinner and drank less in those days; he was just married to Doris, and the four of us were inseparable for a while—all of us young and poor and just starting out. Roger wasn't interested in changing society; his dreams were more suburban. But we felt right together, and when, after a couple of years, he suggested starting our own criminal law firm, I was willing to listen. Liz was certainly in favor; she hadn't married a Harvard Law grad so that she could live on hot dogs and Franco-American spaghetti. Besides, the baby was on its way, and we were going to lose Liz's teaching income.

So Roger and I hung out our shingle, and we began to see another, wealthier brand of guilt. It was interesting and remunerative, if unexceptional, work. I might still be doing it today if Paul Everson hadn't called me up one day and once again changed my life forever.

CHAPTER II

Paul Everson and James O'Connor, Act Two

"You saved me once, Jim. I need you to save me again," he said over the phone.

We hadn't kept in touch since college. I read about him in the papers, of course, and occasionally compared my own middling progress with his spectacular success. But that was about it. So I was surprised that he knew all about me and what I'd been up to. I shouldn't have been, I found out: Everson made it a point to know as much as he could about everything and everyone; that was how he stayed ahead of the competition. He wanted someone young and smart and energetic to represent him. Above all, he wanted someone who would believe in him. He said that I fitted the bill perfectly.

Now I wasn't about to downgrade my own abilities. I had become a good lawyer, always well prepared, naturally eloquent and quick thinking, and yes, they tell me my appearance made quite an impression on the female jurors. And Paul Everson certainly had reason to think kindly of me. But even so, I was a little surprised when he dropped his case in my lap. It wasn't simply the murder case of the year in Suffolk County; it was the murder case of the decade.

131

Everson was going to need all the help he could get if you believed the newspapers. The facts of the case looked grim. He and his wife had been involved in a bitter divorce, one that would have cost him millions. It was the kind of divorce, filled with charges and countercharges, that makes the tabloids goofy with joy. Who is Paul's mystery woman? How much does Alice actually spend on shoes? Which of them will get custody of Kubla Khan, their beloved Lhasa apso?

And then Alice was found dead—stabbed through the heart on the floor of her bedroom. All clues pointed to one suspect: her estranged husband. Whose fingerprints were on the knife? Who else could get into their mansion without setting off the security system? Who else could keep Kubla Khan from barking so much that the housekeeper would wake up? Who had a better motive?

If the divorce made for great reading, the murder drove the tabloids to rapturous excess, even by their standards. Alice went from being the ditzy spendthrift to the tragic victim. Paul went from glamorous financier to sinister murderer. Corporate executives he had thrown out on the street were delighted to provide quotes about how ruthless he was, how little he cared about anyone besides himself. He became a robber baron, a symbol of the collapse of America's values. The photo of him being led away in handcuffs after his arrest, smiling cockily, wearing a cashmere blazer and suede Gucci loafers, seemed to say it all: Here is a man who thinks he can get away with murder.

What lawyer wouldn't want this case? Only a lawyer so convinced of Everson's guilt and so disgusted by his crime that he couldn't give his client effective representation. But that certainly wasn't me after my first meeting with him. It wasn't simply that he told me he was innocent; all my clients told me that. It was that I found myself so much *wanting* to believe him. Because when he talked to me, he wasn't the tabloids' personification of Satan; he was a scared young man in over his head—not so very different from the kid who stood next to me as the police marched toward University Hall. "Everything looks terrible, Jim, I know that," he said to me. "And I know I won't make a very sympathetic defendant. But Jesus, murder? No, Jim. I didn't do it. In my own way I'm as moral as anyone. You've got to believe that."

"The most important thing you can do to help yourself is to tell me the truth," I said. "Otherwise I can't do my job." This was the standard admonition I gave my clients. They rarely paid any attention to it, but I felt obliged to make the effort.

"I'll do whatever it takes," Everson said. "Trust me."

I trusted him, and I set to work.

Oh, what a trial it turned out to be! Not the least interesting aspect of it, at least to me, was the prosecuting attorney. Not surprisingly Cavanaugh had decided to try this one himself. Cavanaugh never met a camera he didn't like, and there would be plenty of them focused on the Everson murder trial. The Monsignor was getting ready to make a run for attorney general, and the publicity of personally winning the case would give him the statewide exposure he needed to sew up the election.

We met once or twice in pretrial maneuverings, and we conducted ourselves with the exquisite courtesy of men who detested each other. The idea of a plea bargain was in the air—Roger, for one, was in favor—but Cavanaugh didn't offer any deals, and I wouldn't have accepted any. He needed the trial to get the headlines, and I needed the trial to get the acquittal my client deserved. So we prepared for a showdown.

Cavanaugh had every reason to be confident, even if you got past the sensationalized coverage to examine the facts. Everson had an alibi, but it was next to useless; his mistress claimed he was with her the night of the murder. Who would believe Dawn Majewski, ex-model and would-be next Mrs. Everson? She might have the IQ of a potted plant, but she clearly had brains enough to realize that she had everything to lose if her beloved was shipped off to the state penitentiary for life with no parole. Cavanaugh didn't have an overwhelming amount of circumstantial evidence, but he had the murder weapon with Everson's fingerprints on it, he had the impossibility of anyone else breaking into the mansion, and he had as good a motive as you could want. He had enough.

I never worked so hard preparing a case. The strategy I finally decided on was so risky it almost gave Roger a heart attack, but I didn't see that I had a choice. I decided to pin it on the victim.

Alice Everson wasn't the world's stablest, happiest woman to begin with, and the breakup with her husband had depressed her even more. She couldn't believe she was being abandoned. She started drinking heavily. She talked to her friends about how empty her life would be after the divorce. So perhaps she had put an end to that life before it became intolerable.

But suicidal women don't stab themselves to death with a

kitchen knife, Roger objected reasonably. They take pills or stick their head in the oven. True, but what if Alice wanted to have her death effectively put an end to Everson's life as well? One night, more despondent than usual and still angry at the husband who has left her, she takes the knife he had used when he was still living with her—the knife that still bears his fingerprints—and plunges it into her already broken heart, knowing that he will be the first and only person anyone would suspect of killing her.

My strategy was risky because, as Everson himself pointed out, he wasn't going to be a sympathetic defendant, and this approach would undoubtedly make jurors like him even less. The guy murders his wife, then tries to say she did it herself. How much more rotten can you get? I had to hope that the jurors would understand enough about reasonable doubt to put their dislike of Everson aside when it came time to vote.

So when the trial started and Cavanaugh presented the state's case, I tried to raise all sorts of questions about the angle of the wound, the placement of the fingerprints on the knife, the alcohol level in the victim's bloodstream—confusing, technical stuff, but necessary for our defense. Cavanaugh for his part did a competent, thorough job. When it was our turn, I tried to build a case against Alice, calling witness after reluctant witness to testify about her wild state of mind in the weeks preceding her death. Cavanaugh objected strenuously, but the judge let me go. The jurors eyed me with suspicion; they didn't like what I was doing, but they were listening. I didn't bother calling Dawn; she was a lost cause. But I did finally call Everson himself—one final risk. I needed to show that he wasn't an ogre, that he didn't eat babies for breakfast. The jurors could hate me if they liked, but I wanted them to think of Everson as a human being on trial for his life.

He listened carefully to my advice beforehand; he even took notes. I made him wear a muted gray suit and no jewelry; he looked like a prosperous businessman, nothing more. On the stand he was low-key, courteous, reflective. He didn't hate his wife, he said; he had simply fallen in love with someone else. He looked on the divorce wrangles as inevitable for someone in his position; he'd had far more bitter fights in his business dealings. He didn't kill his wife. *No, sir. So help me God.*

Then I handed him over to Cavanaugh. And Cavanaugh laid into him. This was the high point; this was what he had been waiting for all his career. *Do you admit that you once punched her in a drunken brawl? Do you admit that you threatened her in the presence of both divorce lawyers? Do you admit that you stood to gain millions of dollars from her death?*

Everson admitted what he had to, but he didn't crack. And then the Monsignor asked him one final question, with all the sanctimoniousness he could muster: "And I ask you, sir—this obscene, ridiculous accusation that Alice Everson committed suicide in order to implicate you. Did you put your lawyer up to it?"

"No, sir, I didn't," Everson replied quietly. "In fact, I agree with you. I don't think Alice would have done something like that. We had our problems, but neither of us wanted to hurt the other. I honestly believe that. And I simply can't imagine her committing suicide. I don't know who killed Alice, but I believe with all my heart that she didn't kill herself."

Cavanaugh was dumbfounded. The defendant had just trashed his own defense. But in doing so he had sounded awfully nice—almost gallant. So what should the poor prosecutor do next? He decided to leave well enough—or bad enough—alone, and with a dismissive, disbelieving wave of the hand he ended the cross-examination.

I was as astonished as Cavanaugh. After mulling it over, I decided that I was pleased. I had made the points I wanted to make, but Everson had effectively dissociated himself from them. Conceivably, the jury could believe me *and* believe him—believe, at any rate, that he was still loyal to his spouse after her death. I rested my case, and in my closing argument I made sure they understood that this was an option for them.

And then all our futures were in their hands.

I happened to share an elevator with Cavanaugh while the jury deliberated. "You prick," he said. "Everson's answer was your idea, wasn't it?"

"No, but maybe it should have been, except I wasn't smart enough to think of it. Besides, you can't coach that kind of response. He was sincere."

"Sincere, my ass. He's laughing at all of us."

"The years have made you cynical, Francis. Have some faith in human nature."

"Everyone is guilty, O'Connor. You should know that by now."

I smiled. "I leave such matters up to the jury. They know best."

Cavanaugh simply rolled his eyes. Then the elevator opened its doors, and we went our separate ways.

The jury took its time, but eventually the moment arrived. We stood erect and listened as the verdict was announced and our fates were determined.

NOT GUILTY! the tabloids screamed, and everyone in America knew who they meant.

Not guilty. There's nothing like winning a case you're expected to lose. Danny had his upset victories on the football field, I'm sure, but the feeling couldn't have been the same; the stakes were so much smaller. My career, my fortune were made; if I could get Paul Everson off, I could work my magic on anyone. I was the one lawyer everyone in America would want.

That night Everson brought me up to his penthouse at the Ritz—a quiet celebration just for the two of us, he said. I drank champagne that tasted as if it should be drunk only by gods, and I gazed out at the lights of the city, feeling that the beverage suited me, at least tonight. "A long way from college, eh, Jim?" Everson said, standing next to me.

"A long way from the Revolution."

He shrugged. "We make our own Revolution, if we have enough balls."

"You should know. You've got more balls than anyone."

Everson smiled and filled my glass. "I suppose that's accurate." He sat down on the sofa and stared at the sparkling liquid in his glass. "I told you that I'm a moral person in my own way, right, Jim?"

"Right."

"Well, I believe in telling the truth. Some people I've dealt with may scoff at that, but it's a fact. They're so suspicious of me that they assume I'm lying, they proceed on that assumption, and they never quite realize that what tripped them up was their unwillingness to believe that I might be telling them the simple truth. I won't deny that sometimes I lie, but the potential return has to be large enough to warrant it, because lying makes me feel bad." He paused for a long time. "I feel bad right now," he murmured finally.

I turned away from the city and looked at him. There was some sort of paradox in what he was saying, and it confused me. "You're lying about telling the truth?" I asked.

He shook his head. "I was lying at the trial," he said.

"The business about not believing that your wife committed suicide? Well, I guess it's understandable. You were facing life in prison, after all."

He stared at me, and I stayed confused. Even after he said the words, I stayed confused. It couldn't be right. The champagne, the excitement, the exhaustion . . .

"I killed her, Jim," he said. "She was driving me crazy. I gave her everything, and it wasn't enough. She wanted me, and she couldn't get it through her head that she wasn't going to have me. That night I decided I couldn't stand it anymore, so I went there and took a knife out of the kitchen and I murdered her. I won't try to justify it, because I can't. I felt awful about it afterward. I'll always feel awful about it. But not awful enough to confess, frankly—except to you. Now, when it's too late for me to be punished. I certainly don't feel awful enough to go to prison for it.

"I know I shouldn't tell you any of this," he went on. "It can't make you feel very good, after you worked so hard to get me acquitted. But it helps to know the truth. You can hate me if you want, I'm used to being hated. But you should also know that if you ever need help—financial, whatever—you just have to ask. You've saved me twice, and now it's your turn."

It helps to know the truth. Do I believe that today? I didn't at the time. I had talked to murderers before; I had defended them and listened to them lie to me, just like Everson. But I had never believed any of them when they lied. And none of them had finally bothered to tell me the truth. *It can't make you feel very good.* That was an understatement. I felt like becoming a murderer myself. I felt like calling up a tabloid.

But I couldn't. Ethically I was bound to keep silent. If I did talk, it would ruin my career and do absolutely nothing to Everson. He had been tried and found innocent. He was free to go back to making his millions, and there was nothing I could do to stop him.

"I hope you feel better now that you've unburdened yourself," I said.

Everson merely shook his head.

I couldn't stand being in his presence anymore, so I put down the glass of champagne and left the penthouse. I drove home— to my beautiful new house in Hingham—and I kissed my wife and baby. And I thought: Everyone is guilty. The Monsignor's hard-earned wisdom. So why bother defending them? Because the system requires that they receive a defense? Well, the system didn't require that James O'Connor defend them. Because that's where the money is? That was the real reason. Cavanaugh would make less in a year than I had made on the case I had just won. Was it worth it? At that moment I sure didn't think so.

I had to tell someone, so I told Liz. That was a mistake. I wanted sympathy; instead I got rage. She didn't understand or care about legal ethics and double jeopardy. She demanded Everson's head, and she was furious with me for refusing to bring it to her. We went to bed angry, and I didn't bother to bring up the qualms I was feeling about my career.

She learned about them soon enough.

The snow has given up for the day, and now the wind has decided it needs some exercise. The panes rattle; the door of the toolshed bangs. It's dark, and I don't feel like going outside to latch the door shut. There are probably bears lurking out there. I can't figure out how to do some things with this computer. If Kathleen were here, my problems would disappear.

I'm lonely.

But that's beside the point. I have work to do, so I should just do it.

More coffee, and on to Act Three.

CHAPTER 12

I didn't want anything more to do with Paul Everson after that night, but it was impossible to avoid him once I entered public life. It wasn't worth the effort to return his checks when he contributed to my campaigns. It wasn't worth the rumors that might start if I spurned his handshake when we met at a political or charitable function. If Cavanaugh was right and everyone is guilty, then Everson was just more so. Or not even that—I was just more aware of his guilt. I knew that the hand I shook had blood on it; everyone else's sins were still hidden from me.

So we chatted politely at the fund raiser or the cocktail party. He asked after Liz, and I asked after his latest wife. He congratulated me on my latest success and reminded me that if there was ever anything he could do . . . But there never was; I made sure of that. I didn't want the scales to be balanced because that would somehow make me as guilty as he was.

But now things were different.

I didn't need Everson's money, but I figured I needed some information, and he was the best source in the world for information. One of the secrets of his success, he told people, was that he knew more than anyone else. If he was thinking about buying a company that made doorknobs, he would find out everything about the company: not just how many doorknobs it was going to sell but who its best employees were, how its president treated his mistress, what the food in its cafeteria was like. And somehow out of this morass of facts he would find what he needed to make the right decision.

Not all his information could have been obtained legally; that was the kind of accusation his enemies were forever making, at least. But the charges never stuck. He was good at what he did; I knew that from personal experience.

So I figured, if there was ever a time when I could use his help, this was it. I didn't have the luxury of worrying about whether this would balance the scales. I had to know what was going on.

When I arrived at my office the next morning, I had Mrs. Sullivan call Everson. He was out of the country, but his staff promised he would call back as soon as possible. Of course, that turned out to be when I was on the Senate floor. I never did catch up to him that day, and by the time I returned to my apartment I was having second thoughts. Even if Everson could come up with the answers I was looking for, what could I do with them? They would either set my mind at rest or confirm my worst fears, but they wouldn't give me a course of action. I had just called him because it was something to do, and I didn't want to feel helpless.

The next day I came back from a meeting, and the people in the office looked a little stirred up. "Paul Everson's here," Mrs. Sullivan said.

I wasn't listening closely, and I didn't understand. "I'll pick it up in my office," I said.

She shook her head. "He's *in* your office," she said. "I thought it'd be all right—" She stopped, uncertain, seeing my own uncertainty. Even in a Senate office Paul Everson was a big deal.

"That's great, Mrs. Sullivan," I said. "Exactly the right thing to do." I looked at the card that had my schedule for the day printed on it. I gave her quick instructions about shifting my appointments around, and I went inside.

Everson was standing in front of the bookcase next to my desk, examining the shelves full of Massachusetts knickknacks people had given me over the years. He turned when he heard me enter. "Jim," he said. "Your secretary—"

"Of course. How are you doing, Paul?" I went over and shook his bloodstained hand.

No blood to be seen, actually. He was perfectly groomed as usual. The suit was tailor-made; the white shirt was starched; its cuffs were monogrammed. He wasn't exactly handsome—the nose was too thin, perhaps, the face too broad—but he was as good-looking as money and good taste could make him. And he had that aura of power that is sexy in and of itself. No wonder my staff was in a tizzy.

"I'm doing just fine, Jim. Just fine. Admiring your memorabilia."

"People like to give me things. I accept 'em if they're cheap enough."

He nodded. "Plaques, yes. Jaguars, no."

"That's the idea. Have a seat."

We sat in the armchairs in the corner of my office—where Amanda and I had sat for our first meeting. "I got your messages," he said, "but we couldn't seem to connect. I happened to be in the neighborhood, so—"

"You flew in especially," I said. "You don't have to be in Washington unless some committee's subpoenaed you."

Everson laughed. "All right. I apologize. I read the papers, Jim. I know what's going on. And when you called, I figured, after all these years maybe I'll finally be able to give you some help."

"Yes, well, this murder case has been worrying me just a little."

"I can't imagine why."

I smiled, although I didn't really feel like it. "Cavanaugh's been waiting for ten years to get me," I said. "Now he has his chance."

"You don't have an alibi," Everson said. "And they have that witness who saw someone that looked like you going into the building. And there's your . . . interesting relationship with the victim."

"Yes," I agreed. No need to go further into the relationship.

"But Cavanaugh won't do anything," Everson said. "Not unless Finn tells him to. And Finn won't. He'd be crucified if they trumped up a charge against you."

"Who's to say what's a trumped-up charge?"

"Well, I'm no lawyer, but it sure doesn't look to me as if they have enough yet."

Unless they knew about Jackie Scanlon. So what should I tell Everson? He wanted the truth, obviously. He was so fond of the truth. But like any client, I wanted to tell him only what I thought he needed to know. "Have you heard that the police have some tapes of interviews she did?"

He nodded.

"One of those tapes, I believe, is of my brother."

"Danny."

"That's right. I need to know if the police have that tape or Amanda Taylor's notes of the interview."

He looked at me. Considering how deeply he should probe, I figured. Wondering how much truth he deserved. "What is it that you want me to do, Jim?" he asked finally.

"Anything you can find out about the investigation will help," I said. "But mainly I just need to know about the interview with Danny."

"I see."

"And of course, we can't have anything you do be traced back to the campaign."

"Of course."

He was silent again. This was as awkward as I had feared it would be. I wasn't going to tell him anything more about the interview. He would either help me or he wouldn't. "Do you think you'd be able to, uh, do something like that, Paul?" I asked.

"No question," he responded quickly. "No question. I don't have any sources in the Boston Police Department—it's not the level at which I generally operate—but I'm sure I'll be able to come up with something. I can find out more than you, at least."

"Whatever you can do," I said.

Everson nodded and looked out the window. I don't have much of a view; views come with seniority. "My opinion is that you shouldn't worry about any of this," he said. "Once again, I think Cavanaugh is too smart to touch this case."

"I wish I could believe that," I said. "But I'm sure that if Cavanaugh can come up with a plausible motive, he'll have me arrested."

"This tape—" Everson began, then stopped and began again. "The thing to do, I guess, is to make sure you don't have a motive."

"Yes," I said. "That's correct."

Everson stood up abruptly. "You only have to ask, Jim," he said. "You know that."

I stood up, too. He was used to being the one to decide when meetings were over. So was I. "I know that," I agreed.

"I'll give you a little unsolicited advice, though. If you want to solicit more, that's up to you. My advice is to ignore this murder. Go on the aggressive and stay there. That's the way to beat Finn. Oh, and I'd look into his war record if I were you."

Finn's war record? Whatever for? I wanted to ask, but I didn't. The fewer favors I received from Everson, the better I would feel. "Thanks, Paul," I said. "I'll do that."

"Good. I'm on your side, Jim. I want to make sure you understand that."

He reached out his hand, and I shook it once again. And then he left.

I felt ill at ease after his departure. The whole conversation had been stilted, painful. I had known that it would be painful for me, but I had expected something different from Everson. Here was his big chance to return the favors he thought he owed me. Why did he seem so unsure of himself?

Perhaps, I thought, he already knew that the police had the tape, and he wanted to spare me the truth. But then what was the point of advising me to be aggressive in the campaign? If he knew what was on the tape, then he knew there was no campaign.

I shouldn't have called him, I thought. This was only making things worse.

My black mood was interrupted by Mrs. Sullivan on the intercom. "Senator Hutchins on oh-one," she informed me.

I forced myself to think about my job once again. I picked up on 01. "Carl, thanks for getting back to me," I said. "I'd like to discuss my prison aid amendment with you."

"Yes, yes," he agreed in his sonorous voice. "Meet me at six-thirty. We'll have a drink and talk about jail cells."

Seniority isn't what it used to be in the Senate, but it still has its rewards. A view is one; another is a secret office in the Capitol, a hideaway where you can escape from the bustle and tension of Senate business but still be close enough to the action to avoid missing anything important. There's no set order of precedence for obtaining these offices; I don't even know how many there are or who has them. All I know is that one day the secretary of the Senate calls you aside and hands you a key and you become one of the privileged few.

Carl Hutchins's hideaway had a crystal chandelier and Oriental rugs and a balcony that looked out onto the reflecting pools of Constitution Mall, the Washington Monument, and the Lincoln Memorial, just barely visible in the distance. It was a view to take a patriot's breath away.

At six-thirty he led me down a dim corridor into the office, as he had many times before. I sat on an upholstered sofa and admired the view while he poured us each some whiskey. A lot of whiskey, I noticed. "Here's to the Senate," he said.

I raised my glass.

"In a couple of months neither of us may be here," he noted. "You've got your governor, and I've got my congressman with his big smile. The people speak, and all this is taken away from us." He motioned with his glass at the office, the view. Then he drank half his whiskey.

"It's not a permanent institution," I agreed.

"Every two years friends disappear," he said. "So after a while you stop making friends. What's the point?"

He was afraid he was going to lose, I decided. "I'm your friend," I responded. "You can be as crusty a curmudgeon as you want, but you've still got a lot of friends around here."

"Then I've made a mistake. We should just do our business and forget about the rest. Anyway, the new fellows don't want friends; they want sound bites. They want photo opportunities."

"Then they're just the kind of people you want to deal with. You can't have it both ways, Carl. Do you want the nice guys or the plastic guys?"

"I want people to stop abusing the rules around here. I want more respect for the institution. I want people to vote for things on their merits, not on how the vote will look to the folks back home. I want something we do around here to matter once in a while." He suddenly started laughing. "I want that congressman to wipe that stupid grin off his face."

I laughed, too, grateful that he wasn't becoming maudlin. "Look, Senator," I said, "I'd like to come back here next January, and you could really help out the cause by voting for my amendment when it comes up. My campaign's going to focus on law and order, and this'll be a good issue for me."

"People love the idea of prisons," Hutchins said, "but they'd prefer them in someone else's state. Right next to the nuclear waste dump."

"True, but this amendment doesn't mandate that a prison be

located in any particular site. It just helps make the process more palatable, that's all."

Hutchins got up and poured himself some more whiskey. He held the bottle out toward me, and I shook my head. "You know," he said as he sat down again, "President Kenton is scared of you. Of all the potential Republican candidates, he thinks you'd be the toughest to beat."

"He's a smart man, for a Democrat," I said.

"He's a good politician, at any rate. He'll do whatever he can to stop you."

Did that make the President a suspect in Amanda's death? Kevin Feeney would probably think so. "All the more reason to support me on this amendment," I persisted. "I need to beat this governor of mine before I take on the President. Pushing this amendment through will increase my prestige, make me look like a can-do kind of guy."

Hutchins scratched his cheek and looked out the window at the twilit Washington Monument. As usual he hadn't shaved very well. "I ran for President once," he said. This wasn't news. "Damn near killed me. Emma wanted me to do it, said, 'You owe it to the nation, Carl.' Said it often enough that I started to believe it. Of course, no one had heard of me, according to all the polls, but money can take care of that. Money can take care of most anything. So I raised some money, from the folks back home mostly, and I went around to all these little living rooms in Iowa and New Hampshire, and I participated in about a thousand debates where the bunch of us said the same things over and over again, till we could have traded places and recited each other's lines. And these were good guys, for the most part, and we agreed on the issues, more or less, but we had to score our points against each other, and after a while we started getting nasty, and I hated it. I was flying all over the country and getting up at dawn to have earnest conversations with millworkers and farmers and auto mechanics, and every one of 'em told me to cut taxes and increase services, and it was always about twelve degrees out and snowing. And when they finally counted the votes, I got beat worse than I ever got beat in my life. The money dried up then and I had to drop out of the race, and I figure that was the best thing that ever happened to me."

"Carl," I said, "are you trying to imply that you didn't enjoy running for the presidency?"

Hutchins laughed. "At least I could tell Emma that I'd done my best. It broke her heart, but it sure didn't break mine. Tell you the truth, I wouldn't've made a better President than any of the rest of 'em. Probably worse than some. I can swing a few votes around here, but I couldn't inspire the nation. Nowadays I'm not sure I can even inspire myself."

"You shouldn't let this congressman get you down," I said. "We need you."

He shook his head. "I leave, and someone else gets this office, and the Senate goes on. A few of you might miss me for a while, but you'll be too busy fighting some new battle to spend time remembering a fellow who fought the old ones with you."

He fell silent. The hand holding the glass of whiskey was trembling slightly, I noticed. He was trying to get used to the idea of not being here, it seemed to me, and he was finding it hard. I sympathized with him; I was finding it hard, too.

I thought about bringing up my amendment one more time and trying to get a commitment out of him. But I didn't bother. Hutchins didn't want to think about prisons. He understood my situation; he would do what was right.

I finished my drink and left him alone in his office as darkness fell. It was time to take home the memos from my staff and prepare for tomorrow's battles.

CHAPTER 13

"I'm Jim O'Connor. You know what I did as attorney general: cleaned up government, protected the consumer, put violent criminals behind bars. I've kept on doing these things as your senator. My investigation of kickbacks and mismanagement at the Pentagon saved taxpayers millions. On the Judiciary Committee I've insisted that judges consider the victim's rights first—not the criminal's. And I've sponsored a bill that will help us build more prisons to keep these criminals off the streets.

"Meanwhile, what has Robert Finn been doing about crime? Murders—up thirty percent. Rapes—up twenty-five percent. Assaults—up thirty-eight percent. Not one new jail cell built, despite a prison system that's filled way beyond capacity. Not one new initiative in law enforcement, despite a crime problem that's crying out for innovative solutions. It's business as usual in the State House, while people are afraid to leave their homes at night.

"And now Bobby Finn wants a promotion." Pause. "I think you're smarter than that."

Fade to the name, white against black: O'Connor. Fade again: Senator.

End of tape.

Sam Fisher was standing next to the TV. "The key here is to keep the focus on the senator," he said. "People like the face, like the voice. They like it that he can make his pitch one-on-one. You know: 'Here are my arguments, now make up your mind.' "

"I think there are too many facts and figures," Marge Terry complained. "People will tune out." Marge liked to criticize Sam's work: as a consultant he made a hell of a lot more than she did, and she resented it. She would undoubtedly end up as a consultant herself someday, however, so no one felt especially sorry for her.

"I think it's *important* we stick in a lot of information," Sam countered. "We're gonna run this spot all over the place. We don't want people getting bored with it. Every time they see the thing, they should absorb something else."

"There's a problem with the rhythm of that sentence about 'business as usual,' " I said. "Are we trying to contrast the State House with people's homes?"

"Something like that," Sam said warily, not wanting to defend the sentence too strongly if I was going to demolish it.

"Well, the contrast isn't coming across. It should go like this: 'In the State House it's business as usual; in people's homes it's something something something.' See what I mean?"

"I suppose we could massage the sentence," Sam offered, "but I think it works pretty well the way it is."

"All right, let it go," I said. "Just the English major in me."

Everyone looked at Harold. It was his decision ultimately. In this sort of thing I was just the actor. "Go with it," he said. "We've already got the English majors."

We all laughed, and Sam took the tape out of the VCR. We'd preview it for the media to get some free mileage out of it and then start running it on stations around the state later in the weekend.

"On the same subject," Harold said, "I've finally got the Finn campaign to agree to a debate."

"Excellent," Kevin said. "We'll slaughter him."

"Don't let reporters hear you say something like that," Sam cautioned. "This is as dangerous for us as it is for Finn. People expect the senator to do well in a debate; he's the lawyer after all. If Finn manages to put two coherent sentences together, the pundits will say he held his own."

"Still," Marge said, "he's the one more likely to come up with the stupid sound bite."

"True," Sam agreed. You could crush your opponent in a debate and still end up a loser if you said something inane that was replayed endlessly on the eleven o'clock news. Bobby Finn had a hard time keeping his foot out of his mouth when the camera was on him.

"What do Steadman's figures look like?" I asked, changing the subject.

"Holding steady," Harold replied. "Undecideds are high for this point in the race, with two well-known candidates. People are reserving judgment."

"The mail and the phone calls have been very favorable," Kevin pointed out.

"And the media have been okay," Sam said, "all things considered."

"They can't figure out an angle," Marge said. "If they get an angle, that could swing it either way."

"If the police don't come up with something soon, that's their angle," Sam replied. "We'll make sure of it."

People were silent for a moment, and I decided that was enough. I stood up. "Thank you all," I said, ending the meeting. Everyone filed out except Marge.

"I have to talk to you," she said.

I had figured we'd need a talk sooner or later. "Okay," I said. "Let's go to your office."

Her office was tiny, but at least it had a door, which couldn't be said for most of the other little cubicles at campaign headquarters. A whiteboard on the wall had a "To Do Immediately" list with about thirty items on it. The lamp on her desk was covered with little yellow Post-Its and pink While-You-Were-Out messages. Names and phone numbers, all with "Urgent!!" scrawled after them. The ashtray between the lamp and the sleek new computer was filled; she was at it again. The only personal item I noticed was a framed photograph of her being interviewed by some famous network correspondent on election night six years ago; she looked awfully young, and so excited that even the jaded correspondent seemed happy for her.

Marge shut the door after us. I deposited myself in a molded plastic chair, and she sat behind her desk. She immediately picked up a pencil and started twirling it nervously between her fingers. "Oh, for God's sake, smoke," I said. "It's a free country. You're allowed to poison whoever you want."

She shook her head. "It's okay," she said. Marge isn't pretty, but she has what I'd call professional good looks: her hair cut fashionably, her figure kept as thin as smoking and intermittent starvation could force it to be, her face a tribute to discreet makeup that highlights her best feature (her big green eyes) and downplays her worst (a mouth that doesn't sit quite straight on her face). But she never looks quite comfortable in her make up and her designer clothes; she is a ponytail, jeans, and sweatshirt woman stuck in a job that requires her to be something else entirely.

Marge kept rolling the pencil. Her fingernails were bitten to the quick, I noticed. All the manicures in the world couldn't cure her of that habit.

"How's Alan?" I asked. Alan was her latest boyfriend. He managed an academic bookstore in Cambridge. He had a beard and wore tweed jackets with elbow patches. He looked down on us Republican political types; the couple of times I had met him there always seemed to be a sneer lurking just behind his polite phrases. I thought he was a jerk. But, then, I thought that about all her boyfriends; she doesn't have very good luck with men.

"We split up," she said.

"I'm sorry to hear that."

"He's a jerk."

"Of course he is. And I'm actually glad to hear you split up."

Marge waved the subject of her love life away. "I can't take this anymore," she said. "I quit."

"Marge," I said.

"Don't give me that," she responded. Give her what? "I know what you're going to say. 'You can't do this to me, Marge. We're at the most critical point in the campaign, Marge. Think of how bad it'll look in the papers. You and me, we go back a long way. We mean something to each other. You're not going to throw all that away, are you, Marge?' "

I thought for a moment before responding. "I'd say, 'You and I, we go back a long way.' Not 'You and me.' "

"Yeah? Well, it's 'poison whomever you want,' not 'whoever you want,' so up yours, Senator English major O'Connor." She reached into a drawer and took out a pack of Chesterfields. She grabbed a cigarette from the pack, lit it with a Bic lighter on the third try, and started puffing on it fiercely.

"Do you want to talk about it?" I asked.

"No," she said. "I just want to quit. I want to forget all about spots and media buys and tracking polls and all about you. I want to move to New Mexico and throw pots. I want to become a nun."

She puffed some more. "Why did you have to fuck that bitch, Jim?"

"Why do you think she was a bitch?" I responded. "I'm not being argumentative, Marge. I genuinely want to know."

"Oh, for God's sake, you men are so stupid. A person just had to take one look at her to know she was dying to get her claws into you. The handsome, roguish senator, on the outs with his wife—what a catch."

"Marge," I said softly, "that's not exactly grounds—"

"Oh, shut up, Jim. Don't make it worse."

I sat back in the uncomfortable plastic chair. Harold marched to some drummer that only he could hear; Kevin marched to whatever drummer I chose. But Marge and I—Marge and I always seemed to be in step, even without a drummer. I never had to explain myself to Marge; Marge could do the explaining for me. That made her perfect as a press secretary or media coordinator or whatever fancy title we wanted to give to what she did, which was to tell the world what Jim O'Connor thought. There was no need to worry that she'd misrepresent my position or misunderstand my strategy. But it made her more than that as well.

She worked in Washington for me before the reelection campaign brought her back to Massachusetts. After Liz left Washington, I started accepting invitations to Marge's apartment. As later happened with Amanda, it was all business at first: take out Thai food while we worked on a speech or pizza while we plotted a media event. But we knew each other too well not to realize that more was going on: that I was lonely and Marge was the obvious choice to ease that loneliness. She was so obvious that it seemed predestined. No need to rush; it was just a matter of time.

I wasn't really expecting it when it did happen, but even that wouldn't have been surprising if I had thought about it. We were huddled over the text of a statement, eating pizza and disagreeing about a dangling participle, and then we were kissing—a long, probing kiss that left us both breathless. She tasted of pepperoni; she felt great. We gazed at each other afterward, and Marge smiled a crooked, expectant smile—and abruptly I knew I couldn't go any further. I put my hand over hers as she started to unbutton her blouse.

"Why not?" she whispered, her big eyes filling with tears.

"I can't do it to Liz."

"Why not?" she repeated.

And it was only at that moment that I could say why not. "Because I love her," I said.

"You love *me*, god damn it," she said, pulling back from my hand. "You know you do. You're just feeling a spasm of Irish Catholic guilt. It's like indigestion. It'll pass."

"I wish you were right," I responded. "But when you smiled just now, I thought of the way Liz smiles when we're about to make love. No—I *saw* Liz, I *saw* the smile. We've had our problems, but that doesn't mean I can't still love her."

"You love *me*, Jim. Say it."

"All right. Yes, I love you, too. But you're not the one I'm married to. You're not the mother of my child."

"So it *is* guilt. Mr. Morality. Let's pass a bill: Stone the adulterers. Off with their cocks." She leaned forward and grabbed my hand. "No one will know, Jim," she whispered. "No one but God, and He doesn't exist. I'm not asking you to leave Liz. I just want to make love with you."

I was tempted—oh, so tempted. But I didn't. I left the apartment to the sound of her crying.

I half expected her to quit after that evening, but she hung on. Hoping I would change my mind? Because she wasn't likely to get another job as challenging and exciting as this one? I don't know. We fell out of step a little bit then; I didn't want to ask, and she certainly wasn't going to tell me.

Was I a fool to pass up the opportunity Marge offered me? Or a saint? That was, of course, the question she wanted my answer to. I had spurned her and had fallen instead for that tramp, that lying blond bitch with the toothy smile. If I really was Mr. Morality, if I really did love my wife, Marge could have stood it—but not if I was just a jerk, like Alan with the beard, like every other man she had ever met.

"Did you love her?" Marge asked after a while, as we sat in her office.

"I don't know," I said. "I had the hots for her. I was seventeen years old again."

"You were never seventeen."

"No, probably not."

"Did she love you?"

I shrugged. "She said she did."

Marge lit up another cigarette. "You can imagine how this makes me feel."

"I know, Marge. And I'm sorry. And I know you must hate me, but right now I need you to see this thing through. The convent will still be there in November."

Marge appraised me. "Beg," she said finally.

I went over next to her desk and got down on my knees. "Please, Marjorie," I said, my hands clasped in front of me. "I've never asked you for anything before, and I'll never ask for anything again, but now I need you. Please remain as the highly paid media coordinator for the Campaign to Reelect Senator O'Connor."

She leaned forward and blew a lungful of smoke in my face. "I've always wanted to do that," she said.

"Bless you," I replied. I kissed her kneecap and stood up. "It's going to be a wonderful few weeks. Wait and see."

She shook her head. "It's going to be hell on all of us. It's already hell."

"The worst is past, Marge. I have a feeling."

She smiled a weary little smile, and then the smile faded, and she gave me a look filled with, dripping with, sympathy. "Jim, things are more complicated than you know. More complicated than you can imagine."

"Then enlighten me."

"I can't. Forget it. You've got me, and that's all you're getting."

What did she mean? What did she know? "Marge," I said, "you can't just drop a hint like that and leave it."

"Yes, I can. I can do anything I want, at least until I take my vows. Now go away and let me do the job for which I'm so highly paid."

I knew her well enough to know that I wasn't going to get anything out of her. Marge had her little secret, and she was going to keep it. "I'll never forgive you," I said.

"Then we're even," she said, smiling once again. I left her office.

It was Friday night. What a difference a week made. I had flown up from D.C. in the late morning, taped the commercial and had the regular Friday afternoon meeting, and now I was driving home from campaign headquarters—I really was. I had the night off. "A chance to get reacquainted with your wife and daughter," Harold had said in that annoying ironic way of his.

I sat in my car in the expressway traffic and thought: Something more has to be done. They'd had a week to arrest me, and I was still a free man. I couldn't understand it, but I wasn't going to complain; it meant I still had a chance to control events. But I couldn't control them unless I understood them, and so far I wasn't even close. In fact, understanding seemed to be getting further away from me all the time. What was Marge's damn secret? And Finn's war record. What was that all about? Like Everson in one of his business deals, I needed information.

Asking Everson to help was a start, but it had felt all wrong. He hadn't gotten back to me yet, and I wasn't optimistic that he would come up with anything. So much for the favors he owed me.

Something more.

Jackie Scanlon, of course. I hated to do it, but I had to see him again.

More than that? Yes, I thought, I would probably need more than that.

After a while I forced myself to stop thinking about it and turned on a talk show. I drove home listening to what my constituents had on their minds.

Domestic life. A quiet, home-cooked meal in the dining room—pot roast and apple pie. It occurred to me that Liz had gone to some trouble to prepare it, what with the tough course she was taking, and it also occurred to me to thank her. Liz blushed. "Kathleen did most of the work."

"Well now, Kathleen," I said in my imitation brogue, "you'll be making some lucky man a wonderful wife one of these fine days."

"Not likely," she said. And I wondered: Were we souring her on marriage?

"Some boy asked her for a date," Liz informed me.

"And are his intentions strictly honorable, Kathleen?" I asked.

"He's a dex," she replied.

"What's a dex?"

"You know, a nerd, a dweeb."

"One of the Hingham Dweebs? Excellent stock. Shall we invite the parents to brunch, get better acquainted?"

"She turned him down," Liz said.

"What? And jeopardized the union of our two great clans? I

won't have it. The nuptials will take place next spring, young lady, whether you like it or not."

"He picks his nose in French class," Kathleen said.

"Oh. Well then. The nuptials are off, I guess."

Kathleen rolled her eyes. She didn't seem especially interested in kidding around. Perhaps this was the wrong subject to be kidding about. I had seconds of the pot roast.

After supper Kathleen went over to a friend's house, and Liz and I were left alone to clean up. "Boys," I said. "Can't we keep her away from them for another ten years or so?"

"I'd certainly like to," Liz replied. She looked distracted; that wasn't unusual.

"So how's school?" I asked. "How's the mystic tradition?"

"Fine," she said, turning away from me to scrub a pot.

"Great." I tried to think of something else to say about the mystic tradition, but I could only come up with jokes, and I knew by now that Liz's education was also not a subject to kid about.

After the dishes were done we watched *Washington Week in Review* and *Wall Street Week* in silence together, and then Liz went to bed. She seemed to need about twice as much sleep as I did.

I went into my office and called Roger. Roger never came to our Friday afternoon meetings: too busy with his law practice, he said, although I assumed that he just wasn't interested enough. He was happy to work on fund raising, but he didn't seem especially excited about the cause; he was simply doing a favor for an old friend. Politicians expect total commitment, of course, and so this occasionally irritated me. But then, a lot about Roger irritated me nowadays.

It was since Doris died, actually. Yes, that had been tragic; she was only forty when the cancer got her. And yes, it takes awhile to recover from the ordeal. But it had been a couple of years now, and Roger still seemed stuck in the doldrums. There were no kids, and he had plenty of money. So apparently he couldn't see the point of doing anything—except maybe drink. I found this attitude extremely frustrating, because Roger was as smart as I was, and he was too young to just give up.

Well, I didn't have the time to solve his problems, but perhaps he could help me solve mine. I asked him what he'd heard about the investigation.

"Word is," he said, "that Cavanaugh wants to remove our friend Jerry Tobin from the case and take over himself."

I didn't like the sound of that at all. "Roger, do you think he hates me enough to arrest me even if he doesn't have a case?"

"Mackey wouldn't let him do that."

"Mackey can be replaced."

"Sure, but what's the point? It hurts Cavanaugh and Finn more than it does you if he can't make the charge stick. Right now he doesn't have a prayer of getting an indictment. So you don't have an alibi, half the world doesn't have an alibi. Maybe if this witness ID'd you—but obviously she couldn't, or we'd know about it."

"I'm not talking logic here, Roger, I'm talking hatred. The Monsignor can't see straight when it comes to me. What if he gets it into his head that he's got enough to pull me in even if—"

"Jim, take it easy. Pour yourself a stiff drink and go to bed. This isn't going to happen. Even if he is a bit unhinged about you, he's got to deal with Finn, and Finn isn't going to let him screw up the election."

Exactly what Everson had told me. "I certainly hope so," I said.

"Trust me. Now, how's Liz? Last Saturday, before the press conference—"

"Oh, you know Liz. She hates it, but she comes through."

"This must be especially tough on her."

"At least she has the spirit world to comfort her, Roger."

"Well, it's good to have something to comfort you. Night, Jim."

"See you."

I sat in my office and stared at the phone. Roger wasn't worried; Everson wasn't worried. I was the only one who was worried, but then, I was the only one who knew the truth. It was possible that Cavanaugh didn't have the tape of Danny's interview; it was possible that Amanda didn't leave any notes about me and Scanlon. But even so, if Cavanaugh took over, he would probe and probe and probe, and he would find something, and then he would try to destroy me. Finn might be able to stop him if the case looked shaky, but what if it didn't look shaky?

Something more has to be done.

I called up Kevin Feeney.

Roger should take lessons in total commitment from Kevin. There are two kinds of Irishmen in politics. There are the conventional hard-drinking ward heeler types, who are attracted to politics because so much of it involves simply sitting around and talking and doing favors for one another. And then there are those who are looking for a cause, who need to submerge themselves in an organization that is greater than themselves. These men don't want to talk; they want to serve. Kevin is such a man.

In the old country, in another era, Kevin might have been a priest, preaching the Vatican party line about sex and marriage to village maidens, content to have his every thought and belief provided for him from on high. Until lately in America he would have ended up a Democrat, but the times are changing, much to my father's chagrin. Kevin embraced the conservative philosophy as a young man, and then he embraced me. He was a volunteer in my first campaign, and he immediately made himself indispensable. I gave him a job in the AG's office, and he has been with me ever since. He seems to disappear into the woodwork for long stretches, rarely speaking at our opinionated staff meetings, but he's always there when I need him.

He was there that night when I called. "Kevin," I said, "I'd like to ask you for a favor."

"Anything, Senator."

"Remember at Harold's last Friday night, when you said we should be investigating Amanda Taylor's murder?"

"Of course."

"Well, I've been thinking maybe you were right. And I think you're the man for the job."

"I knew it, Senator," Kevin said, exalted by my agreement. "I bet someone like Donato—"

"Now, Kevin. Let's not get hung up on your theory about the Democrats. You may be right about that, too, but it could be a blind alley. The important thing is to get this murder solved. And of course, we want to keep the police from finding out we're doing this, if possible. And Kevin?"

"Yes?"

"We also want to keep the rest of the people in the campaign from finding out. I don't think they'd approve, and I don't want any battles with Harold and Marge just now. This is just between you and me."

"Okay, but how am I—"

"Hire people if you need to, but the fewer, the better. Pay them yourself, and I'll reimburse you. You can also tell Harold you're sick and take some time off from the campaign."

"But I never call in sick."

"It's okay, Kevin. You won't go to hell. You won't even go to purgatory."

"I know, but Harold might suspect something."

"Then I'll take care of Harold. All right, Kevin?"

"Of course, Senator. You can count on me."

"I know I can, Kevin. Thank you."

I hung up. There. Everson was on the case, and now Kevin. If Kevin came up with anything terrible about me, well, he would also come up with a way to not believe it. And if he managed to find out something about the murderer that the police didn't know—because Cavanaugh was keeping Mackey on too short a leash, for example—then we might be able to forestall the arrest that I knew Cavanaugh was itching to make.

Not likely, but it was worth the effort.

And now for the toughest phone call.

Kathleen came home as I was about to make it. My hand froze over the receiver as she stuck her head in the door. "I'm in," she said.

"Hi. Thanks for supper. Great pot roast."

"We should do it more often," she said meaningfully.

"I know," I said. "I know. Good night."

She waved to me and went upstairs. I picked up the receiver and made the call before I lost my nerve.

A woman answered.

"Jackie, please." The less I said, the better.

"Who's calling?"

"Tell him it's about the *Sea-Star*."

"Hold on."

I held. At least he was home. I didn't relish the thought of trying to track him down. He came to the phone almost immediately. "Yeah," he said. His voice was low. He knew who it was.

"We've got to talk."

"I figured. When?"

"Sunday evening. About six."

"Fine. Just park. I'll find you."

"Have the police—"

"No, nobody."

"All right," I said. "I'll see you Sunday." I hung up and breathed a sigh of relief. Fast and cryptic, but it had done the job.

And I couldn't think of anything else to do until Sunday

evening. I sat in my office for a while and then went up to bed.

Liz was asleep in pajama tops and panties. I got in next to her, as I had thousands of times before, and read for a few minutes before turning the light out. A week ago, could I have imagined that domesticity would settle in again so quickly? It wouldn't have surprised me then if I never slept in this bed again.

Well, it was at best old habits reasserting themselves, or a truce arranged by Kathleen. Liz could hardly have forgiven me so soon. It was hard to imagine that she ever would. I looked over at her and sighed, and then I put the book down, set the alarm, and went to sleep next to her.

We made love the next morning. I awoke in a fog when the alarm went off. It was dark out; the bed was warm, the house was cold; I didn't want to get out of the bed and go make a speech to a bunch of businessmen. I snuggled up to Liz; she snuggled back. And then we were kissing, and then we were making love the way we had been making love for twenty years—silently, our hands moving over each other's bodies, the two of us kissing hard, then breaking off as we gasped for air. And when it was time, I held her more tightly and plunged more deeply into her, and she gasped one final time, and it was over.

I remember the first time we made love, on the floor in my apartment, and she gasped just like that as I came. "Did I hurt you?" I whispered.

She smiled and shook her head. "It just took me by surprise."

"What did?"

"That it finally happened. That you made love to me."

"Was it worth the wait?"

And she just kept smiling.

Now, in the darkness, in our home, I stayed where I was for a while, looking at my wife. She opened her eyes and briefly returned my gaze before turning her head away. She waited until I rolled off her and then immediately put on her robe and went into the bathroom. I lay back for a moment and tried to figure it out.

It was just your basic married sex. We were both adults, and we hadn't been getting any lately.

It was something more than sex. But what? A yearning for a simpler past: Eat supper, watch TV, go to bed, wake up early and have a pleasant roll in the hay? Or a silent agreement about the future: We've managed to stay together this long; let's keep trying awhile longer?

I didn't know. We could talk about it, but I didn't have time, and Liz probably wasn't interested. She returned from the bathroom, got right back into bed, and closed her eyes. I got up and went about my business.

When I came back into the bedroom after taking my shower, her eyes were still closed, but her face was wet with tears.

I didn't feel like asking her where my cuff links were. I went searching through bureau drawers, and in one of them I saw her gun.

I hadn't thought about that gun in years. It was a Colt Python .357 Magnum, recommended to me by some cop when Liz decided she didn't feel safe with my going off to work every day as the chief law enforcement officer of the commonwealth. What if a mobster decided to get even with me? I couldn't really blame her, although I figured she had been in more danger when I was a defense attorney and occasionally lost a case that my scumbag client had expected me to win. She got her permit and practiced with the thing for a while, and then it found its way into a drawer and sat there, awaiting the crisis that had yet to arrive.

Coming across it like that made me uneasy. The past hadn't really been simpler; there had always been danger lurking somewhere. And the danger still existed, waiting for us even as we ate pot roast and joked about our daughter's would-be boyfriend. I could live with it; in a way I thrived on it. But not Liz.

Poor Liz. She had known what she was getting into when she succumbed to my blarney and married me, but she had gone ahead and done it anyway. And now she was crying in bed, and I was off again for another day of campaigning, and there seemed to be nothing she could do about it.

I found my cuff links in the next drawer. "I'll be back late," I whispered as I finished dressing.

Liz didn't reply.

I went and kissed Kathleen good-bye, and then the long day began.

CHAPTER 14

*H*arold picked me up instead of Kevin, appearing out of the mist in his red Porsche. "What's the story?" I asked.

"Kevin called and said he was sick," Harold replied. His tone of voice suggested that this behavior was totally unacceptable. He had a couple of coffees and a bag of doughnuts on the passenger-side seat. Did he know my favorite kinds, like Kevin?

I moved the food onto the floor and got in. "Is it serious?" I asked innocently.

"It better be. Let's go."

He carefully made his way through the light early-morning traffic and onto Route 3, which took us down to Cape Cod. Everyone was going about twenty miles an hour faster than we were. It seemed ridiculous to be poking along the uncrowded highway in a sports car, but that was Harold, and I had known him too long to take much notice of his peculiarities. I handed him his coffee, and we drove in silence, trying to wake up. After a while he began prepping me: where we were going, who we were meeting, what I should say. There was a full day on the Cape ahead of me, followed in the evening by the main event back in Boston: a speech before the annual meeting of the Massachusetts Police Patrolmen's Association. Harold had the speech ready for me, and I glanced through it. I couldn't get interested.

"The two of us on the road together—just like the old days,"
I said.

Harold grimaced. "Don't get maudlin," he said. "There's too
much work to be done for you to start reminiscing."

"Except for the Porsche," I went on, ignoring him. "What did
you have back then—a Dodge Dart or something?"

"I had a Fiat, and I loved it."

"You have to admit it was fun the first time."

"It was fun because it was so easy," Harold said. "I wish it
was that easy now."

"If it had stayed easy, we'd be stale. You wouldn't have a
challenge."

"There are some challenges I don't need."

Harold clearly wasn't about to wax nostalgic. So I did it without him.

Harold White came into my life after the Everson trial, when
Roger and I had more work than we could handle, and I was
getting my first taste of glory and riches. He paid for an hour of
my valuable time. When he showed up—in his blue blazer and
gray slacks and bow tie—I tried to imagine why he needed a
criminal lawyer. Securities fraud? Embezzlement? He had to be
guilty of something, I assumed. "What can I do for you, Mr.
White?" I asked.

"I am a recent graduate of the Yale Law School," he began,
"and—"

I raised a hand to interrupt him. "If you're looking for a job,
just leave your résumé with my secretary. We'll get back to you if
we're interested."

"Mr. O'Connor," he said, "I have no intention of ever practicing law."

"Well, good. That leaves the field wide open for guys like me
that have to earn a living. If you don't want a job, you must be in
trouble. So tell me about it."

"It's not me who's in trouble, sir, but this state—and this
nation. And you are the person who can save it."

Harold never had any difficulty in thinking big. "How do you
propose that I save the nation, Mr. White?"

"You can begin by running for the Republican nomination
for attorney general of the Commonwealth of Massachusetts."

"I see. And do you represent the Republican party?"

"No, sir. But I believe that if you so much as lifted an eyebrow as an indication of interest, the nomination would be yours."

I thought about it. He was probably right. The state GOP in those days wasn't exactly crawling with people who wanted to run for the lesser constitutional offices. "So what's your stake in this?" I asked Harold.

"I want to be your campaign manager."

"Why?"

"As I mentioned, Mr. O'Connor: I believe in you."

"You don't even know me. You don't even know if I'm a Republican."

"But in fact, I know a good deal about you, sir." And he then proceeded to recite virtually everything that was in the public record about me. He quoted from a speech I had made to some law students. He listed the candidates whose campaigns I had contributed to. He even knew about the time my grandmother had been mugged.

"Well, I can see that you've done your homework," I responded. "But that still doesn't tell me why you believe in me."

"Because I watched you during the Everson trial," Harold said. "And it was clear from your performance that you are destined for greatness. And I am enough of a judge of character to know that you feel the way I do about crime, about morality, and about civilization."

I laughed. "I'm not sure I know how I feel about those things myself," I said. "Why don't you give me your opinions, and I'll see if I agree?"

He nodded and settled in to give his lecture. "I believe that the only way America can hope to survive as a nation is by stopping its moral decline. Government can't make people better, it can't force people to be moral, but it can make sure that they take personal responsibility for their actions. And that means swift, sure punishment when they transgress the boundaries of civilized conduct."

"People steal because they need to eat," I said in my argumentative fashion. "People do drugs because their lives are hopeless. Liberals would say you should be solving those problems instead of building more prisons."

Harold waved away the liberals. "They are asking too much of government, and that's why their programs always fail. Government can't make people rich, and it can't make them happy. It can't make whites love blacks or Arabs love Jews. And it probably can't make the punks sitting across from you on the subway train leave you alone. But it might make the punks think twice about hassling you if they know they'll go to prison for it."

"Sounds like you're proposing a police state. We already send a greater percentage of people to prison than almost anyplace else."

"We're a violent nation," Harold replied. "That helped make us great, but it also threatens to destroy us. People fear those punks on the subway more than they fear some hypothetical foreign invader we spend billions protecting ourselves against. Why not spend as much protecting ourselves against the punks as we do on the military?"

I shrugged. "Maybe because it's easier to protect ourselves against foreigners than it is to protect ourselves from each other. But anyway, I'm a criminal lawyer. A lot of people would say that guys like me contribute to this problem."

"But you don't want to be a criminal lawyer, Mr. O'Connor," Harold replied. "You want to make a difference. And the best way of doing that is in government."

"How do you know I don't want to be a criminal lawyer? If you followed the Everson trial, you could at least see I'm pretty good at it."

Harold simply shook his head. "You're just going to have to learn to trust me," he said.

It was an amazing performance. I couldn't decide whether to laugh at him or be in awe of him. I didn't agree to run at the end of his hour, but I didn't charge him for the hour either. The cynical lawyer in me believed he was trying to snow me with his talk about saving the nation. He was really trying to land a job as a campaign manager, I figured, and to do that, he was trying to manufacture his own candidate. A clever idea, but not easy to pull off. Why would I give up the chance to make my fortune as a lawyer in order to go into politics?

Except that he was right about me, damn it. Right, at least, about me and criminal law. I didn't want to help set more people like Paul Everson free. Was that a lucky guess on Harold's part? Cunning flattery? Or did he really understand me? I have always been inclined to believe that Harold White doesn't understand the first thing about me—and, furthermore, doesn't care. I am the clay he thinks he is sculpting; I am the empty vessel into which he has chosen to pour his own dreams and ambitions. If the clay thinks, if the vessel has dreams of its own, that is a trifling annoyance, an imperfection in the raw material.

But I may be wrong. A lot of people have underestimated Harold over the years, thinking he is too cerebral, or simply too weird, to survive in politics. He has ignored them and done things his way, and no one—least of all me—can argue with the results.

He certainly knew what to do after our first meeting. He went to the Republican leadership and told them he had interested me in running, but I needed convincing. The head of the State Committee met with me; Harold leaked news of the meeting to a friendly reporter, and the rumors started flying. Soon every Republican in the state (there weren't that many, actually) was importuning me to run.

But if I ran—and I began to find the idea more and more appealing—why make Harold my campaign manager? I was a neophyte, and I would need a pro to guide me; Harold was just a kid. That's what I told him the next time we met. And that's when he produced his Master Plan.

He had already written my position papers and my speeches. He had already mapped out the advertising campaign. He knew how much money we would have to raise and how we could raise it. He knew whose endorsements we needed and how we could get them. For two hours he led me through every step of the process by which he would make me the next attorney general.

Perhaps a pro wouldn't have been impressed, but I was. I'm always impressed by good preparation. When I finally told the Republicans I was a candidate, Harold was part of the package.

They handed me the nomination, and then there was just the little matter of defeating the Democratic candidate. His name was Francis X. Cavanaugh.

Needless to say, handling the Everson prosecution turned out to be a major mistake for the Monsignor—especially when I entered the race. Everyone in the state knew his name now, but they knew him as the loser of the big case he was supposed to win. If the Democrats could have come up with another candidate for attorney general, I'm sure they would have. But Cavanaugh had laid his groundwork too well; he had the commitments from the delegates at the nominating convention, and the party bigwigs couldn't talk him into releasing them. They tried to get someone to run against him in the primary, but my reputation was already scaring potential candidates away. So they were stuck with Cavanaugh. He ran a straightforward, old-fashioned Democratic campaign: Get the union endorsements; get the big-city machines behind you; aim for the ethnic vote, the working-class vote, the intellectual vote. It worked when he ran for DA, and it might have worked this time. But he didn't have the money, he didn't have the charisma, and he didn't have Harold. He tried to make the case that he was the experienced prosecutor and I was just a flashy kid trying to capitalize on one fluke victory. No one listened. I had defeated him in the courtroom; I now proceeded to trounce him in the voting booth.

It's easy enough to say that he should have dropped out of the race; he probably could have bided his time, let people forget about the Everson case, and won the job four years later, when I ran for the Senate. But a politician never knows when his opportunities will show up. If I hadn't been around, he might have been the one in the Senate now.

I wonder if a day goes by when he doesn't think about that.

At any rate Harold and I had started on the road to saving the nation. And here we were, ten years later, and we had traveled quite a distance. If we could only get past a roadblock named Bobby Finn, who knew how far we could go?

The first event on the Cape was a disaster. How many businessmen wanted to attend a breakfast meeting early on a Saturday morning? No reporters bothered to come, and that was even worse. All the businessmen were going to vote for me anyway; at least the reporters might have spread the message to some people who were undecided. I gave a quick speech, drank some watery orange juice, shook a few hands, and got out of there.

"Sorry," Harold murmured. "Have to have a word with the scheduling people."

I didn't want to think about the tongue-lashing the scheduling people were in for. "That's the glamorous life of a politician," I replied. "What's next?"

Next was a nursing home, where we had arranged an informal meeting with the senior citizens. A couple of radio stations covered it, and we had our own video crew there, in case we wanted to use footage for a spot. I talked about my grandmother, who raised me after my mother died, and my father, struggling to stay independent in his retirement, and it all went over very well. People

don't necessarily demand that you agree with them; they do like
it, though, when you can show that you understand and sympathize with their problems.

No one brought up Amanda's murder, and I took that to be
a good sign. If the issue were still alive in people's minds, then
the media would not let me get my message out. They'd cover my
response to the questions about it and ignore everything else I
said or did.

From there I went to talk to the members of a local elderly
affairs council. They were a tougher audience. Why was I opposed
to this bill? Why did I vote for that one? What solutions could I
propose for every problem that old people faced nowadays? I
regurgitated my position papers for them, but I knew I wouldn't
be able to charm them. Finn would promise them heaven on earth,
and he would get their endorsement.

Next stop was lunch with the editorial board of a leading
Cape Cod newspaper; its endorsement I was counting on. The
board members brought up the murder, but mainly as a potential
problem for the campaign. Did I think it was going to cause me
difficulties?

No, I honestly didn't.

Would the Democrats try to keep it alive as an issue?

You'd have to ask the Democrats about that. I certainly
wouldn't want to see a murder investigation become politicized.

After that, a couple of media events with local politicians. A
fund raiser late in the afternoon on a CEO's estate overlooking
the ocean. And then the long drive back to Boston for the speech.

It was a typical day on the campaign trail. The pace can be
killing, but you can't let up, you can't give in to your exhaustion,
because your opponent is working just as hard as you are, and
any of it can make the difference: the elderly vote; the Cape Cod
vote; the sound bites chosen by some radio station; the endorsement of some newpaper. Carl Hutchins was undoubtedly back in
his home state doing exactly what I was doing. I wondered where
he would find the energy or the interest. He's in trouble, I thought.
People sense it when you're tired, when you're going throught the
motions. At some level you can't *just* be acting; you have to believe
in your role. And Hutchins no longer did.

"How was I?" I asked Harold.

"Okay." Harold didn't like to praise me; it might make me
complacent. "You should be studying your speech."

"Is Finn speaking tonight?"

"He's probably delivering his oration at this very moment."

"Do we have someone there to find out what he said?"

"Of course."

Stupid question. And here was something else he would think was stupid: "Harold, I want you to put someone on Finn's war record."

He glanced at me. "What in the world for?"

I wasn't going to tell him about Everson, but I figured I didn't have to. The idea made sense on its own. "I'm vulnerable over Amanda's murder because I'm so big on morality and crime issues," I said. "Well, we can apply the same reasoning to Finn and his war record. He's supposed to be such a big hero, and he's so promilitary—well, if there's something bad in his record, that would really hurt him."

"But why would there be something bad in his record?" Harold asked. "Finn's been around for years. People have looked at him pretty closely."

"We're supposed to do things better than other people. Maybe we can find something no one else has been able to."

"Sounds like a waste of time."

"Humor me."

He shrugged and studied the road. He would ignore my suggestion if he thought it was too stupid; he had done that before. But I had a feeling he'd go along. It didn't hurt to look, and Harold, like me, approved of being thorough. I would have agreed that it was a waste of time, except that Paul Everson didn't drop hints like that just for fun. And if there was something out there, we had to know about it.

We got to the Hynes Convention Center in the Back Bay a few minutes before I was scheduled to speak, and Harold immediately found our campaign staffer, who briefed us on what had been going on. Good speech from Finn, warm reception from the audience. No mention of the murder case. Friendly faces surrounded me as I made my way toward the hall where I was going to speak—burly cops who believed in me, who in their own way loved me.

I was on the up escalator when I saw Bobby Finn and his wife getting on the down escalator. "This is symbolic, Governor," I said as we passed.

Finn laughed his hearty laugh. "You read too many books, Senator," he called out.

He waited at the bottom of the escalator, looking up. I looked back at him, smiled, and took the escalator back down.

Mr. and Mrs. Robert Finn. The odd couple, columnists called them: Bobby, the stout Irish charmer; Elsa, the slim Cambridge heiress. But there is one thing at least that they have in common, and that is Bobby's political career. Elsa is not the kind of heiress who donates her time and money to chic charities that save cute animals or teach the poor how to keep from procreating. She is nothing if not practical, and in Bobby she found what Harold had found in me: the means to the kind of power and influence and prestige that money can only partially buy.

I shook her hand first. "Mrs. Finn," I said. "Good to see you. You look wonderful, as usual." And she did; she had the the regal presence that comes from old money; a presence that improves with age.

"Why, thank you, Senator. And how is your wife?"

"Terrific, thanks." Unlike Elsa, Liz wouldn't dream of coming to an event like this. I wondered if Bobby ever envied me. If I had a wife who didn't care enough, he had one who probably cared too much. A lot of people were surprised when he announced that he was going to run against me. He enjoyed being governor so much; why would he want to give it up? It didn't surprise me, though. Elsa wanted to go to Washington as much as Liz wanted to stay home in Hingham.

I turned to Bobby next. "Governor, we've got to stop meeting like this," I said. "There'll be rumors in the *Herald*."

He laughed. "I wowed them in there, Jim. It'll be a tough act to follow."

Finn may not be especially handsome or well bred or articulate, but you only had to spend a minute in his presence to know why he would have been a successful politician even without his wife's money. There is a vitality about him that ordinary politicians, like Cavanaugh, lack. It surrounds him even when he is silent. It is an aura; it is a magnet. It draws people to him. He is overweight, but he is graceful and energetic; he seems to be in motion even when he is sitting down. He is going bald, but he still has a military crew cut—a reminder of his days as a war hero. He is only a few years older than I am, but women think of him as the father they wish they had, while I am the lover they are a little afraid of.

"We had spies listening to your speech," I said to him. "They said your plan to let prison inmates hold down part-time jobs at convenience stores and all-night gas stations didn't go over too well."

Finn laughed as if I had just told the killer joke. "I bet they'll like it better than your proposal to institute the death penalty for double parking," he replied.

I smiled. "People have to be taught a lesson," I said.

"Maybe we'll have a chance to discuss our proposals in the big debate."

"Ah, yes, the debate. I'm looking forward to that—unless the Monsignor throws me in jail first."

"By the time I'm through with you," Finn said with a smile, "you'll wish you'd been arrested before the campaign even started."

"That sounds like a challenge, Bobby," I responded.

"Well, this ain't exactly a courtship, Jim."

"You're right about that. So you'll have to excuse me while I go blow your socks off, Governor."

"You're welcome to try, Senator."

We shook hands, I said good-bye to Elsa, and I headed up the escalator once again.

"You shouldn't talk to the opposition," Harold said, hardly for the first time. He didn't want me personalizing the race. My feelings toward Bobby Finn—good or bad—might interfere with the execution of our strategy. To the campaign Bobby Finn should exist not as a person but only as a bundle of perceptions in voters' minds, perceptions that it was our job to make as unfavorable as possible.

"Sorry," I said. "Were we obnoxious back there?"

"You were like a couple of teenage boys insulting each other in front of a girl. I could almost smell the testosterone."

"Well, your Porsche can beat his limo anytime. Let's challenge him to a race."

"Sure. Right after you give your speech in front of every cop in the state."

We talked to a few officials to make sure everything was in order. And then we hung around, waiting for the moment to arrive. Harold didn't have to tell me that I had to make a good speech. We needed the endorsement of every law enforcement organization we could find. None of them were likely to endorse Finn over me, but they might vote to stay neutral if he could put enough pressure on them or if I managed to screw up. So I couldn't screw up.

Someone signaled, and I made my entrance. The crowd jumped to their feet with a roar of recognition and approval. These were my people.

I stood at the lectern and let them roar for a while, and then gestured for silence. It was only as I opened my mouth that I decided to forget about the prepared speech and wing it. This is risky, and it sends Harold into cardiac arrest, but it's often a good strategy; people are more likely to pay attention when you speak directly to them. They enjoy the sense of drama when you throw aside the sheets of paper you brought with you and put your faith in your native eloquence. And I've done it often enough that I don't have to worry about running out of things to say.

I began with some standard generalities about the importance of law enforcement and the problems police officers face. I talked about what I've tried to do to help them in the past and what I proposed to do in the future. Straightforward stuff, but the crowd was with me. Abruptly I decided to talk about the murder.

"Last week, as I'm sure you all know, I discovered a murder victim, a young woman brutally stabbed to death in her own apartment. Now, I've been involved with the legal system for my entire adult life, but never so personally as this. And I felt the way everyone must feel when confronted with such a violent crime: There was a sense of outrage and also a sense of helplessness. I could only think of one thing to do, and that was to call nine-one-one. The police responded immediately and began doing what they're trained to do. And my sense of helplessness turned to gratitude. Gratitude for their professionalism. Gratitude for the concern they showed the victim. Gratitude, above all, because they were there, to do an unpleasant job that nevertheless civilized society demands be done.

"I have no grand insight to give you from my experience. You've been out there; you know what it's like. I have no idea when or if this young woman's murder will be solved, but I know that the people assigned to this case will work as hard as they possibly can to solve it. They may make mistakes; everyone does. But I just wanted to publicly express the gratitude I felt—and still feel—for the police I met that night and for all of you here in this room. My job is to make your job easier, and I intend to keep trying. Thank you very much."

Once again the crowd rose to their feet, cheering. They loved me; I loved them; we all loved each other. The cheering didn't stop. I waved and grinned and shook hands. The endorsement, I knew, would be laid at my feet, an offering from my adoring subjects.

"Not a bad idea," Harold murmured on the way home. As always, he was lavish with his praise.

"I didn't plan it," I said. "I just did it."

"As long as it works."

I was exhausted. Another month of eighteen-hour days. Of charges and countercharges. Of spots and press conferences and interviews and debates and debates about debates. Of worrying about Jackie Scanlon and Francis X. Cavanaugh and Marge Terry's secret. Of thinking about Amanda.

No, the thinking about Amanda would last much longer than a month.

"Do you still believe I murdered Amanda Taylor?" I asked Harold.

He glanced over at me. "I never said I believed you murdered her," he replied. "I simply asked you a question that night."

"You knew I was having an affair with her."

"It was pretty obvious."

"Did she interview you?"

"Oh, she was too smart to try and do that," Harold said. "Actually, when a couple of people in the campaign told me she'd been after them for interviews, I went to her and tried to get her to stop."

"When was this?"

"A few weeks ago."

"Why did you want her to stop?"

"Because I didn't trust her. Because I didn't trust *you*. You were obviously infatuated with her. You were sitting around all summer mooning about her. And she was obviously hoping to use your infatuation to get some sort of scoop. So I told her it wouldn't work, that I'd make sure she didn't get anything worth writing about."

"What did she say to that?"

"She told me I didn't have to worry, she wasn't going to write about you. She said she'd fallen in love with you, and she was just trying to understand the man she loved. So that's why she was talking to people, pretending to interview them. Would you have believed that if you were me?"

Of course not. Still, it was the explanation I wanted to hear. "What did you say to her when she told you that?" I asked.

"Nothing, really. Why bother, if that was the best story she could come up with?"

"So when you heard Amanda was murdered, you figured: The schmuck found out she didn't love him, was just using him, and he killed her in a jealous rage."

This time he didn't answer.

"Your problem, Harold, is that you don't understand human passion," I said. "And you're frightened of what you don't understand."

"You're absolutely right," he replied. "I don't understand why someone would risk throwing away a career like yours over a dreary little affair with some blonde fifteen years younger than he is. And I haven't devoted ten years of my life to your career only to have you turn into another Gary Hart."

Ten years, I thought. And we weren't even friends, were perfectly willing, in fact, to suspect each other of murder.

If I were Cavanaugh, I could have worked up a perfectly respectable case against Harold, I figured. Motive? Get rid of the tramp who was threatening his candidate's—and therefore his own—career. Opportunity? He had been at the Friday afternoon staff meeting with the rest of us. We all had time to get to the Back Bay and kill her. Harold had even been the one who made sure the meeting ended on time; he said he had an appointment in the Back Bay he had to get to. Perhaps he was the mysterious stranger seen entering Amanda's building. He then confronts her one final time, demanding that she get out of my life, not knowing that she has already left my life. She gets angry at him. Perhaps she blames him for my attitude toward her. I had certainly talked enough to her about Harold and the way he had molded me into a politician. They quarrel, and then . . .

But the theory seemed less and less persuasive as I considered it. If Harold were going to commit a murder, he would have done a better job. He wouldn't have announced his intentions of going to the Back Bay. He wouldn't have left a weird message on her computer. And he would have made absolutely sure I had an alibi. Why not wait until I was in Washington, for example?

It could have been a crime of passion, I supposed, but it was hard to imagine Harold in the grip of that kind of passion.

"Harold, who was your appointment with after the staff meeting last Friday?"

He glanced over at me. "I figured you'd bring that up sooner or later."

"Idle curiosity," I said.

"I suppose I'd better tell you," he replied. "It may come up. I went to see Mort Blumenthal."

I took a moment to think that one over. Mort Blumenthal is the publisher of *Hub*. A big contributor to conservative causes, although his conservatism didn't seem to affect the conventional liberal bias of his magazines. "What did you and Mort have to talk about?"

"Amanda Taylor. What else?"

This didn't sound good at all. "Go on," I said.

"From what I could figure out, it looked to me as if she wasn't necessarily trying to destroy you," Harold said. "She was just stuck where she was at *Hub* and hoping to use her relationship with you to get her big break. I thought I'd see if I could fix it so she got her break without writing something nasty about you. So I talked it over with Mort—without going into details—and he said he could probably give her an assistant editorship at one of his other magazines, you know, with the more or less implicit proviso that she lay off Jim O'Connor."

"Blumenthal would do something like that?" I asked. "I thought he was pretty hands-off with his magazines."

"You'd be surprised how fond Mort is of you," Harold said. "And he knows what it's like to be caught with his pants down. He thought the situation was pretty funny actually."

It wasn't funny now. The problem was obvious. I had made a big deal to the press about the book Amanda was writing and how the campaign was cooperating with her. If it got out that she was really writing a kiss-and-tell exposé, which my campaign manager was trying to quash, then I was going to look very bad, no matter what else the police came up with. "Have you talked to Mort since?" I asked.

Harold nodded. "The next day. He's not happy. He says he won't go to the police on his own, but he won't guarantee that he'll lie if they find out about the meeting and want to talk to him."

"Will they find out about the meeting?"

"I don't know. We didn't make any special effort to hide it. But I can't think of any reason why they'd necessarily be interested."

"Have they talked to you?"

"Yeah. It seemed pretty routine. Just checking out that what you said was true about the book."

"And you lied?"

"Of course."

I sighed.

"Sorry, Jim."

He wasn't apologizing for lying, that was for sure. It bothered him about going to Blumenthal. Had he made a mistake? Not given his understanding of the situation. But you never know everything in politics, so you have to be judged by your results. And these results were not good. "It's all right," I said. "I'll talk to him, try and keep him happy."

"That might be a good idea," Harold admitted.

I closed my eyes and leaned back in the seat. One more thing to worry about. I wished Harold would drive faster; I was exhausted. I wondered if Kevin had made any progress. "Why did you drive me today, Harold?" I asked. "There's a dozen people you could have gotten to take Kevin's place. Were you trying to recapture the spirit of the old days?"

"Don't be absurd." Harold was silent for a while before he spoke again. "I wanted to make sure you were okay, that's all," he murmured.

"And what's your expert opinion? Have I cracked? Can I still get the job done?"

"You could be worse."

"Bless you for those kind words."

We didn't speak again until Harold pulled into my driveway, and the long day was over. He turned to me and recited Sunday's schedule while I nodded numbly. When he was finished, I got out and watched him disappear into the night. Then I trudged inside and collapsed into a chair in my office, happy to be alone at last. I listened to the messages on my machine. Nothing from Everson. Nothing from Kevin.

Tomorrow, I thought, Jackie Scanlon.

I was already afraid.

CHAPTER 15

Kevin made a remarkable recovery from his illness and was back on the job the next day. "I hired a private detective," he said as we drove to our first event. "His name is Sharpe—honest to God. I checked up on him, and the word is that he's very discreet. You've gotta be if you're in that line of work, I guess."

"What'll he do for us?"

"Standard stuff. Interview neighbors, relatives, people who knew her. Try to piece together her life, see if she had any secrets. See if he can come up with anything the police miss."

Swell, I thought. "It'll be hard for him to do that without the police finding out," I said.

"True, but they won't find out he's working for you, because Sharpe doesn't know it himself. He thinks I'm a free-lance journalist writing a book about the murder, and I've hired him to help out with the legwork."

"Kevin, what are you doing driving me around for a living? You oughta be, I don't know, president of a multinational corporation or something."

Kevin flushed with pride. "I like my job just fine, Senator."

*　　*　　*

177

The Sunday events went well enough, considering that my mind was far away. As usual I dropped Kevin off in the early evening, and I was alone.

I drove around the corner, stopped the car, and called my father. "It's me," I said. "Looks like I won't be able to make it tonight."

"No problem," he replied immediately. "I'll just read some more about you rotten lawyers."

He was disappointed, I knew. My visit had to be the highlight of his week. But he wasn't going to let on that he was disappointed; that would be a show of emotion and therefore unacceptable. "The campaign, you know," I felt obliged to explain. "I'm flat out."

"I understand. That Finn guy is starting to say some nasty things about you."

"Not as nasty as the things we're going to be saying about him. At least, I hope not. Did Danny get his car?"

"Oh, sure. Melissa, actually. She came over on Monday. He's been sick, I guess. I hope he doesn't lose his job."

"Don't worry about him, Dad. It doesn't help."

"You're right, you're right. I just wish he'd take better care of himself, that's all. He's got a family to think about. Anyway, a policeman came to talk to me the other day."

"Was he nice to you?"

"Oh, he was fine. His name was Mackey. He seems to like you."

"And you said nice things about me, right?"

"As nice as I said to Amanda Taylor."

"I appreciate it. Listen, Dad. Enjoy your Dickens. Have a bourbon for me. And forget about Danny."

"Okay. See you next week?"

"Count on it."

"All right, then."

I love you, Dad.

I love you too, son.

Oh, well. I suppressed the usual twinge of jealousy that he was more worried about Danny than he was about me. It was stupid; he always had reason to be more worried about Danny.

Until now. So the police had talked to my father and my campaign manager—but not to Danny. Clearly they were focusing on me, which I had expected, but they hadn't found my most vulnerable spot. Why not?

I couldn't figure it out. I started the car and headed for South Boston.

South Boston is its own little universe. I've lived in and around Boston all my life, I'm so Irish I bleed shamrocks, yet I still feel like an outsider whenever I go into the place. If you weren't born there, in one of the three-deckers or the grim brick projects or the grand old Victorian houses, you are always an outsider.

They love me in Southie just the same. I may be a Republican, but I speak their language.

Tonight, though, I wished I could be invisible. I had no desire to mingle with the natives. Above all, I had no desire to be seen with Jackie Scanlon.

When I reached my destination, I parked the car next to a fire hydrant, the only empty space on the street. And then I waited in the growing darkness. He had video cameras, I knew, trained on the street, to give him advance notice of unwelcome visitors. I hoped he wouldn't be long.

It was a street crowded with three-deckers, most painted an identical chocolate brown with yellow trim. On the second-floor porch of one, an old man in a sleeveless undershirt was smoking a cigarette, the orange glow of its tip moving metronomically to his mouth and away again. A fat woman walked past, pushing a stroller in which a red-headed toddler lolled. She had the ageless look of the obese; I couldn't tell if she was the mother or the grandmother. A man wearing a bowling jacket and a Red Sox cap came out of the first floor of a house across the street and headed toward me. I opened the passenger-side door. He got in.

"Hiya, Jim."

"Hello, Jackie."

"Just start driving, Jim. Gotta make sure we're not bein' followed. I'll tell you when to turn."

He was gray-haired, with bushy sideburns and enormous eyebrows that met in the middle. He had a square face and a stocky build that was starting to go to fat. His hands were thick and callused. He smelled of cheap after-shave. He looked like the foreman of a construction crew or maybe an off-duty cop.

He was anything but.

I started driving.

*   *   *

My conscience is clear.

Every time I think about Jackie Scanlon, my next thought is: *My conscience is clear.* That says something altogether different about the state of my conscience, doesn't it?

And yet, damn it, would my conscience be any better off if I had acted differently?

All right. I'll tell it to this computer that just sits in front of me like a shrink—silent, except for the humming of its fans. It's so quiet in this room that often the humming is the only noise I hear. If I explain what happened clearly enough to the computer, then I'll understand.

Right?

I was a better attorney general than I was a defense lawyer. Many people have called me the best attorney general in a generation. For the first time my heart was really in my work. I hired a bunch of bright, energetic young lawyers and let them do their jobs. What I said in my ads was not exaggerated. We protected the consumer against powerful business interests. We uncovered corruption at all levels of state government and put some influential politicians behind bars, including Tom Donato, the president of the state senate and Kevin's bête noire. We never backed down. I was a shoo-in for reelection, and people were urging me to aim higher. The incumbent senator was planning to retire. Who would make a better candidate to succeed him?

Meanwhile, my brother was struggling to survive.

It was more than an economic struggle. Oh, sure, he had to keep Danny Boy's afloat; he had to find a way to pay the mortgage and the orthodontist and the liquor wholesalers and the Sears charge. But he also had to find a way to keep his self-respect as the years went by and his life went nowhere.

It was in those years that the envy started to surface. For a long time my road was just too different from his for him to take much notice of me. But when my name started showing up in the paper all the time, when my face became a fixture on the local news, when people started asking Danny if he was Jim O'Connor's brother, it began to hurt. Then he began to refer to me as the General; then he began making cracks about my politics and my ambition. Did the General send anyone to the electric chair today? Has the General written his inaugural address yet?

And it was then that he turned into a barroom Irish patriot. A lot of Irish immigrants, legal and otherwise, came into Danny Boy's, and they brought with them their tales of hardship and injustice, their grudges ancient and new, their boozy memories of the auld sod. Like Kevin, Danny needed a cause to believe in. These men gave it to him; they gave him an identity.

We're Irish, but our father was not the kind to make a big deal of it. We didn't have "Honk If You're Irish" bumper stickers or "May the road rise up to meet you" wall plaques or "Erin Go Bragh" beer mugs. We never went to the parade in Southie on St. Patrick's Day. "I've got better things to do than stand around in the cold and have some drunken mick puke on my shoes," my father would say. He never visited Ireland and seemed uninterested in the problems of the Six Counties. He raised us to think of ourselves as Americans.

But Gramma, our mother's mother, was different. She was born in the old country and never really adjusted to America. She would talk endlessly about the morning mists on the green mountains, the flocks of sheep crossing the narrow roads, the thatched cottage where she grew up, the simple life close to both God and the earth. My father would interpose cynical remarks now and then, but she ignored him. He wouldn't understand, she thought, but his children would.

I never did. I thought my father always made perfect sense. If Ireland is such a great place, then why can't anyone stand to live there? If the Irish would put as much energy into economic development as they do into complaining and looking for other people to blame, then they'd have a lot less to complain about.

Well, that's not very charitable—and certainly not something I'd ever say in public. If anyone else said such a thing, I'd feel obliged to boil over with righteous indignation. But that's the way I feel; Republicans aren't romantics.

Danny is a romantic, however. And the Irishmen he listened to in his bar started him dreaming of intrigue, of heroic deeds, of liberation and redemption.

At first he didn't do much more than pass the hat for NORAID on St. Patrick's Day; a few dollars for the Provisional wing of the Irish Republican Army from their brethren, safe and sound in the new country. He also helped the occasional illegal when one of them came his way—a Provo gunman who found things too hot in Northern Ireland, perhaps, and needed a place to stay in Boston for a while before disappearing once again. At any rate he made a few contacts in the IRA, and he found himself on the fringes of a war that had been going on for hundreds of years and will probably continue for that much longer.

And then Tom Glenn came back into his life.

He had been a buddy of Danny's in the Navy. I never met the man, so I have no idea what he looks like. But I have a clear image of his personality. He is a lot like Danny, it seems to me: fast-talking, friendly, sincere, not entirely scrupulous, but you are willing to forgive him because he is so sincere about his unscrupulousness.

A lot like Danny, only a lot smarter.

Glenn appeared in Danny Boy's one night, and it was a wonderful reunion. The whiskey flowed, and so did the memories of their Navy high jinks. Remember the time we got away with this? And what about the time we pulled that? Ah, those were the days.

Finally Glenn told Danny why he had come.

He had weapons. Oh, he didn't exactly *have* them, but he knew a guy in the Army who had access to them, and this guy needed money bad. The Army was all fucked up, and stealing the weapons was as easy as changing a few numbers in a computer and backing up a truck to a loading dock. But this guy had some scruples; he didn't want to sell the guns to drug dealers or terrorists or the mob. So the guy started thinking: Maybe the IRA would be interested. Now there was a good cause that could use some weapons. But how could he get in touch with the IRA? The guy talked to Glenn, and Glenn thought of Danny.

Was Danny interested in helping? Glenn wanted to know. There'd be something in it for him if the deal went through.

Danny was more than interested. This was the chance of a lifetime. He could help the cause he believed in so fervently and help himself as well. The General wasn't the only one in the family who could be a success.

Danny introduced Glenn to his IRA contacts. They were naturally suspicious. They had been burned too often by government agents to trust this glib stranger, even though Danny vouched for him.

They were suspicious but tempted; weapons were hard to come by. They finally agreed to a trial run. They would buy a small shipment of arms from Glenn. If everything seemed okay, they would come back to him for more. And Danny was to serve

on the crew that would ship the weapons across the Atlantic to
Ireland. Danny was overjoyed at this. He was an old sailor; his
experience would be invaluable to the cause. I don't think it occurred to him that the Provos might have wanted him around as
a kind of hostage, in case he was thinking of cheating them.

At any rate, they bought a ship called the *Sea-Star* and out-
fitted it as if it were going to be doing some swordfishing off the
Grand Banks. They made a down payment to Glenn, with the rest
to be paid on delivery. And they waited nervously for Glenn to
deliver.

He did: a couple of vanfuls of weapons, mostly M16's with
their serial numbers carefully filed off, along with a few thousand
rounds of ammunition. They paid Glenn the rest of his money,
loaded the weapons onto the *Sea-Star,* and several of them took
off early in the morning from a pier in South Boston.

Danny had told Melissa he was going on a fishing trip with
some people who might be interested in investing in his bar. She
didn't believe him, but she couldn't stop him, and wasn't sure she
wanted to. He seemed happy for once, full of energy and purpose.
She was willing to live with lies if the lies would somehow help
make their lives better.

The *Sea-Star* made the crossing without incident and met up
with an IRA vessel about a hundred miles off the west coast of
Ireland. Danny and the rest of the crew transferred the weapons
on the open sea, and the other ship disappeared into the fog with
its deadly cargo. Success.

The *Sea-Star* returned to Boston safe and sound. The Boston
Provos were ecstatic. Nothing had gone wrong in Ireland, they
informed the crew; the weapons had made it. This was the first
successful shipment of arms from North America to the IRA. Get
hold of Tom Glenn, they told Danny. Let's do it again.

Danny was happy to oblige. Negotiations were more complicated this time. The Provos wanted as many weapons as they could
get their hands on. That increased the risk, Glenn pointed out.
It would cost a lot more, and he would need a higher percentage
up front. The Provos finally agreed to his demands. He had come
through for them once, after all. They would trust him to come
through again.

They made a down payment of four hundred thousand dollars. Not a huge amount in some criminal circles, but for the IRA
it represented a lot of hats passed on St. Patrick's Day, a lot of

rural banks robbed back in Ireland, a lot of secret contributions from wealthy Irish-Americans seeking to soothe consciences made guilty by success. But the Provos figured it was worth it. If they could buy that many weapons, for the first time they would have an arsenal capable of inflicting real damage on the British forces occupying their land.

They rounded up the cash and gave the down payment to Danny, who delivered it to Glenn. "I'll get back to you as soon as I can," Danny's old friend said as he walked out of the back room of the bar lugging the suitcase full of cash.

He got into his car and drove away, and they never saw him again.

This seems utterly predictable in hindsight, of course. One more fiasco for the IRA, which makes a habit of shooting itself in the foot. One more disappointment for Danny to add to his list. Oh, but this time it was supposed to be different! Danny's cut would have come out of the final payment, and it would have been enough to pay off the note on his bar. At last things would start to improve for him.

Instead things got considerably worse. As the days passed with no word from Glenn, the Provos began to freak out. This was a catastrophe, and it was Danny's fault—or, worse, it was Danny's idea. After all, Glenn was Danny's friend. What if they had agreed to split the money somewhere down the road, after the furor subsided? The Provos wanted their four hundred thousand dollars back. They wanted it from Danny. He tried to explain to them. He was as devastated by this as they were. He didn't have any money: Look at how he lived; look at his bank statements; look at the nasty letters from his creditors. The Provos weren't interested. This is war, they said. You know what the penalty for treason is. They beat him up—just a little, just enough to show him what his real punishment would be like. They gave him a week to come up with either the weapons or the money.

So what could Danny do? Ask me for the money? He'd rather have died. Besides, I didn't have it. I was a public servant now; no more six-figure incomes for me. Run away? He wouldn't know where to go. He wouldn't know what to tell his family. Find Glenn? But Glenn could be anywhere. Ask the police for protection? Sure, and explain that he was an international arms smuggler; they'd be very interested in that. Suicide? No, I don't think Danny considered suicide. He's not the type.

Danny had no options, it seemed.

Ah, but as Danny pondered his plight and cursed his fate, an angel of mercy was preparing to descend. The angel's name was Jackie Scanlon.

Back then Jackie was the fourth- or fifth-biggest mobster in New England, with most of the non-Mafia crime in South Boston under his control. If you expected to do any drug selling or book-making or prostitution in Southie, you had to be prepared to deal with Jackie's organization. Jackie had his contacts among the Provos, and it stood to reason that before long he would hear about how they had been double-crossed. And so he paid Danny a visit. "I heard you got a problem," he said. "I'm here to offer a solution."

The solution was simple. Jackie would pay the Provos their money. In return all he wanted from Danny was a signed statement admitting his gun-smuggling activities on behalf of the IRA.

Danny is far from stupid. He understood what Jackie was up to. But he also knew that he had no choice. His life was at stake. He agreed. They worked on the statement then and there. Jackie handed the money over to the Provos a couple of days later, and Danny signed the statement. He was safe.

He then came to see me and explained what had happened. He was drunk; he was frightened; he was contrite. He begged my forgiveness. He said he'd understand if I didn't help him out. He didn't mind going to prison; he probably deserved to go to prison. But Melissa. The kids. Dad. It would be so hard on everyone. If I could see my way clear . . .

I threw him out of the house. He was lucky I didn't kill him.

The next day I got a call from Scanlon. It was brief and polite. Would I like to meet him on a matter of some urgency? We agreed on a place and time. And that was how Jackie Scanlon came into my life.

Neither of us wanted to be seen with the other, and Scanlon was terrified of being bugged—with good reason. So we set up a meeting in the parking lot of the South Shore Plaza in Braintree early on a Sunday morning. He pulled up next to me in the deserted lot and motioned for me to get into his car. It was a Ford Crown Victoria, the kind all the police departments use for their cruisers. I got in. He offered his hand; I ignored it.

His appearance did not impress. But I knew scum like him. A lot of street smarts can be hidden behind a construction worker's face.

"I wonder if you'd mind if I searched you, sir," he said.

"I'm clean," I replied. I didn't like the way he called me *sir*.

"You can't be too careful in my business," Scanlon said. He waited. I shrugged and raised my arms. He patted me down, feeling for a transmitter. "Thank you, sir," he said when he was satisfied. I wondered if I should search him, but I figured the transmitter could be anywhere in the car if he wanted to record the conversation. So I didn't bother. Scanlon leaned back in his seat. "I guess you know what this is all about."

"Not really. The feds are the people you have to be concerned with."

"Sure, but they gotta let you know about things. They gotta have everyone cooperating, make sure you're not stepping on each other's toes. I hear they're planning a big offensive against me. Well, I'd like to find out something about it, naturally. In case it hurts my business."

"Naturally. You think you can blackmail me with a piece of paper my brother is supposed to have signed."

"Well, no, I agree that's pretty flimsy. I like to be more thorough than that." He opened a beat-up briefcase. "Maybe you'd like to take a look at these pictures. And I got this tape, too. I can play it for you if you want."

They were photographs of the guns being loaded onto the *Sea-Star*. Danny's face was recognizable in the gray light. Scanlon slid the tape into the cassette deck. A babble of voices discussing payment, the weapons, weather conditions for the voyage. Danny had as much to say as anyone; he loved being an expert. He sounded like an old hand at arms smuggling.

"See, they made the mistake of leaving from Southie," Scanlon explained when he stopped the tape. "Nothing goes on in Southie without me knowing about it."

I handed the photographs back to him. "Voters are smarter than you give them credit for," I said. "They won't necessarily hold a candidate accountable for the sins of his brother. Nobody has a perfect family. Danny's willing to go to prison for this. So why shouldn't he?"

"I dunno," Scanlon said. "I only know, if it was my brother, I'd help him out. Don't you love your brother?"

"Politics is a business. Would you help him out if it hurt your business?"

"Sure I would. Only a jerk wouldn't help his brother."

"I could have you arrested for attempted bribery," I pointed out. "I bet the feds would agree not to prosecute Danny if he testified against you."

"And maybe at the trial I testify that you were the one doin' the bribing. You told me to fork over the four hundred grand to your brother in return for you goin' easy on my operations. I refuse to do it, and you turn me in to the feds."

"No one would believe that."

Scanlon shook his head. "You really do have a lotta faith in the voters. I don't know what they'll believe, but I figure it'll all end up sounding awful messy, and maybe the Republicans won't be quite so eager to make you their candidate for senator."

We sat in silence for a while as I tried to think it through. And then Scanlon said, "Listen, I gotta get back home or I'll be late for mass. I'll give you a few days to make up your mind. I'll be in touch." Scanlon held out his hand once again; again I ignored it. I got out of the car, and he drove off. He'd be home in time for the ten-thirty at Gate of Heaven, I figured. I got back into my car and sat in the parking lot for a long time before returning home.

The next Sunday I met him again and agreed to feed him information. Scanlon was delighted; it would be a wonderful relationship, he assured me. And for the rest of my term I told him whatever came my way about the feds' operations against him. They tried several times to plant bugs at his office, in his car, at his favorite table in his favorite restaurant. Somehow he always managed to find out. They turned one of his dealers, who gave them the information they needed to raid one of Jackie's marijuana-filled warehouses. When they got there, the place was so clean they could have performed surgery in it. They began to suspect there was a leak, but they assumed it was some low-level functionary on the take, or maybe an Irishman in their office with divided loyalties. Jim O'Connor? Don't be absurd. But as long as I was attorney general, their investigations got nowhere, and Jackie Scanlon flourished.

Why did I do it? Why flout my principles to cover up Danny's lame-brained crime? The reasons were both good and bad. To this day I'm not sure which mattered most.

I did it for Melissa and the kids. He wasn't a very good father, but he wasn't a terrible one either. And they all loved him, despite his drunken rages, despite the financial mess he had gotten them into. Who was I to say they would be better off with him in prison?

I did it for Danny. I wasn't inclined to do him any favors at that point, but Scanlon was right, after all. Only a jerk wouldn't help his brother. I could rage at him, but I couldn't feel good about letting him be ruined.

I did it for my father. That was actually a much stronger motivation. Everyone else might get something positive out of Danny's disgrace—he might straighten himself out, Melissa might find the courage to start another life—but there was nothing in it for my father. It might not have killed him, but surely it would have darkened the rest of his days. He *worries* about Danny. All the time. Even on a cozy Sunday evening with me, relaxed and sipping his bourbon, a part of my father is worrying. Is Danny drinking too much? Is he in trouble at work? Does he need money? I've always tried to do what I can to soothe his soul. This was just an extreme case.

I did it for my career. There was danger either way, but if I sacrificed Danny, the problems were real and immediate. I was sure it would cost me the Senate nomination, and I badly wanted that nomination. The voters might not have minded my brother being a reprobate, and they would probably have believed my version of the events over Scanlon's, but I didn't think they'd feel good about me turning in my only brother to the cops. It would leave a sour taste in their mouths; they might agree with me morally or intellectually, but they would no longer like me.

My probable opponent in the Republican primary for the Senate race was a desiccated Boston Brahmin with a limp, lord-of-the-manor handshake and the usual distinguished career of public service—all in appointed offices. He was a lousy campaigner; he seemed to believe that the Republican nomination should be his by divine right. Harold didn't think he'd give us much trouble. But Yankees still had clout in the state GOP, even if it was no longer their exclusive property. It was clear that a lot of Republicans would feel more comfortable voting for him than for me if I began to look like just another scandal-plagued Irish pol.

Finally, *I did it for me.* Because it made me feel superior to Danny. He expected me to be a sanctimonious prig and send him off to jail. I think part of him *wanted* me to do it, so that I could be the convenient villain to explain the wreckage of his life. But

I fooled him; I threw out my principles and broke the law and risked everything I had achieved so that he couldn't find a way to blame me for what he alone had done to himself.

That about covers it. Were my reasons good enough? To this day I don't know. I shouldn't have done it. I did it. Life went on.

One good thing about going to Washington was that I couldn't do much for Scanlon there. He asked a couple of times, and I turned him down; it wasn't part of the agreement, and I didn't see how I could live the rest of my life in his back pocket. Surprisingly, he didn't complain or make any threats; a deal was a deal apparently. He did well enough without my help; perhaps he had other sources of information, recruited God knows how. Whatever the reason, the feds never laid a glove on him. He thought about becoming respectable; perhaps he fancied himself turning into another Paul Everson. But Southie had too much of a hold on him. The years passed, and he didn't change. He stayed in the same three-decker, running the same rackets. On Thanksgiving and Christmas his people passed out baskets of food to the needy; he fancied himself a one-man welfare system. I supposed he still went to the ten-thirty mass Sundays at Gate of Heaven.

And when he called me a couple of days before Amanda was murdered and said he had to see me, my blood froze, and I thought: It's starting again. But I was wrong. Something far worse was starting.

We drove out to Castle Island and parked in front of Fort Independence. There wasn't much traffic; the ocean was peaceful. Out on the causeway a couple of men leaned over fishing poles; a bearded man on RollerBlades whizzed past them. Scanlon made himself comfortable in the passenger seat and sighed with happiness. "Look at that view," he said, waving at Pleasure Bay and, beyond it, the Kennedy Library and the buildings of UMass. "What a great town. Who'd wanna live anywhere but Southie?"

We had parked not far from here for our previous conversation. I had been furious, and I was prepared to turn down his request, whatever it was, even if it cost me the election. His blackmail wasn't going to work anymore.

I hadn't been prepared for the real reason he wanted to see me. "This woman reporter's been nosin' around about you and me," he said. "I figured I'd better warn you."

Amanda had tried to interview Joe Costello about my relationship with Scanlon. It probably seemed to her like a reasonable, if risky, choice; for years Costello had been the number two man in Scanlon's organization, but he was rumored to be on the outs with Jackie. My brother could take the story of my involvement with Scanlon only so far; he couldn't confirm that I had actually let Scanlon blackmail me, because I never told him. Someone like Costello might be able to finish the story, might have the proof that I broke the law.

Unfortunately for Amanda, her choice turned out to be a bad one. Costello knew nothing about me—Scanlon, too, had kept that information to himself—but Costello, in spite of the rumors, was still loyal to his boss and, because of the rumors, was eager to prove it. So he had nothing to tell Amanda but plenty to tell Scanlon afterward. And Scanlon then had plenty to tell me.

Now there was more to talk about, and none of it was good.

"Have the police been to see you about her murder?" I asked, ignoring Scanlon's praise of Southie.

He shook his head. "Don't worry, though. I won't tell 'em nothin'."

I hadn't expected him to. "This is big trouble," I said.

He nodded. "For both of us, Jim," he said. The "sir" had long ago disappeared. "Anyway, I hope you don't think I had anything to do with it."

"No, I don't think you had anything to do with it. And that's why this is big trouble. The worst thing would be if it's just a random killing, and the police come across her notes about us while they're investigating."

"Nothing's happened yet," Scanlon pointed out. "That's encouraging, isn't it?"

"I guess. I was thinking—Costello. If he's so eager to show you he's loyal, maybe he killed her, you know, then stole all the notes and tapes, thinking he's doing you a favor."

"That occurred to me," Scanlon said. "Thing is, Joey isn't the brightest guy in the world, and I can't believe he'd type some weird message on a computer."

She had to die. I shivered. "Pretty simple message," I said.

"Simple or not," Scanlon replied, "I don't think Joey has written anything but his name since the fourth grade. If he wanted to murder someone, this just isn't the way he'd do it, Jim. Anyway, I've talked to him, and I think he's straight."

"Any other ideas?"

Scanlon shook his head. "I've been askin' around, but I don't wanna seem too interested. I mean, why should I care why this broad got murdered? There's nothin' on the street about it that I've heard."

"Any idea who told her about you and me?"

Scanlon looked surprised. "I assumed it was your brother."

"Danny talked to her, but he swears she knew about us already, says he was just trying to defend me."

"Well, meaning no offense, Jim, but—"

"I know, I know, Danny could be lying. But if he isn't, I have to know who told her. Because I sure didn't."

"Me neither. And I don't know of anyone else who knows about me and you."

I wasn't surprised, but it was still disappointing. Scanlon wasn't exactly being a font of information. I considered asking him if he knew anything about Finn's war record, but didn't bother. Not Jackie's area of expertise.

We sat silently in the gathering darkness for a while, looking at the lights come on in Dorchester and Quincy across the bay. We were like old friends who have outlasted the need to speak, I thought. We certainly weren't friends, but over the years I had come to realize that I didn't hate Jackie Scanlon either. He is scum, but he had lived up to the deal we made. Unlike Paul Everson, he had never tricked me. I made the deal with my eyes open, and these were the consequences.

"Cavanaugh's gunnin' for you, I guess," Scanlon remarked.

"A lot of people are gunning for me," I replied.

"It's tough bein' on top," Scanlon said. "Look at me. I'm fighting every day. The local cops, the feds, young guys think they're smarter than me and indestructible to boot, out-of-state bosses lookin' to expand. There's always someone I've gotta beat."

"You're saying we're not that different, huh?"

"That's it exactly."

"Well, fuck you, Jackie."

Scanlon laughed. "Excuse me. I forgot. You're the guy's on the side of the angels."

"I can be on the side of the angels without being an angel myself," I said.

"No one's an angel, Jim, and no one's a devil," Scanlon replied. "I'll keep my ears open, let you know if I come up with any-thing."

"Thanks." There was nothing left to say; I wasn't about to debate ethics with Jackie Scanlon. I drove him home in the dark-ness—two old friends returning from a trip to the beach.

Then I got out of Southie as fast as I could.

CHAPTER 16

$\mathcal{T}$wo days after my chat with Jackie Scanlon, I was chatting with the President of the United States.

Things were getting hectic on Capitol Hill. The Senate majority leader was threatening to keep us in session around the clock to accomplish all the remaining business, and the staff had brought cots and blankets into the cloakrooms as a precaution. Meanwhile, the usual senators were tying us in procedural knots in order to wring every last advantage out of everyone's desire to get the hell out of the place.

I was baffled by the federal legislative system when I first saw it in action. How could anything ever get accomplished? Carl Hutchins set me straight. "Son, it isn't *supposed* to work well," he told me. "If we were more efficient, we'd make a hell of a lot more bad laws." We were participants in a legislative process of natural selection; only the strongest bills could make it through the sub-committees and the full committees and the behind-the-scenes bargaining and the votes on the floor and the joint conferences until they made it to the President's desk. It is frustrating to be part of this process, however, and never more so than at the end of the session, when a year's worth of work can go down the drain because your favorite bill has a killer amendment tacked onto it, or it gets filibustered to death, or time simply runs out before it can even be considered.

This was the first time I'd had to face a reelection campaign at the end of the session, and now I learned how uniquely frustrating that can be. While I was bogged down in Washington, Bobby Finn was back home kissing babies and cutting ribbons and promising everything to everyone.

Actually, though, to most voters I was now more of a presence than I had been at any time during the past six years. The latest wave of ads was running, the direct-mail pieces were starting to arrive, and bumper stickers and lawn signs were appearing across the state. I was also taking every opportunity to get free publicity; I was more than willing to be interviewed from the Capitol steps live via satellite on the six o'clock news about whatever momentous event had taken place that day, and reporters from local papers who hadn't been able to get ten minutes of my time previously now found me available for in-depth interviews.

Did my physical presence make a difference then? I believed that it did. It energized the staff, it provided the campaign with a focus, and of course, my charm and wit undoubtedly swayed some of the voters I did meet in person. So I needed to get home.

My fear of imminent arrest was diminishing as the days went by, but it hadn't disappeared altogether, and that made it even more difficult to concentrate on Senate business. That, and my increasing puzzlement over Amanda's murder. My talk with Scanlon certainly hadn't cleared it up. How had Amanda found out about him? What, if anything, did that have to do with her death?

Was the person who told her getting ready to tell someone else?

And on Tuesday the President asked me to stop by for a chat.

It wasn't unusual. Charles Kenton is at his best one-on-one, and he knows it. He can appear stiff and defensive in front of groups—when talking to congressional leaders, for example, or in press conferences. But when he gets you alone, with that soft voice of his and those dark eyes boring into you, he is almost hypnotic. You want to listen forever. You feel disappointed in yourself for not agreeing with him, for not giving him what he wants. Some of us manage to resist, however.

He wanted to talk about his farm bill. Now I am hardly an expert in agricultural policy. We have some farmers in Massachusetts—wonderful people, salt of the earth—but there aren't

enough of them to make much of a difference in an election, and
I'm not the kind of guy who likes to don his overalls and plow the
back forty in his spare time. But my vote counted as much as that
of a senator from Iowa, so Kenton wanted it. He was making
inroads in some of the traditionally Republican farm states, and
he needed to solidify his support there to get reelected in two
years.

There is nothing like the ego gratification of being summoned
to the White House—except if you are the one doing the sum-
moning. I have gotten used to many things in my career, but I
have never gotten used to that. To enter the Oval Office and have
the President's face light up as he strides across the room to greet
you: "Jim, Jim, good to see you, good of you to come . . ." The
paralyzing handshake, the arm around the shoulders, the offer
of something to drink . . .

It was all a crock. Everyone knew that Kenton didn't like me.
More to the point, he was afraid of me, as Carl Hutchins had
pointed out. I was a potential rival, and everything he said had
to be interpreted with that in mind.

Politics and policies aside, I don't like Kenton much myself.
Most politicians tend to relax when they are alone with their own
kind—no need to act when you're with other actors. But Kenton
never let up, at least in my presence. Always the sanctimonious
defender of the rights of the little guy. Always the seeker of justice
and equality for people of all races. Never admitting that politics
might conceivably influence his decisions. There were two possible
interpretations: Either he really believed that the role was the
reality, in which case he was a menace, or he didn't think I was
smart enough to realize he was acting, in which case he greatly
underestimated me.

We sat in overstuffed chairs on either side of the fireplace; a
fire was burning, even though it was warm out. He crossed his
legs, and I could see an inch of white skin; he should get longer
socks, I thought. The flickering of the flames was reflected in his
glasses.

"Jim," President Kenton began, "I wanted to talk to you about
the farm bill that's coming up for action tomorrow." He spoke so
softly that I had to lean forward in my chair to hear him, a good
technique for ensuring that people pay attention. I've used it on
juries a few times, but Kenton is a master of it. He had a five-
minute spiel that he delivered flawlessly, his handsome face dark-

ening as he spoke of the problems that today's small farmer faced, then brightening as he explained how his bill would solve them, his arguments marching resolutely to the only possible conclusion: America needed this bill. We would be lost without it. His hands reached out to me as he pleaded for my support: "This isn't a partisan issue, Jim. There's real suffering on America's family farms, and we now have a chance to do something about it. Can I count on your vote?"

It was a wonderful performance even if you didn't know what he was talking about. *Mr. President, I don't give a shit about your bill.* That's the sort of thing I wanted to say, but it wasn't quite right for the Oval Office—at least not when talking to someone like Kenton. "I'm afraid that this *is* a partisan issue, Mr. President," I responded. "The minority leadership has come out against this bill. I generally defer to their judgment on matters like this— unless I'm given a strong reason not to." In other words, *What's in it for me?*

"Jim," the President said, "I assure you that these issues affect many citizens of Massachusetts as well as those of other states." *There are votes in it for you.*

I decided to be a little blunter. "Farmers vote Republican in Massachusetts, Mr. President. Your bill won't make enough of a difference with them for it to be worth my while bucking the leadership."

The President smiled. He has wonderful teeth: white and even. But to me his smile always has a phony, Nixonesque quality to it. He smiles because that's what the role calls for, not because he finds something funny. "Well, Jim," he said, "we're not above doing a little horse trading here, if it comes to that." *Heh-heh. See, I can be a regular guy, too.* "I understand that you're going to offer your prison aid plan as an amendment to the crime bill."

"That's right. Are you suggesting that you might support the amendment?"

"Now you know I can't do that, Jim. We've made our position clear, and it wouldn't look good to flip-flop. However, I think I can swing a couple of votes your way. Dayton, for example, and Larmore. If I could tell them this would get your vote on the farm bill, I believe they'd be happy to oblige."

It was a good deal: two votes for my bill in return for one vote for his. The two votes might be enough to get it passed. The deal was so good that I had considered trying to pull off something like it myself. It wouldn't have been hard; vote trading like that goes on all the time. But the very fact that Kenton was offering the deal made me reconsider. If the bill was so important to him, perhaps it was important to me that it not pass. Not now, certainly, but down the road, if I were to face him in two years.

But how could I be worrying about the next election when I was in deep trouble in this one? I could use a victory on my amendment. Besides, I hadn't come close to making a decision about running against Kenton. I had forbidden Harold even to bring up the topic in my presence. I had enough to worry about without planning a run for the presidency.

Still, I thought, if I had Carl Hutchins on my side, my amendment could make it even without Dayton and Larmore. And I didn't feel like doing Kenton any favors, whether or not he would ever be my opponent in an election. I shook my head. "Sorry, Mr. President. I wish I could oblige."

Kenton raised an eyebrow. He was still smiling, but his dark eyes became a little harder, his language a little blunter. "Your amendment isn't going to pass without some help, Jim," he pointed out.

"Oh, I think it has a good shot. Besides, anything can happen at the end of the session."

"That election of yours is going to be tough. Getting your amendment passed would give you a boost."

"Not really. I've got the law and order vote. This isn't going to change any minds." I didn't believe that, but I wasn't going to let Kenton know what I believed.

And then I had an awful thought: What if Kenton knew about the tape, knew about Jackie Scanlon? What if they all knew? It wasn't impossible. If Cavanaugh had the tape of Danny's interview, he would certainly tell Finn, and Finn might tell the President. Perhaps they had all sat around thinking about how to use the knowledge to inflict the most damage on me. If that were true, Kenton would know that he had nothing to worry about from me; Cavanaugh makes the tape public after the session ends, and my career is finished. And the longer they waited, the tougher it would be for the Republicans to field another candidate if I had to withdraw. In the meantime, why not give me my little amendment if in return I could help Kenton with his farm bill?

Maybe I would end up inside one of those prisons my amendment would help build.

"Jim," the President said, "I hate to say this, but I've heard that Bobby Finn is coming on strong up there in Massachusetts." He didn't look as though he hated to say it. "My political people were opposed to me offering you any help on your bill," he went on, "because they think we've got such a great shot at taking your seat, and they didn't want me giving you any advantages. But I feel so deeply about the importance of this farm bill that I over-ruled them. So I'm asking you one more time for your support. What do you say, Jim?"

"I say that you'd better get some new political people, Mr. President, because Bobby Finn isn't going anywhere. He's been down eight to ten points for weeks, and even this supposed scandal I've had to deal with hasn't helped him much. To have any shot at beating me, he'll have to give the Gettysburg Address at our debate. And frankly he's lucky if he can say his own name without making a grammatical error."

The President shrugged. "Well," he said, "who knows what can happen when you've got a scandal to deal with?" And what did that mean? I didn't respond; I just gave him a cold stare. The President smiled his just-one-of-the-boys smiles. "Anyway, I get the picture, Jim. I guess I'll just have to win this one without you." He stood up and extended his hand. "Give my regards to your lovely wife, Elizabeth."

"I certainly will, Mr. President." Obviously he had been briefed before our meeting. Not very well, though: No one called Liz "Elizabeth," even though she hated her nickname. But was bringing her name up some sort of oblique dig about Amanda?

Kenton can be had, I thought as I left the White House. Mediocre political advisers, bad staff work—and he himself just wasn't very likable. But would I be the one to take him? I had the feeling he was sending me messages all through our chat. Or was I just becoming paranoid?

Back at the office Mrs. Sullivan reported that there had been four urgent calls from Harold. Was this it? I wondered. Had the bad news finally arrived? I shut the door of my office and called him back.

"We've got him," Harold said.

"Who?"

"Finn. The war record. Just like you said. How'd you do that? We've got him, Jim. We've got him."

I had never heard Harold so excited. He couldn't have

sounded happier if the Supreme Court had thrown out the exclusionary rule. "Take a deep breath, Harold," I said, "and tell me what you found out."

"Not over the phone. You've got to come back. You've got to talk to this guy."

"What guy?"

"Not over the phone. He's no Gary Cooper, but I've done some checking, and I think he'll do. You've got to come back."

"Look, Harold, I can't possibly get out of here. The place is crazy. I just got in from talking to the President, and the bells are ringing for a vote on the floor, and I'm up to my ears. Can't it wait till the weekend?"

"Fuck the President, Jim. Fuck the vote. This is important. This is the election."

"I really can't do it tonight, Harold. Maybe tomorrow—"

"Tomorrow night then. I'll charter a private plane for you, bring you into Hanscom Field; that'll be closer. Fly back afterward, you won't even lose any sleep. Except you'll be too excited to sleep."

"This better be good, Harold."

"It's good, Senator. Trust me."

I did trust Harold. If he thought we had Finn, we had him—except that, unknown to Harold, Finn might also have me. And where would that leave the two of us?

I talked to the majority leader, who assured me that the crime bill wouldn't come up before the end of the week at the earliest. So there was no reason not to make the trip back to Massachusetts.

Except that I was scared. Scared of a private plane flying in the darkness and rain and fog, for one thing. Too many members of Congress seem to crash in the damn things. And scared of the decisions I might have to make after I had heard what Harold's prize discovery had to say. It would be good news, apparently, but even the best of news would complicate a situation that was already getting far too complicated.

The plane managed to land without going up in flames, and I was at Hanscom Field in Bedford, northwest of Boston. Harold was waiting for me, and we drove off in his Porsche.

"Where to?" I asked.

"Waltham," he replied. "Massachusetts Gear Works."

"Gear Works?" I said, not quite sure I had heard right.

"Gear Works. Somebody has to make the things."

"This guy works there?"

"Uh-huh."

"Second shift or something?"

"Or something. Remember, he's not the most impressive specimen you've ever seen, but I think he's okay."

"How did you find him?"

"Wasn't difficult. He wrote us a letter after Finn was nominated. It got ignored, wouldn't you know, but someone decided to save the thing, and it ended up in a miscellaneous file on Finn's background. I went through the file after you brought up this war record business."

"And you checked out his story?"

"Working on it. I'll tell you after you've talked to him."

We drove along Route 128 in silence; then Harold turned off the highway into Waltham, an industrial city a few miles away from Bedford. Massachusetts Gear Works occupied a dreary brick building along a street filled with dreary brick buildings. Rows of chrysanthemums blooming along the front walk showed that someone cared, but a couple of boarded-over windows on upper floors showed that nobody cared very much. There were few lights on in the building. "Not a very big second shift," I said.

"He *is* the second shift," Harold replied.

We parked in a visitor's space next to the front door and got out. Harold pounded on the door, and a few moments later a guy in a security guard's uniform was peering at us from inside the building. He unlocked the door and let us in.

The guard was a big man, but it was an unhealthy bigness; he could have been a hundred pounds overweight. His hair was thin and greasy and combed straight back. His eyes were dark and peered out at you like distant black holes from deep inside the flesh on his face. He was sweating and breathing heavily, apparently from the effort of coming to answer the door. He looked to be in his forties; I wouldn't have bet on him reaching his fifties.

"Larry Spalding, this is Senator Jim O'Connor," Harold said.

"I'm honored to meet you, sir." The security guard shook my hand; he had a limp, sweaty grip. His voice was strangely high for such a big man. "Let's go back to the office."

We followed him past a receptionist's desk and into a small room with a metal desk and imitation wood paneling. A calendar from a plumbing supply house hung on the wall; the desk was bare except for a copy of the *Herald*, open to the comics. Spalding sat behind the desk on a swivel chair that looked ready to break under his weight. Harold and I sat on metal folding chairs on the other side of the desk. Spalding opened a drawer and produced a flask. "Anyone like a drink?" he asked.

We both shook our heads. I was not impressed.

He looked at the flask for a moment, then put it back in the drawer. "I shouldn't," he said. "Should keep my head clear. I'm kinda nervous. But see, if I don't drink, I think I'll hafta smoke." I suppose we couldn't hide our reactions because he hastened to add, "I know it's obnoxious, but see, this isn't gonna be easy, and I can use all the help I can get."

He looked at me as if for permission. "Larry," I said, "I want you to do whatever you need to do. And I also want you to understand that I appreciate you talking to us like this. It must take a lot of courage."

I had no idea at this point if it did or not, but that seemed to be what he needed to hear. Spalding smiled at me in relief. "Thank you, sir." He took a pack of Marlboros out of his pocket and lit up. I thought of Marge and her damn secret. Everyone had a secret; only this guy was going to tell me his. He was the picture of unhealthy living, sitting there with the sweat pouring out of his flesh and the smoke pouring out of his lungs, and he realized it. "I guess if the diabetes doesn't get me, then the lung cancer will, right? Or maybe it'll be the booze." He shook his head. "Didn't think I'd end up like this. But who does? It just sort of happens. You guys weren't in Vietnam, right?"

"That's right," I said. I braced myself for a you-can't-know-what-it-was-like speech, but I didn't get one.

"Then you're lucky—or smart," he said. "Prob'ly smart. Jeez, it sure screwed me up. I used to think about becoming, like, an engineer or something. Study electronics maybe. But it's all I can do to hold on to a job like this, where you basically don't have to do anything but show up and not get too drunk. People run out of sympathy after fifteen, twenty years, you know? Can't really blame 'em. Especially when there's nothing wrong with you except what you do to yourself. Vietnam didn't make me fat exactly. And I could always go on a diet, right? Some guy lost his leg over there, he ain't gonna grow it back."

"I talk to a lot of Vietnam veterans' groups," I said. "We could be doing more to help you guys."

Spalding shrugged. "Ah, that's all right. If it hadna been the war, it probably woulda been something else. Some guys make it, some guys don't. You know?" He lit another cigarette.

"Bobby Finn," Harold murmured.

"Right. He was my second lieutenant, okay? God, he was somethin'. He was the only guy I knew really seemed to like it over there. Slogging through the jungle with the heat and the insects, and every second you think you're gonna die. You stop thinking about it for a while—you smoke some dope, or you start talking to someone about back home—and then it hits you like, oh, Jesus, I stopped thinking about dying. Like you made a big mistake, let your guard down or something. But Bobby Finn wasn't like that. He seemed to think it was all some big adventure. Like we should be grateful for the opportunity the government gave us to go marching through a rice paddy ten thousand miles away from home and catch some tropical disease and get our ass shot at.

"It was the weirdest thing. See, my theory is that he didn't believe he could get hurt. Like he was indestructible or something. And for a while there it looked like he was. He'd lead us into the heaviest fighting and come out without a scratch. 'Men,' he'd say, 'you're just as likely to die if you're cowards, so you might as well be heroes.' Which makes absolutely no sense, right? But some of the guys believed him. And they'd end up in a body bag, a lot of them. He still gets away with that sort of thing today, ask me. He's got this force about him, this determination, and people just go along because he looks like he knows what he's doing. Well, I didn't get it back them, and I don't get it now."

This struck me as a very accurate analysis of Bobby Finn, but it was clear that we would have to keep Larry Spalding focused. "What was it then," I said, "that—"

Spalding nodded. "Right. Okay. I'm sorry." He stubbed out his cigarette and lit another. "See, his luck didn't hold. We came into this village was supposed to be deserted. Of course, you never believe that, you're always on your guard. But Finn was out front as usual, and he was the guy who got hit when someone opened fire from one of the huts. So a couple of us dragged him out of the way while everyone else returned fire and leveled the hut. It was some kid, figured he had nothing to lose, I suppose, we were going to find him anyway, so why not take one of us out first?

"He hit Finn in the shoulder. It wasn't serious, but Bobby went wild. Not just because of the pain, see, but because it was like his illusion was shattered. This war really could hurt him. Sid Blomberg and I tried to bandage up the wound, but he was too angry to let us. He went stompin' off, shootin' his gun in the air, and swearing at, you know, the friggin' gooks, that sort of thing, with Sid and me trailing along behind, trying to calm him down while the rest of the guys were still attacking that hut.

"And that's when we heard a noise from another hut. We tried to get Finn down, you know, let someone else handle it, but he was too angry, he just marched right up to the hut and went inside. Sid and I followed him.

"It was dark in there, and it took a coupla seconds for our eyes to adjust, and then we saw a little Vietnamese woman squatting in the corner. She was kind of whimpering, you know? Not quite crying, but she couldn't keep quiet either. She was too scared to know what to do, so she just crouched there, lookin' at us.

" 'C'mon, Lieutenant,' I said. 'Let's get outa here.' But he didn't pay any attention to me. He just took his rifle and aimed it at the woman and blew her away."

Spalding fell silent. The little office was hot, and the air was filled with smoke. It was becoming difficult to breathe. Spalding had started to cry, his tears mingling with his sweat so that his face glistened with moisture; it looked as if it were melting. Harold handed him a handkerchief, and he wiped himself off. "Take your time, Larry," I said. "I know this must be very difficult for you."

"Just blew her away," he repeated. "Squattin' there one second, the next second she was just, like, a heap. A bloody heap. Sid and I looked at each other like *I can't believe this.* And then we looked at Finn, and he was just staring at the woman, with his rifle up, like he was ready to shoot again if she moved. But she wasn't gonna move. And then he seemed to come out of it, and he looked at us, and I guess he must've seen how, you know, horrified we were, because he brought the rifle down right away and he said, 'I thought she had a gun. I saw metal. It was dark in here, and I thought I saw metal.'

"But he didn't see any metal, Senator, he didn't see any gun. He was mad 'cause they hurt him, so he wanted to hurt them back. That was all. He thought he was indestructible, but no one's indestructible. Not even Bobby Finn."

Spalding mopped his face again and lit another cigarette. "Tell the senator what happened then, Larry," Harold prompted gently.

"Nothin', really. Everyone else came running, and they

wanted to know what was goin' on, and Finn just kept repeating about the gun. No one believed him, but what are you gonna do? It was dark in there. He was the officer, and he was so damn sure of himself. That sort of thing happened all the time, I suppose. But that doesn't make it right."

"So no one made a report or filed charges or whatever?" I asked.

Spalding shook his head. "We just bandaged him up and left the village. Guys asked me and Sid about it, and we told 'em what we saw, but that was it. We all went back to fighting the stupid war and thinking about dying. Finn got his ribbons and his Purple Heart and then he goes into politics and he's a big war hero and he becomes governor. And here I am. I don't think I've been right since that day. It just sort of took somethin' out of me, seeing him kill that woman like that. I understand about war, and I realize you've gotta have soldiers, and sometimes things get out of hand, but what he did wasn't right. And it isn't right for him to be a senator either."

"It's been a long time since this happened, Larry," I said. "Why did you finally want to talk about it now?"

"Because I've been scared," Spalding said softly. "I don't wanna get mixed up in anything. Finn's a powerful guy. I see how things happen. You make charges, get your face on TV, all of a sudden people are rootin' around in your life, tryin' to prove you're crazy or something. All I want is to lay low, stay out of trouble. I got enough trouble just gettin' out of bed every day. But you're a good guy, Senator, and he shouldn't take your job away from you."

"Well, this is very brave of you, Larry, and I certainly appreciate the sacrifice you're making."

Spalding stubbed out his cigarette. He looked a lot calmer now that he had told his story. "Did you have any luck finding Sid Blomberg, Mr. White?" he asked.

"Not yet," Harold replied. "We have gotten in touch with some of the other men in your platoon, though."

"And they remembered, right? They told you I wasn't lying."

"Some of them remembered. But you and Sid were the only ones to witness the actual killing, so it's important for us to find him and make sure he can corroborate your story."

"I understand. I wish I could help you, but like you say, it's been a long time. Sid could be anywhere. Could be dead." Spalding's tone suggested that the latter possibility was not unlikely.

"We'll keep looking," Harold promised.

"What do you think you'll do with—with all this?" Spalding asked.

"First we have to think over the situation very carefully," I responded. "Politics is a tricky business, as I'm sure you understand. This is a serious charge, and we wouldn't want to make it recklessly."

"I'm willing to, you know, do what I can."

"Thank you, Larry." I stood up. "And if we can do anything for you—"

Spalding struggled up from his swivel chair. "No, no. I don't want money or anything for this. That's not why I'm doin' it."

He led us back to the front door. His keys jangled at his side. His shirt was soaked with sweat. I shook his hand again before he let us out. "We'll be in touch, Larry."

"Thank you, sir. I've always admired you, you know. You've always been a straight shooter."

I smiled, and Harold and I left the darkened building.

The rain was heavier. We raced over to the Porsche and got inside. Harold started the car. "Interesting thing about Massachusetts Gear Works I found out today," he said.

"What's that?"

"Seems it's a subsidiary of Everson Enterprises." He gave me a glance.

"Small world," I said. "But doesn't Paul Everson control just about everything?"

"I suppose that's true."

We pulled out of the parking lot and left Larry Spalding to his lonely job of guarding one of Paul Everson's many possessions.

"So what did you think?" Harold asked.

"He seems like a really nice guy. It's sad."

"True. But the story. It's perfect, isn't it?"

I knew what he meant. If I had a weak spot, it was that many people perceive me as being soft on defense. This was consistent with the philosophy I shared with Harold. I would rather spend some of the Pentagon's billions on programs that would help improve life in America—not necessarily the same programs that liberals supported, but the line of argument was the same. What's the point of being impregnable against outside attack, if we collapse from internal rot?

When I was assigned to the Armed Services Committee, I wasn't exactly antimilitary, but I was death on waste and fraud. I used the investigative experience I had built up as attorney general to poke around the Pentagon budget. My staff uncovered some shady dealings, and we made some headlines, and I acquired a reputation.

It wasn't a bad reputation to have—who's in favor of waste and fraud?—but Bobby Finn, the war hero, decided he had an issue. He was overseas fighting for our country while I was attending that pinko university in Cambridge. And now I was crippling our nation's defenses by second-guessing the people who were trying to protect us. This tactic didn't go over well with the liberals in Finn's own party, but that didn't matter; they would have to hold their noses and vote for Bobby anyway. But it did strike a chord with veterans' groups and other patriotic types who would normally vote Republican. I might not be evil, but Bobby was one of them.

But Larry Spalding's story undercut Finn's patriotic appeal; this wasn't the way we wanted our heroes to act. Furthermore, it went to the heart of many people's doubts about the governor. Sure, he was fatherly; sure, everyone liked him. But everyone also knew that he had a temper, that his staff hid beneath their desks when things didn't go his way. He admitted it; he joked about it. That was part of his charm. But murdering an innocent woman wasn't charming at all.

If we could back up Spalding's story, Governor Finn was history.

Unless, of course, he had a worse story to tell about me.

And it would be worse, in every way. I had abused my office, then (people would surely infer) murdered a young woman in cold blood to keep her from revealing my secret. Finn's murder had occurred during wartime, when he was under terrible stress. And he could conceivably wriggle out of the charge. It was his word, after all, against that of a not very articulate and not very prepossessing security guard. And Sid Blomberg, perhaps, wherever Sid was. If Finn insisted he had seen a gun, who could prove he was lying?

If the Democrats were toying with me until after the session, they would stop toying once we told the world what had happened in that Vietnamese village over twenty years ago.

"Well?" Harold didn't like my silence.

"I think we have to find Sid Blomberg," I said.

"I disagree," Harold replied. "Surprise is crucial when you drop this kind of bombshell. Someone from the platoon may be talking to Finn right now, telling him his opponents are asking nasty questions. That gives him a chance to figure out a defense. What if *he* finds Sid and convinces him to contradict Spalding, offers him some low-stress job at the State House in return? Even if Finn doesn't do anything, we still don't want to wait too late in the campaign to come out with this. People are liable to think it's a smear, and it might backfire."

"Those are chances we have to take then. This is just too risky. I want more than one guy's word on it."

Harold pounded the steering wheel in frustration. "Damn it, you could lose this election," he said. "Steadman's polls still show that people are on the fence. If any evidence comes out that Amanda Taylor was your lover, Finn will cream you. You're walking a tightrope, Jim, and this is your net."

We reached the airport. The rain came down in sheets. SENATOR DIES IN PRIVATE PLANE CRASH. SECRET CAMPAIGN TRIP BLAMED. I couldn't argue with Harold about this; better to just lay down the law. Let him think I was a cretin; nothing would change between us. "Harold, I want you to keep looking for this guy," I said, "at least until after the weekend. A few days won't hurt. We'll reassess the situation then."

"This is idiocy."

"And don't go behind my back and leak the story to some reporter. Understand?"

"Why? Why? Why?"

"Understand?"

Harold shook his head and looked out at the rain. "Did you bring an umbrella?"

"I left it on the plane."

"Then you can borrow mine."

"Thanks."

I took his umbrella and got out of the car.

"Don't forget to bring the damn thing back!" Harold shouted to me as I walked toward the administration building, where I would find my pilot and then head back into danger.

I waved to Harold without turning around.

CHAPTER 17

I survived the flight to Washington. Back in my apartment, and feeling guilty, I called Kathleen. I could fly up to Massachusetts to see a security guard, but I didn't have time to see my daughter, my only child. We chatted about school and the campaign, but the whole time I was trying to keep from apologizing. After the election, I promised myself. But I had made promises before.

When I had said good night to Kathleen, I called up Paul Everson. I had the private number for his retreat in the Berkshires. Shangri-la, it was called; I had never been there, but I read an article about it once in one of the decorating magazines Liz buys. It had been built by some movie magnate, who had given it the banal name. I vaguely recalled an indoor basketball court and swimming pool, an oak-beamed dining room large enough to hold the U.S. Senate, and a row of antique autos gleaming in a spotless garage.

I got an answering machine; I left my name and was about to hang up when Everson came on the line. "Jim," he said. "Sorry I haven't gotten back to you."

"Have you come up with anything?" I asked.

"I'm working on it, Jim. As I said, this isn't my turf, and anyway, this case is so political that people are afraid to say any-

208

thing. Their careers are at stake. But I wouldn't worry about it. Did you look into Finn's war record?"

"As a matter of fact, I was chatting tonight with Larry Spalding. I understand he's one of your employees. How did you come up with him?"

Everson laughed. "If I told you my secrets, you'd be a wealthy man, and obviously you don't want to become wealthy. Let's just say he's talked about Finn before, and I have people who are paid to listen for talk like that. What did you think?"

"He mentioned a guy named Sid Blomberg who was also supposed to be a witness. Does Sid work for you?"

"Not that I know of. Want me to find him for you?"

"All right. Harold is looking for him, too."

"So you're going to use Spalding?"

"I'm not sure yet. I'd like some supporting evidence. Spalding sounds like he's telling the truth, but I don't want to get burned."

"You can trust him, Jim. Go after Finn. Forget about the murder. Forget about that tape. You'll be all right."

I wanted to believe him, but he wasn't giving me much reason to. "How are things in Shangri-la?" I asked.

"Lonely," Everson replied.

I tried to remember if he was married at the moment. "What about that starlet? Didn't I read—"

"You haven't kept up on your reading. The starlet is in Cancun, probably screwing her divorce lawyer. I've got an army of M.B.A.'s who come in by day and make money for me, but at night it's just me."

Poor little rich kid. I couldn't manage to feel sorry for him. "Well, if you come up with anything—"

"Of course, Jim. We'll find this guy Sid for you. Don't worry."

I hung up. Don't worry, don't worry. I replayed my messages. There were two from Kevin. "It's very important, Jim," the second one said. "Please call me back no matter how late." It must have been important for him to call me Jim. Had he and his private eye come up with something already, while Paul Everson was still running into brick walls?

I called Kevin. He answered on the first ring. "Kevin, what's up?"

"Oh, Senator, well, there's good news and there's bad news."

"All right, bad news first."

"Do you remember that obnoxious reporter at the funeral home? Brad Williams?"

"Sure." He had slipped out of my mind, but now he returned, with his cologne and his slicked-back hair and his insinuating whispers on the church steps.

"Well, it turns out he's investigating the murder, too. He's looking for dirt, Jim. Sharpe says he's trying to prove you and Amanda Taylor were lovers."

"Yeah, I sort of figured he was going to do something like that."

"What should we do?"

"I don't know. Let's talk to Harold. We ought to be able to handle someone like Brad Williams. What's the good news?"

"Well, Sharpe talked to the woman who saw that man coming into the building around the time of the murder. Her name is Henrietta Perlstein, and I guess this is just about the most exciting thing that ever happened to her. Anyway, he couldn't get anything more out of her about the man, but he came up with something else. It seems that Henrietta saw clips on the news of that press conference you and Liz gave, and she told Sharpe that she recognized Liz; she ran into her in the lobby a few weeks before the murder."

I took a deep breath. "She saw Liz in Amanda's apartment building?"

"That's right. Isn't it great?"

"Um, tell me your thinking here, Kevin."

"Well, the Democrats and reporters like this guy Williams are trying to insinuate that you had a, you know, romantic involvement with the victim. But you keep pointing out that Liz was the one who was friendly with her and, really, introduced the two of you. So this just proves you were right; they were still getting together long after you started working on the book with Amanda Taylor. But of course, we don't hear anything about this from Cavanaugh because he's too busy trying to figure out how he can charge you with murder, right?"

"Right. Well, thanks for keeping me updated, Kevin. I appreciate it."

"Anytime, Senator. Except for this reporter I feel very good about the case, don't you?"

"We're in great shape, Kevin. Great shape."

I hung up. Everson reassured me, and I reassured Kevin. And nobody knew what the hell was going on.

What was Liz doing visiting Amanda? Leave it to Kevin to come up with the best possible interpretation for it.

We were back more or less to normal, Liz and I. Staying on the surface. Ignoring everything but everyday life. I'd just as soon have left it that way. There was too much churning beneath the surface for me to want to probe any deeper in the midst of all my other problems. But now I realized that I couldn't afford not to.

I remembered Liz's silence as I told her about the affair, about the murder. What had that silence meant?

What did Liz know that she hadn't told me?

In the morning I wander through the empty rooms of this fancy house before I settle down in front of the computer, and I miss my daughter—miss the sound of her hair dryer and her rock station, the steam pouring out of the bathroom after her endless showers, the trail of clothes and cassettes and dirty dishes she always leaves in her wake.

And, strangely, I find that I miss Liz, too. Miss the economy-size store brand toothpaste she buys, miss the way she furrows her brow as she concentrates on a textbook she's reading, miss the gentle sound of her breathing as I tiptoe around the bedroom while she sleeps.

Strange, because I rarely miss her when I'm staying at my Washington apartment, though Kathleen's absence is always an ache in my heart. In Washington I have always felt a sense of bachelor freedom at being away from Liz—even before I took advantage of that freedom. I didn't have to deal with her unhappiness, her brooding silences; she could brood perfectly well without me.

But here, now, it's different—perhaps because I don't have the press of Senate business to keep me occupied; perhaps because I'm spending so much time remembering, and my memories of Liz are so different from today's reality.

Not all of them are perfect—whose memories are?—but all of them are worth remembering.

We met when I was in law school and she was still an undergraduate at Regis College, a pleasant suburban school for Catholic princesses. Her father was a stockbroker, and her family lived in a big old house in Needham—not the poshest of suburbs, but far more pleasant to me than the dreary urban streets of Brighton. I started spending a lot of time there. Her parents certainly approved of me. I didn't have much of a background, but I had a great future, and I was beginning to lose my bookworm mentality and find out how to make people like me. I was the kind of nice short-haired Irish boy Mr. and Mrs. Whelan wanted for their daughter.

It wasn't a great blazing romance, but I felt comfortable with Liz. I liked trying to break through her silences, getting her to argue about Nixon, contraception, contract law, anything. I liked making her laugh. I liked the way her head fitted against my shoulder when we embraced. It was an astonishingly chaste courtship for the times. For a long while there was nothing more than groping on the sofa. Finally we graduated to making love on the lumpy bed in my apartment in Somerville, but I sometimes got the feeling that Liz wasn't thrilled about this, that she was doing it just because she didn't want me to think of her as a prude. That didn't bother me especially; sex was a gift, a bonus. Mostly I liked just being with her.

And then, at the beginning of her senior year, things fell apart in the Whelan family. To this day I'm not exactly sure what happened. I assume that Liz knows, but she has never confided in me; it is one more thing—perhaps the most important thing—that she keeps locked up inside her skull. Sometimes I have gotten the impression that her father had been misappropriating his clients' funds; at other times it seemed that he had merely convinced people to invest in some scheme that was possibly illegal and certainly disastrous. Whatever he did, he ended up disgraced and jobless. The scandal was hushed up, but he was ruined. The family had to sell their house in Needham, and Liz had to drop out of college. I don't think she has ever gotten over it.

Coming from a working-class background, I have always had to be aware of money, but it has never been an obsession for me. Unlike Danny, I have never been interested in flashy cars or expensive clothing, and I didn't have a bunch of kids to break my budget. I have no need to be rich, and I'm too smart to be poor; this seems to me to be the perfect combination.

Liz had the money and lost it, and that has made her very different. She grew up without a care—much like Amanda, it occurs to me—and then one day the real world tapped her on the shoulder and introduced itself to her. I never heard her blame her father, but she's not the kind to complain. She's also not the kind to forgive easily, however, and her relationship with her parents has been touchy ever since.

She went to work after dropping out of college, determined to pay her own way through her final year. I didn't see much of her during that period; we both were busy, and besides, I think she was too ashamed—or too angry—to spend time with anyone who knew her before the fall. I wanted to help, but her problems seemed way beyond my ability to solve. I didn't want to lose her, but I didn't know how to win her back.

She finally retuned to school and graduated, on her own. No one was invited to her commencement. I was in the PD's office by then, earning a regular, if meager, paycheck for the first time in my life. I had dated other women, had shared my lumpy bed with one or two, but my mind kept coming back to Liz: her furrowed brow, the clean soapy smell of her skin, the sexy way she ran her hand through her hair as she combed it. Perhaps the time we had spent more or less estranged from each other had increased my appreciation of her; before that the relationship had been too easy, too comfortable. Now that she was finished climbing her private mountain, I decided it was time to pursue her once again.

Liz proved surprisingly difficult to catch. I suppose I was stupid or naïve, but it took me years to figure out what the problem was—and still is. Her father had let her down, and she was determined not to let any other man disappoint her in the same way. If that meant doing without men, well, this was apparently an option. She didn't dump me, but she didn't let me past her guard either. For a while our relationship developed a strange and artificial tone. I somehow became the Irish reprobate trying to ensnare Liz, the virtuous—and rightly suspicious—maiden. The tone seemed artificial, at least to me, because I honestly didn't feel like much of a reprobate—certainly not when compared with my brother. I wasn't used to playing roles back then, and after a while I didn't like this one.

I had to convince her I was real. I had to convince her that *we* were real. I tried at Danny's wedding, I tried at candlelit dinners in fancy restaurants I couldn't afford. I worked at winning Liz the way I later worked at winning public office. Finally I tried in a supermarket. We were in the Stop & Shop one night; I pushed the cart for her while she studied her coupons. This seemed to me to be about as domestic as you could get; do reprobates take their girl friends to the supermarket? "We should get married," I said yet again.

"Trouble," she muttered. A coupon had expired.

"Why shouldn't we?"

"We're too different," she said. "We're opposites, in fact. I'm a Democrat; you're a Republican. I squeeze from the bottom; you squeeze anywhere you damn feel like. I think; you talk. How could we ever get along?"

"You're a woman; I'm a man," I said. "We're not talking about a dating service here; we're talking about love."

"We're not talking about love; we're talking about marriage," she responded. "I don't care where you squeeze if we don't share the same toothpaste."

"But don't you see, Liz? It's the differences that will make us strong, that will make our lives interesting. You wouldn't want to be stuck with someone who sat around and brooded all day, and I couldn't stand it if I lived with someone who talked as much as I do. We complement each other. We need each other. The whole is more than the sum of our parts."

Liz stopped in the middle of the health and beauty aids. Had she never considered this before? Had I produced an epiphany? Or did she simply give in, tired of the struggle? I don't know. I just know that she said yes and threw a huge bottle of store brand shampoo into the cart, and before I realized that she had accepted my proposal, she had already headed for the deli counter.

So we got married, and our new life, filled with old problems, began. I could have avoided a lot of the problems by staying out of politics. Liz wanted to protect her privacy, fearing that her father's scandal would emerge to shame her once again. She also wanted us to make lots of money, so that she could reclaim her lost childhood and never have to worry about tuition bills. But I was the one making the money; grammar school teachers don't get rich, and when Kathleen arrived, we no longer had even that meager source of income. And my ambition and inclination led me in exactly the wrong direction, from Liz's point of view. I didn't take the personal cost of my plunge into politics lightly. I knew it worried her, but I believed her worry was misplaced. "I'm not your father," I insisted, having finally figured out the connection. "I'm not going to let you down. Just wait and see."

Well, it's been more than ten years now. Our problems, like most people's problems, have never really been resolved. I can't live the way she wants, and she can't live the way I want. The differences between us have made our lives more interesting, but they haven't made our lives any easier. So what to do? I don't know. Have an affair. Go to graduate school and study pop psychology. Smile in front of our child, who understands the situation as well as we do. And occasionally make love to each other in the gray light of dawn, searching for the happiness that we still think must be somewhere just out of our reach.

I waited till I was back in Massachusetts again. The last free Friday night before the election. Kathleen was staying in, so I couldn't talk about it at home. "Your mother and I are going for a drive," I announced after supper. "Kathleen, you're in charge until we get back."

"Hot date?" she asked hopefully, but she saw her mother's puzzled look, and she knew this wasn't a date.

"Exactly right," I said. "Watch *Washington Week in Review* for me. Take notes."

She made a face. "I'll tape it," she said. "So where are you guys going—in case there's an emergency or something?"

"Good-bye, Kathleen," I said.

Liz got her jacket and silently followed me out of the house.

I drove to Nantasket, a seaside neighborhood a few miles down the road from Hingham. We didn't speak on the way. I parked near the beach, as far away as I could get from the teenagers hanging out along the seawall, smoking cigarettes and listening to their boom boxes. We got out of the car and sat on a bench facing the sea; the sun hadn't yet set, and the air was warm for a change. I looked at Liz, and she could have been twenty years younger; we could, in fact, have been on a hot date, getting ready to neck to the sound of the surf. "Remember when we used to take Kathleen walking along the beach here when she was little?" I said.

Liz nodded. "I remember that time she found a crab and thought it was *interesting*. She wanted to *study* it. That's when I knew I'd given birth to a stranger."

I laughed. "Sometimes I think it's a bad idea to live in the same area all your life. The memories crust over everything. You can't see things fresh. I remember my father used to take us here to Paragon Park once every summer, and Danny and I would stuff our faces with junk and then go on the roller coaster, and we'd spend the rest of the day trying not to throw up."

"Did your grandmother go, too?"

"Not on the roller coaster. But yeah, she'd come. She had no vices, but she loved cotton candy. Dad would buy us each one when we got here, and Gramma would snarf hers down faster than any of us. I can still see her walking along in that blue-check dress she always wore, with a parasol in one hand and this cloud of fuzzy pink goop in the other. Smiling as if life just couldn't get any better."

Liz smiled, too. She looked out at the ocean. A carload of kids raced by, shouting obscenities. She zipped up her jacket. Once the sun went down it would be too chilly to sit outside—unless we put our arms around each other and started necking, of course.

But I had other things on my mind. "Why did you go to see Amanda in her apartment a few weeks before she died?" I asked.

"She wanted to interview me for her book," Liz responded.

"Bullshit."

Liz looked at me. "You don't want to know the truth," she said calmly. "You just want things to go along. Have your wife and your mistress, have your home and your apartment, have the voters think you're wonderful. Why change anything?"

"Well, things *have* changed, haven't they? Whether I wanted them to or not."

"Poor Jimmy. Let it go. You'll win your election. No reason to worry."

"I've got every reason to worry. What was going on between you and Amanda?"

Liz shook her head. "I made a mistake. I thought she was an airhead, just a blonde with a tan and too many teeth. I thought she was beautiful enough to interest you without being bright enough to hold your interest. I thought maybe she was the right one to help you get it out of your system."

"What do you mean? Get what out of my system?"

"Oh, come on. I'm not as stupid as you think, and you're not as innocent as you sound. I spent enough time watching the two of you together, the way she looked at you, the way you joked with each other. And you were together down there in Washington every day. And of course, you'd have to work late; your job is so important, after all. And your wife doesn't understand you; that damn Liz has been nothing but a problem ever since you got into politics. *She* was the one I was worried about, not some bimbo reporter."

"Marge," I breathed, beginning to understand.

"Marge," Liz mimicked.

"Let me see if I have this straight," I said. "You thought Marge and I were having an affair, and so you—what?—set me up with Amanda to make me forget about Marge?"

She shook her head; her eyes were glistening. "Not an affair. I suppose I could live with an affair. But you and Marge—that was the real thing. You used to talk about how we were opposities and how that was good, it made us stronger as a couple. But you haven't thought that lately. You look at Marge, and you see your soul mate, someone who approves of what you are, of what you do. You look at me, and you see problems. You see judgments. Well, I am not going to be traded in for a newer model. I am not going to be pitied: 'Oh, yes, she's the ex, poor thing. Couldn't hold him. Bearing up awfully well, though, don't you think, for a middle-aged woman with no prospects?' Fuck that shit, Jim O'Connor."

The tears overflowed. I offered my handkerchief. She took it and turned away. I waited until she seemed calmer and then resumed the interrogation. "You figured I'd have an affair with Amanda and that would somehow cure me?" I asked.

She raised her hands in a despairing gesture. "I thought it was worth a try. I don't know. It was a spur-of-the-moment thing. The bitch asked me to put in a good word with you about an interview, and I was going to laugh, her little scheme was so transparent, and then I thought, Why not? Things can't get any worse. Maybe he'll have a fling with her, and Marge will find out and dump *him*. Or he'll get his hormones under control, cure his little crisis or whatever, and realize he doesn't want to spend the rest of his life with an airhead. So I said, 'Why, of course, Amanda, dear, I'd be happy to mention you to my husband. He's been dying to have an affair with a beautiful blonde.' God, how stupid can you get?"

Liz fell silent. "I never made love to Marge," I said.

She flashed me a don't-give-me-that look. I felt a rush of righteous indignation, recalling the effort it had taken to avoid having an affair with Marge. But it wasn't worthwhile pursuing the subject. I was hardly going to convince Liz of my purity and self-denial at this point. It was more important to stick to the main topic of discussion.

"So why did you go to see Amanda, Liz? Did you know we were having an affair?"

"Sure I did. No one had to tell me. I just knew. And then I realized how stupid I'd been. How could I be so sure you'd get over her easier than you'd get over Marge? And if I had to get dumped, I'd rather get dumped for Marge, who at least is right for you. You and Amanda wouldn't have lasted a year if you actually had to live together without the thrill of sneaking around behind people's backs, if she had to wash your underwear and you had to listen to her at breakfast. So I decided to go and have a little chat with her."

A boy and girl walked past, and Liz fell silent. They both wore leather jackets, and the boy's hand was pressed casually to the girl's backside, his thumb in a belt loop of her skintight jeans. The girl was talking animatedly. "So I says to my mother, 'I don't *have* no homework, they didn't *give* me no homework,' and she goes—" Her voice was drowned out by the surf.

"I felt like I was in a soap opera," Liz went on. "The betrayed wife visits the mistress in a vain attempt to win her husband back. What a joke. I was so nervous I thought I'd faint. She's oh-so-pleasant on the phone and invites me over to her sleek modern apartment, nothing out of place, decorator magazines on the glass coffee table, would you like some tea or perhaps a glass of white wine? And she's so sincere, she admits that yes, there was something between you, but that's all in the past, she hasn't seen you in over a month. And of course, I didn't believe her; I saw the way you moped around over the summer as if you could barely stand to be parted from her for a day. And then she starts talking about what a wonderful human being you are, how warm and witty, such a dedicated public servant. And I thought: Maybe they should start the canonization procedures early, while he's still alive. And I thought: He's cheating on his wife. Doesn't that make him something less than a saint? And I started to get angry. I didn't feel like being civilized and understanding. I felt like telling her the worst thing I knew about you. And so I did. I put down my tea and I smiled—not as nice a smile as hers, of course—and I told her about you and Jackie Scanlon."

Liz crossed her arms. The sun had gone down, and she was starting to shiver. I was feeling pretty cold myself. "Let's get back in the car," I said. We left the bench and returned to the Buick. I started the engine and turned on the heat.

I felt like Kathleen when she was younger and we finally gave her the answer to some puzzle she couldn't quite solve. "Why did you tell me?" she would whine. "I almost had it. Don't tell me next time, okay?"

But the answer to this puzzle just brought more puzzles, and I had no answers for the new ones. "How did you know about Jackie Scanlon?" I asked.

"That night Danny came over to beg for help—I was home, or don't you remember? You went into your office with him. You kept your voice down, but Danny didn't have enough sense to. I could figure out what was going on. You may think I'm just a dumb housewife, but I know more than you give me credit for. When nothing happened to Danny, and then later I read the stories about how they thought someone was tipping off Scanlon about the government investigations, I could put it all together.

"Of course, I didn't expect you to talk it over with me. Why should you? Obviously it's more important to save Danny's ass. It doesn't matter if you risk ruining the lives of your wife and daughter to do it. After all, look at everything Danny has done for you."

Liz stopped talking, and I tried to think of a response. I couldn't come up with one. She was right. I should have discussed it with her. But I couldn't bring myself to do it, couldn't stand the thought of the confrontation that would have resulted. Better just to do what had to be done and hope that I got away with it. And here was the result. "I'm sorry," I said. "What I did was wrong. You have every right to be angry at me. But Liz, telling Amanda doesn't just punish me; it could punish you and Kathleen, too. If the police find out that Amanda knew about Jackie Scanlon, I can guarantee that Cavanaugh will have me arrested for murder. It gives me the perfect motive. If you were fighting for your marriage, there must have been a better way of doing it."

"Well, I certainly didn't sit around plotting how to tell her," Liz responded. "It just happened. Besides, I'm not the one you should be blaming. If she really was in love with you, why was she planning to use that information?"

"Do you know that she was planning to use it?" I asked.

"Of course she was. I gave her the biggest story she was going to see in her life. She was more interested in the story than she was in you. *I'm* the one who stood by you, even when you betrayed me."

I had to get to the bottom of this. "Did she say anything to indicate that she was going to do something with what you told her?"

Liz looked at me in disbelief. "You still love her, don't you? You're still trying to believe she was innocent. Why did she tape those interviews they mentioned in the papers if she wasn't working on a story?"

"I don't know," I said. "I was just wondering what you know."

"I know you're a fool, for one thing. As soon as you become a successful lawyer, you throw away your law career so you can be a big man in politics. You risk throwing away your political career to help a no-good brother, and then you have an affair with a tarty reporter looking for an exposé. Not to mention what you risk losing in your wife and daughter. You're a fool, and you deserve to lose this election. And maybe that's not all you deserve to lose."

I decided that she didn't know anything, and it was futile to push her any further. All she wanted to do right now was hurt me, and she was too good at that. "Why, Liz?" I asked instead. "Why did you agree to stand by me after the murder if this is how you feel?"

She shrugged, and I could feel her retreating from the battle. "I don't know," she said wearily. "It just seemed easier to go along. Get it out of the way, think about it after the election. Let's go home, Jim. I've had enough of this."

Liz put her hand to her brow as if to keep her head from bursting. I looked out at the ocean. And for some reason I thought of President Kenton calling her Elizabeth. And how that had gotten me thinking I could beat him. Poor Liz. A senator's wife can stay out of politics. A presidential candidate's wife really can't. How could I dream of subjecting her to that?

Well, I had.

"Liz, did you mean what you said about me at that press conference?"

"What did I say?" she asked.

"That I was a good senator and a good man."

She was silent for a long while. "Did you kill her?" she asked finally.

"No," I replied. "I swear to you. And Amanda was telling the truth: It was over between us."

Liz didn't believe that any more than she believed that I hadn't slept with Marge. "But you just happened to still have the key to her apartment when you went there the night she was murdered," she pointed out. "You're a fool and a liar, Jim," she said. And then, after a pause: "But I guess you're not a killer. And I guess you do the best you can." She paused. "And so do I," she whispered. Then she turned away from me and stared out the window.

Not a ringing endorsement, but apparently it was the best I was going to get. I started the car, and we drove back home in silence.

CHAPTER 18

I awoke in the middle of the night convinced that Liz had murdered Amanda.

It was an eerie feeling, as if I had been visited in my sleep by one of Liz's astral presences. More likely my subconscious had simply worked through the ramifications of what I had learned from Liz earlier that evening. Now a lot of things I apparently hadn't wanted to think about were buzzing around my brain.

I looked at her, asleep beside me: the familiar blond hair splayed against the pillow; the familiar features—the small nose, the big ears that she hated and tried to keep hidden beneath her hair—the familiar, gentle rise and fall of her chest. How many times had we breathed since we met? I had known her half my life, more or less. But what did I know?

I remembered her silence, her lack of surprise when I told her about Amanda's death. She hadn't even asked me if I was the murderer. Granted, she had asked me in Nantasket a few hours ago, but that was different. The first reaction was the important one; everything afterward could be just pretense.

Had she not bothered asking me because she knew who the murderer was? Had she agreed to play the role of the supportive wife because that was the best way to protect herself? The reason Liz gave in Nantasket hadn't been especially convincing. It was

222

much more likely that she needed to keep people from believing that Amanda and I were having an affair because that would give her a stronger motive even than my own. The scorned wife, lusting for revenge. The tabloids would love it.

Did I really believe that Liz was capable of murder?

It hardly seemed possible. But she had just confessed that she told a reporter the most damaging thing she knew about me, and I wouldn't have believed she could do that. It was bizarre; it was self-defeating; it was irrational. But then, Liz had never been rationality's biggest fan. Hell, she was getting a doctorate in irrationality, as far as I could tell.

Words were one thing, though; stabbing a person to death was something else entirely.

But then I remembered the time she had asked for a gun after I became attorney general. "Do you honestly think you could shoot someone?" I asked her.

"If he was trying to break in here and harm Kathleen, I'd rip his heart out with my bare hands," she responded, with an intensity that was utterly convincing.

I shivered, imagining the two women together. A dark Friday afternoon. One more confrontation, Amanda would think. Was she worried, upset, bored? Was she thinking: Why do I deserve this? I'm not even seeing her husband anymore, and still I'm being harassed. She tries to persuade Liz: It's over. We were too different. We couldn't get past the roles we were playing.

But Liz doesn't believe her. She has come here ready to fight. She's fighting for more than her marriage; she's fighting for her *self*. She hates this woman. Amanda is the focus of all her frustrations with me, with our marriage, with her life.

Amanda, too, becomes angry. She doesn't have to put up with this.

The emotions finally explode. Liz comes after Amanda, who retreats to the kitchen. She picks up a knife. Liz wrests it from her. She attacks. Then, in a panic, she tries to make it look like a robbery, like the work of a psycho, like anything but a banal crime of passion committed by a jealous wife.

Oh, God.

I got out of bed and groped for my robe and slippers in the dark. It was a cold night, and Liz refuses to turn on the heat until we can see our breath indoors. I put on the robe and slippers and padded silently downstairs.

At the bottom of the stairs I stood for a moment, hand on the newel post, and wondered what to do next. Get a glass of milk? Go for a drive? Call Marge or Kevin or Roger? They'd be happy to hear from me, even at this hour, but I didn't feel like it. I went into my office; the light of the answering machine was blinking, as it usually was, notifying me of messages that were undoubtedly of vital national significance. I ignored it and sat down in the leather chair behind the desk.

The room is small and jammed with lawbooks that I never glance at anymore. Its one window looks out on the driveway. Kathleen used to wave to me as she and her mother pulled up from doing the shopping; it was my signal to come help with the bundles. Next to the window is my framed law degree, which I brought back from the practice after I was elected attorney general. The wallpaper was starting to peel beneath the window, I noticed. The sight made me terribly sad.

This was the first room we redecorated after we bought the house. I was starting out in private practice, and Liz wanted me to have a professional-looking office in which to do my work at home. Ah, that was a wonderful time! I don't think Liz has ever been happier: new baby, new house, lucrative new career for her husband. We were the perfect American family. Roger and I would become filthy rich, and everyone would live happily ever after.

Roger and Doris came over to inspect the room when it was finished, bringing champagne to toast our future success. Liz was still breast-feeding and only had a sip, but I can remember looking into her eyes as we clinked glasses and seeing more sparkle there than in the whole bottle.

And what had come of it all? We could not have been more successful. But now, I thought, Doris is dead. She was always a meek little creature, and when the doctors diagnosed her cancer, she seemed to accept her fate as her due, and then she shriveled up and finally disappeared, as if grateful to no longer be taking up space in this strange, harsh world. Now Roger sits home alone nights, drinking and getting fat, with nothing to keep his interest in life. And now Liz, if she isn't a murderer, is at least willing to destroy me, along with whatever it is that we have created together.

And Jim?

Abruptly I had an awful vision of myself, perhaps sent to me, once again, by one of Liz's mystical entities. I had spent my life restlessly pursuing one goal after another: get into Harvard; convince Liz to marry me; become a successful lawyer; win the election for attorney general, then U.S. senator; get reelected . . . and then? Perhaps none of these goals had meant anything to me. Perhaps I was just mindlessly trying to exorcise my childhood demons, over and over again. See, Dad, I'm a good boy; I was worth bringing into this world, even if Mom had to die. See, Danny, I can be as successful as you, even if you're older and more popular and better at sports I couldn't care less about anyway.

And that was why I was so eager to give up my law career, just when I was assured of success. Where was the challenge in that case? It couldn't be very hard if I was that good at it. In politics, at least, you are never assured of success; there is always another election, another chance to fail.

I thought again about Danny and about Liz's charge that he meant more to me than my wife and daughter. In a way she was probably right, if only because your childhood demons are so much stronger than any of the other demons in your life.

I found myself remembering a beautiful Saturday in fall when I was twelve. As usual I spent most of it in my room reading, but I finished my book and got bored. My bedroom was as jammed with books as my office is now; I read whatever I could get my hands on: science fiction, lives of the saints (to Gramma's delight and my father's chagrin), history, even adolescent sports novels. *Buzzer Basket. Triple-Threat Quarterback.* But that day was just too beautiful to stay indoors, and I decided to go for a ride on my bike.

I ended up in a park near where we lived. There was a touch football game going on; Danny was playing, and of course, he was the star. He was only average in size, but he was faster, trickier, and stronger than all the other kids; he seemed to be playing in another league altogether.

I watched for a while, not having anything better to do, and then the players were motioning to me. One of the kids had to go home; they needed me to take his place to keep the sides even. I shook my head. "I don't play," I said.

"Come on. What are you, a sissy?"

"I'm not a sissy. I just don't play."

Danny came over to me. "You're playing," he said.

I wanted to run away, but it was too late. I couldn't face down everyone; I had to play. I joined the huddle. Danny was on the other team. He grinned at me. I knew what was coming.

It took a few minutes. We were on offense, and I had nothing to do but make feeble attempts at blocking the pass rush. Then we punted, and Danny's team got the ball. Now I was supposed to defend against one of their wide receivers. I stayed on the opposite side of the field from Danny, who caught everything that was thrown to him. But after a few plays their wide receivers crisscrossed, and Danny was coming straight toward me. The ball came spinning through the clear blue sky from the quarterback. I stayed back and let Danny catch it; I didn't want him to get past me and score.

He started to run. I got ready to tag him. He slowed down in front of me. He feinted left and right. I tried to match his feints, tried to be as graceful and clever as he was. I reached out for him—and he wasn't there. I lost my balance and fell to the ground as Danny trotted in for the touchdown.

"Nice try," he muttered as he walked past me, but he was grinning once again, and my teammates looked at me with disgust.

I played for a while longer to keep from acting like a sore loser, and then I made up an excuse and left the game; no one bothered to stop me. I rode my bike home and went up to my safe, familiar bedroom. I tried starting another book, but the words blurred on the page. And then I was crying, hot, despairing childhood tears over the injustice of life and the impossibility of change. This was it. This was the way it would always be. Why had I ever been born?

I didn't cry again until I saw Amanda's corpse.

Well. That was long ago. I stood up. No sense getting maudlin. It's too tempting for an Irishman. Besides, it just wasn't fair. Sure, I had my childhood demons, but damn it, they didn't rule my life. Did they?

If I couldn't figure out the truth about myself, how could I figure out the truth about Liz?

I decided to get a glass of milk. I went into the kitchen and took the carton out of the refrigerator. As I did, I felt something on my ankles and looked down; Angelica was curling herself around my legs, acting more friendly to me than she had in months. "Aren't you supposed to be asleep?" I said. She started purring. "Milk isn't good for you, did you know that?" She didn't know that. I got a saucer and poured some milk into it. Angelica jumped up onto the counter, and I let her lap it up there, flouting one of Liz's sacred household rules. Then I decided, what the heck, and I flouted another, drinking directly from the carton. "Don't tell a soul," I whispered to Angelica. She didn't respond, but I knew I could count on her.

As I put the carton away, I noticed the calendar taped to the refrigerator door. On it was the household schedule: dentist appointments, Kathleen's gymnastics lessons, Liz's classes, my comings and goings. I looked at the schedule for the day Amanda was murdered. From two-thirty to five-thirty Liz had her course on mysticism over at Cabot. Kathleen had penciled in "Dad Back" underneath.

So Liz was in school when it happened. She had an alibi.

That was fine with me. I didn't want to be a jerk; I didn't want Liz to be a murderer. I leaned my head against the cool metal of the refrigerator door. For some reason I felt like crying again. Angelica whined for more milk. I gave her some, then carried her upstairs and set her gently down in Kathleen's room. She jumped onto the bed and settled in. I returned to my own bed and did the same.

When I woke up again, it was morning, and I realized that I would have to check out Liz's alibi before I could let the matter rest. But how?

Kevin picked me up in the campaign car, and we were off on a long day of campaigning. Kevin had no more news to report from his private eye. "Sharpe will come up with something, though," he promised as we drove from one event to the next. "Did you mention to Liz about how we have a witness that saw her at the victim's place?"

"Yeah. She was thrilled. Listen, Kevin, you remember driving Liz over to school after Amanda Taylor's funeral? She mentioned a course that she was taking—on the mystic tradition?"

"Sure."

"Her professor—what was his name?"

"Zacharias," Kevin replied promptly. It was part of his job to remember names.

"Right. Liz mentioned his name again this morning, but of course, I forgot it right away. The thing is, she said this guy knew how friendly she was with Amanda, and maybe we ought to talk to him."

"Great. I'll tell Sharpe to track him down."

"Well, I was thinking instead maybe I'd like to talk to him

myself. Liz is forever telling me about him. I want to take an interest in her studies, you know."

"No problem, Senator. I'll get his number for you."

"Thanks, Kevin."

The next stop, as luck would have it, was a Catholic youth convention, where I had to give a speech about "Family Values." It was boiler plate, which was a blessing, because I couldn't keep my mind on it. I cut it short after a few minutes and let the fine young nonvoting Catholics ask me questions. Most of the questions, as I expected, were powder puffs, but I finally got a zinger from a stocky, serious-looking girl who demanded to know if I had ever been unfaithful to my wife. Some people in the audience hissed. The poor girl turned red but stood her ground. She'd make a great nun, I thought, and my heart suddenly went out to her. No one would ever lust after her the way I had lusted after Amanda. "The short answer is no," I replied. "The long answer is: I really shouldn't answer you, because I don't think it's any of your business."

"But why isn't a candidate's character our business?" the girl persisted. "Lots of us wouldn't vote for someone we knew had committed adultery."

"Fair enough. But how does asking me the question help you decide? If I'm an adulterer, why couldn't I also be a liar? And if I honestly believe it's none of your business and I refuse to answer, then you think I'm ducking the question and you mistakenly decide I'm guilty. So I believe the public is better served if candidates simply aren't asked that kind of question. Judge us on our public records; that way you're much more likely to judge correctly."

The girl looked as if she wanted to defend herself, but the priest who was running things hustled her away from the microphone and gave someone else a chance. I didn't feel very good about my response; Harold certainly wouldn't have approved. Too abstract; too argumentative. That's what happened when I wasn't sufficiently tuned in to what I was doing. I tried harder for the remaining questions, but I didn't get any better.

Kevin was waiting backstage when I finished. "Got the number," he said as we headed off to our next stop. "The guy lives in Belmont—Bobby Finn territory."

"Belmont has many fine citizens, I'm sure," I said. Kevin grinned. "Thanks, Kevin."

He grinned some more. "Anytime."

I called the number from my car phone while Kevin was using the rest room at a gas station. A young girl answered. When I asked for her father, she dropped the receiver without a word and went off in search of him. "Hello?" a deep male voice answered finally.

"Is this Professor Zacharias?"

"Indeed it is." He had the kind of voice that could make a weather report sound profound. I pictured a middle-aged guy with a goatee, threadbare jacket and chinos, battered briefcase, abstracted air of brilliance. The students at Cabot were no doubt suitably impressed.

"Professor, this is Senator Jim O'Connor. Perhaps you've heard of me?"

Of course, he'd heard of me. "Yes, why, certainly. My goodness. What can I do for you, Senator?"

So how could I approach this? *Professor, can you help me clear my wife of murder?* "Professor, you probably know that my wife is taking your course on the mystic tradition at Cabot."

"She is?"

Let's not get too absentminded, Professor. "My wife, Liz," I said. "Elizabeth O'Connor. Blond, good-looking, early forties."

"One moment please, I have my class list here somewhere." Rattling of papers. "No, I thought not. There's no Elizabeth O'Connor registered. Are you quite sure you have the right course?"

I looked out the window at the gas pumps, the squeegee in the pail of water, the used car for sale. Automatic, AM/FM, Factory Air. Kevin was approaching from the rest room. It was starting to rain. "A history course," I said, "about Greek myths and such. Zeus. Athena. Right?"

Professor Zacharias chuckled. "No, no. Not the mythic tradition, the *mystic* tradition. St. Teresa of Ávila. Swedenborg. William Blake. That's my course. You must have misheard your wife."

I chuckled back. "Oh, how stupid of me. Of course. The mythic tradition. I'm so sorry to have disturbed you, Professor."

"Not at all. I'm not one of your supporters, but I do admire the forthrightness of your positions."

"Well, thank you very much. Perhaps I'll be able to change your mind by election day. Good-bye now."

I hung up. Kevin got back in the car. "Ready for the next one, Senator?" he said.

Liz wasn't taking the course. I smiled. "Ready."

She had lied to me, and she had no alibi. Worse, she had lied about her alibi. Kevin started up the car, and off we went in the rain.

My wife had lied about her alibi, and she had a motive, and for the life of me I didn't know if she was capable of committing murder.

So how was I supposed to campaign for the Senate with that on my mind?

CHAPTER 19

*T*he case against Liz seemed pretty strong until, for some reason, I decided to look at it as her defense attorney. Then it began to crumble.

Liz hated Amanda, hated being the scorned wife. Okay, granted, that's your motive, but there's plenty of hatred in this world, and most of the time it doesn't lead to murder. Surely telling Amanda about me and Jackie Scanlon was enough to satisfy her hatred.

Liz lied about taking the course. But how could that relate to Amanda's murder? Liz is an intelligent woman. If she were trying to construct an alibi for the murder, what did her phantom course accomplish? Nothing, because one phone call was enough to prove that she was lying. Less than nothing, in fact, because her lying casts suspicion so readily on her. If she's a liar, people may think, why not a murderer? So why lie so gratuitously?

Liz said she'd murder to protect her daughter. And she's a licensed gun owner. These random observations occurred to me, but I immediately dismissed them as irrelevant. Her desire to protect her daughter had nothing to do with murdering her husband's lover. And if she really was planning a murder, why not use the gun instead of brawling with Amanda in her kitchen?

And furthermore:

What about the man seen entering Amanda's apartment building? The case against Liz made him utterly extraneous.

Why was Amanda's apartment ransacked? Liz had no motive to do that.

What about the missing tape? No help there.

How could Liz stab Amanda to death? I suppose she had the physical capacity to do it—but not without sustaining some damage herself. I saw her hours after the murder, and I didn't remember any bruises, any scratches, anything at all to indicate that she had just been in a fight to the death with her archrival.

Having poked plenty of holes in the case against Liz, like any good defense attorney, I cast around for other suspects. Was the case against her any stronger than the case against them?

What about a nameless minion of the Democratic party, out to incriminate me?

Or, for that matter, Bobby Finn himself, who had certainly shown himself capable of murder.

Or an ex-con like Tom Donato with a grudge against me.

Or Harold White, the campaign manager who saw Amanda Taylor as a threat to his future and perhaps even to America's future. All right, he had an alibi, but he could have hired someone to do the dirty work for him.

Or Kevin Feeney, the loyal aide eager to protect his boss from the scheming adventuress who had ensnared him.

Or Brad what's-his-name, the evil reporter and would-be lover whom Amanda spurned.

Or Marge Terry, the virtuous, highly paid media coordinator who was as jealous of Amanda as Liz was. She at least had a bruise on her arm the night of the murder, a fact that I had somehow managed to forget until I found myself mentally trying to exculpate Liz.

Obviously there were suspects and doubts aplenty. With me as her lawyer, no jury in the world would convict Elizabeth O'Connor of Amanda Taylor's murder.

I was sure I could convince a jury, but I wasn't so sure I could convince myself. The heart ignores the niceties of reasonable doubt.

I sleepwalked through the rest of the day and finally realized that I needed to talk to Marge. I insisted on dropping Kevin off and then headed for her apartment in Cambridge. I thought about calling first but decided against it. Surprise might work in my favor.

I needed to know what her damn secret was. "Things are more complicated than you know," she had said. "More complicated than you can imagine." Did she know something about Liz that she didn't want to tell me, that had somehow eluded my feeble male awareness?

Or did she know something about herself that she wouldn't reveal? My mental defense of Liz had uncovered Marge as a suspect. Hadn't occurred to me before. But if I was willing to consider Liz, then why not Marge, whom I knew so much less well, but whose motive was equally strong? Where had *she* gone after our staff meeting that Friday afternoon when Amanda was murdered?

Marge rented the first floor of a two-family house near Central Square—real Cambridge, where the streets were lined with hardware stores and pizza parlors instead of the boutiques and cafés of Harvard Square, a mile down the road. It was a neighborhood where the houses were built inches apart, where elderly couples living under rent control tended tiny gardens, where grad students camped out in comfortable squalor, where yuppies like Marge braved urban life until they got married and had a kid or simply got tired of the crime and the noise and the lack of privacy and headed for places like Hingham. Legal parking places were nonexistent on her street, of course. I parked in a residents only space without feeling much guilt. This was campaign business, sort of, and the campaign would take care of any ticket.

There were lights on in her apartment. Her doorbell had been broken ever since she moved into the place, so I rapped on the glass of the door. A few moments later the lace curtain was drawn aside, and Marge stared out at me. She rolled her eyes and opened the door.

She was holding a baseball bat. "I was ready for you," she said, hefting it.

"I think I deserve at least a forty-four Magnum," I replied, stepping inside.

"You flatter yourself." She was wearing pajamas, a pink terry-cloth robe, and white athletic socks. She ran a hand through her hair; it wasn't nice of me to show up without giving her a chance to get dressed. "What's happening?" she asked.

"We have to talk."

She tilted her head a little, appraising me. "About what?"

"About what you know and I don't."

Her face hardened for a moment, and then she seemed to yield. "Give me a minute to, um, get decent," she said. "Pour yourself a drink if you want." She waved toward the living room, then headed down the hall.

I walked into the living room: white walls, gleaming hardwood floor, long sectional couch, large-screen TV, stereo speakers the size of Kathleen. Papers were scattered on the coffee table in front of the couch, along with a full ashtray, a half-full bottle of white wine, and an almost empty pack of Chesterfields. I glanced at her work. She was editing one of the position papers my Washington staff had written for me. I wondered how many people were spending their Saturday night helping to get me reelected. You become used to it; you start to think of it as natural, as your due. I brought the ashtray and the cigarettes into the messy kitchen, where I emptied the ashtray and tossed the cigarettes into an overflowing wastebasket. I found an almost clean glass, rinsed it out, went back to the living room, and poured myself some of the wine. Then I sat on the couch and waited for Marge.

She returned a few moments later, wearing a green cable-knit sweater and jeans. The sweater looked good on her. I could smell her perfume from across the room. "Do you ever read your position papers?" she asked, sitting at the far end of the couch.

"Religiously," I said.

"What's your stand on import quotas?"

"I'm very glad you asked me about that," I responded, "because I believe it's one of the most important issues facing America today." And then I gave her three perfect paragraphs about the balance of trade, international economics, and the competitiveness of American industry.

"You're good, there's no doubt about that," she said, shaking her head.

"You sound as if that pains you."

"Just envy, that's all."

"I don't feel particularly enviable at the moment," I said.

"Why not? Still miss Amanda?"

I leaned back into the pile of striped cushions. Marge was no more interested in being tactful than Liz was. "I have to find out who killed her," I said.

"Why? Why not let it go? As long as Cavanaugh doesn't try to nail you—"

"Cavanaugh *is* trying to nail me. He's been trying to nail me since you were in junior high. And besides, I—I need to know."

"Poor Jimmy." Marge came over and searched the coffee table for her cigarettes. She saw the empty ashtray and looked at me. "Asshole," she said.

"You didn't kill her by any chance, did you?"

She sat back down, a little closer now, and still looking at me. "You flatter yourself, Senator. Do you honestly think I'd murder Amanda Taylor out of jealousy?"

"Beats me. But I couldn't help noticing that bruise on your arm the night of the murder. As if you'd been in a struggle with someone."

Marge took a long time to respond. Then she left the room and returned a moment later with the baseball bat. I admit that made me a little nervous. "You think I keep a baseball bat next to my door because I live in a bad neighborhood?" she asked.

"I don't know, Marge."

She rolled it in her hands. "You know my ex-boyfriend Alan."

"The jerk."

She looked at the bat. "I guess you could say he's a little more than a jerk. It annoyed him that I've been spending a lot of time at work lately. Couldn't imagine why I'd have to put in some overtime during an election campaign—especially when I was seeing him. His needs came first. He's a man after all. We had a little discussion about it after the staff meeting that Friday. His idea of a discussion is to whack the woman around, try and slap some sense into her. Frankly, Jim, you're lucky I'm not in jail for murdering *him*, never mind Amanda."

Her mouth was pursed; she was trying to keep from crying. "I'm sorry, Marge," I said.

She shrugged. "I can take care of myself," she said. Then she got up abruptly and went into the kitchen.

I drank half the glass of wine, feeling like a heel. Poor Marge. She was tough, but not as tough as she wanted people to think she was.

Marge, like me, had more or less created herself. Her father owned a hardware store in upstate New York. Typical small-town chamber of commerce "I Like Ike" Republican. She should have become a teacher, married a lawyer, helped him run for town council. Or she should have rebelled, worn flat shoes and braided her hair and demonstrated against nuclear power. But she had turned her father's values into a philosophy and ultimately into a career. She had transformed herself into a slick professional woman and moved to the big city, where she could join the battle for America's soul. She enjoyed the battle. Most of all, she enjoyed winning.

Which meant, of course, that she didn't like losing to Amanda. But that was hardly reason to accuse her of murder.

And she certainly wasn't going to make up an alibi as painful as that one had to be.

She returned, puffing away at a cigarette. "After the election," she said. "I'm definitely giving them up after the election." She emptied the bottle of wine into her glass. "Now, where were we?" she asked with mock pleasantness.

"Well, I guess I was quizzing you about Amanda. Did she interview you?"

She shook her head. "We talked on the phone once. This was a couple of weeks before—"

"Right. What did you talk about?"

"She was perfectly nice in fact. I got the impression that she knew about you and me—not that there's anything much to know. You told her about us, I suppose. She said she didn't want to talk about that, just about you: what you were like, what made you tick, that sort of thing."

"What did you say?"

"Oh, I don't remember exactly. Something catty at any rate. Like: You seem to be doing a perfectly good job of finding out what makes him tick. You don't need my help."

"What did she say to that?"

"Not much." Marge drank some of her wine and stared at the glass. "Actually, she started to cry."

"Did she say why?"

"Well, you know, I didn't get into it, Jim. I just couldn't seem to work up much sympathy for her."

"We had broken up. Did you know that?"

Marge shook her head. "I suppose I might have dredged up a little sympathy if I had. Did you dump her?"

"Not really. It was that article you showed me. After a while it just made things too complicated for us. I think we were both lying a bit, and the lying caught up with us. Or maybe not. I don't know."

"You think she only got interested in writing about you once you'd split up?"

"Yeah, I guess so. But I'm not entirely sure she was going to write about me. Did she say anything to suggest that?"

"I don't recall. I mean, I sort of assumed it. Why else was she trying to interview me? But then she burst into tears. That caught me by surprise. Did you love her, Jim?"

"I don't know, and if you're going to ask me if I killed her, the answer is no."

We fell silent. Eventually Marge finished her wine and stubbed the cigarette out in the empty glass; I cringed. "You know," she said, "some women might find cause to be offended by all this," she said. "Jesus. Guy comes over unexpectedly late one night, finds this attractive young woman in her pajamas. Instead of bashing him with her baseball bat, which is what any self-respecting attractive young woman should do, she invites him in, offers him a glass of wine, puts on some perfume. And what does he do? He takes away her cigarettes, asks her if she's a murderer, and starts talking about his dead lover."

"I'm sorry, Marge," I said. "This is important. You didn't have anything more to do with her?"

"I tried to not even think about her, Counselor. Until Harold calls me up one night when all I want to do is get drunk and maybe kill a few men, and he tells me to get my butt over to his place, our beloved employer is in deep doo-doo and we have to find a way to get him out."

"Then what's the big secret you wouldn't tell me last week?"

Marge sighed. "I won't tell you the secret," she said, "but I will tell you the name of the person who owns the secret. And then you will leave, so I can resume enjoying the wanton pleasures of my Saturday night. All right?"

"Thanks," I said.

She stood up. "Go talk to your old buddy Roger Simmons," she said. "And leave me out of it."

Roger? "Why Roger?" I said.

Marge picked up her bat. "Good night, Jim."

She headed for the door, bat in hand. I followed. I was desperate to learn more, but I figured I had worn out my welcome. "Thanks, Marge," I said.

Her big green eyes stared at me for a moment, and she gave me a quick hug. "Good luck," she whispered, and then she opened the door and shoved me out of her apartment.

CHAPTER 20

Roger?

I tried to imagine Roger as a murderer. No good. Roger was just too damn nice. It was a problem he'd always had as a lawyer. I would take the cases that required a little meanness, where I'd have to go after a witness and maybe ruin a reputation. Roger was better at getting the jury's sympathy. People tend to underestimate him because he is so nice, and his pudgy face and slightly befuddled expression make them think he doesn't know what he's doing. In court he knows exactly what he is doing.

But even if Roger were a trained killer, what could his motive possibly be? The best I could come up with was jealousy. I was the one who had made a name for myself. I was the one whom beautiful women like Amanda wanted. Roger, meanwhile, lingered in the background. I had thought he'd simply lost interest in things after Doris died. But perhaps there was something festering in his soul, some resentment against my success, my home life, my sex life, against me.

Amanda calls and asks him for an interview. He goes to her apartment, meets her for the first time, is awed by her beauty. He realizes that I've been screwing her, just one more pleasure thrown into my already rich life, while he sits at home nights wifeless, childless, nothing to do but drink and contemplate the emptiness of his life. His resentment overflows, and he lashes out, destroying this perfect creature that he can never possess. . . .

No, not Roger.

I thought about giving him a call, but I didn't. I was tired. I had too much to think through. I would deal with it tomorrow.

The next morning I went into my office after breakfast. Instead of calling Roger, I called his secretary. Sally O'Malley is living proof of why some women should keep their maiden names after marriage. Actually I think she likes the rhyme; she's a sociable sort, and it gives her an easy opening for conversations with strangers. She had been with Roger since we started the firm, and she adores both of us. "Hi, Sally," I said. "It's Jim O'Connor."

"Oh, Senator. Oh, my. How are you? It's good you caught me. I was just on my way out the door to mass."

"I'm sorry, Sally. Don't let me keep you."

"No, no. There's plenty of time. How are you, Senator?"

"Just great. And how are things in the valley, Sally O'Malley?"

"Oh, stop." I could feel her blush over the phone. I had used that line on her a thousand times.

"Sally, the reason I called is, I wanted to ask you for a favor."

"Anything, Jim."

"It's about Roger."

"Yes?"

And how would the clever sleuth handle this one? "Well, I have this notation here about a contribution from a guy named Paul Despino. It says Roger talked to him—I think it says September twenty-fourth, P.M. The thing is, this guy Despino has ties to organized crime. Harold—you know my campaign manager, Harold White?—well, he gets pretty steamed about things like this. It's the sort of thing that Roger should have been aware of, and if he wasn't, he'll get in big trouble with Harold. Now I think the notation may be a mistake, and it wasn't Roger who talked to this guy. If I can find this out before Harold gets wind of it, I might be able to smooth things over. But I don't want to ask Roger because it could be kind of embarrassing. So I was wondering if you could take a look at his schedule for that afternoon, tell me who he saw and so forth, and get back to me."

I took a deep breath. Had that sounded totally ludicrous? "September twenty-fourth in the afternoon?" Sally said.

"That's right. A Friday, I think."

"Then I can't really help you, Jim. Roger wasn't in the office that afternoon."

"Are you sure?"

"Oh, he hasn't been working Friday afternoons for some time unless he has a trial. Didn't you know that? He said he was doing it because of those staff meetings over at your headquarters."

"Of course. That's right. How could I have forgotten? This notation must be a mistake then. I'm so relieved. Listen, Sally, I'm sorry to have bothered you. I could have figured this out on my own."

"Nonsense. You must have so much on your mind. It's wonderful of you to be thinking of Roger. Poor dear, he does get distracted now and then. You know, since Mrs. Simmons died. It's been hard on him. Anyway, good luck in the election, Senator. I'll be praying for you."

"I appreciate that. Now go to mass. And don't dally, Sally O'Malley."

"Oh, stop."

I hung up and stared at the peeling wallpaper. Roger always told us he was too busy to attend our Friday afternoon meetings. Too busy doing what?

I made it to my father's that evening. He had finished *Bleak House* and was in the middle of *Hard Times*. "You should read it, you hardhearted Republican," he said.

"I *have* read it," I replied. "And be nice to me. Even Republicans have feelings."

"A Republican is only happy when his boot is on a working-man's neck. I think I'll have another drink."

"I'll get it. Mind if I make a phone call?"

"Go ahead. Call your strikebreaking henchmen. I'm too old and feeble to stop you."

I grinned and picked up his glass. In the kitchen I set the glass down next to the bottle of bourbon and stared at the phone. I had been avoiding this all day. Roger lived in Newton, not far from my father. I had to talk to him. I didn't want to talk to him.

I called him up, hoping he wouldn't answer. He answered.

"Roger. Jim," I said.

"Jim, you got my message?" he replied.

No, I hadn't. "I've been with my father," I said. "What's up?"

"Jerry Tobin's off the case. Cavanaugh's going to handle it himself."

More good news. "I'm surprised he waited this long," I said.

"Well, Cavanaugh knew he and Finn would be better off if Tobin could get you on his own. But time's running out now, and your crime ads are having an effect. They need some results."

"Should we make a fuss?"

"See what Harold says, but I think we can stick with the usual line for now: You know, we welcome all efforts by the DA's office to solve the crime, we'll do everything in our power to help them, and so on and so forth. Cavanaugh will probably haul you in again, to remind people you're a suspect, and then we can start complaining."

"That sounds right. I bet Cavanaugh's just itching to get his hands on me."

"I'm afraid so. You ought to know that there've been some reporters nosing around."

"Brad Williams," I said, remembering the name. "I met him at the funeral. A real slimeball."

"There may be some bad publicity coming up, Jim."

"We'll just have to roll with the punches. Listen, I'd like to come over and talk if you're not busy."

"Not busy at all. I'd be delighted."

"Fine. I'll be right over."

I refilled my father's glass and brought it back to him. "Problems?" he asked.

"Always problems. 'Fraid I have to go."

My father rubbed his nose, a sure sign that he was trying to avoid getting emotional. "You are going to win this election, aren't you, Jimmy?"

"I don't know. We're ahead, but anything can happen."

"You'll destroy that guy in the debate."

"That's what everyone expects."

"Irv Goldfine next door sent you a contribution yesterday. He says he'd vote for anyone but Finn."

"Tell Irv Goldfine his support is heartwarming. See you, Dad."

My father raised his glass to me. "Good luck."

I drove to Newton, not knowing whom to worry about most: Cavanaugh, Liz, Roger, Brad Williams . . . The list was getting too long.

Newton is one of those suburbs where the rich people live

who don't want a long commute into the city. Urban life without urban worries. Brighton kids always despised the stuck-up Newton kids, but none of us with any brains would have turned down a chance to move there. Roger lived in a mock-tudor brick house on a pleasant little street glowing with the autumn colors of its maples and oaks.

Roger had let the place go since Doris died. The flower beds had turned into crabgrass; the driveway was mapped with cracks and fissures; the once carefully sculpted bushes were now scraggly and misshapen. I was surprised the neighbors hadn't sent a delegation to complain; perhaps they had, and he'd greeted them looking befuddled and apologetic, and they decided to leave the poor grieving widower alone.

Roger was at the door when I pulled into the driveway. He was wearing lime green pants and a white Izod sweater—the official leisure uniform of the professional class.

"Hey, Roger," I said, getting out of the car.

"Hey, Jim."

I followed him inside. The house was dim and musty, filled with unused furniture—like my father's house when he finally sold it, only Roger's furniture was much more expensive. "You should buy a condo," I said. "Get rid of all this stuff. Simplify your life."

"Oh, well, I just seem to be too busy."

Doing what?

He led me into the spacious living room, lined with bookshelves and dominated by a grand piano that no one played anymore, I remembered sitting there and listening to Doris, grim-faced, work her way through a Schubert waltz while Roger looked on proudly. Today some baroque string piece issued from the stereo. A jug of Chivas Regal, a silver ice bucket, and a couple of glasses were set out on a side table. "Are you drinking?" Roger asked.

I shook my head. "Had one at my father's." His face fell, and I immediately changed my mind. "Maybe a small one."

"Okay. Great. Just a small one."

I sat in a leather recliner. Roger poured a medium one for me and a somewhat larger one for himself. His hands shook a little, I noticed, as he used the ice tongs. "Cheers," I said, raising my glass.

"Cheers." He downed about half his drink. "We don't get a

chance to do this anymore," he said. "We had some good times in this room, though, in the old days. Didn't we?"

"Sure did. Just too busy nowadays."

He nodded. "Especially now. This business about Cavanaugh worries me, Jim. There's just no telling what's going to happen."

"People are unpredictable."

"That's certainly true."

I sipped my drink. We had never really had an argument, the two of us. Different personalities, different backgrounds, but somehow everything had meshed. He had been brokenhearted when I won that first election and left the firm. "I can't make it by myself, Jim," he had said. "You're the heart and soul of this place."

"You'll be fine," I had responded. "You'll blossom. You'll never look back."

I had wanted that to be true, to keep from feeling guilty. And it was true—or at least it seemed to be. He dropped the criminal stuff for the most part and concentrated on civil. He was great at arbitration and negotiation. He was great at keeping clients happy. His association with me didn't hurt him in drumming up business, although he was scrupulous about not trying to use his influence. It wouldn't have done him any good to try; I, too, was scrupulous, at least about that.

I didn't know how to bring up the subject of my visit, so I tried avoiding it at first. "Remember that day you and Doris came over to see my study after Liz and I finished papering it?" I said. "I was thinking about that just yesterday."

Roger smiled but I could tell he didn't remember. "Good times," he said. "Good times. And remember that surprise birthday party we had for Liz here? She thought it was just going to be another evening of boring legal shoptalk, and then everyone piled in from the kitchen and started hugging her. I don't think I've ever seen her so happy. There's nothing like a surprise party to make you feel wanted."

"Liz hasn't been looking very happy lately," I said.

Roger finished his drink and poured himself another.

It was time to stop reminiscing. "Roger, how come Sally O'Malley thinks you're taking Friday afternoons off to go to our strategy meetings, and we think the reason you don't come to the meetings is you're too busy at the office?"

The blood drained from his ruddy face. I thought he was

going to keel over in his chair. His hand started shaking so badly that an ice cube spilled from his drink as he set it down. He couldn't have looked more guilty if he were a bad actor on the witness stand at the end of a *Perry Mason* episode. "I, uh, that's really none of your business Jim, now is it?" he managed to blurt out finally.

"I don't know. Is it?"

"Of course not."

"As far as I can tell, that leaves you without an alibi for Amanda Taylor's murder. That's of some concern to me."

His guilt turned to puzzlement. "You think *I* murdered her?"

"I don't know. Did you?"

"That's absurd. It's outrageous. You're out of your mind. What a thing to suggest."

He picked up his drink and managed a sip. The string piece finished on the stereo, and an announcer began to drone. I knew it was absurd. But then I thought of something slightly less absurd.

I don't know why. No, that's not true; I do know why. It was the memory of Liz's face in that room as everyone yelled "Surprise!"—her face aglow with the delight of knowing she was loved, all barriers down for once before this sudden onslaught of affection.

It made no sense for her to lie about her course in order to have an alibi for murdering Amanda. But it made perfect sense if she had something else to do with her Friday afternoons, something that she wanted to keep secret from everyone, but especially me.

"Roger," I said, "never mind Amanda. Let's talk about Liz."

His lips quivered. His hand squeezed the glass. "You're just toying with me," he said belligerently. "How long have you known?"

I shook my head. "I don't know anything, Roger," I whispered. "I don't know anything."

He sighed and reached for the bottle of Chivas, then changed his mind. "No one wanted to hurt you, Jim," he said, his tone mournful. "These things happen."

He was going to be nice, I realized; he was going to be adult; he was trying to spare me. It made me furious. "Yes, I know, I know," I said, barely restraining my anger. "So why don't we assume we've uttered all the clichés and get to the facts?"

Roger nodded; he looked frightened. "Well, what do you want

to know? Dates? Friday afternoons mostly. Places? Here mostly. When did it start? This spring. Do I feel guilty about it? Yes, of course I do. But not very. You've treated Liz shamefully, Jim. You know what I'm talking about."

"She's using you to get back at me," I said.

That caused his anger to overcome his fear. "You would think that, wouldn't you?" he said. "But the world doesn't revolve around you, Senator—pardon the cliché. Isn't it at least possible that I can offer her something that you can't or won't: attention, affection, companionship, sympathy? Isn't it possible that she could fall in love with someone who isn't witty or handsome or a United States senator, but someone who loves her back, who thinks she's more than just a campaign prop?"

I remembered the day after the murder, the press conference outside our house. She hadn't wanted to go through with it. She wouldn't listen to me or Sam Fisher. But there was Roger—loyal Roger—to talk her into it. "Why hasn't she asked for a divorce then?" I said. "Why is she still making up phony courses and sneaking over here on Friday afternoons?"

"After the election," Roger said. "We were going to tell you then. We didn't want to jeopardize your career. And of course, it would have looked even worse after the murder. You know, it isn't just sex, Jim. That's probably not even the main thing. Sometimes we just sit here and talk. She's a very intelligent woman, and you've never given her a chance to demonstrate it. You don't listen to her opinions about the issues. And you do nothing but make fun of her graduate program."

"I do not. I keep my opinion to myself."

"And you think she's too stupid to know what your opinion is. Or you don't care if she knows; the whole thing is just not important enough to consider."

"What would Doris think?" I said, trying to hurt him. "In her own home."

"Doris is dead," Roger replied. "You're the one who's always trying to convince me to get on with my life. Well, that's what I'm doing. Doris is dead, and I'm alive, and Liz loves me. And that's the way it is."

I wanted to attack him some more; I wanted to defend myself. But everything I had to say seemed pointless and demeaning. My best friend was fucking my wife, and all my oratorical skill wasn't going to change that. Roger looked much better now, with the secret revealed: sitting up in his chair, arms crossed, color back. He had probably rehearsed this conversation a million times, and now he was getting through it quite well, thank you. So why shouldn't he look good? He had defeated me in the most primitive struggle of them all. He should have been swinging from vines and beating his chest in triumph.

So if I wasn't going to trade clichés with him, what should I do? I thought of Liz telling Amanda the worst thing she knew about me. What was the worst thing I knew about Liz? Damned if I could think of anything especially bad. She brooded. She was a cheapskate. She didn't put enough mayonnaise in the tuna. She understood me too well.

She was having an affair with Roger.

I certainly couldn't act self-righteous. *How dare she!* Perhaps I should have felt relieved, since this could erase some of my own guilt. Ours was just another modern marriage that had gone sour. No one to blame. People change. Let's shake hands and go on with our lives.

Perhaps I could do that eventually, but not now. Now there was just pain and rage and a numbed sense that my life was spinning totally out of control.

I couldn't think of anything to do, so I stood up. "Thanks for the drink, Roger," I said. "See you around."

Roger got to his feet, too. "Are you okay, Jim?"

He was triumphant; he could afford to be solicitous. "I'll live," I muttered. I headed out of the living room.

"Let's talk about this some more, Jim. I don't want you to—"

But I was out the door and racing toward my car. I had to leave that house. I had to leave Roger and his sympathy.

But I couldn't leave the pain.

I thought about going to stay with Marge, but I decided I was angry with her, too. She had known, and she hadn't told me. Was that her revenge for my affair with Amanda? Who else knew? Was I the laughing stock of the political world?

No matter what her reasons for not telling me, I figured Marge, too, would be full of sympathy if I showed up; she might even be expecting me to come. Where else would I go? Well, I wouldn't give her the satisfaction.

And then I thought: What if she doesn't want me on the

rebound? What if she doesn't want me at all? Maybe I didn't understand her any more than I understood Liz or Roger. Or Amanda.

It started to rain. I pulled the car over and closed my eyes. I felt safe and protected as the raindrops pounded the metal roof inches above my head. The phone rang; I ignored it. Wouldn't it be nice to just keep driving? I thought. Go to an ATM and clean out an account, then point the car toward an entrance ramp and disappear into the interstate highway system. Spend the night at some Motel 6 where the the proprietor never looks up from his *National Enquirer,* wouldn't recognize me if he did. Watch dirty movies on cable. Forget about the crime bill and Bobby Finn and tracking polls and murder investigations. End up in some anonymous midwestern state and become a farmhand, a short-order cook, a day laborer, get any damn job where I didn't have to be quick-witted and golden-tongued, where the whole world didn't seem to be depending on me.

I remembered dancing with Liz under that rotating globe at Danny's reception. Oh, Liz, we were such a couple. The world sparkled for us then like that globe. I remembered our own wedding reception—smaller than Danny's, because we had to pay for it ourselves and we were still poor, but big enough, because Liz insisted on doing things right. "Gotcha," I whispered to her as we danced our first married dance.

"I'm making the biggest mistake of my life," she whispered back, but her eyes were aglow, and she kissed my chin, and I knew that this couldn't be a mistake for either of us.

The rain let up. I was cold and tired and confused. My car suddenly seemed like a terrible place to be. I decided to go home.

Liz was in bed, awake. She knew. Roger must have called her. *Watch out, darling, he's in a state!* Perhaps her gun was hidden beneath the pillow, just in case. One glance at her lying there, and I knew she had passed already from the fear-of-my-reaction stage to the what-else-did-you-expect stage. Or, more likely, she had skipped all the early stages and gone directly to this one. I sat down on the Boston rocker next to the bed; Liz had nursed Kathleen in it a lifetime ago. It needed to be reglued.

"Do you love him?" I asked.

She gestured vaguely. "Roger is solid," she said. "He's reliable. He cares about me."

"You could be talking about a dog, not a lover."

That wasn't such a smart thing to say. Liz glared at me. "Roger is a wonderful man."

"Yes, I know. I'm sorry. I agree. Roger is wonderful. I owe him more than I can ever repay. But I'm not interested so much in Roger right now as in you. What you're thinking, what you're feeling. What you're going to do."

"Well, isn't that novel?" she said. "Senator O'Connor is interested in his wife."

This wasn't going well. I thought about my conversation with Liz the night Amanda died. I understood that conversation a lot better now. "Liz," I said. "I apologize again. Tell me what you want me to do. Tell me what you want me to say."

She shook her head. "You fool. If I tell you, it doesn't count, now does it? Oh, who cares anyway? I want you to tell me that you love me desperately, you hope it's not to late, you'll do anything to win me back. But you can't say it now because I've already said it for you; it'd just be an act, like everything else you do. How will it play with the voters? How will it play with the wife? You aren't real anymore. You stopped being real when you became a politician."

She turned away from me. I stifled the urge to defend myself, as I had stifled it when talking to Roger. Instead I got up, went around the bed, and laid my head on her lap. She was wearing one of my pajama tops; I could feel that her legs were bare beneath the covers. It was freezing in here, and she was still wearing the outfit I had once told her was sexy. Her chin was quivering. "Are you going to leave me?" I asked. "I don't want you to, if that matters."

"Of course, you don't want me to leave. What would that do to your popularity ratings? How would it affect the presidential primaries? Even Roger worries about that. After the election, after the election, as if it matters if America has one more hypocritical politician who's against crime and taxes and in favor of good wholesome family values."

"Liz," I said carefully, "I think you might give me credit for being a little more complex than that."

"Why should I? Who cares?"

"Are you going to marry Roger?"

She started to cry, her head still turned away from me. "Damn you. Of course I'm not going to marry him. Damn you."

"Why not?"

She choked back a sob. "Because I'm still in love with you," she said, an ache in her voice, as if her love for me were a disease from which she was desperately trying to recover.

I moved forward on the bed and tried to kiss her, but she pushed me violently away. "Go," she said. "Get away from me. Get out."

I thought about staying. Struggling against her struggles. Perhaps we would end up making love, as we had before. But I knew it wouldn't make any difference. If I didn't leave the room, Liz would. If things were to work out, it would take much more than a single moment of passion.

And perhaps they would never work out. Her love was almost indistinguishable from hatred at this point. And my love—was it just a habit? Or worse, an act, as Liz believed?

I didn't know. I retreated from our bedroom. I got a couple of blankets out of the linen cabinet and took them downstairs to the living-room couch. It would be nice, I thought as I lay on the couch, if I could get up early and keep Kathleen from seeing me here. And then I thought: What if *she* knew about good old Uncle Roger and her mother? She was no dope; she could pick up vibes that a stupid male like her father would be unaware of. Oh, Lord. What a picture of adult life she was getting. No wonder she didn't want to go on a date; it was a miracle she didn't run away from home.

I settled down on the couch, but I couldn't sleep, couldn't even close my eyes. There was a sudden movement, and Angelica was staring down at me from the top of the couch.

I took a deep breath. "Trying to give the old senator a heart attack there, huh, Angelica?"

She continued to regard me suspiciously. This wasn't right, and she knew it.

"Better get used to it," I said. "No telling when things'll get back to normal. Maybe never."

She meowed, then jumped down and padded off into the darkness. I lay back against the small pillow perched against the hard arm of the couch. My neck would ache in the morning, I knew. I tried to think about something constructive, but nothing came to mind. Instead I wallowed in thoughts of Roger and Liz. Their little love games. The stolen caresses in public when they hoped no one was looking. Roger's pity for me. Liz's grim revenge.

I thought about the old days. Had the spark always been there between them? I remembered one time when we were all a little drunk, walking across the Boston Common and looking at the Christmas lights on the trees. Liz slipping on the ice and Roger helping her to her feet. His arm around her, her look of gratitude. Doris standing meekly by, smiling at her husband's gallantry. Had he always longed for her? Had she always thought: What if . . . ?

I thought of Roger at Amanda's apartment the night of the murder and the way I had told him to take off his silly rain hat. How laughable that must have seemed to him when he had just come from cuckolding me that afternoon, when his senses were still suffused with the smell and taste and feel of my wife. Sure, he'd take off his hat. It was the least he could do for the poor guy.

And then I thought: The damn hat. The witness—what was her name? Kevin had told me, and I immediately forgot—didn't she say the man she saw going into the apartment building was wearing a hat? Yes, a white man, wearing a hat, carrying a black umbrella.

Could have been anyone. Could have been Roger. I thought of how nervous he had been when he showed up at the apartment. I had figured it was because he was uncomfortable doing criminal law after all these years. Could have been something entirely different.

Why not?

Well, why? Jealousy—my first stab at a motive for Roger—clearly wasn't right. He had no reason to be jealous of me. In fact, the opposite was true: He was better off with Amanda alive, if he thought, like Liz, that I was still seeing her. That kept me from paying attention to Liz and kept Liz angry at me.

But what if Liz had put him up to it? Clearly he was more enamored of her than she was of him. She sets him a test, and he is eager to pass it, no matter what the consequences. *If you really loved me, you'd murder that bitch my husband is screwing.*

No, too crude. What if it was rhetorical? *Who will free me from this turbulent priest?* Like the knights listening to King Henry, he mistakes a bitter question for a command from his liege. He cannot believe his good fortune in possessing Liz. He knows she still has feelings for me. He longs to prove his love for her, to prove that he is every bit the man her husband is. So after Liz leaves him that Friday afternoon, he goes immediately to Amanda's apart-

ment, while his blood is still hot. Perhaps he has a drink or two
first, to keep his courage up. Amanda doesn't know what to make
of his visit. She is a little afraid, but mostly she is amused. She
knows Roger Simmons only through my eyes, after all, so what is
there to worry about? But his courage stays with him, and he
strikes. Afterward, scarcely able to think, he bumblingly attempts
to make it look like a robbery, he leaves the message on the computer—a message to Liz, to his beloved.

And then, triumphant, does he tell Liz? Perhaps not. His
courage has deserted him by then, especially when he sees the
problems the murder causes for me. Liz suspects, but she is afraid
to ask. The murderer could be either her husband or her lover,
and she doesn't want to find out which.

I pulled the blankets more tightly around me in the cold living
room. Roger couldn't be a murderer. But then, I wouldn't have
thought he could be an adulterer either. Not with my wife at any
rate.

No more theories, I resolved suddenly. It was clear that I
didn't know anything about anyone, so what was the point of
speculating? *"Everyone is guilty,"* Cavanaugh had told me. Or perhaps no one is guilty. *"No one's an angel, and no one's a devil"*: That
was Jackie Scanlon's analysis. I was beginning to have reasonable
doubt about the entire universe.

I closed my eyes, and there was Amanda's corpse staring at
me. I turned and pressed my face into the rough fabric of the
couch, praying that I would go to sleep and stop thinking. Enough
was enough; I needed some peace.

But when I finally slept, there was still no peace. I dreamed
I was a bird, or perhaps a ghost, and I was watching myself watch
Roger screwing Liz, his flabby white body working away on top
of her while I stood by, helpless to stop them. I—the bird, the
ghost—plunged to earth to join my other self, to somehow rouse
me to action. Finally I moved, in the lead-limbed way of dreams,
and I reached out toward the beast with two backs. Liz turned
her love-glazed eyes to me as I approached, but it wasn't Liz, it
was Amanda, and her eyes were wide with terror, and I realized
that my hand held a knife. "No! No!" I shouted to myself, but it
was too late, the hand was already in motion through the heavy
air, the knife flashed in the darkness as it descended, and when
I looked again, oh, God, it was no longer Amanda but my mother,
and she screamed as she must have screamed giving birth to me,

and I screamed, too, as I realized what it was that I could not stop myself from doing.

And then through bleary eyes I saw something orange.

Kathleen was holding a glass of juice out toward me. "I think you were having a nightmare," she said.

I took the glass from her and struggled to a sitting position. It was morning. Kathleen was dressed for school. She had a "Senator O'Connor" bumper sticker on her book bag. "You should read the *Globe*," she said. "Finn is running a rotten ad about how you're weak on defense."

I couldn't work up any interest in Finn's ad. "Okay," I said. I gestured at the rumpled blankets. "Your mother and I had a— a—" I couldn't bring myself to describe what it was that we'd had.

Kathleen looked as if she'd had enough of this. "Are you two going to get a divorce or what?"

"I don't know," I said. "Things are—" I also couldn't bring myself to describe how things were.

"Things suck," Kathleen said.

I shuddered. She was right, but it hurt to hear her say it. "I'm sorry," I said.

For once she didn't object to my apology. She just looked at me, waiting for more.

"After the election," I said, begging for a reprieve. "Everything will get thrashed out after the election."

She shook her head, unappeased. "I've gotta go," she said.

"Me, too."

She reached out a hand. I took it, and she yanked. I was up. Ready, more or less, to face another day. "Thanks for the help," I said.

"Don't mention it. You look like you can use all the help you can get."

She was certainly right about that.

CHAPTER 21

*H*arold got hold of me in the car on the way to the airport. "You saw the ad," he said.

"Yes."

"You realize we could cut Finn's legs off if we produced Larry Spalding."

"What about his friend—what's his name, Sid? Have you found him yet?"

"No, but—"

"Find his friend, and then I'll consider going public."

Harold was silent for a moment, then changed the subject. "There's a reporter trying to get an interview," he said. "I think he's out to prove you had an affair with—"

"I know," I said. "Roger mentioned him. Stall him for a few days, okay? I don't feel like dealing with that right now."

"If he's got dirt, Jim, we're better off having it come out sooner rather than later. There's not much time left for damage control, you know."

"He won't have any dirt. He'll have inference and conjecture. I'm not worried about him."

"Then talk to him, for God's sake. Roger tells me Cavanaugh has taken over—"

"I know. That scares me more than this reporter."

"Cavanaugh and Finn are going to try something, Jim. I can feel it."

"I don't see what we can do to stop them."

"Larry Spalding," Harold said. "Larry Spalding."

I hung up. Not a good start to the week for either of us.

The day didn't get any better when I spotted Brad Williams lying in wait in the departure lounge at Logan. He approached me, smiling, hand extended, like an old friend or a life insurance salesman. He was wearing a double-breasted suit and shiny black loafers. His hair looked even greasier than before. "Senator, I thought I might run into you here."

I ignored his hand. "You would've gotten your interview," I said. "No need to ambush me."

He continued to smile. "You've got to understand, Senator, I'm under deadline pressure here. I'd hate to go to press without getting your comments. This is a very serious matter."

I sat down. Williams sat next to me. He produced a pocket tape recorder. "Who's going to print your story?" I asked. "*Hub* can't run it before the election. And what's the point afterward?"

"I'm free-lancing it for the *Real News.*"

The *Real News* is a weekly paper that aspires to be both respectable enough to attract advertisers and outrageous enough to appeal to counterculture types who scorn the dailies. It has always despised me. "Don't you think that might damage the credibility of your story?" I asked. "Most people would automatically suspect anything that paper printed about me."

"I think the facts will speak for themselves, Senator. Shall we begin?"

I wasn't thrilled to be doing this in an airport, but I figured I might as well get it out of the way. "Whenever you're ready," I said with an air of bland confidence.

Williams turned on the tape recorder and began the interview. And I began lying. He started with some straightforward questions about Amanda and our book interviews. Nothing that hadn't already been asked, nothing for which I didn't have a ready, if not entirely satisfactory, answer. He made a big deal about my having a key to Amanda's apartment. He made it clear that he didn't believe my explanation, but so what? He was out of the Mike Wallace school of tough-guy interviewers: "Are you seriously asking people to believe that you're no longer a drug-crazed wife beater?" Interviewers like that don't worry me nearly as much as the Barbara Walters oozing-sympathy kind, the ones who make you think that telling the world about how you beat your wife will somehow cleanse your spirit and make you a better person. The only thing you can do in either case is stick to your game plan and hope for the best.

After the preliminaries Williams brought up San Francisco quickly and unexpectedly: "Were you at a criminal justice conference in San Francisco in early April, Senator?"

No denying that. "Yes, I was."

"Did you meet Amanda Taylor while at that conference?"

So what was my game plan for this? I knew that I should have expected questions about it from somebody. If I said I had met her, then I was admitting to something that looked awfully suspicious. But it was easy enough to prove that we both were there, and it would strain credulity to suggest that we hadn't met—even if there were no witnesses. My general rule is to stick as close to the truth as possible, and that's what I decided to do now. "Yes," I replied. "It turned out that she was at the conference as well, so it seemed convenient to schedule an interview out there. I don't recall the circumstances offhand."

Williams couldn't hide the triumph in his expression. He hadn't had the proof, but now he didn't need it; I had confessed. "Don't you think it's strange Amanda Taylor would attend that conference?" he asked. "She never showed any interest in the topic before."

"I don't know about that. She wanted to write a book about me, and criminal justice is an issue I'm closely identified with."

"She paid her own way to the conference; she wasn't on assignment from the magazine," Williams pointed out. "And she didn't subsequently write about the conference for any other publication. Doesn't that suggest that attending the conference was just a pretext for meeting you?"

"Well, in the sense that she was trying to be as accommodating as she could to ensure my cooperation on the book, sure. Clearly the book she was writing about me meant a lot to her career, and my free time is quite limited. But that's all supposition on my part."

Williams smirked. "Are you asking people to believe that she followed you across the country to do an interview that she could as easily have done in her apartment, like all the others?"

"I'm telling you that she was a good reporter, and she saw this book as her big break. So it doesn't surprise me that she went to some lengths to make sure she got her material."

"And yet you were the one who was accommodating her by going to her apartment. And it was her annoying habit of being late for these supposed interviews that caused you to demand a key to her apartment. Doesn't that sound somewhat inconsistent, Senator?"

"But who says life is perfectly consistent? I tried to be accommodating to her when I could, and on a couple of occasions she wasn't as professional as I believe she should have been. That's the way things go."

"Were there any other instances when you met Amanda out of town?"

"Not that I can recall offhand." Did he know about her trips to Washington? If he did, let him bring them up. My flight was called, and I stood up immediately. "Have enough?"

Williams turned off the tape recorder and got to his feet. "Oh, I think so, Senator. Thanks. Can we go off the record?"

I shrugged. "If you make it quick."

He leaned close. I recalled his cologne from when we stood on the footsteps of the church after the funeral; it hadn't improved with age. "This article is going to be devastating to you, Senator," he murmured.

"If you say so."

"No doubt about it. I've got dates and places. I've got your own admission that you met her in San Francisco. I've got my own personal observations of Amanda. Senator, I think you might consider what it's worth to you to keep this article from appearing."

"You've got to be joking."

"We're talking about your political career, Senator. Not to mention a possible murder charge."

I glared at him. "Listen, you little prick, go ahead and print the article. Maybe you'll win the Pulitzer Prize and become rich and famous. Or maybe you'll end up an unemployed and unemployable muckraker with enemies in high places. Take your chance. But you're not going to blackmail me. Understand?"

Williams reddened and started to reply, but I didn't wait to hear what he had to say. Instead I strode off toward my plane, full of righteous indignation. Who was he to think I would submit to blackmail?

*   *   *

San Francisco. It had been a risk, but we couldn't resist. The affair had been going on for a few months; the initial excitement was waning, and the stolen evenings had begun to seem insufficient for the danger they entailed. This would be more dangerous, but it also gave us more time—time we could use to figure out what was real and what wasn't about our relationship. I had a keynote speech to give and a couple of panels to sit through. Other than that I was on my own. And I spent all my free time with Amanda: riding the cable cars, wandering through Golden Gate Park, feeding the pigeons in Union Square, taking the ferry across the bay to Sausalito.

And making love. Yes, Brad. Yes, Mike. Yes, Barbara. In her room, in my room. In the shower and on the bed and on the carpet next to the bed. Lying and sitting and standing up. We made love till our loins ached, till our mouths were sore, till our brains reeled.

The whole experience was suffused with guilt for me, but I couldn't seem to help myself. The risk just seemed to make it more exciting; the knowledge that it had to end just made me determined to enjoy it more.

Now, on the plane to Washington, it all seemed childish and irresponsible. If we had stuck to occasional trysts in her apartment, Williams wouldn't have had a story. But San Francisco would look bad even if no one had seen us holding hands on a cable car. So Williams had his scoop, and God only knew what Cavanaugh would do with it.

And I wondered: What was Liz up to while I was having my fun? She probably knew perfectly well what the trip to San Francisco was all about. Perhaps that was when she started her affair with Roger. He calls, looking for me, and she answers, lonely and bitter. She invites herself over to his place for a drink. He is confused, frightened, excited. She arrives, and one drink leads to another. They reminisce about the good old days. They talk about their loneliness. She leans against him. He gives her a fraternal hug. She looks up at him . . .

I closed my eyes. It was all too plausible.

I would have to talk to Harold about the article and how to deal with it. But not now, not now.

*   *   *

In Washington Congress lurched toward adjournment, and the crime bill finally made it to the floor of the Senate. Art Chandler remained doubtful about the chances of my amendment passing. "If you've got Hutchins, maybe," he said.

"I think Hutchins will be okay," I replied.

"Did you get a commitment?"

"Well, not in so many words."

"Then you haven't got anything."

Still, I was confident. Denny Myers had grudgingly redrafted the amendment so that it cost less, and that meant fewer Republicans could complain. And even with President Kenton opposed to it, some Democrats might go against him in order to look tough on crime just before an election. He couldn't afford to veto the bill, even with my amendment attached. So I thought I could come up with a slim majority.

The bill's floor manager, Glenn Courtney, was scared that last-minute amendments would derail the whole thing. He was right to be scared. Anything can happen in the last days of a session. Some liberal senators might manage to get an amendment restricting the sale of handguns passed, for example, and all the senators who were wholly owned subsidiaries of the NRA would then feel obliged to filibuster the entire bill to death. But Courtney recognized that my amendment was serious and not especially threatening, so he agreed to let it be considered early in the process, before there was a chance that the bill would be moved for a final vote.

I went over to Carl Hutchins in the cloakroom beforehand. "How's it going, Carl?" I asked.

He shrugged. "I'm down by ten. That congressman just has too many teeth. How about yourself?"

"Up six, but it's still volatile—lots of undecideds. I wish I could get the hell out of here and press some more flesh back home."

Hutchins nodded, but he didn't look as if he shared my desire. He much preferred the cloakroom, the private Senate dining room, his hideaway office with the majestic view.

"Carl, I need to know if you're with me on this prison aid amendment. It's coming up in a few minutes."

He looked at the floor, and I knew I had a problem. "The congressman is in favor of your amendment," he said.

"So what? You don't have to disagree about everything. Bobby Finn and I have the same position on something, I forget what it is."

"Well, we're going the tax-and-spend route against him. So my people say I should line up on the opposite side on all these big spending bills."

"But Christ, this is spare change. Fifty million or so. We spend more than that designing the men's room in the new bomber."

Hutchins looked up. His eyes were bloodshot, I noticed. "Will it make a difference?" he asked.

"I'll lose without you, Carl."

"To America, Jim. Will it make a difference to America?"

The arguments in favor of the plan popped smartly into the foreground of my consciousness, clean and well dressed and ready to do their job. But suddenly I couldn't bring myself to utter them. Suddenly I was confused. How did I know what was good for America if I couldn't figure out that my wife was having an affair with my best friend, couldn't figure out whether my lover really loved me or was planning to destroy me for a scoop? Everything had seemed so clear to me once; every*one* had seemed so predictable. What had gone wrong? Or, perhaps, what had been wrong before that was now painfully righting itself?

"I don't know," I said to Senator Hutchins. "But maybe it's worth a shot."

"Maybe," he agreed, but he didn't seem convinced.

And then it was time to offer my amendment.

I got to make a speech. Speeches rarely change votes. They're mostly for the *Congressional Record,* for the TV camera, for the gallery. But occasionally a thoughtful senator will listen and be persuaded—or he'll decide that you don't know what you're talking about. So it pays to do a good job.

It's better if you can speak extemporaneously, but that was no problem for me on this issue. I knew the facts. I had my arguments and the rebuttals to my opponents' arguments. I didn't need a speech writer.

But I needed passion. And on the Senate floor that day I couldn't find any. *One more hypocritical politician who's against crime and taxes and in favor of good wholesome family values.* That's what the person who knew me best thought of me. And who was I to disagree with her? This amendment might help me get reelected, but I had no more idea than Carl Hutchins if it would help America. And did I care? Oh, it would be nice if it reduced the crime rate and put people to work and improved our way of life. But that all seemed so unreal as to be almost not worth thinking about. Whereas this election and the presidential primaries after that . . . they seemed very real to me.

My speech was bland and dry. No one stopped to listen, as people sometimes did, impressed by my eloquence; business went on as usual in the aisles as votes got traded and deals made. I noticed that Hutchins wasn't on the floor. No chance of persuading him. And then I understood: He couldn't vote with me, but he wouldn't vote against me. He just wouldn't vote.

That might salve his conscience, but it also doomed my amendment. After I was finished, a few other senators had their say. Larmore and Dayton, the guys whose votes the President had offered to deliver to me, spoke against the amendment. And then the roll was called. It was over in a couple of minutes. I lost by five votes. And then the next amendment was offered, and the business of the Senate continued.

I went over to Denny Myers and Art Chandler, who were standing in the back of the chamber. Art was okay; he'd been around long enough to take these things in stride. But Denny was new, and this had been his idea, and it was dead, at least for this year. He was trying to look professionally blasé, but I knew he was hurting. "Small consolation," I said to him, "but you did a good job. We just couldn't pull it off."

"Where was Hutchins?" Art asked.

"Hutchins took a walk. He's fighting for his life back home, and this figured in. That's the way it goes."

"We'll do better next session," Denny said, trying to be upbeat.

"That's right." I glanced at Art, and I knew what he was thinking: Let's hope there is a next session for us. I went back to vote on the next amendment.

I found Hutchins later in his hideaway office, staring out at the Washington Monument. His tie was loose, and he had a glass of whiskey in his hand. He motioned to the bottle, and I poured myself a small drink. "Alcohol is boring, but it's predictable," he said. "It does the job."

"If the voters knew how much drinking goes on in this town, they'd never reelect any of us." I sat down next to him.

"I never drank much when Emma was alive," he went on.

"Never minded the pressure. I'd just talk everything over with her when I got home, and then we'd go to sleep holding on to each other, and that was better than any amount of liquor."

"My marriage seems to be going to hell," I said after a while.

He glanced at me. "A lot of that goes on down here, too," he remarked.

"How did yours become so strong?"

"I've often wondered that, and the only answer I've come up with is that I was the luckiest man alive."

There were tears in his eyes. I suddenly felt like crying myself. Carl's luck had passed, as everyone's must, and mine—well, perhaps I had kicked mine away. Now the session was ending, and the stretch run of our campaigns was about to begin. And what were the odds that the two of us would sit in this spectacular room together again? "I can make an appearance for you," I said, "if you think it'll help."

He shook his head. "Stay home," he said. "Take care of yourself. Take care of your wife. I've got some tricks left. I'll pull it out. And if I don't, the world won't come to an end."

And then I realized: It wasn't that Hutchins was afraid of losing; his problem was that he was afraid of winning. He was tired of it all and didn't want to admit it. Emma wouldn't have approved. "We need you," I said.

"No one is irreplaceable, Jim. Anyway, I'm sorry about that amendment."

I shrugged. "What amendment?"

And then we sat in silence for a long time, sipping our drinks in the darkness, taking one final break before our final battles.

CHAPTER 22

So You Think You Know Jim O'Connor!

Take this simple quiz and find out about the *real* Jim O'Connor.

How many major defense bills has O'Connor voted for in the past three years?

How many pieces of legislation authored by O'Connor have become law?

How many meetings of the important Governmental Regulations Subcommittee—of which O'Connor is a member—did he attend in the past session of Congress?

How is O'Connor rated by the prestigious National Foundation for Women's Issues?

How much federal aid has O'Connor obtained for the commonwealth's financially strapped cities and towns?

If you answered 0 to all these questions, then you know the real Jim O'Connor. A guy who talks a good game but fails to deliver. Who has consistently opposed efforts to maintain America's military strength. Who has shown a callous disregard for the needs and rights of women.

The real Jim O'Connor has been hiding out in Washington for six years, hoping we wouldn't notice. On Election Day, tell Jim O'Connor you weren't fooled. Enough is enough.

Robert Finn.
Because the Times Demand a Tough Leader.

"What do you think?" Sam Fisher asked as we examined Finn's latest print ad.

"I think they could have found a worse photograph of me," I said. "One where my finger is inserted all the way up my nostril."

"Yeah," Marge agreed. "And your little finger would've been more effective than your index finger. These guys are just not on the ball."

"Still," Harold said, "the prestigious National Foundation for Misleading Political Advertising gives the ad a ninety. Marge, you'll have to hold a press conference to heap scorn on this reprehensible piece of demagoguery."

"Right."

"Now, Jim, what about this piece that's coming up in the *Real News?*"

"Well," I said, "there'll be a problem with that. The piece will say that Amanda and I were in San Francisco together at a convention over the Easter recess."

Sam groaned. "Can we deny it?"

"Sorry, no. I admitted it to the reporter."

He groaned a bit louder and ran a hand through a mass of frizzy hair.

"It was all perfectly innocent. She was chasing after me to get material for her book."

Marge and Harold stared at the table.

"I was beginning to hope this would go away," Sam said, ignoring my protest.

"It won't go away," I said. "Even without this article the Democrats were bound to try something before the election. They can't just let the case drift along. We've made too big a deal of the crime issue."

"But what's the motive?" Kevin demanded. "I mean, I thought

their theory was that she was going to print something nasty about the senator, and he killed her to stop it. Sounds like this article will suggest they used to be lovers. They can't have it both ways."

"Why not?" Marge asked. "What if Jim thought he and Amanda were lovers, and then he found out she was really just using him so she could write nasty stuff about him? Or they were lovers and had a falling-out, and then she starts with the nasty stuff. That sounds like a pretty good motive to me."

Me, too, unfortunately. "Well, I don't know what to do about it," I said. "Maybe see if we can come up with something on this reporter. He strikes me as being pretty sleazy."

Sam paced. "Thank goodness the story isn't coming out till after the debate," he said.

"But it'll blow away any good publicity we get from winning it," Harold pointed out.

"Probably won't be all that much good publicity anyway," Marge said. "Everyone expects Jim to win."

"It'd be nice if we could get *some* good publicity for a change," Sam muttered.

Marge was glaring at me. I'd had enough. "Let me know what you come up with," I said. "I have to study up for the debate." And I left the glum meeting.

There comes a time when it gets to you: the endless pressure, the sniping from the press, the attacks from the other side. You think you're immune, you're all pros and can handle it, but one day all the news is bad and the coffee is cold and the doughnuts are stale and you start wondering why you're doing this to yourself. We had reached that point in the campaign.

Only for me it was much worse.

The session was over. The crime bill ran out of time and died in conference, so all my work on the amendment would have been wasted anyway. I threw out the half-empty cartons of Chinese food and headed home from Washington—possibly for good. In Hingham I was still sleeping on the couch. Liz and I were civil, and we stayed out of each other's way. Kathleen didn't come out of her room much; her computer was probably better company than either of us.

Now that the session was history, I figured there was nothing to stop Cavanaugh from arresting me. President Kenton couldn't hope to squeeze anything out of me, and it was far too late for the GOP to come up with another candidate. But still nothing happened, and that only increased my tension.

Paul Everson didn't return my phone calls, and eventually I stopped trying to reach him. Kevin had nothing to report from his private eye. "We're going to try some new approaches," he said. "Don't worry." I worried. The countdown to the election was measured in days now, not weeks, my lead was scarcely beyond the statistical margin of error, and whether or not Cavanaugh had come across the Jackie Scanlon angle to the case, I just knew he was going to pull something before the first Tuesday in November.

It was the afternoon of the debate, however, when things *really* started going downhill.

I was driving back to Boston with Kevin. I was looking forward to a few hours in the office by myself, to glance through the briefing papers one last time and prepare myself mentally for my performance. We had already gone over my talking points, the catch phrases that I was supposed to fit in every chance I could get. Marge had written Lincolnesque openings and closings for me, and I had them down pat. Sam Fisher had videotaped my delivery and dissected it gesture by gesture. Everything had been done that could be done. But now I just wanted to be alone for a while to get focused.

Melissa called on the car phone. When I heard her voice, I assumed that Danny was up to something. She wouldn't bother me unless it was serious. Just like him, I thought. "What did he do now?" I asked.

"No, no, it's not Danny," she replied. "It's your father. He had an accident, Jim."

He's dead, I thought. But no, he couldn't be dead. He hadn't finished rereading Dickens; he was only up to *Hard Times*. Or was it *Little Dorrit*? "What's the matter?" I managed to say.

"He's all right, Jim. Really he is. He smashed up his car. He broke his arm, and he's got some cuts, but he's okay. Except he's pretty upset. We thought it'd be a good idea—"

"What hospital is he at—the Faulkner?"

"Uh-huh. He said not to bother you, but you know him. I wouldn't have called, but—"

"I'll be there in—twenty minutes?" I looked to Kevin for confirmation; he nodded. "Twenty minutes, Lissa. You were right to call."

"Thank you, Jim."

I hung up. Kevin headed for the hospital.

Liz was there, along with Kathleen. And Danny, looking tired and sullen. So why was it Melissa who had made the call? Was she the only one who felt like talking to me? They were all sitting in the lobby, as if waiting for me to make things happen. "He threw us out," Melissa explained.

"He must be all right then," I said. "What room is he in?"

Melissa smiled. "Four-twelve. He'll throw you out, too."

"Let him try." I took the elevator up to the fourth floor. One of the advantages of my position is that even doctors leap to attention when I arrive. The guy who had treated my father was an earnest-looking young resident with thick tortoiseshell glasses. He was explaining Dad's condition to me within a minute of my appearance on the floor. My father would live, although his left arm would probably never be the same. More worrisome was what had caused the accident. He couldn't remember anything about it. One moment he was driving along Center Street on his way to do some errands; the next he was parked partway inside a bank, with several frightened customers and employees gaping at him.

"Alzheimer's?" I asked. "A stroke?"

"Too soon to tell," the doctor replied, in typical doctor fashion. "We'd like to run some tests. It could be nothing more than old age: Your reflexes slow down, you mistake the accelerator for the brake. It happens."

"Well, he's a menace, no matter what caused it."

The doctor nodded. "I think he realizes that, even if he won't admit it."

"Can I see him?"

"It should be okay. Don't get him too excited, though."

I went into the room. He was in the bed by the window. Nearer the door was another old man watching a *Hogan's Heroes* rerun. The old man seemed to think it was hilarious, and every time he laughed he went into a spasm of coughing. He didn't glance at me as I walked past. My father was staring out the window.

He's going to die, I thought. Not necessarily from the accident. I was simply pondering his mortality. I was so used to denying it when he brought up the subject that now I felt as if I'd had an insight. He's going to die, I thought, and I never really knew him.

Or perhaps I did. Perhaps what I knew was all there was to know. A simple, quiet man who worked at the Post Office for forty years, then retired and did what he really wanted to do: sit by himself and read books all day. He wasn't interested in his job; I can't remember him ever talking about it. He gardened grudgingly, as if it were a homeowner's responsibility to have a few tomato plants. He was hopeless at all but the most basic home repairs. He liked to talk about politics, but never seemed especially passionate about the subject; he never worked for a candidate or a party. He drank a little but never went to bars, never got noticeably drunk. He seemed content.

Was he? I always assumed that my mother's death had taken something out of him, crushed his ambition, made him turn away from other people. But perhaps he was like that anyway; perhaps the loss of his wife hadn't really changed him at all, and it was only my own ambition or guilt or imagination that made me think he must once have been different.

The hardest people to understand are the ones you've known the longest.

"I hate hospitals," he said when he noticed me standing there.

"Then quit driving into banks, unless you're inside an M-1 tank or something. Are you in any pain?"

My father ignored the question. "The doctor's a jerk," he said. "And he can't be more than eighteen."

"Well, he needs the practice then." I went over and sat down next to him. He had a bandage over one eye. His left arm was in a cast. He looked terribly vulnerable away from the familiar surroundings of his apartment. This is it for him, I thought. The end of his independence. And that is the beginning of the end of everything. The question was how to handle it. The patient in the next bed hacked as the laugh track roared.

"You shouldn't be here," my father said. "You've got that debate tonight."

"I can outdebate Bobby Finn in a coma," I said. "Don't worry about me."

"Well, don't you worry about me. It was the car, I'm pretty sure. I never liked that power steering. Too loose. You can't control the thing."

"Look," I said, "I could beat around the bush, but what's the point? You don't have to decide right away, but I want you to think about moving in with us."

"Ha! That'll be the day."

"Just consider it, okay?"

"You and Liz have enough problems without an old divil like me kicking around."

"Me and Liz? Problems? Nonsense."

"Your house is too small. Where would you put me?"

"I was thinking of sticking you out in the toolshed, next to the lawn mower. Look, we can deal with this, okay? I have an office on the first floor that I don't use much anymore. Or we can put up an addition. Or, what the heck, we can move into the White House. You can share a room with Lincoln's ghost. How would that be?"

"I like where I am."

"Yeah, well, life goes on, right?"

"That's very profound. You should save that up for the debate."

I laughed. "I'm glad I'm not debating you."

My father didn't laugh back. And then he started to reminisce—a sure sign that things were serious. "I remember when your gramma moved in," he said. "Neither of us wanted it, but what could we do? I had two of you in diapers, and the Post Office sure didn't pay me enough so's I could afford a maid. It was awful. Here I'd been, expecting a nice life with my wife and two beautiful babies, and suddenly she's dead and I'm stuck with my mother-in-law instead."

"You always seemed to get along with Gramma," I said. "More or less."

"Oh, by the time you fellows were old enough to notice we'd pretty much figured out how to make it work. But you know, I don't think she ever liked me."

"That's hard to believe."

He nodded solemnly. "It's true." His gaze drifted out the window again. "She never wanted Kathleen to marry me. Thought I was a dreamer, always with my nose in a book. Didn't think I could be bothered supporting a family. She couldn't figure out a way to blame me for Kathleen dying, but I bet she felt that if her daughter'd married someone else, she'd still be alive."

"Then Gramma wouldn't have had the pleasure of raising Danny and me," I pointed out. I couldn't remember the last time my father had referred to my mother as "Kathleen."

My father looked back at me. "Yes, and what a thrill that was," he said. "Funny, we always thought you were the one who took after me—the dreamer, you know. I guess we got that wrong. Anyway, I know what it's like to have an old person come to live with you, and it's no fun."

"We're not talking fun here, any more than you were talking fun forty years ago. We're talking survival." My father closed his eyes momentarily, and I figured I'd badgered him enough for one day. I stood up. "Just keep it in mind," I said. "And don't worry. You've got friends in high places."

"Do you think I should rent the TV to watch you tonight?" he asked.

"No, no. What does it cost—two, three dollars? That's way too much money to see your son demolish the governor of the commonwealth. Maybe your buddy here will be watching."

My father rolled his eyes as the old man in the next bed gasped for breath. I leaned over and kissed my father on the forehead, next to his bandage. He let me, but then, he didn't have much choice. *The Beverly Hillbillies* was starting as I left the room.

When I returned to the lobby, Danny, too, was reminiscing; this was a much more normal state of affairs. He started up whenever he was around Kathleen, trying to impress her, I figured. "Oh, those were great times," he was saying as I approached. "Great times." He looked up at me. "I was just telling Kathleen about how we used to sneak onto the Beacon Street trolley and go downtown to watch the Red Sox play."

"You're not suggesting that I broke the law as a youth, are you?"

"Aw, come off it, Jim. We got into our share of trouble back then. Admit it."

He was inventing a past for us. Partners in crime. Take the senator down a peg. As far as I could remember, he had forced me to sneak onto the trolley once to go to the ball park with him, and that was it. I had hated doing it, and I had hated the baseball game. Didn't matter now. "Well, anyway, the patient is not happy, but he'll live," I said. "And now Danny and I want to take a walk and have a little chat."

Danny winced. What did he think I was going to do to him? He followed me out of the lobby into the cold late-afternoon air. "You don't mind me talking about the old days, do you, Jimmy?" Danny said. "Time like this, you can't help but think back."

I knew what he meant. "I don't mind," I said.

"You know who I was thinking of the other day?" he went on. "Old lady Billings. Remember she had that little poodle, and we used to throw snowballs at it and it'd go nuts? What was that poodle's name?"

I shook my head. I had never thrown snowballs at Poochie. Danny hadn't shaved very well, I noticed. His eyes were bloodshot; his raincoat—the one Liz had given to Melissa—was rumpled. "How's work?" I asked.

"Work's fine. Just fine. And you? How's the campaign?"

"Fine."

"The, uh, you know, the murder. What's going on with that?"

"Beats me. I take it the police haven't talked to you yet?"

He looked down at the ground. "A guy named Mackey came by a few days ago. I was gonna tell you, but . . ."

I suppressed a groan. "What happened?"

"Well, it really wasn't much; it seemed sort of routine. He didn't ask me about—you know, anything dangerous. He said you mentioned that she'd interviewed me. Why'd you do that, Jim?"

"I was trying to find out if he had a tape of the interview. He didn't ask you anything that suggested he did?"

Danny shook his head emphatically. "Honest to God, Jim. It was like he was fishing, seeing if I knew anything that could help him."

"And what did you say?"

"Nothing, Jim. Honest. I just said, you know, I talked to her about growing up with you, what a great guy you are, stuff like that."

"You think he believed you?"

"Why not?"

I tried to imagine Danny up against Mackey. Not a fair fight. It had been a mistake to tell Mack about him. Still, if Mackey didn't know what he was looking for, maybe it was all right. Maybe it *was* just routine, and he'd chalk up Danny's nervousness to a hustler's natural fear of the police. But why didn't he know what he was looking for?

"All right, Danny," I said. "I guess that's good news." And then I tried to focus on my real purpose for the conversation. "Look," I said, "Dad's going to need help when he goes home. He can't drive, and he doesn't want to be a burden, but he has to be able to get around or he'll go nuts. So you have to help out.

I've asked him to come live with Liz and me, but it'll take awhile to talk him into it, and obviously I've got a lot going on right now. So meantime, we've just gotta make do. Okay?"

"Of course. Jesus, Jim, what do you think—you're the only one who's responsible around here? You're the only one who cares about him? Shit, Lissa and I spend more time with him than you do anyway, even if it's a big deal when you show up. He's already asked me to take care of the bills and the insurance stuff and so forth, and I said fine. Don't worry."

"Okay, okay. I'm sorry. I just don't want him to feel helpless, that's all."

Danny smiled and patted me on the back. "I'll take care of it."

It pleased him to be able to do something that I couldn't; why deny him the pleasure? "I appreciate it, Danny," I said.

He left his hand on my back. The family in crisis. We draw together. Forget about Mackey and Scanlon; forget about blackmail and murder. "We were okay growing up, you and me," he said. "Weren't we?"

Were we? We had certainly gone our own ways. And he had certainly heaped his share of scorn on my bookishness. But overall I realized that I didn't have much to complain about. The envy I had felt was my problem, not his. "For an older brother, you didn't beat me up very much," I offered.

Danny laughed. "I wasn't older, not really. We're twins, remember? Irish twins."

"You have to admit we weren't very close, though. It's not as if we snuck on the trolley together every day."

"You don't have to hang around together all the time to be close," Danny said.

He was getting maudlin over Dad, I figured. We were both having intimations of mortality. "Look," I said. "Why don't you come to the debate tonight? It's just over in Cambridge. It might be fun."

I could feel him stiffen. His hand fell away from my back. "Oh, no, I don't think so," he said. "You don't want me there."

"Why not? As long as you promise not to tell the reporters about me throwing snowballs at defenseless poodles."

"No, I don't think so," he repeated. "A debate's not—it's not the sort of thing—"

"All right, Danny," I said. "Just a suggestion. Let's go back inside."

Danny looked relieved. "Sure, Jim. I'm glad we had this chat." "Me, too."

When we were back in the lobby, Kevin glanced meaningfully at his watch. I nodded. "Well, it's time for me to go win this election," I said. "Liz, Kathleen, I'll see you there?"

Kathleen had a special dispensation to attend a political event. Liz was going as well, probably because Roger had asked her to. "Good luck, Daddy," Kathleen said. She hugged me.

"Thanks, kitten."

She stuck her tongue out at me. I pecked Melissa on the cheek. "Thanks for calling me," I said to her. She looked as though she were taking this worse than anyone else. She bit her lip as if holding back tears and said nothing. Kevin waved at everyone, and we headed quickly out to the car.

Kevin had already started the engine when I heard the rapping on my window. Melissa was standing outside, panting from the exertion of running after us. Alarmed, I lowered the window. "Did something happen?" I asked.

She shook her head, gasping for breath. "Danny's in the men's room. He'll kill me if he finds out I—" She paused to compose herself. "He got fired, Jim," she said finally. "Excessive absenteeism. I told you how he's been sick. Anyway, he just wasn't doing his job, so finally they let him go. I know I shouldn't bother you with it, especially on top of everything else, but—"

I put my hand on top of hers. "This isn't a bother, Lissa. Of course you should have told me. How's he taking it?"

"I don't know, it's sort of scary. He didn't even tell me for a week or so. He went off like usual in the morning, and then he just drove down to the beach or someplace and stayed there until it was time to come home. When I found out, I expected him to carry on, you know, blame the company, blame me, blame you. But he didn't. He just doesn't want to talk about it. And of course, he doesn't want to talk about getting a new job, no, we're not allowed to bring up that subject until he's got through brooding about the old one, and God knows when that'll be. I don't know, Jim, sometimes I get so angry with him I think I'll—"

I squeezed her hand. "I know the feeling, Lissa. How are you fixed for money?"

"Oh, he got some severance pay. We're all right for a few weeks, I guess, and then there's the unemployment, although—"

"Can you hold out until after the election?"

She nodded. "I think so."

"Well, if there's a problem, be sure to let me know. Otherwise we'll put our heads together after the election and see if we can find something for him."

"Jim, I swear I'll make him straighten out. Give up the booze, start exercising again, take care of himself so he doesn't get sick all the time. He's just got to do it."

Best of luck to you and the Red Sox, I thought. "You're a good woman, Lissa," I said.

She shook her head. "I'm stupid, Jim. Stupid and stuck, and I don't know what to do about anything."

"Me neither, but I'll try to help."

Melissa leaned over and kissed my hand, and then she ran back toward the hospital.

I raised the window, fell back in my seat, and closed my eyes. Kevin put the car in gear and headed out of the parking lot. "Are all families like this, Kevin?" I asked.

"Pretty much," he replied. "Mine is bigger, so it's worse."

I sighed. "I'm sorry to hear that. So who's this guy I'm debating tonight?"

"Try to relax, Senator. We've got awhile. Clear your mind. You'll be fine."

"Christ, I hope so." But I knew that clearing my mind wasn't going to be easy. Danny out of work, my father hurt and frightened. What next? Breast cancer for Melissa? Kathleen knocked up by a dweeb?

And I thought suddenly: What if Danny murdered Amanda?

I had sworn off theories, but this one seemed worth considering. He was physically capable of stabbing Amanda to death, and when he was drunk he could get angry enough to do almost anything. But what was his motive? To get the tape of the interview back? If anything, he had seemed rather pleased by the problems the tape was causing me. It wasn't as if *he* were going to get into trouble over it; the government would be wasting its time if it tried to prosecute Danny for his gunrunning. The case was just too stale; the witnesses were far away or dead, the evidence no longer existed; all the prosecution would have was his confession to a reporter, which he could easily recant. He might have been embarrrassed by the revelation of the way he had to come crawling to his brother to get out of the jam caused by his gullibility, but I didn't think so. He might even be pleased that people knew about his dealings with the underworld. His stature in the eyes of his drinking buddies would undoubtedly be raised.

And if he had killed Amanda to get the tape, why mention its possible existence to me and risk looking stupid, risk having me explode at him?

And then I remembered that Danny had an alibi as well. Melissa had told me he was home sick that day, and she had been forced to take care of him. And surely Melissa was too angry at him to lie in order to protect him.

Well, good. One less problem to worry about. But there were plenty without it. And no time left to think about them. The most important event of the campaign was just ahead, and I had to get ready for it.

The brain trust was waiting for me at campaign headquarters. Kevin and I arrived there half an hour later.

CHAPTER 23

Sam Fisher paced along one end of the conference room. "Maybe you can use this as a human-interest story," he suggested. "You know, they ask you about health care, the elderly, so on, work in about how you just came from visiting your aged father in the hospital, you saw what wonderful care he was being given, and your reforms to the medical system would provide every senior citizen with the opportunity for the same kind of care."

I rolled my eyes. "I'll keep it in mind," I said.

"You've got to stay personal," Sam warned. "You have a tendency to come across as a know-it-all. People can't digest strings of statistics in a debate; they like anecdotes."

"Welfare mothers using food stamps to buy heroin," I said. "OSHA inspectors shutting down pro football 'cause it's dangerous to the employees."

"And don't be a wiseass. You can be witty, but don't get nasty, and don't go over people's heads."

"And above all, be myself," I said.

"Well, that goes without saying," Sam replied, and I wasn't sure he got the joke.

"Perhaps we could go over the main points one last time," Harold said.

The debate, we figured, would be the campaign in a micro-

cosm. Each candidate had his themes; they'd been tested on countless focus groups and honed to a fine edge by master political
craftsmen. They didn't have a great deal to do with policies and
issues, which made some op-ed types gnash their teeth, but they
weren't entirely devoid of content. We both stretched the truth
in support of our themes, but they were close enough to reality
(they had to be) that people wouldn't notice or care if we fibbed
a bit.

Bobby Finn's main theme was that he was in touch with the
people of Massachusetts. Their concerns were his concerns. He
was the guy you could go have a beer with and talk about your
sewer bill, your car insurance rates, your kid's drug problem. He
wasn't the handsomest or wittiest politician around, but he understood how to make government work for the average citizen.

The corollary of this was that Jim O'Connor was out of touch
with people. Out of touch philosophically, since many of my positions were not shared by the majority of voters. And out of touch
as a senator, hobnobbing with the rich and famous and planning
my run for the presidency instead of taking care of the voters'
business. Bobby Finn wanted to be senator so he could serve the
people, not so he could gratify his own ego.

Our main theme, on the other hand, was that I was the candidate who had the stature to be the United States senator from
the commonwealth of Massachusetts. I had the leadership skills;
I had the experience; I had the intelligence; I had that extra
something that made me a worthy representative of the Bay State
in the world's greatest deliberative body. You might not always
agree with Jim O'Connor, but don't you feel proud that he's your
senator?

Our negative theme, therefore, was that Bobby Finn was just
not "senatorial." He hadn't done a good job as governor, and he
wouldn't do a better job as a senator. You might go out for a beer
with him, but can you imagine him debating the great issues of
the day on the floor of the Senate?

Our debate would be a contest to see who would do the better
job of getting across his themes. I would stress my accomplish-
ments and try to project my senatorial image—without sounding
too intellectual—while portraying Finn as just another local politician who was in over his head. Finn would try to come across
as the friend of the workingman—without sounding too inarti-
culate—while portraying me as distant, uncaring, interested only

in my own career. And the one who had the edge might see a spurt in his tracking polls, and that spurt, if properly nurtured, might be enough to win the race.

I listened to all the advice as Harold led the last-minute strategy session, but I didn't pay much attention. Harold, of course, noticed. He cornered me in the men's room afterward. "You're not here," he said.

"I'm on my way," I responded.

"Would you please make sure you show up? I mean, I'm sorry about your father, I'm sorry about your marriage, but this is important. This is crucial."

He knew about my marriage then; Marge had probably told him that she had given away the secret about Liz and Roger. "Doing my best, Harold," I murmured. "Honest."

He gazed at me, helpless. A campaign manager can take care of a lot of things, but he can't step out in front of the TV cameras for his candidate and debate the opposition. We flushed in unison and washed our hands, and it was time to go.

The debate was held at the John F. Kennedy Institute of Government at Harvard University. More or less neutral territory, since I was a Harvard grad and Finn claimed to be a JFK Democrat. My entourage pulled up at a side entrance, and we made our way to the auditorium. A burly Cambridge cop was guarding the stairway to the stage. He beamed when he saw me. "Hey, Jim, good luck tonight!" he said as we approached.

"Thanks very much," I replied with an automatic smile.

"I'll never forget you writin' those book reports for me in high school. Sure saved my ass."

I stopped and looked at his name tag. *Doherty.* "Billy?" I said.

He grinned. "Been a long time, huh, Jim?"

"Sure has." Since that gray dawn when you punched Paul Everson in the face and might have killed him with your nightstick if I hadn't kindled some spark of human feeling in your soul. Do you remember, Billy? Or have you conveniently forgotten—like Danny, rewriting the past to make it fit what he needs to survive the present? "Gee, it's good to see you, Billy," I said. "You're looking great."

"Ah, I've put on the weight. Too many beers. But we're all rootin' for you, Jim. You're doin' a great job."

I shook his hand. "I appreciate it, Billy. We had some good times in the old days, didn't we?"

"Sure did."

"Senator," Kevin murmured.

"Gotta go, Billy. Give my regards to the family."

I went onstage, to cheers from my half of the audience. Bobby Finn was there already, along with his wife. They were talking to the moderator, an anchor emeritus at one of the Boston TV stations, which trotted him out for important occasions like this. Gobs of makeup and a toupee made him presentable on camera, but in person they couldn't disguise the passage of time; he seemed tired and bored, as if he had attended one too many of these things in his career. Mrs. Finn looked cool and handsome in a navy blue silk dress and pearls. She also looked psyched up for the big event; I was glad I was debating her husband instead of her.

Finn's forehead was already beaded with sweat, and his palm was moist when he came over and shook hands with me. He made no secret of his dislike of debates. "Don't worry, Senator," he said with a tense smile, "I'm gonna go easy on you tonight."

"No, no, gimme your best shots," I replied. "We don't want people upset because they gave up reruns of *The Cosby Show* to watch us."

Finn shook his head. "Okay, you asked for it."

I looked around for Liz. She was already in the audience; Kathleen waved to me, and I waved back. Liz didn't want to come up onstage, and I didn't blame her.

So we killed time chatting with the moderator and the panelists, who were going to ask the penetrating, provocative questions to which we would respond. We went over the ground rules. We tried to control our nerves. It felt like a prizefight; it felt like a trial. The difference was that there was rarely a clear-cut winner in a debate. Finn would win if he did better than people expected; I would win if I came up with better sound bites or if he said something outrageously stupid. The polls might show something, but most likely the message would be mixed. And the battle would continue until election day.

The director started giving orders. The audience quieted. I went over behind my lectern, where Kevin had arranged my notes. Everyone waited. Then the red light over the camera came on, and the debate began.

*   *   *

I gave the first opening statement. "Six years ago you elected me to the United States Senate. It was the greatest honor of my life. Not a day has gone by since then that I haven't reflected on the responsibilities that go along with that honor. Not a day has gone by that I haven't tried to live up to the trust you have placed in me . . ."

I could tell immediately that I wasn't right. I had hoped that my personal problems would take an hour off while I did my job; they had generally cooperated in the past. But instead I felt the way I had on the Senate floor when making my futile speech in favor of my amendment. The words were all there, but the passion was missing. I couldn't focus on what I was saying. Instead I saw my father in his hospital bed, or Liz in Roger's arms, or Amanda dead on her kitchen floor. I wondered if Melissa and Danny would survive their latest crisis; I wondered if I would share Liz's bed again; I wondered how much all this was hurting Kathleen. I tried to banish such thoughts, but apparently I was no longer in control.

Would the voters notice? Would the pundits and the spin doctors? Perhaps not. I was a professional, after all, and my opening, no matter how absentminded, was still smoother than Finn's; Bobby stumbled a couple of times and looked as if he'd rather have been single-handedly battling the entire North Vietnamese Army. And this was the easy part for him: just say what he wanted to say, without having to respond to some tricky question. So maybe I would be all right, at least by comparison.

The first question was about crime. Doesn't matter what the specifics were; reporters spend hours crafting their questions trying to trip us up, and then we go ahead and answer the unasked question we feel like answering. Finn overpraised his own record and belittled mine. For all my tough talk, what had I accomplished as a senator? He brought up the failed amendment. All talk, no action; that was Jim O'Connor. I gave my standard response, ticking off all that I had done and all that Finn had failed to do. Too many facts, Sam would say. Well, did he want me to bring up Amanda?

The next reporter brought her up for me. Did I think her death and my relationship with her should be a factor voters should consider in deciding whether or not to vote for me?

We had figured out how to handle this one. "Her tragic death is an issue," I said. "But so is every other murder in this state." And then I simply ignored Amanda and laid into Finn again.

Finn gave a careful response, which indicated to me that his people still didn't know how to handle the situation. The matter was under investigation, it would be inappropriate to comment on the case until the investigation was complete, blah, blah, blah. If Cavanaugh had something on me, wouldn't Finn at least have dropped a hint?

And so it went. Neither of us was particularly effective, I thought. Finn made a moderately controversial statement about taxing Social Security, but I failed to follow up on it. He garbled his syntax, but I tossed off too many statistics.

And then came the easiest question of them all. "Could you each recount for us one incident from your early life that helped form the person you are today?"

Finn went first. As usual he didn't answer the question; instead he talked about how important his family had been to him. Good old middle-class Democratic family values. Big deal. While he blithered, I thought. My standard response to this sort of question was to talk about the time my grandmother had been mugged, beaten up by a couple of punks for about seven dollars in cash. She lived for a few years after that, but she never left the house again, except to go to a nursing home to wither away and die. The punks were never caught.

But I didn't feel like talking about Gramma. God love her, I had gotten enough mileage out of her suffering. What then? Just one-up Bobby Finn on families? Mine was more working-class than yours, so there! I could bring in my poor dead mother and probably my injured father—Sam Fisher would be pleased—but I didn't feel like doing that either.

What about the time Danny scored the touchdown off me and made me cry? Not very senatorial, unfortunately. But I wasn't feeling especially senatorial. I was feeling . . . strange.

Something was happening inside me as I stood at my lectern and listened to Bobby Finn—some shifting of my internal continents, some rearrangement of my constellations. It had started when I talked to Carl Hutchins in the cloakroom and realized that I didn't know if my amendment was worth passing, or perhaps it had started even before that, when I found out about Roger and Liz, or when I saw Amanda's body on her kitchen floor.

I don't know when it started. I only know that at that moment

I felt reckless; I felt reborn. I felt as if true wisdom were within my grasp if only I could recognize it.

Finn had stumbled to a finish. "Senator O'Connor," the embalmed moderator intoned.

I opened my mouth, and I swear I had no idea what was going to come out.

"One morning in April 1969 I was present when the police evicted a group of demonstrators from University Hall in Harvard Yard," I heard myself say. "This was at the height of the antiwar movement, when campuses across the country were in turmoil. The police cleared out the hall without much trouble, and then some of them proceeded to riot in Harvard Yard, indiscriminately bludgeoning helpless onlookers. I saw fellow students, male and female, with blood streaming down their faces. I saw a boy being dragged from his wheelchair and beaten with a nightstick. I saw the fierce, unreasoning eyes of the police as they attacked these kids who despised them."

So what did that teach you, Senator? How did that form the person you are today? It had better be something good, or you've just thrown away the election. "It would have been easy enough," I went on, "to become a left-wing radical as a result of that experience, to mindlessly despise all authority, to see everyone in uniform as the enemy. That's what happened to many of my classmates. But I think that eventually I learned some deeper lessons. First, that all authority must be tempered with restraint. It must not simply please the majority; it must be absolutely fair to the minority, or else authority will become tyranny. Second, that you must give the people in authority the tools and the training and the support to do their job effectively; otherwise you risk having them lose control the way the police did that morning. And finally I learned the importance of tolerating diversity, of seeing someone else's point of view. I was a student, but I was also a local boy; those cops were my neighbors. So I was pulled in two different directions. But in life I've found that you can be pulled in many more directions than that. You choose the path that you think is right, but you always have to keep in mind that there are other paths, and other people who firmly believe that those paths are correct."

I stopped. Had that been ninety seconds or ninety minutes? I felt as if the whole world were staring at me with its mouth open; Bobby Finn certainly was. Was that Jim O'Connor, *the* Jim O'Connor, talking about a "police riot"? About them beating up a kid in a wheelchair, for God's sake? Had my explanation of the lessons I had learned saved my skin or just dug me in deeper? And had I really learned those lessons, or was that just the politician in me talking?

The next question arrived, and I answered it on automatic pilot. Everything else was an anticlimax now. The TV stations had their sound bite; the columnists had their angle. And I had one more problem to add to my list. Before long I was making my closing remarks, and then Bobby and I were shaking hands as the moderator declared the debate history.

"You kinda surprised me there, talking about the police," Finn said.

"I'm full of surprises."

"You don't think you shot yourself in the foot?"

"Just wait and see, Bobby. Just wait and see."

Then it was time to greet the family, who were obliged to come onstage as the closing credits rolled. "I thought you were great, Daddy," Kathleen said, giving me a hug.

"I've been better," I said.

Liz was looking at me oddly. "You never talked about that incident in Harvard Yard before," she said.

"Saving it up for the right moment."

"It was very moving," Kathleen said.

"See? I've clinched the fourteen-year-old vote."

On the way offstage I saw Billy Doherty staring at me. We didn't speak.

Sam Fisher kept on pacing. "They don't know what to make of it," he said, referring to the pundits. "Some of 'em think it's a cynical ploy to get the liberal vote. Most of 'em think you're off your rocker, although they're afraid to say so."

"It reminded me of one of those Saturday morning cartoons," Marge said. "You know, where the stupid lumberjack saws off the limb he's sitting on?"

"I think it'll go over well," Kevin said. "It'll make the senator appear more human, less—less . . ."

"Arrogant?" I suggested. "Cocksure? Condescending? Isn't that what you wanted, Sam?"

Sam threw up his hands. "I wasn't suggesting that you spit in the face of your core constituency."

"Just what were you thinking of, Jim?" Marge demanded.

I shrugged. "I don't know. It seemed like the thing to do at the time. Maybe I was wrong. Do you people want a real live candidate or a robot?"

"A robot, of course," Marge replied. "Especially if the real one is going to start reminding people that he was a draft-dodging police-bashing Harvard pinko while Bobby Finn was over in Vietnam heroically defending his country."

Harold glanced at me. I smiled at him. He looked away.

"This is bad," Sam muttered. "This is very bad."

"Well," Kevin said, trying desperately to look on the bright side, "things can't get much worse."

"The *Real News* comes out tomorrow," Harold said.

I stood up. "I guess we'll have to have another meeting tomorrow then," I said wearily.

No one replied, so I left the conference room and went home to sleep on my couch.

CHAPTER 24

This is a story of murder and deceit. I don't know who is guilty of the murder, but I know who is guilty of the deceit. I have a small part to play in the story, so perhaps I can't be as objective as a reporter is supposed to be. But I will try to tell the story as accurately as I can, and I'll let you come to your own conclusions.

On a foggy afternoon in late September, someone entered the Back Bay apartment of Amanda Taylor, a 26-year-old reporter for *Hub* magazine, and stabbed her to death. The murderer then apparently ransacked her apartment, stole her money, and left the message "She had to die" typed over and over again on her computer. Her body was discovered several hours later by U.S. Sen. James O'Connor, who has since claimed that he was there to be interviewed for a book the victim was writing about him.

O'Connor's involvement in the case makes Amanda Taylor's murder *important*. The careers of powerful men are involved. The future of Massachusetts is at stake, and perhaps of America as well, given O'Connor's ill-concealed presidential ambitions. What tends to get lost in the gossip and the innuendo is that a woman has died:

a bright, beautiful, hardworking woman who had a terrific future ahead of her. She died, I believe, because she fell in love with the wrong man.

Amanda Taylor was a friend of mine. We were both staff writers at *Hub*. Our relationship was never romantic, although we grew to be something more than just co-workers. We were kindred spirits in a way. We were young; we loved our profession; we wanted to make our mark on the world.

And then, around the beginning of this year, Amanda began to change . . .

You get the idea. It was a typical *Real News* piece, suffused with a sense of its own importance, decrying the gossip and innuendo of others while indulging in the same things itself.

The book was a cover for our affair, according to Williams's thesis. Amanda was an innocent who succumbed to my oleaginous charms; I was a sinister hypocrite who enjoyed having my way with her. Pretty plausible so far, I guess. But he went on to theorize that as the election approached, the affair—and Amanda's very existence—became an issue for the even more sinister behind-the-scenes types who actually have the power in America. They were grooming me for the presidency, and they didn't want a cheap affair to blemish my clean-cut image. Williams concluded that these shadowy fiends had ordered Amanda's murder to keep her from destroying my career. But the plan had backfired: The actual murderer had been supposed to make the crime look like a run-of-the-mill robbery, but he had bungled the assignment or gotten carried away, and by bad luck I didn't have an alibi, and as a result, I was in deep trouble.

The theory fitted in nicely with the paper's paranoid view of the way America is governed. But it didn't help the believability of the article as a whole, and that was fine with me. Williams played up the San Francisco episode, and he had some nasty quotes about me from Amanda's sister, Lauren. He built a reasonably strong case that Amanda was in love with me. But he didn't produce a smoking gun. There was nothing that proved we were having an affair: no love letters, no secret copy of the Polaroid of us kissing, no sworn statement from a bellhop who saw her sneaking out of my room at four in the morning. So people would still have to make up their own minds about what had really gone on between us.

Smoking gun or not, there was enough in the article to put Amanda's murder back on the front pages—along with my instantly famous "wheelchair shocker," as the pundits referred to it. What was going on? Was the O'Connor campaign falling apart? Tracking polls showed my lead dwindling into statistical insignificance after the debate. Williams's article made it disappear altogether. What was more ominous, contributions dried up almost immediately. The people with the money were waiting to see if I continued to self-destruct.

And what was the candidate's response? Well, I had no response at all. My braintrust decided that if I couldn't be a robot, they would do without me altogether. My father's accident was a perfect excuse for them to hold me incommunicado for a couple of days while they worked on damage control.

They'd had a chance to get ready for the article, so they were able to strike back as soon as it hit the stands. Harold had decided to follow my advice and shoot the messenger. It turned out, not surprisingly, that Williams didn't have the best of journalistic reputations; in fact, he had been fired from one job for making up a source. And he had clearly exaggerated his relationship with Amanda; there were plenty of fellow staffers at *Hub* who were willing to state that she had despised the guy. They were also willing to state that they despised him themselves.

Of course, our campaign couldn't say stuff like this; we couldn't be seen stooping to his level. So Harold leaked the information to a friendly columnist at the *Herald,* who was glad to stoop for us. When Marge faced the press, she dismissed the whole story as an outrageous and unprofessional attack from a fringe periodical. When pressed on the San Francisco bombshell, she denied that it was a bombshell. After all, Senator O'Connor had freely admitted it to Williams, hadn't he? It hadn't come up before simply because no one had asked. Was the senator supposed to detail for the press every moment of every meeting with the woman? Amanda was a professional. She had a big story. She was interviewing a busy man. Why shouldn't she go to San Francisco to track him down?

Marge, wily media person that she was, managed to imply that it was sexist and demeaning to women to suggest that the only reason a female reporter would cross the continent to meet a male senator was that she had the hots for him. I thought this was a particularly clever tactic. People might not have any qualms about accusing me of being a lecher, but they might feel guilty about thinking that the murder victim had nothing better to do than to be the object of a lecher's attentions.

The strategy for dealing with the wheelchair shocker was more difficult. Voters couldn't figure out how to react to it any more than the pundits could. The statement had been too articulate to suggest that I was becoming unhinged, but it seemed too out of character to be a campaign ploy. So what did it mean? Harold and company didn't know; I couldn't or wouldn't explain it to them. So they had to make something up.

They tried to float two separate and not quite contradictory interpretations of what I had said. In the first, they made the case that it represented nothing new. I had always been opposed to police brutality. I had always been willing look at things from the other person's point of view. I had always been honest in my responses to questions.

In case people didn't buy that, the braintrust offered a second interpretation: Yes, Jim O'Connor has grown in his years in office. He is no longer the doctrinaire law and order Republican he might once have been. Look, for example, at his iconoclastic positions on defense. O'Connor's ability to grow is one of his great strengths.

This latter interpretation had the advantage of quite possibly being true, although Harold couldn't have had any idea why. The problem with it was that it left me open to the charge of political expediency. Was I growing, or was I just trying to make sure my appeal was broad enough to get myself reelected? I needed liberal votes to win in a state like Massachusetts; maybe this was just a cynical ploy to claim some of them.

There was no real way of defending against that sort of charge, except to make people trust me. If they trusted me, they would see everything I did or said in the most positive light. And that kind of positive perception of me was just what we were in danger of losing because of Amanda's murder and Williams's article.

The Democrats did not decline the golden opportunity I had offered them, of course. Cavanaugh chose this moment to strike, and he hauled me in for further questioning. So Roger and I had to make our way once again past the TV cameras into the courthouse building.

This time we assembled in Cavanaugh's own office rather than a bleak conference room. Photographs of the enemy grinned at me from every wall. Cavanaugh shaking hands with Finn. Cavanaugh shaking hands with President Kenton. Cavanaugh, the Chamber of Commerce's Man of the Year. Mackey sat in a corner, expressionless; this was the Monsignor's show.

Roger—my faithful friend—began with the obligatory protest. "This is pure politics, Francis, and we resent it. And the people of Massachusetts are going to resent it, too."

The Monsignor nodded, hands folded on his chest, as if he were relaxing after a hearty meal. He looked content, as if the dream of a lifetime were about to come true.

It would be easy enough for us to make the case that it was pure politics, I reflected. We could point out that if Finn became senator, the lieutenant governor would become governor, and the current attorney general might then run for lieutenant governor in two years. And that would finally open up the AG's job for Cavanaugh, after I had snatched it away from him so long ago.

But looking at Cavanaugh, I couldn't believe that he was interested. He was getting old; his time had passed. Revenge was more important to him now than ambition. He wasn't going to let this opportunity slip away.

"Your client was the one who failed to reveal pertinent information to our investigators," Cavanaugh replied to Roger's charge.

"It's not our job to determine what you might possibly consider pertinent," Roger said. "Do you want to know what Jim had for breakfast the Tuesday before the murder? Does his brand of socks make a difference? We're not mind readers. Ask us specific questions, and we'll be happy to respond."

"Clearly the nature and extent of your relationship with the victim is of interest to us," Cavanaugh said to me. "You don't need to be a mind reader to figure that out."

"I have already explained the relationship," I replied.

Cavanaugh shrugged. "Maybe we don't believe you."

"Then arrest me for obstruction of justice or something. I don't have to sit here and be called a liar, Francis. Especially by a Democrat."

Cavanaugh grinned. Roger laid a hand on my arm. "Specific questions, Francis," he said. "Otherwise we won't get anywhere."

Cavanaugh turned to Mackey. "Take him through it, Mack," he said.

Mackey looked at me with the expression of a public servant just doing his job. "Jim," he said. "Every meeting. From the beginning."

It was torture. The only point to it was to see if I would lie, and I was smart enough not to. They had all the records of her charge cards. They knew when she had been to Washington and where she had stayed. So I admitted to those meetings, and that was that; there was still no smoking gun. She had taken a couple of other trips; Mackey quizzed me on those, but they had nothing to do with me, and I knew I could prove it.

And then Mackey brought up something new. "Your second meeting with Amanda Taylor—you said it was at a café in the Back Bay?"

"That's right. But honest, Mack, I can't remember the name. One of those little places on Newbury Street."

"Doesn't matter. We've talked to your waiter. He remembers the two of you vividly. He even overheard some of your conversation."

I didn't change expression. The jerk had wanted to argue with us instead of serving our food. "Did he now?"

"Yeah, he says Amanda was talking like a Ronald Reagan clone. The thing is, Jim, you told us before that you knew about her politics. Sounds like she was lying to you in this restaurant."

"I don't remember it that way at all," I said. "We found some areas of agreement. Even liberals believe in individual responsibility."

"Isn't it possible that you only found out about her real politics later? And wouldn't that have made you pretty angry?"

"Angry enough to kill her? Come on. I'm a professional, Mack. Ask Harold White and Marge Terry. I had them run a check on her before I even met her at that café. I knew what I was doing."

Mackey shrugged. It was shaky, but if he was looking for a motive, that might help him establish one. Actually it made me feel a little better that they were still fishing around for a motive. "Jim," he went on, "can you tell us why, if the victim was working on this book since the first of the year, she apparently didn't interview anyone before late August?"

"She interviewed me," I said.

"Interviews for which we have no tapes and only very sketchy notes."

"Haven't we been through this before?" I said. "I don't know anything about her writing methods. Maybe she was too busy to interview anyone else until August. Maybe she wanted to get to know me better before she put anything on paper. I really don't see what this has to do with anything."

Oh, yes, I did. Mackey didn't press the issue, but he didn't have to. A jury could decide if I was lying about this supposed book.

Cavanaugh had little to say during the interrogation. It was clear that he was letting Mackey take care of the details. Perhaps the details didn't even matter at this point. After an hour Mackey gave up. He had a little new information, but surely not enough for an arrest. Not unless they were still playing games with the tape of Danny's interview.

Not unless Cavanaugh wanted to make an arrest no matter how little evidence he had.

"Francis, mind if I speak to you in private for a minute?" I said as the meeting ended.

Cavanaugh looked a little surprised, but he simply said, "I'm at your service." Mackey and Roger left us alone in the office. Cavanaugh sat back in his chair. "Now what can I do for you, Senator?"

"There's something I've always wanted to know, Francis. Why didn't you hire me when I applied for a job here? I would have worked hard. I would have shown up on time."

Cavanaugh smiled. He looked as if he'd just sunk a birdie putt. "Been gnawing away at you all these years, huh, Jim?"

"I've been curious," I said. "Sure."

"Thought you were gonna be God's gift to the DA's office, right? Thought we should roll out the red carpet for you as soon as you consented to work for us, right?"

"I thought I met the employment qualifications. And I didn't drool or pick my nose during the interview."

Cavanaugh nodded. "You were a swell candidate all right. I got some heat from the assistant DAs for turning you down."

"So why did you do it?"

He steepled his palms and looked out the window. "Because," he said softly, "I knew what you were up to—even if you didn't know it yourself. You were going to come in here and set the place on fire, and after a few years you'd start feeling stifled, you'd get the urge to move up, but there'd be nowhere for you to go. So you'd decide the old man didn't have it anymore—he's out of touch, the place needs new blood—and you'd run against me. And probably you'd win."

I had never thought of that. "You thought I'd be another Francis X. Cavanaugh," I said.

"Spittin' image," he agreed.

"Well, even if you were right, not hiring me was still the worst mistake you ever made," I told him. "If you'd taken me on, you'd have had a clear shot at attorney general, and I'd have run for DA to succeed you."

Cavanaugh nodded. "And maybe I'd be the senator today, and you'd still be the DA."

We sat in silence for a moment, brooding about the road not taken. I wondered just how much time Cavanaugh spent brooding like that nowadays.

"Even so," he said after a while, "it wouldn't have made a difference if you hadn't pulled that stunt with Paul Everson."

"I didn't pull any stunt," I said. "Everson did it on his own."

Cavanaugh gave me a disbelieving look.

"Are you going to arrest me?" I asked.

"I'm going to let you twist slowly in the wind," he replied.

"There's not that much time left for twisting," I pointed out. "The election's less than a week away."

"You can do a lot of twisting in a week."

"Do you think I'm guilty?" I asked.

Cavanaugh smiled again. "Everyone is guilty," he said.

Outside the courthouse I made a brief statement to the reporters. I didn't bother with subtlety. The DA was playing politics with the case, I said. He was harassing me to cover up the police's inability to solve it. I reminded everyone that Cavanaugh had a grudge against me that went back many years. I expressed my hope that the voters would realize what Cavanaugh and the rest of the Democrats were up to.

I didn't wait around to take questions.

My father was feeling better, but he was still in the hospital, grouchier than ever. When I visited him, he was worried about the insurance, the car, the overdue library books, the unpaid rent.

Danny had promised to take care of everything, but that didn't stop my father from worrying. I offered to look into things.

"No, no, it's too much trouble, you've got enough to do," my father said.

"Actually I don't," I said. "I've been pulled off the campaign trail for a couple of days for various reasons."

"I never heard you talk about that riot at Harvard," he said.

"Kids weren't supposed to talk to their parents back in the sixties."

"They say you brought it up just to get votes."

"Everything I do is to get votes. The only reason I'm gonna take care of your insurance is because I want to make sure of yours."

"Oh, Danny'll handle it."

"And maybe I'll get Danny's vote, too. Although that's a lot more doubtful."

"Danny." My father sighed.

"I'll be back tomorrow," I said.

I drove over to my father's apartment and let myself in. Just as he seemed diminished outside his apartment, it seemed smaller and more ordinary without him in it. The armchair where he always sat looked worn and shabby; the rugs were threadbare, the dishes chipped and mismatched. It didn't feel right being there without him.

I went upstairs and sifted through the papers on his desk, looking for his auto insurance policy. But I couldn't concentrate. I started to think about having to clear out this place when my father finally left, as he would have to, sooner or later, one way or another. What would he want to take with him; what *could* he take with him, as his world shrank yet again? Would he care about his armchair, his favorite mugs, this worn oak desk at which I had once sat to do my homework? Or would he take nothing—except, perhaps, the photographs of Danny and me in our moments of triumph?

And I remembered the other time he had moved—out of the old house in Brighton—back when Danny was starting his bar and I was starting my law career, and it was clear that no one was going to be living with him there ever again. I wanted no part of Brighton, and Danny had bought a two-family a couple of blocks over, convinced that he was going to make a fortune in real estate in addition to being a successful businessman. We all spent a sweaty summer weekend sorting and packing and—mostly—throwing away. In a corner of the attic I found an old steamer trunk, and in it was a yellowed gown, carefully folded. I suppose I knew its significance immediately, but I brought it downstairs to my father for confirmation.

He took it from me and fingered a sleeve. "Well, this would be your mother's wedding gown," he said.

"Want to keep it?" I asked.

He looked at me, and I realized that I shouldn't have asked, should have simply pitched it myself or packed it up without his permission. Because now he had to choose, and this was the kind of choice he had never before had to make.

He looked back down at the gown, and what he saw when he looked at it I will never know, because I wouldn't dream of asking him and he wouldn't dream of telling me. "Not much use to anyone now, is it?" he said.

I took it back from him. "I'll take care of it," I said. He nodded.

It is sitting in my attic now. I never told him; he never asked.

I decided that I needed a drink. I went back downstairs, and I saw my father sitting in his armchair.

It wasn't my father, of course. It was Danny, looking more like my father than I would have believed possible. We were now about the age that he had been when we were growing up, and the trials of living had etched themselves in our faces—Danny's more than mine. But it wasn't his face so much as his posture, the way he slumped in the chair, like an old man who had gone through too much. He's giving up the struggle, I thought. He's falling into old age. My father, for all his talk of dying when he finished Dickens, was at least still struggling. "I didn't hear you come in," I said.

"I saw your car outside," he replied. "Didn't want to disturb you."

"I was just, uh—"

"You were just doing what I promised Dad I'd take care of. After I talked my boss into giving me the afternoon off to come over here."

Sure you did, I thought. You lie well enough to be a politician. "I haven't done anything," I said. "Really. It's all yours."

Danny shrugged. "I don't care. I just don't want you treating me like I'm totally irresponsible."

I sat down. "Lighten up," I said. "This is hard on all of us. I was just remembering when we moved him out of the old house. What a job that was."

"Won't be so hard this time," Danny said. "The junk we collected in that old place. All those books of yours."

"All those baseball cards of yours."

"Probably worth a fortune now. Wonder where they all went."

I thought some more about the old days and the junk that accumulates. "Danny, do you remember one Saturday afternoon when I played touch football against you over at the field? There was one play where you caught a pass and put some fakes on me. You left me standing there as if I was stuck to the ground. I'll never know how you did that."

Danny brightened. That was his kind of memory. But then he shook his head. "I don't remember ever playing football against you. You always said you hated games." He considered. "That made me think you were a wimp sometimes. But I knew you weren't, not really. Actually I sort of admired you."

I was surprised. Surprised that he hadn't remembered his triumph over me, and even more surprised at his admission that he had admired me. "Well," I said, "maybe I made it up."

Danny grinned. "That's okay. I've been known to make up a thing or two myself." He arose from the chair. "I better go upstairs and take care of business."

"Okay," I said. "I'll see you, then."

"See you."

Danny went upstairs. I hung around for a moment, staring at the lonely pair of photographs on the wall. Something had happened just then, but I wasn't sure what it was. I gave up trying to figure it out finally, and I got in my car and drove home.

There wasn't much happening at home. Liz was out—at school, I hoped—and Kathleen was working on her computer. "Wanna rake leaves with me?" I asked her.

She looked up from the computer. "Don't you have something important to do?"

"Hey, don't blow your chance for some quality time with the old man."

"If you don't get out there and win this election, I'll have plenty of chances for quality time," she pointed out.

"True," I said, "but they also serve who only stand and rake."

"What does that mean?"

"I don't know. C'mon, let's go outside."

We found a couple of ancient rakes and some plastic barrels in the toolshed, and we set to work transferring the leaves from the front lawn to the woods behind the house. There were hundreds of barrels' worth of leaves to be moved, and the lawn beneath them was scarcely worth exposing; I never had any time to work on it, and Liz had lost interest since she went back to school. But I felt so wholesome performing the chore—on a crisp fall day, with my perfect daughter helping and the cat sitting on the front steps supervising—that its futility didn't matter. "Sometimes I think normality is within our grasp, Kathleen," I said.

She looked at me. "Have you told the police you were having an affair with Amanda Taylor?" she asked.

So much for normality. "No, I haven't," I admitted.

"So you've been lying to them."

"Um, I have to empty this barrel. I'll be right back." Kathleen had been brooding, obviously. So what could I do about it? I emptied the leaves onto the ground and returned out front. "Yes, I've been lying to them," I said.

"What if they come and question me? Should I tell them the truth? You told me you were having an affair, remember?"

"They won't question you, Kathleen," I responded gently.

"But suppose they do?"

"Then you should tell them the truth."

"Why is it okay for you to lie to the police and not me?"

I leaned against my rake. Kathleen's cheeks were ruddy in the cold air. Her jeans had holes in the knees. The laces of her sneakers were untied. Was that the fashion, I wondered, or just her sloppiness? My love for her was heart-stopping. "I didn't say that what I'm doing is okay," I replied. "I would like for you to be a better person than I am, that's all. I'm just sorry I can't set you a better example."

"I'd be a better person by turning you in?"

"You wouldn't be turning me in. I didn't murder the woman."

"But the police would arrest you if they could prove you were having an affair with her. That's why you're lying to them, right?"

"Yeah, I guess so. But your job isn't to protect me from the consequences of my sins."

"Then what is my job?"

"To rake leaves. To obey your father. To tie your shoelaces."

Kathleen looked down and scuffed the ground with her

sneaker. "Sometimes I just don't feel like growing up," she said.

"Sometimes I know how you feel," I said.

She knelt and tied her shoelaces. A car came up the driveway. Not an ordinary car. A gold Jaguar, low and sleek. Backlit by the setting sun, it looked like a chariot of fire. I figured I knew who it belonged to.

"Nice car," Kathleen breathed as it pulled up next to us.

"Do you have some homework to do?" I asked.

"Nope."

"Then go play with your fractals."

She continued to gawk at the car. "Who's that?"

"He's the new hired hand. He'll finish up the raking."

Kathleen stuck her tongue out at me and returned to the house. The Jaguar's door opened, and Paul Everson got out.

He was impeccably dressed, as usual, from his mohair topcoat to his tasseled Gucci loafers. I held the rake out to him. "I could use some help," I said.

He grinned and walked toward me. "Was that Kathleen?" he asked.

"I think she wants to marry you. Or at least go for a ride in your car."

"Anytime, Jim. Anytime."

Not on your life, I thought. "So what brings you to my happy Hingham home?" I asked.

"Harold White said I'd find you here. I have news."

News? I became a little excited. He wouldn't show up in person unless it was good news. Had he actually come through for me? "What is it?"

He took a tape out of the pocket of his topcoat, and I became more excited still. "Sid," he said.

Sid? It took a moment for me to remember Sid. The other witness to Bobby Finn's atrocity in Vietnam. I didn't want to know about Bobby Finn. "How is Sid?" I asked.

"Not well," Everson replied. "He's in a VA hospital in Fresno. Liver trouble, I understand. But he remembers our governor all right. And what he remembers supports Larry Spalding's account. You've got him, Jim."

"That's great," I managed to say.

Everson stared at me. My lack of interest was not hard to discern. "You've won the election," he said. "It's in the bag. Even with the stuff that's been happening lately."

"Right."

His stare turned angry, then exasperated. "You're not going to use this, are you?" he said.

I shrugged. "I haven't decided."

"Well, you won't get out of it easy, because I gave Harold a copy of the tape, too. He's not going to let you simply forget about it."

"Harold won't do anything with this if I tell him not to."

Everson kicked at the leaves with one of his expensive loafers. He shook his head, as if despairing of me. "Why are you destroying yourself, Jim?" he asked softly. "The Harvard Bust—why did you have to bring that up in the debate? That was a lifetime ago."

"It was a big event for both of us."

"So what? Jesus, I'm no politician, but even I'd know better than to talk about the police beating up a kid in a wheelchair."

I scooped up some leaves and put them in the barrel. I didn't need political advice from Paul Everson. "Find out anything about Danny's tape?" I asked him.

"Forget about the tape!" he said, throwing up his hands. "There is no tape. Look, you don't want to hear this from me, but—well, I understand. I know what you're going through. And believe me, you have to get beyond it. And fast. What's done is done. Life isn't going to wait for you to decide that it's okay to go on living."

What the hell was he talking about? What did he understand about me? I could imagine him knowing the truth about Amanda and me, with all his spies. I could even imagine him knowing about Jackie Scanlon. But could he know that my wife was having an affair with my best friend? Could he know that my father was afraid of dying and my brother was afraid of living? Could he know that the man I respected most in the Senate was just giving up, unable to see the point of it all anymore?

It didn't matter. I didn't need advice from this man; I needed favors. I thought of Larry Spalding, guarding one of Everson's many companies. "You know my brother Danny," I said.

"Of course."

"He's an alcoholic, more or less, and he just got fired from his job, but he's not stupid, and he's not a bad guy. He's got four kids. I was wondering if you could find him a spot somewhere."

"No problem, Jim."

"Maybe something in sales—but not liquor sales. And we've got to do it without him finding out I'm involved."

"Don't worry. These things can be made to look completely innocent."

"You do this often?" I asked.

"For friends, sure." He paused. "I've done terrible things, you know, but that doesn't make me a terrible person."

I didn't know how to respond to that. "Thanks," I said. I scooped up some more leaves.

Everson stood there for a moment, as if wondering if he should say more, and then he returned to his golden car and drove away.

I lugged the barrel behind the house and emptied it. Kathleen intercepted me as I trudged back out front. "Kevin Feeney's on the phone," she said. "He says it's urgent."

What now? I wondered. Maybe Harold had told him what we had on Finn, and he was calling to share the triumph with me. Poor Kevin. I went inside and picked up the phone in my office. "Yeah, Kevin."

"Jim, you'll never guess," he said. He was calling me Jim again. His voice was quivering with excitement.

"What's that, Kevin?"

"Jim, we just found out who murdered Amanda Taylor."

CHAPTER 25

*T*he Lynn Arms. Even the name sounded depressing, and I was not surprised when I found it wedged between a plumbing supply house and a driver's ed school, on a dismal side street near the center of that dismal city. It was a narrow brick building, with the name inscribed over the doorway and two small weathered concrete lions on either side of the entrance. Someone had blackened the eyes of both lions. The walk was littered with Doritos wrappers, a supermarket advertising supplement, the remains of a broken beer bottle. The place had once been genteel, perhaps, when Lynn was thriving and people wanted to live downtown. Now the stores were closed and everyone had fled to the suburbs, and you'd live in such a place only if you had to. I shivered and went inside.

Surprisingly, the inner door was locked, and I had to ring the bell of the man I was looking for. The intercom didn't work, apparently, or else he didn't care who he let in; he simply buzzed the door open, and I walked up the steep stairway.

I heard TV noises as I climbed: guns firing and tires squealing, a gleeful laugh track. A woman shouted in rapid-fire Spanish. I smelled onions being fried. A cardboard Halloween skeleton was taped to a door. I had forgotten about Halloween.

The man I had come to see was waiting for me on the third floor—older but still easy to recognize, even in these surroundings. His thatch of hair was white now, but it still fell over his forehead in that way women (I am told) found endearingly boyish. The narrow face, the Roman nose, the mouth twisted into a half-sneer or half-smile, depending on your point of view: all that hadn't changed.

But he had changed, in ways that couldn't be blamed merely on the passage of time. In the old days who would ever have caught Tom Donato wearing a shapeless acrylic sweater—with a hole in it no less? And the way he stood was different. He had always been on the balls of his feet back then—because he wanted to look a little taller, perhaps, or because he had so much energy pent up inside him that he simply couldn't stand still. Now that energy was gone, and his body sagged. The energy had left his eyes, too, the eyes that had once sparkled with the joy of doing battle. It was depressing.

Still, when he caught sight of me, his eyes did seem to come to life a little, and he started to laugh. "Well, if it isn't Senator O'Connor, paying a call," he said. "What a wonderful surprise."

"Hi, Tom," I said. We didn't shake hands. He just stared at me for a long moment, and I began to wonder if he really believed I was there.

"Come on inside," he said finally. "Let me show you my spectacular dwelling place."

I followed him into his apartment. There was a tiny kitchen to the left, and one large room straight ahead, crammed with a bed, a TV, a couple of armchairs, and a rolltop desk. The bed faced a walled-over fireplace; on the mantel were photographs of three smiling teenage boys. The bed was unmade; the TV flickered soundlessly. In the corner a parakeet whistled and chirped in its cage.

"Excuse the mess," he said. "Maid's day off, wouldn't you know. I've given up the booze, but I think I have a bottle here somewhere—" He went into the kitchen and started rummaging in a cabinet.

"That's fine, Tom," I said. "I'll have whatever you're having."

He nodded and poured us each a small glass of orange juice. Tom Donato drinking orange juice! I followed him into the bedroom, and we sat down in the armchairs. He reached over and switched the TV off; the parakeet continued to chirp merrily. "Cheers," he said, raising his glass to me.

"Cheers."

He smiled and put his glass down. "I notice that things don't seem to be going well in your campaign," he remarked. "So I assume you're here looking for my endorsement."

He still had his sense of humor. But the time was long past when we could trade quips. "You know Kevin Feeney?" I asked.

"Of course. How is Kevin?"

"You know Amanda Taylor?"

He shrugged, still smiling. "I read the newspapers. I keep up, God knows why."

"I had Kevin hire a private investigator to look into Amanda Taylor's murder," I said. "Just in case the police investigation was a little—well, slanted."

"With the Monsignor in charge? My, you're a suspicious person."

I shrugged. "The guy didn't come up with much to begin with. But Kevin had this theory, you see. He thought Amanda Taylor was murdered by someone trying to get back at me. Someone who hoped the murder would somehow destroy my career the way I had destroyed theirs. So Kevin got hold of photographs of people he thought were likely suspects, and he gave them to the private eye, who started showing them around. No one in the apartment building recognized any of them, but the UPS guy did. Remembered you going into the apartment building while he was there. He even talked to you, shook your hand. Turns out he had a cousin who got a job from you once. Small world, huh, Tom?"

My host kept smiling.

"So what do you think of Kevin's theory, Tom?" I went on. " 'Donato's the one, Jim,' he says to me this afternoon. 'After all, who fell further? Who's got more reason to hate you—except maybe the Monsignor?' Thomas Donato, senate president, the most powerful man in the commonwealth back then, according to some people. Perhaps the next governor. But then the ambitious young AG decides to go after him and catches him taking a bribe. And he ends up Thomas Donato, jailbird, the latest symbol of political corruption in Massachusetts. Does that make Thomas Donato, ex-con, capable of murdering to get his revenge on the ambitious AG who destroyed him?"

My host downed the rest of his orange juice. "Sounds like a pretty good theory to me, Senator. I'd have this guy Donato arrested. Send him back to prison where scum like that belong. What do you think?"

"I don't know. I'm reserving judgment on everything nowadays."

"And that's why you're here: to interview the suspect in person? You're pretty fearless. What if I decide to kill you, too?"

I took Liz's gun out of the inside pocket of my jacket. "The possibility occurred to me," I said.

Donato laughed. "Good old Jim O'Connor. Always prepared. Always has the angles covered."

"So what were you doing there, Tom?"

"Same as everyone else apparently: She was interviewing me about you. She offered to come visit me here, but the maid was on vacation that week, wouldn't you know, so I said I'd go into the city instead. Feels good to get back to the city. Of course, I don't have the parking space behind the State House anymore. But then again I don't really need it because I don't have a car either. This was about a week before the woman was killed, though. No one saw me there the day of the murder, right?"

"Kevin's theory is that you got the idea the first time you went there, then returned another day to actually commit the crime."

Donato shook his head. "Kevin's a treasure. I used to have aides like him. A couple of them still think you framed me."

"Did you murder Amanda Taylor, Tom?"

Donato got up and went back to the kitchenette. I studied the parakeet, which hadn't shut up since I arrived. I wondered why Donato liked keeping something in a cage. Had he turned into the birdman of MCI Concord? Maybe he wanted to treat a prisoner better than he himself had been treated. He returned with the carton of orange juice and offered to refill my glass. I shook my head. He poured some more into his own glass, then sat back down in his armchair and leaned forward. His eyes were totally alive now, staring into mine with all the intensity of the politician I had once known. "Senator, I have no desire to destroy you," he said. "And if I did, it'd be a lot easier for me than committing murder. All I'd have to do is pick up the phone, call my old buddy Francis Cavanaugh, and tell him about you and Jackie Scanlon."

I hadn't expected that. I returned his gaze, but I could feel myself start to sweat. "Did Amanda tell you about Jackie Scanlon?" I asked him finally.

"Nope. A guy named Tom Glenn did."

Tom Glenn. The man who had walked off with the IRA's

money. This could not have been worse. "Where did you meet him? In prison?"

Donato nodded. "He was in for insurance fraud. Funny the friends you make in prison. Of course, we had mutual acquaintances, more or less."

"What did he tell you?"

"Well, it was a great story. It started out with him having some guns to sell; I think you probably know that part. What you might not know is that he went to the IRA people first. Jackie Scanlon found out because he finds out about everything that goes on in Southie. And he also found out that Glenn was an old Navy buddy of your brother's. So he got together with Glenn and the IRA people and offered them a proposition. He'd front the money for the guns if they'd do things his way. It was too good a deal for anyone to pass up, so they agreed."

Donato sipped his juice, a satisfied look on his face. I looked blankly at the gun in my hand. Poor Danny. Poor me. "So it was all a scam?" I managed to say.

"I'm afraid so, Senator. They arranged it so your brother would think he was in the hole four hundred thousand dollars to a bunch of desperate terrorists, and Jackie Scanlon was the only man who could save him."

"Four hundred thousand dollars is a lot of money to spend, even for my influence," I said.

"That was the beauty of it, though," Donato replied. "It didn't cost Scanlon anywhere near that much. The first shipment of guns was the only one he bought; they were the only weapons Glenn had. He loans the IRA the four hundred thousand. The IRA hands it over to Glenn for the bogus second shipment, and he hands it back to Scanlon, minus a few thousand for his trouble. Then Scanlon hands the same money over to your brother in return for his confession, your brother hands it over to the IRA to save his life—he thinks—and they hand it back to Scanlon. The IRA gets their guns, Glenn gets his money, and Scanlon gets you. Pretty neat, huh?"

Pretty neat. I sighed. The big adventure of Danny's life, and it was all a con game to trap me. "So how come you didn't tell anyone when you found out about it?" I asked.

Donato leaned back and ran a hand through his white hair. "It occurred to me, Senator. Oh, yes, it occurred to me. But for one thing, I didn't have any proof that you were involved. Glenn just knew this was how the scheme was supposed to work. He wasn't around to find out if you really took the bait. From reading the newspapers it was pretty obvious to me that you did, but I wasn't sure anyone would believe a couple of convicts, one of whom clearly had a grudge against you."

"Could have done some damage, at least."

"Sure, but here's the thing. In a strange sort of way Glenn's story actually made me like you. At least it proved you were human, and maybe only half a jerk, doing that for your brother. I mean, it's not that different from what I did. Sure I took a kickback to get that courthouse built. But why? I'll tell you why: because I'm not a fuckin' Kennedy. No one gave me a trust fund so I could be a public servant; no one gave me a damn thing. Twenty-five years in politics, and I was making less than some kid a year out of Harvard Law. So I ended up with three sons in college and a mortgage and a wife who never worked a day in her life, and the bills were killing me. I had to provide for my family, and damned if I could figure out how to do it on the salary I got paid in the state senate. I had to make a choice—just like you.

"The funny thing is," he went on, "two of my kids dropped out of college after I went to prison. Not because they didn't have the money, but because they were ashamed when they got asked if I was their father. None of them'll have anything to do with me now. My wife waited till I was paroled, and then she left me. She had to work while I was in the slammer, see, and it didn't agree with her, so she blamed me. So I lost the only two things that mattered to me: my career and my family. I'm to old and tired and stupid to start over, and even if I had the energy, there wouldn't be any point, 'cause I'd just have to hand over everything I made to my wife. I live here free in return for changing the light bulbs and taking out the trash and shoveling the walk. I prepare tax returns for a few of my friends. But mostly I just sit around all day and watch TV. And once in a while—like every half hour or so—I think about the old days, when I mattered."

Donato fell silent. His eyes went dead again. Strange the way the mind works, reducing a complex life to a soothing cliché. *I did it for my family.* He probably believed that. And it might have been true, in a way. But how convenient that he had forgotten about the sultry mistress he kept in a Charlestown apartment and the liquor-soaked trips they had taken to Atlantic City to blow thousands at the blackjack tables. She had dumped him, too, of course. And I thought: It matters to him that my motivation for helping Jackie Scanlon be good and pure because that way he can think of his own motivation as being equally good and pure. We had sinned because we loved too much. "I'm sorry," I said, for want of anything better.

He drank some more orange juice. "How's your brother?" he asked.

"About the same."

"Is he grateful for what you did?"

"If he is, I don't think he'd ever say so."

Donato nodded in sympathy.

"So, uh, you talked about Jackie Scanlon with Amanda, I take it?" I said.

"She brought it up actually. I just hinted at this deep dark secret I knew about you—just to feel self-important, I suppose— and she pounced on it. She seemed to know all about what you did, except for the little twist that Glenn told me in prison. It was sort of disappointing, to tell you the truth. I thought I was going to shock her."

"Did she tape the interview?"

The smile returned to Donato's face. "I didn't think of that," he said. "Yeah, she taped the interview. So does Cavanaugh—"

"The police haven't asked you about it?"

He shook his head. "I wonder what's going on," he said, with the interest of the professional politician.

Mackey had talked to Danny only because I had mentioned him; he hadn't talked to Donato at all. I couldn't figure it out. "So do I," I said.

He stared at the gun, which I still clutched in my right hand, and he grew serious again. "You know," he said, "when I read about the murder in the paper, my first reaction was that you did it. To keep her quiet about Scanlon. And that would explain why the police don't have the tape. You took it when you murdered her."

"But you still know," I pointed out.

"So that means you'd have to take care of me, too."

"If I figured I had to kill you, I've sure taken my time getting around to it."

"You're a busy man."

We stared at each other, two suspicious criminals sizing one another up. Did Donato kill Amanda? The idea had appealed to me when Kevin announced his triumphant solution to the case. If Donato had done it, all my problems were solved along with the case. Now I knew that my problems wouldn't go away that easily. But that didn't necessarily mean Donato was innocent. Did it?

And then his parakeet suddenly started to jabber, "Ex-con, ex-con, ex-con," over and over again, as if it couldn't contain its excitement over the word. We listened to it for a few seconds, and we stared at each other, and then we both burst out laughing. I can't say exactly why, but we two criminals had tacitly agreed to trust each other. I put the gun back into the pocket of my jacket. "If I didn't do it," I said, "and you didn't do it, then who-dunit?"

"If it wasn't you," he said, "I figured it was probably one of your friends, trying to protect you. Kevin Feeney came to mind."

I thought about Kevin. It made some sense. I remembered his eagerness to provide me with an alibi for the time of the murder; it hadn't occurred to me then that this would provide him with an alibi as well. What if he figured—along with everyone else apparently—that Amanda was conning me, and he decided to save me from her clutches?

No. Kevin might be capable of murdering for me, but he wasn't capable of being as cool about it afterward as he had appeared that evening. I shook my head. "Not Kevin."

"Well, you've got lots of friends," Donato replied.

"As far as I can tell, everyone in the world had a motive for killing her."

Donato shook his head. "You're not having an easy time of it, are you, Senator?"

I didn't know what to say to that. It seemed strange to have Tom Donato feeling sorry for me. Easy or hard, I was still in the fight, and it was all over for him. I shrugged. "Looks to me like you're having a worse time. What I did to you wasn't personal, you know, or political. I was just doing my job."

"That's okay. If someone does what I did, he's gotta be willing to accept the consequences. You go into politics, you risk losing an election. You break the law, you risk going to jail. Keep it in mind, Senator. Keep it in mind."

I stood up, thinking of Paul Everson. "You're right, by the

way," I said. "I've got lots of friends. One of them might be able to give you a job if you're interested."

Donato shook his head. "Don't bother," he said. He gestured at his tiny apartment. "This is about all I'm good for anymore. Just keep Kevin from coming after me. I don't have the strength left to fend off rabid Republicans."

"I'll do my best."

I reached out my hand. Donato hesitated for a moment and then shook it. The parakeet was still chirping, "Ex-con, ex-con, ex-con," as I left the apartment.

The phone rang in the car. I didn't answer it. It was Harold, I was sure, desperate to go public with the information about Finn. The phone had rung off and on during my trip up to Lynn. He was probably frantic by now.

He could have decided to go public without my approval, I thought. After all, I seemed to have lost interest in the campaign; why not just forge ahead without me? Time was running out. But he wouldn't do anything tonight—would he?

I drove along Route 1, past steak houses and car dealerships and discount furniture stores, barely able to focus on the highway. I hadn't been sure what to do about Finn before my trip to Lynn, but I was sure now. "There is no tape," Everson kept telling me. But he was obviously telling me that just to keep me calm; he was unable or unwilling to find out the truth. I wasn't quite sure of that before, but I was now—now that I knew there was a second tape, one that would be just as damaging as Danny's. I could fantasize that Amanda hadn't really taped Danny's interview; Danny wasn't especially clear about the whole thing, after all. I could fantasize that she hadn't put anything about Jackie Scanlon in her notes. But there was no fantasizing about Donato.

So Cavanaugh had to know, right? He had to be toying with me, savoring my coming destruction. Publicizing what Finn had done would only make the destruction inevitable. I couldn't let Harold do it. There was only one thing I could do with that information, I realized.

I pulled into the deserted parking lot of a water bed store and called Harold. He answered on the first ring. "Hi," I said. "I've been trying to reach you all night. Where've you been?"

"Did Everson talk to you?" Harold replied, ignoring my little joke.

"He did, as a matter of fact. And he gave me a tape. Said he gave you one, too."

"So what are we waiting for?" Harold said. "Let's go with it. Right now.We can't sit around mulling it over. There's not enough time. I've got a strategy mapped out. Get over here and we can start working on it."

I didn't respond, and that was response enough.

"What's the problem now?" Harold demanded, not bothering to conceal his exasperation.

"Harold, we're not going to do anything with that story," I said. "I'm not going to tell you why, and I'm not going to argue about it. And you're not going to leak it behind my back, because if it gets out, I will hold you personally responsible. I will fire you, and I will never speak to you again, and that will end your hopes of saving America and the world."

Harold was silent for a moment as well, and then he said, "It's my future, too, you know."

"We can still win. And even if we don't, you can stay employed for the rest of your life based on what you've done for me already."

"I don't want to just stay employed. I want to work in the White House."

"Think of this as a challenge."

"I don't need the kind of challenges you've been giving me lately. Look, at least you owe me an explanation."

"I owe you a lot more than that, Harold, but you're not going to get one. I'm sorry."

And then, finally, quietly, he said: "You did kill her, didn't you, Jim? That's what this is all about."

The inference made sense if he didn't know about Jackie Scanlon. "I didn't kill her," I said. "I'm sorry. I'll talk to you tomorrow." And I hung up.

I stared out into the empty parking lot. The water bed store was having a gigantic clearance sale. The wind whipped the highway litter past. I turned up the heat in the idling car. The gun felt awkward against my side; I was breaking the law by carrying it with me. Harold might risk my wrath and leak the story, but I didn't think he would. He was too confused, too worried. Even if I wasn't guilty of Amanda's murder, he knew I wouldn't cross him on something like this without a very good reason. But he didn't know what the reason could possibly be, and that would unnerve him. He had already been unnerved by the mistake he had made in going to the publisher of *Hub* behind my back. He didn't want to make another mistake.

It couldn't be helped. I had to do something, and I had to do it right away.

I picked up the phone once again and dialed directory assistance. "In Belmont please," I said. "I'd like the number for Robert Finn."

CHAPTER 26

*I*t was no surprise that Bobby Finn's phone number was unlisted. But I had seen a sample ballot at campaign headquarters, and I remembered his address from it. I had a street map in my car—required equipment for campaign vehicles—so I had little trouble finding the place. It was on one of those serene side streets where half-million-dollar houses smile discreetly at one another from the ends of their long driveways, their security systems turned on, their owners snug and safe inside. Belmont was a rung or two up the economic ladder from Hingham, and Finn's street was several rungs above the one on which I lived.

It was Republican territory for the most part, but it was also home to wealthy people whose consciences bothered them or who had a sense of noblesse oblige—like Elsa Finn. Bobby was as out of place here as he was at the white wine and Brie receptions he went to at the Kennedy School—or as he would be at a cocktail party in Georgetown—but he wasn't about to return to his roots any more than I was.

Unlike me, Bobby had always been a politician. When he got back from Vietnam, he ran for state rep in a district where being a war hero was still looked on as a virtue. He won easily, and he started working his way up the chain of command in the House. He probably would have still been there, a loyal soldier awaiting his chance to lead, if he hadn't met and married Elsa, who apparently saw in him something of what Harold had seen in me. She knew that the House was a dead end for a politician, so she bankrolled his run for lieutenant governor. The race was tighter than his first run for state rep; there were a lot of candidates for the Democratic nomination, and there was little reason to vote for one rather than another. But Bobby's connections in the House helped him win the endorsement at the Democratic convention, and his wife's money helped his name recognition in the primary. He won again, and he was now a statewide figure.

Being lieutenant governor is as useless as being Vice President. But the two positions share one crucial advantage: When the boss leaves, you're the heir apparent. Finn performed his limited duties well; he never upstaged the governor, but he made sure he kept a high enough profile that people didn't forget about him. And when the governor decided to retire, he was ready to make the run. His only serious opposition on the Democratic side would have been Tom Donato, and I took care of Donato for him. The only Republican he had reason to fear was me, and I wisely decided to run for the Senate instead. So Finn was elected governor the year I was elected to the Senate; four years later he was reelected in a landslide. We were now the two most popular politicians in the state; by tomorrow, I thought as I pulled into his driveway, we might have destroyed each other.

I turned off the engine. There were lights on in the house, so someone was probably awake. I hoped Finn wasn't still out campaigning; this was going to be awkward enough without having to wait for him. I wondered if he had state troopers guarding him at home; that would also be awkward. The gun pressed against my side; I took it out and stuck it in the glove compartment. Then I picked up the tape Everson had given me, got out of the car, and walked up to the governor's front door.

I rang the bell, and a few moments later I was facing a teenage boy wearing one olive green plastic soldier earring, a Grateful Dead T-shirt, and Army camouflage pants. He had a spray of acne across his forehead and the glazed expression I associated with kids listening to heavy metal on Walkmans. He stared at me with a vague sense of recognition: Had he seen me on TV or someplace? "Yeah?" he said.

I smiled and held out my hand. "Hi, I'm Senator Jim O'Connor. I'm here to see your father."

He took my hand and gave it a limp, puzzled shake. "Uh, wait here a sec," he said, and he disappeared into the house.

Nice young man, I thought. Maybe I should introduce him to Kathleen. As I expected, his mother was next to show up.

I was used to seeing Elsa Finn at public functions like the policemen's convention and the debate, where she wore outrageously expensive clothes and radiated an energy that was almost sexual. Here at home, however, she had the no-makeup, no-nonsense look of old money. She was wearing faded jeans and a turtleneck sweater; her hair was pulled back from her face, and reading glasses dangled over her chest. She was offstage, I realized. At least she had thought she was.

"Senator?" she said a bit uncertainly, as if I might have been an impostor or a doppelgänger. She wasn't the type to believe in the spirit world, however.

"Sorry to bother you at this hour, Mrs. Finn. I was wondering if the governor was at home."

"Come in, come in, Senator," she said, realizing that I was still on the doorstep. She had a husky alto voice that commanded obedience. I went inside. "Was Robert expecting you?"

She was the only person in the world who called him Robert. "No, this was more of a—a spur-of-the-moment thing. If he's here, I'd like to speak to him. It won't take long."

She looked uncertain. "Well, he's asleep, you see. He has an early schedule tomorrow, and—"

She stopped, realizing that this wasn't some hapless aide she was talking to. "Elsa," I said softly, "I wouldn't be here if it weren't important. I'd appreciate it if you'd wake him up."

"Could you tell me what it's about?"

Didn't she know? I wondered. Wouldn't her husband have confided in her about Donato and Danny and Jackie Scanlon? I shook my head. "I'm sorry, Elsa. If Bobby wants to talk about it later, that's up to him."

She pursed her lips. "Very well, Senator. I'll see if I can awaken him. Would you like some coffee in the meantime?"

"No, thank you."

She nodded and ascended the stairs, leaving me alone to await the governor's arrival. I glanced around. The hall opened up into a vast living room; I glimpsed a hardwood floor, uncomfortable-looking furniture, and white walls with primitive wall hangings on them, all knots and splotches of color. Did she decorate the

place herself, I wondered, or bring in the experts? Bobby certainly
had nothing to do with it. From beneath my feet came the throb-
bing of a bass guitar. Junior was in the basement, I imagined,
expressing his disdain for his parents' life-style.

I thought about Donato's cramped little apartment. What
would happen to Finn and me if we couldn't straighten this out?
Would the people we loved desert us? Would we end up changing
light bulbs for a living and watching *Wheel of Fortune* for entertainment, lying in our lonely rooms and dreaming of the days
when we could park right next to the State House?

Yes, this meeting was going to be important. As important as
any in our lives.

Finn came downstairs a few moments later, buttoning the
flannel shirt he had pulled on. He was wearing slippers and no
socks; his hair was short but still managed to look rumpled. "Don't
tell me, Jim," he said. "You've come to beg for a second debate.
You wanna give away the few votes you've got left. Well, I just
might agree to it if you ask me nice."

"You're too kind, Governor."

"What'll you insult this time? Apple pie? Motherhood? Why
not just burn a flag on camera and do the job right?"

His wife came down after him, evidently hoping for an in-
vitation to join us. She wasn't going to get it from me. "Can we
go someplace and discuss my options, Governor?" I asked Finn.

"Sure thing. Let's go into my office."

Finn led the way without looking back at his wife, who stood
grimly at the bottom of the stairs. I followed him through a spectacular dining room, with sliding glass doors looking out into a
floodlit garden, and into a large book-lined room that made my
little office in Hingham look like a closet. I bet the books had
never been opened.

"Have a seat, Senator," Finn said, and I sat in a leather wing
chair. All I needed was a smoking jacket and a pipe. "Can I get
you something?" he offered.

I shook my head. It was a little disconcerting, seeing my opponent at home, with the heels of his slippers caved in and late-
night stubble on his chin. He looked vulnerable. Just another
quick-witted, street-smart mick at an age when you need more
than street smarts to keep you going. He was a good politician,
but he had also been very lucky: in getting through the war un-
scathed; in finding a wife like Elsa; in having me shoot down

Donato for him. And, I figured, he probably thought his luck was holding strong: He goes up against the formidable incumbent senator, and the senator self-destructs in front of the voters' eyes. He probably thought I was here to beg him not to release Amanda's tapes. But he was about to find out that his luck had run out.

"Now, what brings you to the enemy's lair in the middle of the night?" Finn asked.

"I wanted to play a tape for you," I said.

I watched to see if the mention of a tape provoked a reaction; it didn't. He pointed to a sleek stereo system in the far corner of the room. "What is it, your concession speech?" he asked.

I shook my head. "Sorry." I went over to the stereo and inserted the tape.

"The button on the left," Finn called out as I fumbled with the cockpitlike complexity of the equipment. I pressed the button and returned to my seat, glancing at a wallful of awards as I passed; among them were a couple of framed military decorations. The tape began before I could read the citations.

"All right, I've started the tape," a tinny voice said. "I'll just ask a few of the questions again, okay?"

"Sure. Whatever." There was a background of clattering dishes and muffled loudspeaker announcements.

"Okay. What's your name?"

"Sid. Sid Blomberg."

Sid's voice was rough. He had a phlegmy cough that interrupted the conversation once in a while. I looked at Finn. He closed his eyes as Sid said his name.

"And you were in Vietnam with Robert Finn?"

"Yeah. He was my second lieutenant for a while there."

"Okay. So we want to know about what happened that time you entered the village you thought was deserted, and Finn was shot."

"Yeah, well, the way Larry told it is right. The other guys were taking care of the sniper, and me and Larry and the lieutenant went into this hut, and there was this old woman there, and he just blew her head off like it was, I dunno, a piece of fruit or something."

"Finn did."

"Yeah, Finn did. Fuckin' Governor Finn. I dream about it sometimes, y'know? I'm full of bad memories about them days, but that's one of the worst. She was just sittin' there. Maybe she was VC, but we never had a chance to find out, 'cause he unloaded on her before she even opened her mouth. He shouldna done that. He was just pissed off. Shit, if I blew away someone every time I got pissed off, wouldn't be anyone left in the state of California." He coughed.

"And you're willing to sign a statement to that effect?" the other voice said after the coughing stopped.

"Sure, I'll sign whatever. I bet they all think he's a hero back there in Massachusetts. Some hero. Of course, this won't do any good, you know. He'll get his lawyers and all and say, this guy's a lush, and probably Larry's a lush now, too, or whatever, and it'll get to be our fault somehow. We're lying, we shoulda done something to stop him. But I don't care. What can they do to me? Kick me out of this dump? Might as well tell the truth, see if it does any good."

"Okay, Sid. I think that should do it."

There was more coughing, and then the sound ended abruptly, leaving only the hiss of the tape in the elegant office.

Bobby Finn opened his eyes. He walked slowly over to the stereo and shut the tape off. "We've got a statement from Larry Spalding, too," I said. "He lives here in Massachusetts. He's eager to come forward and tell his story."

Finn looked at me, holding the tape in his hand. "Elsa doesn't know," he said softly. "She really did think you were here to do something crazy like concede. She said you looked like you were at a funeral. Didn't know it was mine."

I didn't say anything. He came back and tossed the tape onto the desk between us. Elsa was probably off picketing draft boards while Finn was shooting innocent women in the jungle; it was common knowledge that his stands on defense issues did not meet with her approval. Was that the thing that bothered him most: the prospect, not of public disgrace, but of his wife's contempt? Somehow that moved me.

"Sid talks about all his bad memories," Finn said. "Strange, but for me there's just that one bad memory of the whole war. That stupid, awful moment. But that was enough. God, I thought I was born to be a soldier. It wasn't just that I was good at it; I loved it. Loved it all, until I went haywire, and I did something so—so evil that it destroyed everything. And I wasn't even man enough to admit what I'd done. I lied, and I got away with it, and I thought it was all behind me, but it isn't, is it? It couldn't be, even if Sid and Larry hadn't been there. Because I can still see the look on that woman's face. I can still feel my hand press that trigger—" He stopped abruptly. "You sure you don't want a drink?"

I shook my head again.

"Think I'll have one myself," he muttered. He reached behind him and grabbed a bottle, but then he put it back down. "Ah, forget it," he said. He looked at me. "You didn't come here to listen to my confession," he said to me. "What is this, a courtesy call? Give the condemned man a little advance notice, let him get his affairs in order? Damned decent of you, old chap, like they say in the movies."

I was surprised. I thought he would be the one to make the offer. Maybe the revelation had slowed his quick wits. "I don't want to go public with this, Bobby," I said.

He looked puzzled and then suspicious. "Why not?"

"Because I want to make a deal. You don't tell people what you know about me, and I don't tell what I know about you."

He continued to study me, searching my face for the catch. "Okay," he said finally. "Fine with me. But why?"

Why? "Because I don't want to be ruined any more than you do."

That didn't seem to satisfy him. "I mean, I know we're both sort of hypocrites, Jim, but the cases aren't exactly comparable. So you were gettin' a little on the side. Big deal. No one really believes you murdered her—even the Monsignor, to tell you the truth, and you rank somewhere between Albert DeSalvo and Charles Stuart on his shit list. But I sure murdered that Vietnamese woman back then."

Was it possible that he didn't know? I tried to figure it out. It didn't *seem* possible, but there it was. He thought I was talking about my affair with Amanda. Maybe Cavanaugh was actually keeping it secret. No, that didn't seem possible either. And Finn couldn't be playing a game with me, not now.

My heart leaped up. If Finn didn't know, then why go through with the deal? Let Harold loose with the information. Destroy the bastard. Finn would destroy me if he were the one with the incriminating tapes and the sworn statements. And his wife would help.

Why indeed?

"Look," I said, "I just want to get rid of the extraneous garbage and focus on the issues. For example, I know in my bones that Cavanaugh is going to try something with the Taylor case before the election. You can do me a favor and make sure he doesn't."

"Of course, Jim. Don't worry about it."

"Great." I reached over and picked up the tape. "We've only got a few days till the election, Bobby. Let's both take the high road and forget about this stuff."

Finn looked a little frightened now. He couldn't figure me out, and that made him nervous. Sparing him certain disgrace in return for him putting in a good word for me with the DA? There had to be something going on that he didn't understand—or else this wasn't the kind of politics he was used to. But so what? He could get used to it very fast if it kept him from losing the election. "Okay, Jim. I don't know why you're doing this, but of course, I accept."

I shook his hand and stood up. "Fine. Now go back to bed and come out fighting in the morning."

"All right. Except I'm not quite sure who I'm fighting anymore."

"I'm not quite sure either, Bobby."

I stopped at an all-night supermarket and bought a bunch of red carnations; the girl at the checkout counter gave me the glazed look of semirecognition I had gotten from Bobby Finn's son. Then I drove to the waterfront and entered Harold's building. The doorman was delighted to see me; it broke up his night. He called up to Harold, and an elevator ride later I was standing in front of my campaign manager, offering him the bouquet. "Let's kiss and make up," I said. "And then let's figure out how to win this goddamn election."

Harold accepted the flowers graciously. He put on a pot of coffee, and I put the carnations in a vase. When the coffee was ready, we sat at a table looking out over the city and set to work with the vase of flowers between us. We didn't stop till morning.

Neither of us mentioned Everson's tape. I think Harold was just grateful that I was functioning again; besides, there wasn't time to argue about settled issues. It felt right that at the end it should come down to the two of us, without the consultants and the pollsters and the staffers; we had started all this, ten long years ago, and it was up to us to finish it.

I convinced Harold that for the final push we should go positive. We had done enough damage to Finn. What we needed now was to shore up my own image. I told him that I liked the approach he was taking with the wheelchair shocker: Jim O'Connor is more complex than you think. Let's go with that, I said. Let's turn the deficits into advantages. Let's make the people believe in me again.

By the end of our meeting we had sketched out the print ads and the TV and radio commercials, and we had come up with a list of talking points for my appearances. The others could organize the media buys and the logistics of the appearances. Marge and Sam Fisher could clean up our prose. Roger could find the money.

"We're going to do it, Harold," I said when I stood up at last to go.

Harold allowed himself to smile, the first smile I had seen on his face in a long time. "I went to bed not believing that," he replied. "Now I think I do."

"See you at headquarters."

"I'll be there."

I drove home to catch a little sleep, going against the rush-hour traffic that crawled toward the city. Finn doesn't know about the tapes, I thought for the hundredth time. I may have shocked Finn by making the deal with him, but I hadn't really shocked myself. He deserved his freedom as much as I did; he certainly didn't deserve to end up someplace like the Lynn Arms. I could beat him without destroying him.

Even in the midst of my relief, however, I could still feel the uneasiness that hadn't left me since the moment I discovered Amanda's corpse.

Cavanaugh was letting me twist slowly in the wind. And there was a murderer out there, still waiting to be discovered. If Bobby Finn didn't know about the tapes, then the murderer surely did. And what was the murderer planning to do with them?

I arrived home to a deserted house. I went to sleep on the couch, and the murderer was there in my dreams. But after a while I awoke, and there was too much to be done to dream anymore.

CHAPTER 27

*T*he election approached, and I twisted in the wind.

For what it was worth, the polls showed that my slide had stopped. All of them gave me a slight lead, but it was within the statistical margin of error. In addition, there were plenty of un-decideds, and even those who had made up their minds weren't as firmly committed as they should have been at this stage of the race. I may not have blown the election, but I had certainly turned it into a cliff-hanger.

If my flowers had mollified Harold, Kevin was inconsolable. "Donato's *guilty*, Senator," he insisted. "We've got to *do* something."

"We've got nothing on him, Kevin," I explained patiently. "So Amanda Taylor interviewed him. That's not a crime."

"But he's got a motive and—"

"And if we tried to make a public accusation, how would it look? Like we were kicking a man while he's down, that's how. That's not the image we want to get across to the voters. Keep your guy on the case, Kevin. But we need something more than this."

My father went home from the hospital. "They did their best to kill me," he growled, "but I guess I was just too tough for 'em." He was carless, but he insisted that cabs were just as convenient, and cheaper in the long run. I pressed him about moving in with us, but the most I could get out of him was "After the election. Maybe we'll talk about it after the election."

Danny had taken care of everything, just as he said he would.

Melissa called. Some company had contacted Danny out of the blue, wanting to interview him for a sales position. Imagine that. She asked if I had anything to do with it, and I swore that I hadn't. She seemed suspicious, but she also seemed eager to believe me. By the end of our conversation she sounded almost proud of Danny.

Liz told me to stop sleeping on the damn couch. If I was going to live in the house, I might as well sleep in my own bed. I asked her if she wanted to talk. "After the election," she said. "We'll figure everything out after the election."

And then Detective Mackey called. When I got the message I thought: Another summons to Cavanaugh's office. But then I noticed that Mackey had left his home phone number. And that scared me even more than a summons.

I called him back when I arrived home after a long day of campaigning. Mackey answered on the first ring. "Mack, it's Jim O'Connor," I said. "What's happening?"

"I need to see you, Senator. It's important."

"Why, Mack? What's going on?"

"Well, for starters, I've been taken off the Taylor case."

Yes, this was going to be bad. "Cavanaugh's about to pull something, isn't he?"

"I'd rather talk about it in person, Jim."

"When? Where?"

He offered to come over to my house right away, and that was fine with me. I thought about calling Finn in the meantime, but I decided I had better get my facts straight before laying into the governor for breaking his promise.

Mackey arrived inside an hour, wearing a windbreaker and chinos. The outfit looked strange on him; I couldn't recall ever seeing him when he wasn't wearing a rumpled suit. We shook hands rather solemnly, then went into my office and sat down. He looked around, drumming his fingers on the side of his chair. He was as nervous as I was; the last thing he wanted was to get squashed in the politics of this case.

"We go back a long way, Senator," he said after we were settled.

"Sure do," I agreed. *Let him take his time.*

"You've always been solid. Even when you were a defense lawyer."

"Even when I became a politician?" I asked.

He smiled. "You may be the only decent politician I ever met."

Then he couldn't know about Jackie Scanlon, I thought, or I'd be on the trash heap with all the rest of them. "Mack, I'm no better than anyone else. It's tough to stay clean in this business."

"It's tough to stay clean in any business," Mackey replied. "But some of us try harder than others." He leaned forward; he was ready. "Jim," he said, "I've been on this case since it started, and I still don't have any answers. It's clear to me you were sleeping with Amanda Taylor, and I think a good prosecutor could convince a jury of it. That book business was just a cover, and not a very good one, or why don't we have tapes of any interviews before September? That suggests the relationship went sour, and maybe that's why she was suddenly interviewing people and taking notes and so on; she was getting ready to do a hatchet job on you.

"So there's bitterness over the end of the affair and fear that she's going to tell the world about it and ruin your career. It's a reasonable motive.

"The trouble is, it doesn't feel right to me. I listen to the tapes, I read the notes, and it sure doesn't feel like that's what's going on. I don't know what she was up to, exactly, but it wasn't a hatchet job. And I don't think a jury would buy it either. They probably wouldn't believe your story, but that doesn't mean they'd believe the prosecution's.

"So from where I sit, you're still a suspect, no matter how much I like you personally. You're our best suspect, basically our only suspect. But I haven't got enough to arrest you, and I don't know if I'll ever get it."

I shrugged. "Fair enough," I said. "I never asked for special treatment."

"The thing is," Mackey said, "Cavanaugh doesn't see it the way I see it. He wants to arrest you for the murder of Amanda Taylor."

"And you refused to go along?"

Mackey nodded. "So he's gonna find someone who will go along."

"Will that be a problem for him?"

"Not really. The commissioner owes Cavanaugh too many favors. If Cavanaugh wants an arrest, he'll get an arrest."

"Does he honestly think he has enough to make a case, or doesn't he care?"

"I don't know. He's not quite rational when it comes to you, Jim."

"Tell me about it. Do you know if he's talked to Finn about arresting me?"

Mackey shrugged. "The Monsignor doesn't take me into his confidence, unfortunately."

"He'd have to clear it with Finn," I said, trying to convince myself.

"You're the expert on that sort of thing, Jim."

If Cavanaugh didn't happen to think it was necessary, then I was sure glad I had the warning, so I had time to call in my IOU from Finn. "Mack, I owe you for this. You're risking a lot to come here."

"I am," he agreed. "The commissioner won't fire me just for refusing to cooperate with Cavanaugh, but he'd get rid of me in a minute if he found out I was leaking this to you or anyone else."

"No one will know it came from you, Mack."

Mackey looked uncomfortable. "If you make it public," he said, "Cavanaugh and the commissioner—they'll know who you got it from. Jim, this job is all I've got—and it's all I want."

"Then I won't make it public."

He nodded his relief and leaned back. "I appreciate it, Jim." We sat silently for a moment, and then he stood up. "Well, I imagine you've got things to do."

"You're right about that, Mack."

Mackey had made it clear enough already, but at the door I decided to settle the Jackie Scanlon issue once and for all. "Mack, you said you listened to those tapes of Amanda's interviews, right?"

"Every one of them."

"No way Cavanaugh could have gotten hold of any before you did?"

Mackey shook his head. "Why, Jim?"

"I was just wondering if there was anything, you know, revealing on any of them."

"You mean, any dirt?"

"Well, yeah."

He considered. "We were looking for dirt, of course," he said. "All Cavanaugh wanted was dirt. But there wasn't really anything the Democrats could use. She was talking mostly to your friends after all. That's part of what made me think it wasn't a hatchet job."

"Just wondering," I said. And I was wondering about something else. "The notes," I added.

"Yeah. There were just a couple of pages. Sort of . . . impressionistic. Like I said, if she was working on a book, I figure there'd be a lot more. Anyway, they're another one of the things that's got me confused about this case."

"I don't suppose it'd be possible for me to see a copy of those notes," I remarked, trying to appear casual.

"I don't know, Jim. Now that I'm off the case—"

"If you can. I'm curious, that's all. Find out what she had to say about me."

"Well, I'll see what I can do."

"Thanks again, Mack."

He disappeared into the night, and I was left behind, staring into the darkness.

I returned to my office and left a message for Finn. He got back to me in twenty minutes. "I didn't have anything to do with this, Jim," he said before I could utter a word. "You've got to believe me. I just heard about it a few hours ago, and I've been trying to talk Cavanaugh out of it." He sounded desperate. He needed me on his side.

"When is he going to have me arrested?" I asked.

"The day before the election is what he told me. That way you wouldn't have a chance to put your spin on it, get some positive publicity."

"He's crazy. It's bound to make you look bad."

"He said for me to hold a press conference and denounce him if I wanted to, say it was all his idea and I didn't believe Jim O'Connor was capable of murder."

That sounded familiar. "Like the Paul Everson trial," I said.

"What? Oh, right. Right. He never got over losing that case, I think."

"But Jesus, didn't you tell him this'll end his career? Talk about spectacular defeats; he'll never win this one. He won't even get an indictment with what he's got on me."

"Jim, I told him that. I used every argument and threat I could come up with. The thing of it is, he doesn't need me on this. He's got Washington backing him."

Washington? "You mean the President?"

"Yeah. If Cavanaugh can help me win, fine. But the main thing is to get you out of Kenton's way for two years from now. The Monsignor's tired of being DA. He's getting old; he doesn't need the headaches. Kenton's promised him some cushy federal job when things quiet down. So he destroys his old nemesis and picks up a President for a friend. It's quite a deal."

I thought it through. They haul me off in handcuffs in time for the six o'clock news. Cavanaugh gives a press conference and makes the case that Mackey had just made to me, only without Mackey's doubts. He swears there's nothing political about the arrest. He conducted a painstaking investigation, he points out, and he points out how much grief he took for not making an arrest even sooner. If it was political, why isn't Governor Finn backing him up? And just to show that he has no hidden agenda, he announces that he won't be running for reelection—or for any other office.

Finn wins or he doesn't; Cavanaugh doesn't care. But Cavanaugh gets his indictment because, despite what I said to Finn, you can almost always get an indictment. He has motive, he has means, he has opportunity; he has enough. The trial would be . . . when? Next summer at the earliest. He strings things out as long as he can.

In the meantime, I can't raise money for the presidential race, I can't build an organization, I can't get any early endorsements. Who would back someone who's going to be on trial for murder?

Cavanaugh lets Jerry Tobin or some other young sacrificial lamb handle the trial, and there's a week of lurid publicity while they bring up San Francisco and my key to the Back Bay love nest and the eavesdropping waiter and whatever else they can come up with. Tobin gets blown away when the case finally goes to the jury because there's nowhere near enough evidence to convict, but by then it's too late for me. I'm damaged goods. I have my freedom but no future. Kenton gets reelected, and Cavanaugh has an IOU as big as the one I had for Finn.

And this was the best I could hope for. The worst was that sometime between the arrest and the trial Cavanaugh stumbles across the truth about me and Jackie Scanlon. Tom Glenn faces

prison again, perhaps, and figures he can cut a deal. Donato decides he could use some help from his old friends and trades what
he knows for a handout. . . .

"This is very bad," I said finally.

"Jim, please," Finn said. "I know it's bad, but you've gotta
believe I'm trying to hold up my end of the bargain. I'll work on
Cavanaugh some more tomorrow. Just don't—"

"All right, Bobby," I said. "All right. Do what you can. But
hurry, would you? For both our sakes."

"Okay, Jim. Thanks."

He hung up. I tried to figure things out for a while, but that
was a waste of time. Finally I went upstairs and got in bed beside Liz.

Amanda's notes, I thought.

And then I fell asleep.

The next day was as busy as the one before. Harold hadn't
found out about Cavanaugh's plan, and I didn't tell him. He would
just want me to launch a preemptive strike and denounce Cavanaugh before he had a chance to arrest me; but I had promised
Mackey I wouldn't go public with the information, and I didn't
feel like going back on that promise any more than I felt like
destroying Bobby Finn.

Any more than I felt like campaigning. The surge of energy
I had felt after the conversation at Finn's house was slipping away,
to be replaced by the brooding confusion that had become my
dominant state of mind before it.

Did I really care if the trial kept me from running for President? Did I really care if I lost *this* election? Maybe, like Carl
Hutchins, I should be afraid to win, afraid of six more years of
decisions and opinions and lies.

How would I act if I were arrested?

How would Kathleen take it?

What would Liz do if I went to trial? She had felt compelled
to tell Amanda about Jackie Scanlon. Would she feel compelled
to tell the world?

Amanda's notes. What was in Amanda's notes?

In the late afternoon I was the guest on a radio call-in show
run by a popular talkmaster whose politics were somewhere to
the right of Louis XIV. He was not happy with the things I'd been
saying lately, and he let me, and his listeners, know it. This was

okay actually; there's nothing like being attacked by extremists to increase your appeal to moderates. The callers sounded angry at me, but I don't think they really were. This guy would stir them up while they listened, but after a couple of beers and a few hours of TV they would calm down and see things my way.

Tony from Revere was on the air, defending the police to me, when I saw Mackey beyond the glassed-in broadcast booth, talking to Kevin Feeney. I longed to go out there and join them, but instead I had to sit and listen to Tony struggle to make his point. "The police, see, they don't, like, it's not easy bein' a cop, right? They're the guys on the front lines, you understand what I'm sayin'? I mean, I think we owe them, like, a lot of support, instead of, you know, puttin' 'em down."

I assured Tony that I couldn't agree with him more, that I had always supported the police and they had always supported me. . . . My eyes never left Mackey. After a brief conversation he handed Kevin a manila envelope, then left the studio. He never looked at me.

During the next commercial I hurried out to Kevin. "Mackey gave you something," I said, unable to make the incident seem unimportant.

Kevin nodded a little sullenly. He was still upset with me. "Mackey said it was personal," he replied, and he handed the envelope to me.

It felt thin. "A couple of pages," Mackey had said. I longed to rip the envelope open right there and read the contents; but the commercial was almost over, and they were signaling for me to come back, and Kevin was looking at me curiously, and I decided to wait until I had some privacy. I returned to the broadcast booth, clutching the envelope, and I talked to Ralph from Somerville about foreign policy.

The privacy didn't come until Kevin dropped me off in Hingham late that night. The house was quiet; Angelica was snoozing on the kitchen radiator; the refrigerator hummed softly. I had been at a cocktail party, a last-minute fund raiser that Roger had organized to see us through the last couple of days of wild media spending. I had eaten soggy canapés and drunk watery Coke, but now I decided that I needed some real food. I opened the refrigerator.

Tuna.

I thought of the night Amanda was murdered, standing in

the same silent kitchen, staring at the same food, afraid to talk to my wife, wondering what was to become of me. Had anything changed since then? I certainly felt different. In a couple of days I could be in a jail cell. Maybe I deserved to be in a jail cell. But maybe America would be losing a great leader if that's where I ended up. I felt different, but I wasn't sure I understood what the difference meant.

I put a little more mayonnaise in the tuna and made myself a sandwich. Then I sat down at the kitchen table, opened the envelope, and looked inside.

I pulled out two badly photocopied pieces of paper; the police had evidently exhausted their budget for toner over at headquarters. The printing was dot matrix; I had no idea if it came from Amanda's printer. There was a yellow Post-it stuck to the first sheet. On it Mackey had scrawled:

All I could come up with. Pls don't show to anyone else.
Mack
P.S. Cavanaugh thought it was interesting about Everson.

I crumpled the Post-it and threw it away. And then I read what was on the sheets.

Who is he? I can't figure it out . . . probably because he can't figure it out himself.

You find a way to come to terms with life. You are successful; perhaps you are even happy. But it's not *you*. The you is buried beneath the quick grin, the perpetual sense of obligation. Not buried, really. It's in the basement of a house of cards, a house that grows more elaborate, and more fragile, with each passing year and each new triumph.

Until finally it collapses, and you have to start over. Paradigm shift.

Did it happen in Harvard Yard?

Surely it happened with the Everson case. Everson tells him he's guilty, and down come the cards. What am I doing with my life? Where did I go wrong? How can I fix what I've suddenly realized is broken?

So he starts over, and he's successful once again, but is he any more real?

Is it happening again?

I think he loves his wife. But which *he* is it? One that he left behind years ago? Or—more likely—one that he *should* have left behind years ago, that he continues to carry with him out of the same old sense of duty?

He is afraid to look too closely at himself, still afraid after all these years that what he will see is a mother killer. Afraid that he will see someone—some*thing*—fundamentally irrational. Guilty before he knows what guilt is.

Original sin.

Irish.

And the rationality is just part of the facade—he fears. The brilliant legal mind means nothing when he's down in the basement.

The foul rag-and-bone shop of the heart.

Part of him wants to escape his own complexity, but he can't do it, any more than he can stop being witty, or being Irish. He wants to *relax*. He thought—he hoped—that I was relaxation. Then he found out I was part of the complexity, and that frightened him away. I have to make him understand that the complexity is all right, that he is all right. That we are all right.

He wants to be President.

He wants to be anything but President.

Oh, Jim.

Imagine writing your biography.

Angelica was sitting on the table now, staring at my uneaten sandwich. "You're not allowed on the table," I informed her. She moved a little closer. I gave her some of the tuna.

I read Amanda's notes a second time, and then a third. *The foul rag-and-bone shop of the heart.* Yeats. I remembered the drunken evening I had recited the poem to her. Champagne brought out the Irish orator in me. Was Yeats right about the heart?

It was certainly starting to feel like it.

I folded the pieces of paper and put them in a locked drawer of the desk in my office. Then I went upstairs and woke up Liz, as I had on that other awful night.

She stared at me groggily.

"I'm sorry to bother you," I said, "but I have to ask you a question. It's kind of important."

"Go ahead," she said, yawning.

"When you talked to Amanda that time about Jackie Scanlon, did you also mention Paul Everson?"

Her face took on that half-defensive, half-aggrieved expression I had become so used to. "I wanted to make sure she knew all the bad things about you," Liz said. "What happened with Everson was as bad as what happened with Scanlon—maybe worse. You should have done something about him, but you never did. Instead you used the case to get yourself started in politics. It wasn't right."

The old arguments sprang to my lips. How could I have done something? It would have been unethical. Besides, that isn't the kind of society we live in. Liz stared at me, daring me to make my stupid rational objections. This wasn't rational, she knew; it was personal. You don't let wife-murderers go free, just as you don't put your family at risk to cover up for your brother's idiotic mistakes.

I didn't accept the challenge. "Thanks," I said. "Sorry to wake you up."

"Why do you want to know?" she asked.

"Just—just trying to fit everything together," I replied vaguely. And then I went into the bathroom to forestall any further questions.

I stared at myself in the mirror.

He is afraid to look too closely at himself.

I was getting old. In the blink of an eye I would look like my father. My world would close in around me as his had, and nothing would be left but my memories—if I chose to remember them. Or, more likely, there would be no choice. Like Donato, like Bobby Finn, I would never be able to escape the consequences of what I had done.

And if only the memories remained, they had better be good ones. I didn't want to end up like Donato or Finn, suppressing the memories or twisting them to suit my needs.

I put on my pajamas and got into bed next to Liz. She had fallen back to sleep; evidently her interest in what I was up to had not run very deep. When she was old, what would her memories be like? I wondered. Would she regret her life with me—except, of course, for Kathleen? Or would there be moments that remained beautiful, not retrospectively ruined by what I later became? Perhaps that night at the Ritz I had sprung for when I was still a penniless law student. Or one of my proposals—at Danny's wedding, or in front of the health and beauty aids at Stop & Shop. Our own wedding day. Or perhaps just a walk along the beach, an early-morning kiss, a gaze full of shared understanding.

I couldn't tell. I couldn't even tell if I loved her, or if it was some other me who longed to take her in my arms and whisper to her how sorry I was.

I didn't do it. She wouldn't understand, and I knew I couldn't find the words to make her understand.

After the election. Everything would get fixed after the election.

Maybe that would be too late.

I stared into the darkness of our bedroom, alone with a thousand memories, trying to see if any of them could tell me what I should do.

I knew now who had murdered Amanda Taylor.

But that was only the beginning.

CHAPTER 28

I sleep alone here. Surprisingly, I sleep rather well. The memories are exorcised during the day, apparently, leaving my dreams to go their own way.

First thing every morning now I go for a tramp through the snowy woods in back of the house. I know them well enough at this point that I'm not afraid of becoming lost and ending up a blue-skinned corpse facedown in a snowbank, food for wolves in the spring thaw. I haven't seen another human being in my travels; I wouldn't know what to do if I did. I am so used to solitude that I might just turn and run. Or I might embrace the startled stranger and burst into tears.

Not likely anyone would recognize me, with the beard I have managed to grow.

There is much more gray in my beard than in my hair.

After the walk in the woods, I make my breakfast: usually fried eggs, juice, and coffee. I am getting quite good at frying eggs. The urge to read a newspaper hasn't gone away, but it's more under control than when I first arrived here. Instead of reading, I force myself to listen to the silence. After breakfast I pour myself another cup of coffee and go upstairs to work.

Some days, like today, I have difficulty getting started. It's almost over now, and that means I have to face the hardest part. None of it has been easy, to be sure, but when I think about what I did, about what I tried to do . . .

No, I can't just think. I have to write. I can't let it escape, any of it. It is all too important. Especially the parts I would rather leave out.

The sun is shining brightly against my computer screen, making it hard to see the words I type. The sun didn't shine at all that day. The fog had returned, and the world was shrouded in gray.

I drove along the Mass Pike in my own fog. It was early Sunday evening, two days before the election. I had called my father and made my excuses once again; that would buy me some time. But I was supposed to be somewhere afterward, and when I didn't arrive, my staff would worry for a while and then panic. Kevin would call Harold, and Harold would call me. And call and call.

But none of that mattered now. I was lost in my fog, and I knew that I was never going to come out.

Traffic was heavy and slow at first, as the Boston drivers coped with the rotten weather; the red brake lights snaked off into invisibility a dozen car lengths ahead of me. Past Worcester the traffic dwindled but the fog got worse, so that I seemed to have the highway all to myself—my personal road to hell.

Occasionally I tried to think, but I couldn't. I was past thinking; I had thought altogether too much in my life. Something more was required now, something that would make the memories tolerable.

The loneliest part of the Mass Pike is the stretch going into the Berkshires, when you have passed the cities—Worcester, Springfield—but haven't reached the posh vacation areas of Tanglewood and Stockbridge. Here there was just the occasional eighteen-wheeler thundering past in the night to remind me that I was still a part of reality. I got off the highway finally and started making my way along deserted rural roads. The Boston Symphony was long gone for the year, the foliage was past peak, and the skiing season had yet to start; there was no reason for most people to be out here. I knew where I was going, although I wasn't quite sure how to get there.

I was headed for Shangri-la.

I found it finally, when I caught a glimpse of a large pseudo-Oriental sign in the fog. I wondered how much Everson had to bribe someone to get the sign approved.

I turned and drove past the sign, up a long paved driveway. I had expected an electrified fence or some other form of high tech security, but I pulled right up to the circular drive in front of the mansion without encountering anything.

I have an army of M.B.A.'s who come in by day and make money for me, but at night it's just me.

It was only as I turned off the engine and started to open the door that the animal came bounding toward me out of the fog like the hound of the Baskervilles. It was a Rottweiler, and it was angry. It barked furiously at me on the other side of the window while I cringed in my seat and wondered about the strength of the glass in a Buick Regal.

After a lifetime there was a shouted command, and the dog calmed down. A heavyset man in a black leather jacket approached, aiming a rifle at my head. I opened the window a crack.

"This is private property," the man said.

"Yes, of course. I'm Senator James O'Connor—Do you recognize me? I'd like to talk to Paul Everson, if he's here."

The man didn't look as if he recognized me. He didn't look as if it would make any difference to him if I were President Kenton. "You don't have an appointment," he said flatly. He knew Everson's schedule.

"Still, I'm sure he'll see me," I replied. "Ask him. I won't be going anywhere."

The man turned and walked away without answering. The Rottweiler stayed where it was. I rolled my window back up and waited.

It was absurd to have thought that Everson would really be alone. Men like him needed guards. Terrorists could kidnap him, after all; disgruntled investors or laid-off CEOs could lob grenades at him. At least he was here, apparently, and that meant he would see me.

After a while the guard returned, now looking appropriately deferential. He grabbed hold of the dog. "Won't you come with me please, Senator?" he said.

I got out, keeping an eye on the dog, and followed the guard into the mansion, which looked Spanish, not Oriental; I wondered if the movie magnate who originally owned it had brought it with him from Southern California. Everson was waiting by the door. "Jim, what a pleasant surprise!" he said. "Come on in. What brings you here?"

He didn't look pleasantly surprised. He looked as if he wanted to invite the guard inside with us. But instead he dismissed him and led me into the marble-floored entrance hall. We stood beneath a mammoth crystal chandelier. "Nice little place you've got, Paul," I said. "Doesn't it make you feel cramped, though?"

Everson laughed, not very successfully. "You've never been here before, right? Like a tour? I have this collection of antique autos—"

"Yeah. I saw some pictures in a magazine once. Actually I'd just like to have a talk."

That didn't make him look any happier. "All right," he said. "Can I take your jacket?"

I shook my head.

"Fine," he said. "Let's, um, go into the office area."

I followed Everson through a wilderness of huge but deserted rooms to one that looked as if it belonged in a military command center rather than a country estate. Unlike Finn's office, it made no pretense of culture; there were no books, no classical music— just an array of electronic equipment: computers and fax machines and printers and phones. The only way you could tell you weren't on Wall Street was by looking out the French doors that opened onto the foggy woods.

"The world's at my fingertips," Everson said. "Want to know current prices on the Nikkei?"

I shook my head.

Everson forced a smile. "Yeah, that's not very impressive. It's the information that other people can't get that makes the difference."

"Like the dirt on Bobby Finn."

"Precisely."

He sat down at a desk in front of the French doors; I sat opposite him. I was as nervous as he was. One of his machines hummed to life, and I jumped.

"Just a fax," Everson said. We waited in silence for the machine to finish. "So," he continued, "you want to have a talk."

I nodded. "About Amanda Taylor."

His expression didn't change. "All right," he said.

"She knew that you killed your wife," I said. "Liz told her."

"That wasn't very nice of Liz."

"I had a private eye looking into her murder," I went on, "since you didn't seem able to come up with anything. I called him today and asked him to find out your whereabouts on the day of the murder. He got back to me a few hours ago. He told me you were meeting with some executives from the Horvath Corporation at the Prudential Center that afternoon. The Prudential Center's about a five-minute walk from Amanda's apartment."

Everson nodded. "Mr. Sharpe does good work," he said. "I'll have to use him someday."

So he knew about Kevin's private eye. Was there anything he didn't know? "A remarkable coincidence, wouldn't you say—your being in the same neighborhood the afternoon Amanda was killed?"

"That's one way of looking at it," he said.

"Of course, what does it matter to you if some reporter knows the truth about your murder case? Double jeopardy is still the law of the land, right? And you're beyond the reach of any exposé. The world already dislikes you, but that doesn't change the way you live your life."

Everson shifted in his chair. "I can't disagree with anything you've said so far, Jim. But I still don't see—"

"Jackie Scanlon," I said. Once again there wasn't a flicker of change in Everson's expression. "I'm so sick of that name," I went on. "It haunts me. It's in my thoughts every day of my life, but I almost never say it out loud. Because if I say it out loud, all my fears might come true. Jackie Scanlon."

"Who," Everson asked, "is Jackie Scanlon?"

But he knew. He could wear his poker face forever, and I'd still know that he knew. It didn't matter how the knowledge had come his way: Perhaps Tom Glenn had sold it to him, perhaps he had tapped Scanlon's phone, or perhaps he had simply deduced it out of a hundred scraps of information about me. All that mattered was that he knew—and he had known on the day he was in the Back Bay taking over yet another hapless company. "Amanda was interviewing people about me in the weeks before she died," I said. "I bet she got in touch with you. She figured you were important in my life, and she was right. And you would have known all about her, right? Because you make it your business to know everything, especially if it has to do with me. Because you still think you owe me. Because you think if you can even the scales with me, you'll somehow find forgiveness for murdering your wife.

"And this was your chance, right? Maybe you even knew about Danny and Tom Donato talking to her about Jackie Scanlon; you knew about the tapes she possessed, tapes that would end my career and put me in prison. You knew that she had lied about herself to make me trust her. So you agree to be interviewed. You go to her apartment. Maybe you try to buy her off—probably not, though. You know she's got money. You know she's just trying to make a name for herself. You know there's only one thing to do, and you know how to do it because you've done it before."

I fell silent for a moment. Everson didn't respond; he was staring intently at me, as if hypnotized. "You're saying I killed her," he murmured finally.

"You made your wife's murder look like a suicide," I said. "This time you try to make the murder look like a robbery or the work of a psycho. You don't do a very good job, though; maybe you're out of practice. I'm implicated, and then I have to come to you for help. Isn't that a strange situation? You want to reassure me, but you don't want to tell me the truth because you're afraid of my conscience, afraid I'll think I'll have to go to the police with the information and ruin both you and me. So you keep telling me, 'Don't worry about the tape, don't worry about the tape,' but you don't tell me why. You don't tell me that you have Danny's tape; you even have Donato's tape, which you think I don't know anything about. You have them, right?"

"Jim, I—"

"*Right?*" And I reached into my jacket and pulled out Liz's gun, as I had at Donato's. This time it wasn't just for protection.

"Oh, Jim," Everson whispered.

"Show me the tapes, Paul."

Everson slowly unlocked a drawer of his desk and took out two cassettes. He tossed them to me, one after the other. I glanced at them long enough to make out Amanda's writing on the labels; that was all I needed to see. "They've been erased," Everson said, "So I'm afraid you won't be able to listen to them. Now put the gun down, Jim, because we've got to talk."

I shook my head. "I don't want to listen to anything you have to say, Paul. You'll say you did it for me. Fine. You'll say she was a bad person, that she conned me. Well, I don't know about that, but I can see where you might believe it. The thing is, nothing you can say matters.

"What matters are my memories. How I see myself when I've got nothing left to do but remember. What matters is that you have murdered two women, and it was my fault you murdered the second one. Because I should never have let you escape unpunished after you told me you murdered the first.

"At first I thought I should come out here and make you turn yourself in. Cavanaugh's going to arrest me tomorrow, see, and I figured that having you confess would solve all my problems. You could tell them you did it to keep Amanda from revealing that you'd murdered your wife. Great. Nothing to do with Jim O'Connor. Cavanaugh wouldn't be able to touch me.

"And then I thought: You'll wriggle out of it. You'll find a technicality or bribe a judge or just come up with another hotshot young lawyer like me to believe in you and make the jury believe in you, too. Oh, you might serve some time, but nowhere near enough to punish you for what you've done.

"I had to do something more. If I kill you, I avenge Amanda, and I also avenge Liz. I start making up to her for all I've done over the years. So what if I go to jail? At least I'll find some peace. There's a lot to be said for finding peace."

Everson's eyes didn't leave the gun. "Jim, you've been under a tremendous strain—

"I've been under a tremendous strain ever since I can remember, Paul. That doesn't change anything."

"I didn't kill her, Jim," he whispered. "If you'll just give me a chance—"

"I'm sorry, Paul. I suppose you think this is unfair, you were only trying to do me a favor. Well, life isn't fair. I can't see any other way out."

Everson kept staring at the gun. I stared back at him, waiting, I suppose, for the trigger to pull itself. And then he stood up. "Shoot me if you have to," he said. "Otherwise, I'm going for a walk." And he turned and headed for the French doors.

Damn you, I thought. I raised the gun and aimed.

But I didn't pull the trigger. Everson opened the French doors and disappeared into the fog.

So why didn't I shoot? Cowardice? Prudence? A sudden attack of rationality? I don't know. But in that moment my latest house of cards started to fall, and I was helpless to stop it.

My immediate reaction, though, was disgust at my inability to do what I had come all the way out here to do. I followed Everson outside.

I shivered in the damp air. The Rottweiler barked in the distance, and I shivered some more. I assumed Everson would stay close to the mansion, on the manicured lawn that surrounded it, but I thought I heard him off in the trees, so I headed toward the sound. The light from the mansion reached only a few feet away from the doors, and soon I was groping in the dark, listening for his footsteps.

Abruptly I was in the woods, and all I could see were the black outlines of the trees as I brushed past them. This is ridiculous, I thought. I should go back inside. I should throw away the gun and return to Boston. But I couldn't. I had come too far. I had to find him.

But where was he? The woods scared me. Never mind the Rottweiler; there were probably bears here. Wolves.

There was a murderer here.

I thought I heard an owl. "Who, whoooo?" I had never heard an owl before.

The gun trembled in my hand. I was lost now. Which way was the mansion? Which way was civilization? Nothing but trees and fog. City boy. I longed for a streetlight. I was helpless without electricity.

"She did love you, you know."

I whirled. It took my eyes a moment to spot him, a black silhouette leaning against a black tree.

"She didn't want to hurt you," he went on. "She just wanted to understand you, particularly after what Liz told her. You had left her, and she was trying to figure out how to get you back. She erased the tapes and gave them to me, to show me her sincerity. She was trying to get in touch with you. She was going to explain everything. But she never got the chance."

"You killed her first," I said. My voice sounded thin and quavering in the darkness.

There was a long silence. The owl hooted again. When Everson finally spoke, his voice was almost pleading. "Jim, you don't have to pretend. I understand; I've been there. When I came out of Amanda's apartment that afternoon, I saw you going in. Oh, you had a hat on, and your head was down and you were obviously trying not to be noticed, but it was you all right. I suppose I should have told you about it when you first came to me for help, but I assumed you had your reasons for this charade. I didn't know what to do. I figured Amanda explained to you about giving me the tapes, but what if she didn't? Maybe telling you the truth would worry you more—knowing that I knew. So I just tried to calm you down. I've been trying to protect you, Jim; that's all I've been doing. But I don't know how to protect you from yourself. I just can't figure you out anymore. It looks to me like you're going to destroy yourself no matter what I do. I suppose that's your right. And if you want to destroy me as well, I guess that's your right, too. But I think you should confront the truth before you do anything."

The truth? I didn't understand a word of Everson's speech. It was as if his meaning were lost in the fog along with everything else. "What is the truth?" I whispered.

"Jim, I know that you killed her."

What?

And in that awful moment I knew that Everson was right. The better the politician, the more he believes in the roles he plays. I had spent this campaign learning the truth about everyone else; now I was learning the truth about myself. *Everyone is guilty,* and no one more than I.

I could feel myself in Amanda's apartment. Feel the hot rage building in me. Feel myself confronting the lover who was only using me, who was about to destroy me. She denies everything, she tries to explain, but I don't want to hear explanations. The rage becomes uncontrollable; my hand reaches out for the knife—

"Who, whoooo?"

The moment passed. What was going on? I wasn't that good a politician (or, perhaps, not that bad a one). I might have been stupid, but I wasn't crazy. Amanda loved me; Everson said so. Even Brad Williams and Harold said so. And I was with Jackie Scanlon when she was murdered. Everson didn't know that, but it was true; I hadn't hallucinated our meeting. So what was he talking about?

And then I understood. I lowered the gun and stood motionless in the fog.

"Jim? Are you okay, Jim?"

I looked at Everson. No, I wasn't okay. I wasn't a murderer, but I wasn't okay. "Can you tell me how to get out of this place, Paul?" I asked.

He pointed.

"Thanks."

I started walking through the woods. Everson may have called out to me, but I didn't pay any attention. Eventually I saw the lights of the mansion. I walked around it to my car. I didn't think about the Rottweiler; I didn't think about what the guard might do if he noticed the gun in my hand. I got into my car and threw the gun into the glove compartment. Then I sat back and closed my eyes.

I had come so close to ruining everything.

But perhaps everything was already ruined.

I started the car then and drove slowly down the road that took me out of Shangri-la.

It was time to start the long journey home.

CHAPTER 29

The journey back now seems like a dream, but it was a car trip like any other. I had to stop for gas; I went to the bathroom; I stood in line to buy a Whopper and ate it as I drove. The car phone rang intermittently; I ignored it. I listened to soft rock on the radio.

My mind, though, was far away. Lost in memories.

The fog started to lift as I got closer to Boston. The toll collector at the Allston toll plaza recognized me and wished me good luck on Tuesday. I flashed my professional smile at him and drove on.

I made my way through familiar streets. The last time I had driven to Brighton I had seen only what was new; now I saw only what I had seen a thousand times before, only what had endured. Look—there's Brighton High, where Danny had his triumphs. Look—there's the library where I spent so many hours that Mrs. Linehan, the sweet old children's librarian, said I might as well just move in. Look—there's St. Columbkille's Church, where we went to mass as long as my grandmother was alive. St. Comical's, my father always called it, to Gramma's dismay.

Look—there's the old homestead. I paused for a closer examination. The hedges we had always hated to trim were gone. There were pots of chrysanthemums lining the front stairs. The

porch had been screened in, the driveway repaved. The place
looked as if it were in better shape than ever.

I drove on. Just a couple more blocks, and a lifetime, to my
destination. It was late, but I didn't care. It was long past the time
when this should have been resolved.

The house was in darkness. I jabbed the bell several times,
and then a light came on in the window to the left of the door, a
silhouette appeared behind the curtain. A few moments later the
porch light came on, and Melissa opened the door. She was wearing a faded terry-cloth robe; her hair was uncombed; she looked
old and tired. My expression told her that I knew, and her eyes
filled with tears. "Can you understand, Jim?" she said. "I had to
lie for him. What else could I do? I love him. After all this time,
after all he's done, I still love him."

She sounded very much like Liz, talking about me.

"I'm sorry, Lissa," I said. I walked past her into the house.

He was standing in the doorway to the kitchen, pulling on a
jacket. He looked at me; his eyes were frightened. "Danny," I said.

He turned and ran.

Melissa grabbed my arm. "Please, Jim," she said. "He'll come
back. He's got nowhere else to go."

Perhaps, but I couldn't wait. I pulled away from her and
followed Danny through the kitchen and out the back door.

He was climbing over the chain-link fence that separated his
tiny backyard from his neighbor's. "Danny!" I called out, but he
ignored me. He dropped down heavily on the other side of the
fence and started running again.

I ran after him.

I ripped my pants and cut my knee on the fence, but I made
it over. I was out of shape—had never really been in shape—but
so was Danny. Gasping, I pursued him past the neighbor's house
and out onto the street.

We must have been a strange sight to anyone who happened
to notice us chugging through the side streets of Brighton: Danny
in his jacket and pajama bottoms, me in my torn pants and wing
tips. Not your average middle-aged joggers. Not your average time
for jogging.

But I didn't feel especially strange, though my lungs were on
fire and my knee throbbed from its encounter with the fence.
These were my streets, and this was my brother, and it could have
been thirty years ago, when running was something that only kids

did, and you would chase one another just for the fun of being alive.

Except that I never chased my brother, because I never could have caught him.

"Why are Danny and me so different?" I asked my father once, thirty years ago or more.

"Different?" he replied, looking at me blankly. "I never noticed any difference."

I couldn't tell if he was kidding. Still can't.

We staggered through a couple of turns, with me gaining ground despite my knee, and then Danny picked up speed as he entered a playground.

No, not a playground, I realized as I followed him. *The* playground, where I had once before tried to catch him, back in his glory days.

Danny ran past the slides and seesaws out to where the big kids played. Onto the football field, which cut across the outfield next to the baseball diamond. He stopped at about the fifty-yard line; I stopped at the twenty. "No more games, Danny," I said, bent over, hands on my thighs, trying to catch my breath. "This is for real."

He didn't reply. Instead he planted his feet, dangled his arms at his sides, and looked to his left—looked, I realized, at an imaginary quarterback barking out the count before the snap. I waited, watching him. And then abruptly Danny was running toward me. He looked back and raised his hands, palms together, caught the phantom pass, and tucked the phantom ball under his arm.

I was the only thing between him and the end zone.

He headed to my right, and I ran laterally to catch up to him. I was a few yards away when he slowed and started putting the famous O'Connor moves on me: a head fake, a dip of the shoulder, a sudden burst of speed.

In his glory days Danny would have left me in the dust. But things had changed. Thirty years had passed; the fakes were still good, but no longer good enough. I lunged and caught him around the waist. He dragged me forward with the desperate strength of a man whose career—whose life—depended on scoring this touchdown. When we both finally collapsed to the ground, I don't know if we were in the end zone. I don't know if he won the game with his last-minute heroics. I only know that we were tangled together, lying in the mud.

And there we lay, my Irish twin and I, wet and breathless, gasping in each other's arms.

If Paul Everson had been watching this time, would he have been able to tell the difference between us?

"Jimmy, I screwed up," Danny said as he regained his breath. "All my life I've been screwing up, but this was the worst." That wasn't sweat on his face, I realized, and it wasn't the rain; he was crying.

"Take it easy, Danny," I said. "Why don't you start at the beginning?"

"I shouldn't have told her about Jackie Scanlon," he said. "But she knew. She already knew, Jimmy. I just wanted to put you in a good light—honest. But after I left, I thought about it, and I realized how bad this was gonna be for you, and I decided I had to do something about it. I know I should've just told you and let you decide how to handle it, but I had the flu and I was lying in bed and I couldn't do anything but think about it, and I thought, maybe this once—"

He stopped for a moment and sobbed. We pulled away from each other and sat up.

"I just wanted to get the tape back," he went on. "And anything else she had that mentioned Scanlon. Sort of put the fear of God into her. I never meant to hurt her. And I sure never meant to hurt you, Jimmy. Or, I don't know, maybe I did. It's all so complicated, you know? One minute I'm jealous of you, and the next minute I'm so proud of you I could burst. One minute I'm grateful for all you've done for me, and the next I resent it that you've had to do so much. I can never seem to figure anything out, you know? I just sorta muddle through."

"I know the feeling, Danny," I said. And then I prompted: "So you went to her apartment"—probably wearing my hand-me-down raincoat, I realized. Head down in the fog, looking enough like me to fool even my old roommate.

"Yeah, well, I guess I stopped to have a few drinks first, to get up my courage. And when I got there, she claimed she didn't have the tape anymore; she'd erased it and given it to this guy Paul Everson. She said she wasn't writing about you, that she was in love with you and was just trying to understand you. But that didn't make any sense. Why would she give the tape to Everson? If she loved you, why was she sneaking around behind your back interviewing people?"

"I don't know, Danny," I had to admit.

"I was just going to threaten her," he said, "but I screwed up. She ran into the kitchen and grabbed a knife. I wrestled it away from her. I was mad at her for lying to me. I was mad at myself for being so stupid. I was drunk, and I wasn't thinking straight. I had the knife in my hand. She was trying to get away from me. And then . . . then . . . "

"It's all right, Danny," I said. "I know what happened then."

Danny struggled to get control of himself and finally went on. "And of course after, I turned the place upside down looking for the tape and it wasn't there, there wasn't anything I could find about Scanlon, and all the time I think someone's gonna show up any minute and that'll be the end of everything. So then I give up and I try to make it look like a robbery, but I was too scared to even do that right. And, I dunno, the computer was on and it was just sitting there, so I just started typing; I was trying to convince myself more than anything—you know, that it wasn't all a waste, a stupid awful mistake. 'She had to die. She had to die.' " He paused. "So then I go home and I get back in bed and I wait for the cops to come and haul me off.

"But you were the one that got into trouble, not me. How was I supposed to know you'd discover the body? And I thought, Jesus, all I was tryin' to do was get him *out* of trouble.

"And then people started talkin' about how you two were probably lovers, and that was the worst. I mean, what if she was telling the truth about everything? But if there was something going on, you were probably just foolin' around with her, right? No way you really loved her—right, Jimmy?"

You idiot, I wanted to scream at him. What do you know about me? Why do you keep trying to drag me down with you? I did love her. And you took her from me before I had a chance to tell her.

And then I stared at my brother, sitting in the mud, dirty and helpless and pitiful, awaiting my answer. And in that moment I learned something about love.

"No," I said. "There was nothing between me and Amanda Taylor, Danny."

He closed his eyes. "I didn't think so, Jimmy. I didn't think so." He sounded immensely relieved. And then he turned solemn. "I'm sorry I lied to you about this. I'll do whatever you want me to do. I'll turn myself in if you think I should."

Did I think that? If he confessed, it might save me. He wouldn't have to bring up Jackie Scanlon; he wouldn't even have to bring up Jim O'Connor. He made a pass at her during the interview, and she rejected him. He was drunk. He was crazy. It was a stupid argument. Second-degree murder, open and shut. Cavanaugh wouldn't even get a trial out of it.

If he confessed, justice would be done. The tide of lawlessness and anarchy that threatened our precious American way of life would be held back just a little. And Amanda's family might find some small satisfaction in knowing her killer had been caught.

If he confessed, my father's heart would break.

I couldn't tell him what to do. I didn't know anything anymore. "Do what you have to, Danny," I said. "Don't do it for my sake."

"The hell of it is," Danny said, "I feel like my life is finally turning around. Did I tell you about this job they called me about—like out of the blue? I really think I'm gonna get it. And I promised Lissa I'd quit drinking, and I know I can do it this time. I hit bottom there for a while—I mean, Christ, *murder*. But now—"

He fell silent. Justice, I thought. Everyone is guilty. Everyone is innocent.

"Let's go home," I said.

Danny looked at me. "Okay, Jimmy," he whispered. "Okay."

I tried getting to my feet, but my knee complained. Danny reached out a hand and helped me up. And then we walked out of the playground and back through the streets where we had grown up, the dull working-class neighborhood that I had been so thrilled to get out of, that Danny felt so trapped inside.

"Born here, and looks like I'm gonna die here," he murmured. "Pretty depressing, huh?"

"I don't know," I said.

"Yeah, I don't know either. The old neighborhood has some great memories—right, Jimmy?"

Most of them had never struck me as particularly great. Danny was just trying to work up a little nostalgia again. But then I changed my mind. The memories were great, I realized, because they were ours. And that was reason enough. "Yeah," I said. "Great memories."

He pointed to a house. "Remember the time that crabby Mrs. Donnelly chased after us with a hockey stick when we were cutting through her yard?"

I had never cut through Mrs. Donnelly's yard. "Great memories," I repeated.

"She's dead now. Most all of 'em are dead. But still."

When we strolled into Danny's house, Melissa was waiting, terrified, in the kitchen. "It's all right," I said to her. "Everything's going to be all right."

She closed her eyes. "Thank God," she whispered.

Danny sat down at the kitchen table. "I've never been so tired in my life," he said.

I sat down at the table next to him. "Anyone got a Band-Aid?" I asked.

Cars littered my driveway when I finally pulled into it, and the house was ablaze with lights. Kathleen came running out to greet me as I got out of the car. She hugged me and laid her head against my chest. "Everyone's so worried, Daddy," she said.

"It's all right," I said. "Everything's going to be all right." I walked inside with my arm around her shoulders.

The brain trust was in the kitchen. They didn't know whether to be relieved or angry—except for Harold. He was angry. "You look like hell," he said. "Where have you been?"

I glanced down at my pants, torn and caked with dried mud. "Playing football," I said. "Sorry I didn't let you know. It won't happen again."

"Don't do us any favors."

"Jim, my sources say that Cavanaugh's going to arrest you tomorrow," Roger announced mournfully.

"Today," Marge corrected, glancing at her watch.

Kathleen looked up at me, tears in her eyes.

"No, he isn't," I said, squeezing her shoulder.

"If you're counting on Finn to help you out," Harold said, "forget it. It was a clever idea, but it won't work. He's been in touch; he thought I knew what you were up to. Fat chance. Anyway, Cavanaugh isn't budging."

"Doesn't matter," I said. "I've got a better idea."

"What?"

"You'll see."

Harold looked as if he were using all his self-control to keep from strangling me.

"I told Harold about Donato, Senator," Kevin said. "I think maybe if we—"

"We're leaving Donato out of it, Kevin. All I have to do is make a phone call, and everything will be taken care of. Tomorrow—today—it's business as usual. One last day of campaigning, and I'm going to make it a good one. I've let you down a lot these past few weeks, but I won't let you down anymore."

People stared at me. They were thinking: It's too late. And I thought: Maybe they're right. But I couldn't let them feel my doubts, or everything would fall apart, and then they would certainly be right.

"You owe us an explanation," Harold said.

"I know I do. But you're not going to get one. I'm sorry, but that's the way it is. Now why don't you all go home and get some sleep? I'm going to make my call, and then I'm going to go to sleep myself."

I kissed Kathleen on the top of the head and walked out of the kitchen. No one stopped me; they were all too dazed. I went into my office, shut the door, tossed my jacket onto a chair, and made the phone call. Afterward I sat behind my desk for a while, listening to the cars pull out of the driveway. Even the cars sounded bewildered. When I came out, the kitchen was empty, except for Angelica, who looked at me expectantly. I smiled and gave her some milk, then I turned out the lights and went upstairs.

Liz was sitting up in bed, waiting for me.

"Hi," I said, starting to undress.

"Hi."

"Sorry for all the fuss."

She looked at me. "For a guy who's going to be arrested on a murder charge in the morning, you don't seem very worried."

"I'm innocent. Justice will prevail. Everything's going to be all right." I was going to keep repeating that until I believed it.

"I happened to notice that my gun is missing," Liz said. "Would you know anything about that?"

I stopped putting on my pajama bottom and looked up at her. "It's in my glove compartment. I'll bring it in first thing in the morning."

"Jim," she said, "you didn't do anything stupid, did you?" Her eyes glistened with incipient tears.

"I've done more stupid things than I can count," I said. "But I think I managed to avoid adding to them tonight."

"Do you want to tell me what's going on?"

I thought: Could I? "After the election, Liz," I murmured. "We'll talk about everything after the election."

That seemed to satisfy her, at least for the moment. She lay back against her pillow. I got in bed next to her, and we fell asleep as if this had been just one more normal day in our normal marriage.

CHAPTER 30

"**I** don't usually speak to the press. But I thought it was important to inform the public why I went to see the district attorney just now, and that's why I've asked you all to come here this morning.

"I explained to District Attorney Cavanaugh that I possessed certain information that I felt was crucial to his investigation of the murder of Amanda Taylor. In fact, I was in Amanda Taylor's apartment on the afternoon she was murdered. As you may know, I was Jim O'Connor's college roommate, and he later defended me when District Attorney Cavanaugh's office charged me with the murder of my wife. So naturally Ms. Taylor was interested in interviewing me for the book she was writing about Senator O'Connor. Since I happened to be in Boston on business that day, I agreed to meet her at her apartment.

"I arrived there at four o'clock. I saw a young man in a hooded sweatshirt leaving the building as I entered, but I thought nothing of it at the time. I rang the bell, but there was no answer. The inner door was open in the lobby, however, so I decided to go up to her apartment and knock on the door in case the bell was broken. Her door was unlocked as well, and it looked as if someone had beaten on it with a hammer.

"I went inside. The apartment had been ransacked. I searched the place, and I discovered Amanda Taylor's body on the kitchen floor. And then, I'm sorry to say, I panicked and left the scene of the crime.

"Why did I panic? It's simple. I had been on trial for murder before, and I didn't want to be implicated in another one, particularly when it bore a superficial resemblance to the death of my wife. I don't know why anyone would think that I was involved, but I didn't want to take any chances. What I did was wrong, and I only hope I have helped to make up for it by finally coming forward today.

"Why did I wait so long? you may ask; certainly this is something the district attorney wanted to know. Well, the longer I waited, the harder it became. Once the police investigation started, of course, I was doubly afraid to come forward since I had no good explanation for not reporting the crime. But finally I began to feel very guilty about my silence. The investigation didn't appear to be making much progress, and I felt that perhaps my information might help get it going again.

"I expect that I may end up in trouble for coming forward. Perhaps some people might even suggest that *I* murdered Amanda Taylor. I assure you that I did not. The best evidence I can give of my innocence is that no one compelled me to do what I'm doing today. Certainly the district attorney's office has not contacted me, and I'm not aware of any press reports linking me to Amanda Taylor or her murder. I only want to see justice served. The district attorney, I believe, received my information in that spirit. I trust that you will, too."

Kevin Feeney received the information in a slightly different spirit. "They're screwed, Senator! The Democrats are screwed!" he whispered to me as I finished an interview with a TV anchor that morning. Kevin looked as if he wanted to kiss me. The station played a tape of the press conference for me afterward. Everson looked contrite, serious, imposing. The questions after his statement were skeptical, focusing on his relationship with me, but he didn't rattle. This had nothing to do with me, he said; as far as he knew, I wasn't even a suspect. Besides, he didn't even know if his statement would help me.

Someone pointed out to him that I had been in a staff meeting until four o'clock on the afternoon of the murder. If Amanda Taylor was already dead at four o'clock, as Everson claimed, then I was in the clear.

Oh, he said. He hadn't realized. But he pointed out that if he had wanted to use this information to help me, he would have come forward much earlier and spared me the weeks of innuendos that I had been subjected to.

They asked about the man in the hooded sweatshirt. Everson couldn't really say much more about him. He had tried to give the district attorney as good a description as he could, but he hadn't had any reason to look closely at the man, so there wasn't much he could offer.

I couldn't have given a better performance.

"Were you behind this, Senator?" Kevin asked after we had left the studio. "Is that what you were talking about last night—you know, the mysterious phone call?"

"Let's just say this isn't totally unexpected."

"Cavanaugh can't arrest you now, right? Not when you have an ironclad alibi."

"Cavanaugh has a history of not believing Paul Everson," I pointed out.

"Okay, but arresting you was going to look pretty political even before. Now no one can believe Cavanaugh isn't playing politics. He'd have to be crazy to try it."

I wasn't entirely sure of Cavanaugh's sanity at this point, but basically I agreed with Kevin's analysis. "We'll just have to see what happens," I said.

"More likely, he'll arrest Everson," Kevin remarked. "It looks awfully suspicious, him finding her."

"But what in the world would Everson's motive be?"

Kevin considered. "I guess you're right. And besides, Cavanaugh tried arresting Everson before. Look where that got him."

"Good point," I said.

We headed on to our next campaign stop.

Not the least of Everson's lies during his press conference was his statement that the district attorney believed him when he said that he only wanted to see justice served by coming forward with his information. In fact, Everson told me later, Cavanaugh threatened to stab him to death. "You're a murderer and you're a liar and I'm going to kill you the way you killed your wife!" he screamed at Everson, who was not perturbed. The only reason for him to visit the DA in the first place was so that he could hold the press conference afterward.

I can only guess at what Cavanaugh did next. There must have been frantic calls to the White House. There must have been a lot of gnashing of teeth and many futile fantasies. When he finally left the office around noontime, the press cornered him, and he was forced to make a statement. He tried to imply that Everson was lying in order to protect me, but it came out sounding as if he were trying to ignore important new evidence. Clearly he hadn't yet figured out what to do.

Meanwhile, we were out there pounding away on the issues, trying to win the election.

In the early afternoon we were stuck in downtown traffic heading for another interview when the car phone rang. Kevin answered, and his jaw dropped. "The White House," he managed to whisper.

I took the receiver away from him. The secretary on the other end let the Presdient know I was on the line; then Charles Kenton was talking in my ear, and I was trying to listen to his sonorous voice while Kevin, shaking with excitement, veered out of our lane and a cabby leaned on his horn and insulted Kevin's mother. "Jim, I just wanted to wish you the best of luck in the election tomorrow," the President said.

"Gee, that's nice of you, Mr. President."

"Not at all, not at all. We have our differences, of course, but I do respect you."

"That's great to know. And of course, the feeling is mutual, sir."

"Why, thank you. Now Jim, a rumor has reached me that your district attorney up there was thinking of pulling some kind of last-minute hanky-panky with regard to that unfortunate murder case."

"Oh, my. That's distressing news."

"Well, I just wanted you to understand that this is not something I condone. I like these battles to be fought fair and square. Governor Finn is a worthy opponent. He may defeat you; he may not. But the voters should decide on the issues, not on some trumped-up murder charge. Don't you agree?"

"I certainly do. And I appreciate your candor and concern, Mr. President."

"Not at all, Jim. Not at all. When you get back to Washington, I'll give you a call. Perhaps we can get together for a drink, let our hair down a little."

"I'd like that very much, sir."

I smiled as I hung up the phone. Kenton had cut Cavanaugh loose. He was on his own now.

"Um, what was that about, Senator?" Kevin asked.

"Oh, politics, Kevin. Just politics."

The day passed in a blur of events and interviews. Six o'clock came and went, and it was too late to get anything on the evening news, and I figured we were home free.

Cavanaugh finally called me as we were on our way back to campaign headquarters. "Francis, good of you to check in," I said. "How are things?"

"You bastard," he replied, "you haven't wriggled out of this yet. I don't care about the damn election. I'll haul you in the day after the election, win or lose."

"The President called me this afternoon, Francis. He's abandoned you. Finn's abandoned you. Everyone's abandoned you. You're the one twisting in the wind."

"I don't care. I don't need Kenton or Finn. I can take care of myself."

"And you can't really expect to convict me, Francis. Not after today. You should be looking for a man in a hooded sweatshirt."

"You think anyone's going to believe Everson?" Cavanaugh scoffed. "I've got the ME to disagree with him about time of death. I've got you saying her door was locked and him saying it was open. I've got a motive for him to lie. I'll tear him to pieces on the stand."

"Well, I would think by now you'd have learned not to underestimate Paul Everson. Look, Francis. You've been a good DA; no one can take that away from you except yourself. If you try to screw me, all you'll do is make people forget about everything you've accomplished over the years. They'll think: Oh, yeah, he was the guy who had the vendetta against Jim O'Connor. Don't do that to yourself. When you're retired, don't have your only memories be of your fights against me. It's not worth it."

"Your concern is heartwarming," Cavanaugh said.

"And the strange thing is, it's real. I'll see you around, Francis."

Kevin looked at me as I hung up. "You're being awfully nice to Democrats today," he said.

"Democrats are people, too, Kevin. Or so I'm told."

Headquarters throbbed with last-minute crises. Harold was

there organizing the get-out-the-vote effort for election day. I went into his office. He was wearing a starched white shirt and a bow tie; his suitcoat was neatly hung on a wooden hanger on the back of the door. He looked like a fussy tax lawyer. He gave me an appraising stare. "Sometimes I think I underestimate you," he said.

"Please spare me the flattery," I replied. "It degrades us both." I sat down. "Think we'll win?"

"Our polls, their polls, everyone's polls have it too close to call," he said. "People are making up their minds at the last minute. They'll go into the voting booth and look at the two names and something'll click, and that'll be that."

"Okay," I said. "It's close. But what do your finely honed political instincts say? What will click when they're in the voting booth?"

"You didn't help yourself by disappearing last night," he pointed out. "We've had an erratic campaign. That sticks in people's minds."

"Bobby Finn's had his problems, too. We've hurt him on crime. He's hurt himself in some of his interviews."

"True." Harold fiddled with a paper clip. "Everson's press conference just might make the difference. Neutralize the murder as an issue. I don't know."

"I don't know either."

Harold tossed the paper clip onto the desk. "I would have resigned a long time ago if I hadn't thought it would doom the campaign," he said.

"Marge was going to enter a convent," I said. "What would you have done?"

He spread his hands. "I have no idea. I guess that's the real reason I didn't quit."

"Well, thanks for sticking around."

"Don't mention it. Now if you'll excuse me, I have a lot more work to do before this election is over."

I left him alone. I, too, had more work to do: one last rally to address, then live interviews with all the Boston stations during the eleven o'clock news. Everything went well. They all asked me about Everson, and I gave a stock response: I was glad he came forward with his information. If it helped convince people I was innocent, that was fine, but the main thing was to bring Amanda

Taylor's murderer to justice. I hoped the new information would help District Attorney Cavanaugh accomplish this.

I saw tapes of Bobby Finn's interviews afterward, and he looked good, too. He said something equally bland about Everson and otherwise stuck close to his campaign script: He was more in touch with the people than I was. My last-minute shifts in positions were a cynical attempt to con the voters. He was confident the voters would be smart enough tomorrow to know who was really on their side.

I went to bed with no idea how I was going to do. I hadn't thought about the election very much lately, and I was having difficulty thinking about it now. I was just doing what had to be done. I wondered if the voters would sense my lack of interest and respond accordingly.

It occurred to me that I hadn't thought about Carl Hutchins very much lately either. A lot of lives are changed forever on election day.

Election day. A politician's whole life leads up to it. When it finally arrives, you are tortured by thoughts of what remains undone, of what was done badly and now cannot be undone. The botched interview; the unintended insult to the union leader; the parade you were too tired to march in. A thousand ways you could have ensured victory, all forever gone. Massachusetts wakes up and takes its shower and feeds its cat and takes its dog for a walk and thinks: What was I supposed to do today? Oh, yeah, vote. I wonder who's running. And you long for one last chance to reach the voters, to talk to them, to make them understand.

But it's too late.

Kathleen was too excited to speak. She wanted to take the day off from school—a first for her—but we turned her down. We pretended to eat breakfast together, but no one had any appetite. Then Liz dutifully accompanied me to the polls. We smiled for the photographers as we went into the high school to cast our ballots. When we came out, a reporter asked Liz whom she had voted for.

She smiled and said, "It's supposed to be a secret," and everyone laughed.

"What are you doing today?" I asked in the car.

"I have classes," she said.

"Kathleen is counting on tonight," I reminded her.

"We'll be there."

Kevin dropped her off at the house, and then we headed downtown.

I had Kevin stop at a couple of polling places so that I could shake a few hands and give some encouragement to the folks standing out in the cold holding my signs, but I was just killing time. When we finally reached headquarters, there was little for me to do but bother the people involved in the get-out-the-vote operation.

It was hard to believe the operation would make much difference. Over a million votes would be cast today. How many would we pick up with all the computerized lists of probable supporters, all the poll watchers checking off names, all the phone people ready to call the supporters who hadn't shown up by late afternoon? Still, it was one of those things you had to do in a modern professionally run campaign. The race was too important to leave anything to chance.

And yet so much of the result would be due to chance—or, at least, to things over which neither candidate had any control. Women liked me, maybe because I'm handsome; what could Bobby Finn do about that? A factory closes in Springfield, and I pick up some votes because workers are unhappy and they take it out on the governor. An old lady in Osterville once knew a fellow named Finn who was a nice guy, so she figures Bobby must be a nice guy, too. Another old lady's Social Security check is always late, and she blames the people down in Washington: another vote for the governor. Over a million people out there, looking at the names on the ballot, making their decisions; over a million different reasons why they choose whom they choose. Candidates spend next to nothing and win; candidates spend millions and lose. It is a strange business. It is the most important business in the world.

I went into Marge's office and went over the victory speech she had written for me. She had circles under her eyes; her ashtray was overflowing. "This part where I thank Liz," I said. "Can't you punch it up? You know, make it more loving?"

"I figured you could do some ad-libbing there," Marge replied. "I don't want to do all the work for you."

"I suppose I can come up with something. Now, where's the concession speech?"

Marge shook her head. "I don't do concession speeches."

"It comes with the territory, Marge."

"You've never lost," she pointed out.

"You've never been my media coordinator during a campaign before."

"And I'm never going to be your media coordinator again. I'm going to become an air traffic controller, some job where I can handle the pressure."

I gestured at the photograph of Marge talking to the Famous Correspondent at the postelection party six years ago. "Still, there's nothing like winning," I said.

"Do you believe that?" Marge asked. "Honestly, Jim. I want to know."

I considered. "Winning matters if you're sure you're right. I guess lately I haven't been so sure I'm right."

She suddenly leaned forward and put a hand on mine. "A politician doesn't have to be right all the time," she said, "but he has to be a good man. You may not believe it, Jim O'Connor, but you are a good man."

I grinned. "Why don't you come up and visit me in my hotel suite tonight."

"I just might do that."

I went back to my office and called my father. "Vote early and often," I said.

"Oh, Danny came over and took me first thing this morning."

"Good for Danny."

"He got that job, you know."

"Even better for Danny. Now if only I can win this election, we'll both have jobs. Are you coming tonight?"

"Well, I don't know. It'll go awfully late."

"No, it won't. I'll be making my victory speech by eight-thirty. Danny'll pick you up."

"Oh, well, I don't know."

I called Danny. Melissa answered. "You're coming tonight, right?" I said.

"Oh, Jim, it doesn't seem—"

"My father's dying to come, and I promised him you and Danny would take him. Bring the kids. Nobody has to talk to a Republican if he doesn't want to."

"Jim, about the—you know. The confession." She whispered

the word. "We talked about it a lot, and we thought, maybe after the election, when it wouldn't hurt you."

"That's up to you two," I said. "Honestly. Anyway, I hear Danny got that job. Tell him congratulations."

"He's really changed, Jim. If only—"

"Come tonight, Lissa. We'll talk about it after the election."

Finally I went to the hotel to await my fate. Kevin and I looked into the ballroom. Workers were putting up a huge banner with my name on it; a technician was checking the sound system, which squealed whenever he tried to speak; a janitor lazily mopped the floor. In a few hours the ballroom would be the scene of either the biggest wake or the biggest party the hotel had seen—well, since the last election.

"They say turnout's heavy," Kevin murmured.

That wasn't a good sign. Casual voters are lower on the socioeconomic scale and therefore tend to vote Democratic. "A snowstorm would have been nice," I said.

We went upstairs to the suite, which was filled with TVs and phones. Liz and Kathleen arrived a little while later. Kathleen started to pace the room as if she had been taking lessons from Sam Fisher. She was wearing a blue silk dress, and she looked so much like a grown-up that I could scarcely stand it. Liz was quiet, distant, preoccupied: the usual. I had room service send up dinner, but our appetites hadn't improved since breakfast. Our minds were on the voters. In the real world people were getting out of work now, finishing supper, thinking: The weather's not bad, TV's lousy, maybe I'll go vote. And at the polling places the lines were getting longer. People were standing there impatiently, thinking: defense, the crime rate, Amanda Taylor, the wheelchair shocker, O'Connor's black hair, Finn's grammar, Amanda Taylor. Thinking: The damn Subaru needs a new muffler; I'm gonna do it, I'm gonna ask Marcia to marry me; Leverett Saltonstall, now there was a senator; my back hurts; this line is too long, I'm going home; all those politicians are the same anyway.

"Can we turn on the TV?" Kathleen asked.

"There's nothing to watch," I said. "No returns to report till after the polls close at eight."

"Maybe they've done some exit polling."

"Where did you learn about exit polling? You must be hanging out with the wrong crowd."

"Daddy."

"The stations are holding back their exit poll data till after eight," I explained, "so they don't influence the vote."

"Well, we can't just *sit* here."

"Eat your chocolate mousse," I said. "That's what I'm going to do."

Once dinner was over, I allowed the parade of visitors to begin. Kevin was the doorkeeper, but there were a lot of people who deserved a few minutes with the candidate on election night, so I let him be lenient in granting admittance to the inner sanctum.

Besides, talking to visitors kept me from becoming as nervous as Kathleen.

Everyone was optimistic; they all told me they were sure we'd won. But what else can you say to the candidate? *Too bad you screwed up in that debate, Jim. Lousy strategy the last couple of weeks, Senator. You really snatched defeat from the jaws of victory.*

I let Kathleen turn the TV on finally, and we saw a report on the mood downstairs in the ballroom. The place was starting to fill up. The perceptive newsman detected an undercurrent of tension in the air. A feeling that we could be in for a long night. He interviewed Marge. And yes, I, too, could detect the undercurrent of tension.

Harold came in. He had been watching in the outer room. "Someone should tell Marge to lighten up," he murmured.

"I hear that NBC News is projecting me as the winner," I said, "based on three absentee ballots from West Tisbury."

"I think I'll go downstairs," he said.

There was a report from Bobby Finn's ballroom next. People there didn't seem any less worried.

And then it was eight o'clock, and there was nothing more anyone could do, short of reprogramming the computers that were already starting to count the votes.

Kathleen gripped the sides of her chair. "Are we going to win, Daddy?" she asked.

"Absolutely, princess."

She didn't even object to her title.

Liz sat silently in a corner of the room, her eyes not moving from the TV screen.

"Channel Four says it's too close to call," Sam Fisher reported from the outer room, just as Channel 5 said the same thing on our set. Sam looked as if he could pace a four-minute mile.

Exit poll data flashed on the screen: Women preferred me;

men preferred Finn. Catholics split evenly. I was getting a majority of independent voters. My percentage of Democratic voters seemed a little low, but in the ball park of what I needed. I didn't see any surprises in the data.

"I'm going to get a little fresh air," Liz said.

I nodded absently, mulling the figures.

Analyzing early election returns is probably as useless an activity as there is in politics, but try stopping yourself if you're a politician. Everything else has been done; now there is nothing left except to study the numbers and try to figure out if all your years of effort are about to go down the drain.

The first returns are always from the big-city precincts with machine voting. The Democrat usually does well in those precincts; the question is whether he will come out of the cities with enough of a lead to withstand the Republican strength in rural paper-ballot towns.

I knew what to expect, but it was still depressing to see the initial vote count appear with Finn in the lead. Kathleen looked stricken. "It's okay," I said. "This is normal."

Sam Fisher popped in again. "Not bad," he said. "Not great, but not bad either."

"See?" I said to Kathleen.

Another report from the ballroom. This time Roger was being interviewed. He was pretty good: rumpled and untelegenic but articulate. He managed to sound confident without sounding banal. It was far too early to make any predictions, he said. The senator was watching the returns closely, and he expected to be watching them for quite a while. I looked around for Liz; she hadn't come back. I wondered if my father and Danny would want to come upstairs. Probably not. Probably wouldn't want to be in the way. I sent Kevin down to the ballroom to make sure they were taken care of.

And then things started to blur for a while. More returns, more precincts reporting. Still too close to call. Sam with a cordless phone pressed to each ear, talking and pacing, talking and pacing. People coming in to offer tidbits of encouragement: We're creaming him in Marblehead; we lost Brockton by a smaller margin than we expected.

I thought of Bobby Finn, sitting in a similar suite in some other hotel, listening to the same kind of encouragement. *You're*

*holding the Democratic vote, Governor. You're holding the cities. He's got
to make up a lot of ground.*

Finn's wife would be sitting by his side, of course, studying
the returns as intently as he was. Would his son be there, too,
bored and sullen?

All politicians are the same.

Where was Liz?

There were reports from other ballrooms, other races. Who
cared? Kathleen started flipping channels, frantically looking for
the latest returns on the Senate race.

And then, slowly, the trend became clear. With 25 percent of
the vote counted we had pulled even; with 30 percent we had
gone ahead. Great cheers from the ballroom. Harold was on TV
now for the first time: calm, authoritative, convincing. He admitted that things were starting to look good. But it was still awfully
early. . . .

But it wasn't, not really. With a third of the votes counted,
Channel 5 put a check mark next to my name, and a shout went
up from the other room. Sam Fisher lit a foot-long cigar, and
Kevin had tears in his eyes as he pumped my hand, and Kathleen
was jumping up and down and screaming, a little girl once
again. . . .

I felt more relief than joy. I had almost let these people down.
But somehow, like Danny, I had managed to muddle through.

I shook everyone's hand and then granted a few brief interviews to the TV reporters, who set up shop outside the suite. Like
Harold, I admitted that things were looking good, but I wasn't
willing to claim victory. I hadn't heard from Governor Finn, and
I didn't expect to, at least for a while; it was still much too early
for him to concede. No, of course, I had no comment on any run
for the presidency; as far as I was concerned, I wasn't sure yet
that I had been reelected to the Senate.

But I was lying, and everyone knew it. The numbers weren't
going to change at this point. The people had spoken, and the
computerized vote totals were their voice. I was up 52 to 48 percent
now, and it looked as if I would hit 53 or 54 by the time it was
over. Hardly a landslide, but against a popular governor in a
heavily Democratic state, it was impressive enough to keep my
name high on the pundits' short list of presidential contenders.
The protocol of election nights said we should wait for the van-

quished opponent to call before we claimed victory, however—as long as he didn't push our speech past the eleven o'clock news. So I settled back to watch more TV and let reality sink in.

"Have you seen your mother, Kathleen?" I asked during a commercial.

She shook her head. "Maybe she's downstairs with Grampa and Uncle Danny?" she offered, although she seemed nervous about making the suggestion.

"Oh. Right. I'm sure that's where she is."

We went back to staring at the TV.

Bobby Finn called at ten-thirty. Kevin answered, then handed the receiver to me with the solemnity of Lee passing his sword to Grant at Appomattox. I shooed everyone out of the room before answering. "Governor," I said.

"Senator," Finn replied. "I'm calling to congratulate you on your victory. Right after I hang up I'll be going downstairs to make my concession speech."

"Well, thank you, Governor. We put on a hell of a fight, I think."

"We sure did. I just wanted you to know, Jim, I did what I could about the Monsignor. I called up Kenton directly and told him if he backed Cavanaugh on this, I'd do everything I could to defeat him when he runs for reelection. He was pretty surprised, but I think I got him to reconsider."

"Thanks, Bobby. I think you did."

"Cavanaugh's still talking tough, but he won't do anything. With the election over, the thrill is gone."

"I sure hope you're right."

"Anyway, I'm kind of glad you won, to tell you the truth. It's much more fun being governor than living in Washington and going to a bunch of committee meetings. Now no one can say I didn't try."

"Funny thing, Bobby: I have this feeling I might have been better off losing myself."

"Why the hell would you feel like that?"

"I don't know. Maybe I just need a vacation."

"Me, too. Although I won't get much of one. And I bet you won't either. A politician's always on the job, right, Jim?"

"Truer words were never spoken, Bobby."

Kevin went down to the ballroom to get things ready for my speech; he took Kathleen with him. I glanced over Marge's text and decided to ad-lib; Marge would understand. I noticed Roger lurking in a corner of the suite, drink in hand. I went over to him. "Thanks for all you've done, Roger. I know I made things tough on you for a while. And it looks like we needed every cent you managed to raise."

"You're welcome, Jim." He finished off his drink. As usual nowadays, Roger acted as if he wanted to be in another time zone when he was in my presence.

"Did you, uh, happen to see Liz downstairs, Roger?"

"No. Wasn't she—I mean, the place is jammed, of course. She could've been there and I just didn't see her."

"Of course."

"Jim, I—that is, Liz and I—I think it's over between us. We haven't seen each other since, you know, when you and I talked. It was—maybe it was just one of those, you know, one of those things. She had to get something out of her system. I don't know."

He seemed intensely embarrassed; I was, too. It wasn't his idea that they stop seeing each other, I realized. "Thanks for telling me that, Roger. Now let's go downstairs. You belong onstage with us."

And off we all went.

There is nothing that can quite compare with the election night celebration of a victorious campaign. The people there have spent all their energy, and often a good deal of their money, working toward this moment, and now they're ready to party for a few glorious hours before they collapse.

The candidate's speech is the focal point of the celebration. It is the easiest speech anyone could possibly give; people will cheer you if you tell them the sun is going to rise tomorrow morning. But you also feel the obligation to reiterate the themes of your campaign, in case the TV audience starts to get the mistaken idea that this was only about winning and losing. By this time, though, you can recite your campaign themes in a drunken stupor, so even that should not be difficult.

I paused outside the ballroom, waiting for the signal that Finn had finished his speech. It was just after eleven—perfect timing, if Bobby didn't get carried away and start thanking each of his campaign workers and relatives by name. I adjusted my tie and shook a few hands, and after a couple of minutes Kevin came out. "We're ready to go," he said. He looked around. "Is Liz, uh—"

"Liz isn't feeling well. She had to go home."

"Oh. I'm sorry. Well, I guess we'll have to do it without her then."

I nodded. "Let's do it."

Kevin held the door open, and I strode into the ballroom. The band was playing "When Irish Eyes Are Smiling," but the cheers quickly drowned it out when people spotted me. It took me five minutes to make my way up onto the stage. Everyone had to be greeted; everyone's hand had to be shaken. I didn't remember the names of half the people pressing up to me, but it didn't matter because no one could hear anything I said.

Onstage I spent a few more minutes greeting people. I embraced my father, who kept rubbing the side of his nose, as if that would keep the tears from spilling out of his eyes. I held out my hand to Danny, who sheepishly accepted it. Kathleen stopped applauding long enough to give me another hug. "I don't know where she is," she whispered in my ear, and she looked a little worried.

"Everything will be all right," I whispered back.

And then I faced the cheering crowd and the mass of TV cameras, and I gestured for quiet. But the crowd wasn't about to be quiet just yet; they were cheering themselves as much as they were cheering me, and they would stop when they were good and ready.

"Thank you very much," I kept repeating until they had settled down. "Thank you. Thank you."

Finally I could begin. "Someone once asked me to name a memorable event from my past that has shaped the person I am today. Tonight I'd like to take another stab at answering that question if I may."

Loud laughter.

"Tonight I would say it was the day a young man named Harold White marched into my law office and told me I should go into politics. Now, as you may know, Harold White can be a very persuasive man."

More laughter.

"If Harold hadn't persuaded me to go into politics, my life would have been infinitely poorer. For one thing, I wouldn't have met any of you folks—the best bunch of campaign workers in the country."

Cheers.

"For another, I wouldn't have had the honor of standing here tonight and thanking the voters of the great commonwealth of Massachusetts for allowing me to serve them in the Senate for six more years."

More cheers. Eardrum-shattering cheers. Cheers that threatened to last till morning. I smiled and waved and smiled some more, and I tried to remember all the people I had to thank, and I wondered where Liz was—

And I wondered if I meant what I was saying: if I could tell the difference between my lies and the truth anymore.

The cheering continued—women with tears streaming down their cheeks, men shouting their undying loyalty—and I wondered if Amanda Taylor was watching on some celestial TV set. Was she joining in the cheers? Or was she shaking her head sadly at this ultimate injustice in the unjust world she had left behind?

I had told Kevin the truth, it turned out. Liz had indeed gone home. Kathleen and I took the campaign car back to Hingham at two in the morning; it was the latest she had ever been out on a school night. She fell asleep in the front seat next to me, a smile on her face. The Buick was in the driveway, as I had hoped it would be. I roused Kathleen to come inside, wishing that she were small enough to carry. Liz was upstairs in bed. She stirred when I got in next to her.

"I won," I said.

"I know," she replied. "Congratulations."

"Thanks. I thanked you in my speech."

"I heard."

"I meant it."

"Glad to help," she said.

"Liz—" I started to say. *The election's over now. All those things we put off*— But it was almost three in the morning, and I still had a lot of thinking to do, and I figured they could wait awhile longer. "Good night, Liz," I said.

She looked as if she had something to say, too, and then decided not to say it. "Good night, Jim," she murmured instead, and turned away.

I slept the peaceful sleep of a winner.

I went to my downtown Senate office later that morning and fielded congratulatory phone calls from across the country. And I made a few of my own; it pays to keep in touch with the winners.

I also called Carl Hutchins; sad to say, he was one of the losers. "I'm sorry, Carl," I said. "The Senate will never be the same."

"Nonsense," he replied. "The Senate will survive. The world will survive. And what's most important, I'll survive."

"Tell me something, Carl. If you'd had to choose between the Senate and your wife, what would you have done?"

He chuckled. "I was a lucky man. I never had to think about such a thing."

"Still," I persisted.

He thought for a moment. "Well, when I was your age, I suppose I would have chosen the Senate," he said. "And that would have been a mistake."

"I see. Well, thanks for the advice, Carl. Thanks for everything."

"I'm not sure I envy you, Senator. Good luck."

That afternoon Harold stopped by the office and dropped a manila envelope on my desk. "What's this?" I asked.

"It's a memo. It explains how I'm going to make you the next President of the United States."

"Harold, couldn't you at least wait till we've gotten over our hangovers from last night?"

"Why? You think your opponents are waiting?"

"I don't have any opponents unless I decide to run."

"Read the memo. It'll explain why you have to run."

"All right. I'll read it."

"And then what?"

"Then I'll make paper airplanes out of it and float them down over Government Center. What do you want me to do?"

"I want you to promise me that you'll think about it."

"Okay," I said. "I'll think about it."

Harold nodded his satisfaction and left.

I sighed. I practiced making a paper airplane out of a leftover sheet of campaign stationery. I opened the envelope and read the memo.

And this, you see, is my way of thinking about it—and everything else.

CHAPTER 31

Now that my ladder's gone,
I must lie down where all the ladders start
In the foul rag-and-bone shop of the heart.

So we know who murdered Amanda Taylor. We know who won the election. All the mysteries have been solved.
All the mysteries remain.

I had plenty of work to do, even ignoring Harold's memo. There was the upcoming session to start planning for, new issues to master, staffing decisions to be made. But I always have plenty to do.

I decided to take a vacation instead. A different vacation from the kind I was used to, one with neither palm trees nor position papers. A vacation where I could think about what happened and what was going to happen and what it all meant.

So I called up my good friend Paul Everson.

"I have the perfect place," he said.

And here I am, in Shangri-la.

Not in the mansion, actually, but in the guesthouse, tucked away in a corner of the estate, far from the M.B.A.'s and the

Rottweiler. No one to bother me, nothing to do but walk in the woods and stare at the computer screen.

Liz thought it was a good idea when I explained what I wanted to do. "We've both got some thinking to do," she said.

Kathleen didn't seem surprised at my plan, but she wasn't exactly overjoyed either. "Could be worse" was all she had to say.

So I packed my bag and headed off along the Mass Pike once again. The fog had lifted somewhat, but it had by no means disappeared.

It made sense to me, the old English major, to write the whole story down instead of, oh, going fishing and hoping to find silent wisdom somewhere between the sea and the sky. But now that I am near the end, with the stack of pages sitting proudly by the printer, now that it is almost time to leave this place, and I need to decide just what it is that I have learned, I realize how few answers I actually possess.

Did Amanda really love me?

Yes, the defense insists. Harold said so; Everson said so; even Brad Williams said so. She loved you all along and was simply trying to figure out a way to get you back. After all, she handed over the tapes to Everson without a fuss. And there was apparently no manuscript of an article, even though she possessed information about me that would have made her a household name. There were only the brief pages of notes, which I have in front of me now. And they are more the musings of a puzzled lover than the outline of a muckraking article. "I was part of the complexity," she says. And who can doubt it?

No, the prosecution responds. She never really loved you; she was lying to you all along, looking for her opportunity, and finally she found it. Or, at best, she was a jilted lover preparing to destroy you. Why did she hand the tapes over to Everson? Out of the goodness of her heart, simply to prove the purity of her intentions? More likely it was out of fear. She knew he was a murderer, and what Paul Everson wanted, he got. Why didn't she tell me what she was up to? Maybe she was going to, with that final phone call, but by that time she had more than enough information to destroy me.

"Imagine writing your biography," she says. Is she remarking on the absurdity of such an idea, or is she showing her excitement at the task in front of her?

Perhaps the truth, as usual, lies somewhere between the defense and the prosecution. She was tempted. The relationship is over, and she has to figure out how to get on with her life, her career. And then Liz shows up and hands her the scoop of a lifetime. She follows up on it and finds out that it's true. Does she publish? Does she confront me with it? Perhaps she finally decides not to destroy me, but by then Danny is sitting in a bar and getting up his courage to confront *her*, and it's too late.

Perhaps. But Amanda is gone now, and I can only guess; I can only hope.

And Liz. She told me she loved me. But if she really loved me, how could she tell Amanda about Jackie Scanlon? Perhaps she secretly wanted me to be destroyed, to validate all the resentment and anger she had built up toward me over the years. What if she has never really loved me at all, just gave in to my relentless courtship and then spent the rest of her life regretting it? What if now she is simply afraid—afraid of losing the last semblance of family life, of becoming the pitiful, discarded wife of the famous politician? Afraid of growing old, alone and eccentric?

What if she does love me, but it is with a love that I am incapable of understanding? What if Roger is really better for her than I could ever be?

And Danny. Oh, Danny. You admitted that you couldn't figure out how you felt about me. How can I be sure that what you told me in the mud of that playground was the truth? Did you really murder Amanda because you wanted to help me? Perhaps you knew that she was my lover and you murdered her out of resentment and jealousy, because an exquisite woman like Amanda would never give you a second look. Perhaps you finally found a way to even the score between us.

Did I make a mistake in shielding you from the crime you committed years ago, and am I repeating that mistake now as you try to find the courage to confess?

Or was I right to lie to you in the playground, to comfort you when I was the one who should have needed comforting? It felt right, but I don't know if I can trust my feelings anymore.

Oh, Danny. I love you because you are my brother, but how can I ever trust you?

*   *   *

And, finally, Jim.

How did you really feel about Amanda, Senator? Did you love her? Or were you in love with a dream that could never become real? "Relaxation," Amanda says. Or lost youth. Or a simpler life. Or just hot sex and a beautiful, admiring face.

And do you still love Liz? Or is that another you, as Amanda puts it? Are you tired of her, or are you only tired of seeing the truth reflected in her eyes?

Your house of cards has collapsed yet again. Will you start building another, or will you do the job right this time?

It is December, and time to go home. I am bored with the woods; I have run out of coffee; if I don't read a newspaper soon, I'll go crazy. The pile of pages next to the printer isn't going to grow any larger. I have no answers, but finally I begin to see that the lack of answers is the point. Like Kathleen's fractals, the closer you look, the more complex everything becomes. The answers are always somewhere beyond the limits of your vision.

But that doesn't mean you should stop looking for them.

EPILOGUE
December 26

I write this in longhand, in my office back home in Hingham. The pen feels primitive, compared with the snazzy computer in Shangri-la, but it will do the job just as well.

The day after Christmas seems like a good time for a final update, one last chance for reflection before the tasks of the new year begin. So I'll give it a shot.

In the outside world there is little to report. The presidential punditry has died down until the holidays are over. According to the conventional wisdom, I'm one of about a half dozen legitimate Republican contenders—if I choose to contend. The conventional wisdom is that I will contend. Harold hasn't pressed me; even he took a vacation.

The Amanda Taylor murder case has disappeared from the newspapers; there are newer murders, newer scandals to take its place. Everson tells me that Cavanaugh dragged him in for an interrogation, but the DA's heart didn't seem to be in it. Mackey says the word is that the Monsignor is talking about retirement; Mack doesn't think the murder will ever be solved.

My own little world has been a little busier. I returned from my vacation, shaved off my beard, locked up the pile of papers I produced at Shangi-la, and got back to work. My heart, too, wasn't in it, but I couldn't stand any more inactivity.

At home Liz was as silent as ever when I returned. The approach of Christmas delayed our inevitable reckoning.

I didn't talk to Danny at all.

At the staff Christmas party Marge Terry resigned—for certain, for good, no foolin' this time. I had bought her a book of devotional poetry—suitable for use in a convent—and when she unwrapped it in her office, she started to cry. "I'm going free-lance," she said between sobs. "It's just no good for me to hang around you anymore."

I gave her my handkerchief. "Free-lance?" I said. "But there are already too many Sam Fishers in this world. You don't want to become another one."

"Don't try to talk me out of it, Jim, because you might succeed, and that'll only make me more miserable than I already am."

And I realized that she was right. So instead of getting down on my knees one more time, I embraced her and we clung to each other while her tears soaked my shoulder.

It was only later that I thought to open her gift to me. It was a gold cigarette lighter. I flicked it on a few times in my car, and then I put it in my pocket, smiling at the memory of the flame.

When I got back from Shangri-la, Kathleen had clearly made up her mind to take one last shot at saving her parents' marriage. One day she herded us into the car to go buy a Christmas tree, and then she supervised as we set it up in the living room. "Isn't this *great*?" she gushed as we hung ornaments on the tree. "It's just like—"

"Just like a normal family?" I suggested.

"Just like the old days," she said, and she stuck her tongue out at me.

Not quite. Liz and I went Christmas shopping together, and it was awkward, as everything seemed to be now. Did Roger stay on our Christmas list? What should we get Kathleen? I thought she wanted software; Liz insisted on clothes. "Computers are just a phase," Liz said. "Boys are the real thing." I deferred to her judgment, but I threw in a fractal calendar just in case.

It took a long time for me to figure out what to give Liz. When I finally made up my mind, life began to seem a lot simpler.

The tradition in the O'Connor household is that after Kathleen goes to bed on Christmas Eve, Liz and I put her presents beneath the tree, then uncork some champagne and exchange our gifts to each other in the living room. I wasn't sure the ritual was going to be followed this year, but I bought a bottle just in case. When I went to put it in the refrigerator, I found a bottle already chilling there. Liz's brand was cheaper.

The three of us spent the evening preparing for the meal on Christmas Day; my father and Danny's family were coming. "It's so nice to be doing things *together,*" Kathleen remarked. It should have been, but I was too nervous to notice.

Once Kathleen finally went upstairs to her room, we quickly got her gifts out of my clever hiding place in the garage and arranged them beneath the tree. Liz put Johnny Mathis on the stereo. I fetched the bottles of champagne and a couple of glasses. "Cheap or good?" I asked.

"Save the good one for the company," Liz said.

I returned my bottle to the refrigerator and popped the cork of Liz's over the kitchen sink. Then I brought the bottle back to the living room and filled the glasses. Liz sat in the wing chair, hands folded, looking tense. She couldn't be as tense as I was, I thought. I gave her a glass. "Merry Christmas, Liz," I said.

"Merry Christmas, Jim."

Our glasses touched, and I sipped the champagne; it was awful. I sat down on the couch opposite my wife. In years gone by we had sat on the couch together, my arm around her shoulders, her head on my chest. Not any more, apparently. I took another sip. Johnny Mathis sang "Hark! The Herald Angels Sing." The lights on the tree blinked blue and red. Liz had turned the heat down for the night, and it was getting chilly. There was no putting it off.

"So," I said. "Here we are again."

Liz nodded. She hadn't touched her champagne, I noticed. She grasped the glass in both hands, like a chalice.

"I decided not to buy you anything this year," I said. No, that wasn't the way to start. What was the matter with me? Liz raised an eyebrow but didn't respond. "I decided to give you something different," I said, hurrying on. "Liz, I'm going to resign my seat in the Senate."

Her mouth opened just a little, and I thought I heard a strangled sound deep in her throat.

There. I had said it, and I couldn't take it back. "I love you," I said, "and I think our marriage is worth saving—not for Kathleen, not to keep up appearances, not for my career, but for us. And this is the only thing I can think of that will save it."

"What would you do instead?" she whispered—croaked, I suppose, would be more accurate.

"Go back to practicing law. What else do I know how to do? Any firm in town would make me a partner just to get my name on the letterhead. I could probably earn three, four hundred grand a year just by staying awake eight hours a day."

"Would you like that?"

"Like what? Being able to send Kathleen to college without worrying about the bills? Having a home to return to every night instead of that pit stop of an apartment? Not having to attend a single fund raiser for the rest of my life? There are attractions to it, Liz. Definite attractions."

"But the presidency," she objected.

"Lots of people would make as good a President as I would. I haven't got a monopoly on virtue, God knows, or on truth. The government will survive without me, Liz, and I'll survive without the government."

Liz stared at her champagne. A single tear made its way down her cheek. "I didn't expect this," she said.

"I didn't expect it either. But that's what thinking will do to you."

She shook her head. She still didn't look at me. "It's kind of funny, I guess," she murmured. "You remember on election night when I suddenly disappeared? I wasn't angry at you or sick or anything, Jim. I was nervous. I was so nervous I couldn't stay there and watch. See, I was afraid you'd lose.

"And that made me angry at myself, really, because wasn't that the best thing that could happen to me? To have you lose, I mean, to have you come crawling back to your old life and forget about Washington and being President and changing the world? But I couldn't help myself. I was listening to the radio while I drove home, and they kept saying, 'Too close to call, too close to call,' and I started feeling guilty about all the things I should've done and didn't, all the events I could've attended instead of going to class or sitting at home, the people I could've convinced to vote for you, and I thought: Oh, God, just let him win, and we'll straighten it all out; somehow we'll straighten it all out.

"And then I got home, and you won—you always win—and I could feel the resentment start up in me again. You didn't need me, you never need me, you're involved in a scandal and you run a lousy campaign and you still manage to win, and now Harold

will talk you into running for President, and another two years
will be cut out of my life. Unless I—unless I—"

Liz stopped and gulped down her champagne. She tried
glancing at me and quickly looked away, as if afraid my gaze would
turn her to stone. That was the longest speech she had made to
me in years. "So you don't have to do anything," I said. "We sit
home nights and watch *Leave It to Beaver* reruns on cable. When
it gets too cold, we let my father in from the toolshed and have
him read Dickens to us. On weekends we can have séances at the
kitchen table and talk to the spirit world. It'll be exciting."

"No, it won't," Liz whispered. "It'll be boring."

"I won't be bored," I replied, getting a little exasperated. "I
promise."

"No, Jim. *I'll* be bored."

I let that sink in for a moment. "More bored than when I'm
away in Washington all week?" I said.

"Well, maybe not. But maybe we can figure that out, too. I
don't want you to quit the Senate, Jim. I can't believe I'm saying
this, but it's true. If you stayed home to watch TV with me, you'd
be a different person, and I don't want that person; I want you.
You'll still be infuriating, and I'll still hate politics, and your career
may still drive me into divorce court, but, I don't know, our marriage is nowhere near perfect, Jim, but I guess I can't imagine it
being any different. Better, sure, but not different."

This was as astonishing to me as my offer to resign must have
been to Liz. How hard must those words have been for her to
speak? I felt relieved; I felt grateful; I felt unworthy. I thought:
Would she feel the same way about my resigning if she knew I
was hiding yet another of Danny's crimes?

I thought: If I want Liz to do this for me, I have to offer up
something in return. There was only one thing more I had to give
her: the truth. And so I gave it to her.

"Danny killed Amanda," I said.

Liz stared at me.

"At first I thought it was Everson, but finally I figured it out,"
I continued. "That's where I went with the gun that night. Danny
thought he was protecting me because Amanda knew about Jackie
Scanlon. I don't know if he's going to confess or not. If he
does—"

Liz came over and sat next to me on the couch. She put a
hand on my thigh. "I know," she said.

It was my turn to stare at her. "You know?"

She nodded. "I suspected Danny all along. I figured your girl friend would try and talk to Danny after I told her about Scanlon. I didn't really think he was capable of cold-blooded murder, but I thought he was capable of, I don't know, bumbling into it. And from what I read in the papers about the murder, it sure looked as if someone had bumbled into it. I went to see Melissa after the election, while you were off communing with nature or whatever you were doing. She told me the whole story. She was glad to have someone to talk to about it. Poor Lissa."

"Poor Lissa," I agreed. I put my hand on top of Liz's. "You gals really got yourselves a pair."

"It's not like I'm totally innocent in this, you know," she pointed out. "If I hadn't blabbed to that woman about Scanlon, none of this would have happened. As soon as you told me she had been murdered, I knew that I was to blame, too. If I hadn't wanted to hurt you so much . . ."

"I guess there's enough guilt around for everyone," I said. "What do you think Danny's going to do?"

Liz shook her head. "I don't think even Lissa knows." She leaned back, and I put my arm around her shoulders. "Thank you for telling me, Jim. That means more to me than you can imagine."

"Sometimes even a politician has to tell the truth," I said.

We were silent for a while, and then she looked up at me. "Do you remember the Christmas when we were engaged? We sat like this on that broken-down couch in your apartment, and I asked you what you wanted to do with your life, and you said you didn't care, as long as you spent it with me?"

I searched my memories, terrified that I might have lost this one. But no, there it was. We had been eating popcorn and watching *The Mary Tyler Moore Show*. The couch was lumpy, and my arm was tired, but I didn't want to move—except perhaps to go to bed. "Why don't we eat popcorn anymore?" I asked.

Liz smiled. "I remember your eyes when you said it," she went on. "I never really trusted you, Jim—even after I fell in love with you. Even now I guess I don't really trust you. But when I looked into your eyes that Christmas Eve, I knew I didn't have anything to worry about. It's moments like that one that make life worth living, despite all the pain and confusion—don't you think?"

"Moments like this one," I said. I kissed her hair, and she snuggled closer, and pretty soon it was midnight, and we had survived another Christmas Eve together.

Kathleen opened her presents the next morning. She was thrilled.

"I picked the clothes out myself," I said.

"Sure you did. Now you guys open up your presents."

She had given us each a framed copy of the campaign photograph taken of our happy family. "Don't we all look nice together?" she asked.

"We're gorgeous," I replied.

"What did you two give each other?" she asked.

"Nothing," we replied in unison.

She looked worried for a moment, but our expressions gave us away, and she grinned finally, and it was as if the spring sun had broken through leaden winter clouds.

Danny and Melissa arrived in the afternoon, bringing my father and their kids. Danny looked clear-eyed and healthy; my father's arm still wasn't working very well, and he still had nothing good to say about doctors, but otherwise he seemed fine. Before dinner we opened the good champagne and had a toast: to my reelection, to Danny's new job. Danny and the kids drank ginger ale. Then we sat down to our turkey dinner—one big happy family, with every reason to celebrate. I felt as if I were in a Norman Rockwell painting.

Afterward, stuffed and drowsy, we opened presents in the living room in front of the tree. Liz put on Johnny Mathis again. My father had an Irish Mist. The kids got rowdy playing with their computer games but miraculously obeyed when Melissa told them to quiet down.

I caught my father in the kitchen later trying to pour himself another shot of Irish Mist. "Must be tough drinking one-handed," I said, uncapping the bottle for him. "How do you manage with a corkscrew?"

"I drink cheap wine," he said. "Twistoffs."

"If you moved in with us, you'd have someone to help you drink the good stuff."

"Oh, the cheap stuff is good enough for me."

I poured myself a shot, too. "How's Dickens coming?" I asked.

"Up to *Great Expectations*," my father said. "They don't write 'em like that nowadays."

"There's not much after that, is there? Are you still planning on cashing in your chips when you finish?"

My father considered. "I could have miscalculated," he admitted. "Maybe I'll start Trollope next."

"Good idea. Why not throw in Henry James and Sir Walter Scott? Keep you busy for another decade or two."

"Oh, I won't be around much longer. I can guarantee it."

"Seems to me I've heard that before."

"Well, you better start believing it."

"When you stop complaining, then I'll start believing. Let's go back into the living room and sing Christmas carols or something."

It was only at the end of the day that I had a chance to talk to Danny. Melissa was rounding up the kids, and he went to warm up the car. I brought out a bag of leftovers that Liz had packed for them, and we stood next to the car in the crisp night air. The sky was clear, and we leaned against the car and stared up at an array of stars so dazzling that it seemed as if I was seeing them for the first time.

"So how's it going?" I asked. "You look good."

"It's going okay. I'm still pretty shaky, to tell you the truth, but I think I'm gonna make it."

"And the job?"

"So far so good." He glanced at me. "You got it for me, didn't you? I wasn't there a week before I found out the company was owned by Paul Everson. Did you think I wouldn't make the connection?"

I shrugged. "I didn't have anything to do with it."

"Well, you're lying. We're a pair of liars. But it doesn't matter. I know how to sell. I just have to stay sober and healthy, and they won't regret hiring me."

"That's great, Danny."

One of his kids came out with an armful of presents. He dumped them into the trunk and hurried back into the house.

"I guess this means I'm not going to turn myself in," Danny said. He looked at me, as if for support. I said nothing. "It's not that I'm a coward," he hurried on, "and it's not that I don't feel guilty. Honest, Jim. It's just that . . . I've hurt enough people in my life. Confessing would only hurt more."

"I'm not looking for anything from you, Danny," I replied.

"I don't deserve what life's given me, even without this."

"I don't know," he said. "Maybe we've both got a lot to be guilty about. But maybe this'll give us a chance to make up for it."

We were silent for a while. A dog barked in the distance. The trees rustled in a chill breeze. "Do you think about her much?" I asked.

"I think about her face all the time," he said. "I see it whenever I go to sleep. At the moment she realized she was going to die. The pain, sure. But also this terrible look of—unfairness. I can never take away the pain, Jim. I can never make it fair."

I looked over at him. His tears glistened in the starlight. I wanted to wipe them off, but I couldn't take away his pain any more than he could take away Amanda's. My brother wiped away the tears himself, finally, as everyone bustled out of the house, and it was time to go home.

Liz went to bed early, as usual; Kathleen was upstairs in her room. I poured myself another shot of Irish Mist and sat in the living room. Angelica was curled up in a corner of the couch, exhausted from chasing ribbons and attacking wrapping paper. I closed my eyes and inhaled the piney scent of the Christmas tree. Below me the furnace rumbled to life.

I thought about Amanda. We don't have the right perspective in thinking about the dead, Liz had told me on the way to Amanda's funeral. They don't care about the same things we care about. I found myself hoping that was true. Otherwise how could Danny and I—and Liz—hope to find forgiveness?

I took my key chain out of my pocket. Amanda's key was still on the chain. Even after she was dead, I never got around to taking it off. What did that mean?

And suddenly I felt her presence, there in the quiet room with me. Not an apparition, but an . . . awareness. The awareness you have in the dark when you hold out your hand and you know that there is something, just beyond your reach, waiting to be touched. I held my breath. "Amanda," I whispered.

There was no sound, only the hum of the furnace.

"Everyone is guilty," I said. "You must know that now. But

everyone is innocent. No angels, no devils. Can you forgive us?"

Silence.

"If you can't forgive, can you at least *understand*? Maybe that's all we can ask of anyone, even the dead."

The silence continued, but it seemed to . . . brighten. I reached out my hand in the dark—and another hand met it and held it for the briefest of instants and then slipped away.

"Daddy? Are you awake?"

I opened my eyes. Kathleen was standing in the doorway, wearing one of her Christmas sweaters and a new pair of jeans; the jeans seemed a little tight to me. "Hi, kitten," I said.

"Hi, puppy."

"You look gorgeous."

Kathleen blushed. "Thanks." She sat down on the couch and stroked the cat. "I thought, um, I thought I might wear this outfit on my date," she said with supreme casualness.

"Oh. Your date. You finally succumbed to the entreaties of the dweeb, the nerd, the dexter?"

"Oh, Dad. Not him. Yucch."

"Yet another admirer then."

"He's in my English class. His name is Jason."

"Jason?" I made a face. "Sounds like an ax murderer. Sounds like a sex maniac."

"Oh, Daddy."

"He's probably a Democrat. He'll carry you off to live on a collective farm."

"We're going to a movie, that's all. And he isn't political. He writes poetry."

I rolled my eyes. "Oh, Lord."

"So, are you and Mom okay or what?" Kathleen asked, cleverly changing the subject.

I smiled. "For now," I said. "I can't promise we won't have any more problems; in fact, I'd be very surprised if we didn't. But we're okay for now."

"That's good," she said. "That's good." She kept stroking the cat. "So, are you going to run for President?"

"He wants to be President," Amanda had written. "He wants to be anything but President."

"Yes," I replied truthfully. "No. I don't know."

"Well, that about covers it," Kathleen said.

"No matter what I do, I've figured one thing out," I said.

"What's that?"

"I'm the luckiest guy in the world."

Kathleen looked up at me. "Just don't forget it then. Or next time you have a problem, let me know, and I'll be happy to remind you."

"Next time," I said, "I will."

Kathleen hugged me and went back upstairs. I sat staring at the Christmas tree for a while longer, then I noticed that the glass of Irish Mist sat untouched on the floor next to my chair. I went out to the kitchen and poured it into the sink. Then I took Amanda's key off the key chain and placed it in the wastebasket, along with the wrapping paper and the empty champagne bottles and the remains of Christmas dinner.

Finally I, too, went upstairs, and I spent the remaining hours of Christmas in bed, in my quiet home, eyes wide open in the darkness, holding on to my sleeping wife.